BLOODY WATERS

Jason Franks

Published by Outland Entertainment LLC
3119 Gillham Road
Kansas City, MO 64109

Founder/Creative Director: Jeremy D. Mohler
Editor-in-Chief: Alana Joli Abbott

ISBN: 978-1-954255-51-7
EBOOK ISBN: 978-1-954255-52-4
Worldwide Rights
Created in the United States of America

Editor: Scott Colby
Cover Illustration: Chris Yarbrough
Cover Design: Jeremy Mohler
Interior Layout: Mikael Brodu

Printed and bound in the United States of America.

Visit **outlandentertainment.com** to see more, or follow us on our Facebook Page **facebook.com/outlandentertainment/**

For Celia.

— PROLOGUE —

1. Badder Than a Bluesman

The bluesman sat at the crossroads wringing music from his scarred old six-string. Just him and the blues and the moon above. The sky was clear, but there were no stars. It was autumn; perhaps they had fallen out of it. The bluesman's voice rumbled low and raw beneath the progression of chords.

A second guitar took up the song, matching him beat for beat, lick for lick. The newcomer did not sing. The bluesman did not look to see who had joined him. When he reached the end of the chorus the second guitarist kicked into a solo.

The soloist's left hand slid down the neck of his instrument, his right picking and raking and scratching over the sound hole. The bluesman strummed rhythm, stomped a beat with his foot, slapped the body of the guitar with the heel of his right hand, hummed deep in his throat.

The soloist's guitar lurched higher and faster and meaner, wailing and screaming and begging. Then it moaned its way down into sadness, despair, and silence.

The bluesman sang the third verse, repeated the chorus one more time. He struck the final chords of the song unaccompanied and raised his head.

The soloist was sitting on a rock with a steel-shelled Dobro across his knee, all the way across the blacktop from the bluesman. "Bad Jack Saunders," he said. The bluesman did not think the rock had been present when he had sat down to play. He supposed that the soloist had brought it with him.

The bluesman inclined his head. "How y'all doing?"

The soloist rose once more. "Doing good, thanks. Yourself?" His face was masked with shadow, though his collar was down and he wore no hat.

"Can't complain," said the bluesman. "That's why I play the blues."

The soloist seemed to smile as he crossed the street. His guitar swung loosely from his left hand; his right was outstretched. The bluesman rose and shook it.

"I'd say it's good to see you again, but ain't nothing good happens when the likes of you an' me sit together," said the bluesman. The rock that the soloist had been using for a seat had disappeared when he wasn't looking.

The soloist grinned through his mask of shadows. "That's the stone truth," he said, "but I enjoy seeing your face." He sat down on the bench beside the bluesman.

"Can't say the same, but I do like to hear you play. You're pretty good, for a white man."

"I'm no more white than I am a man, Jack," said the soloist, crossing his booted feet and settling the Dobro in his lap.

"Well, you dress like a white man," said the bluesman, grinning. "An' I bet you sing like one, too."

"That's why I play the guitar." He raked a chord.

"Fair enough, too," said the bluesman. "Ain't a lot of singers come to you for no favors, I'll bet."

"Just so," said the soloist. "Singing is for good people. Guitars are for the bad."

The bluesman considered that. A nightbird called, somewhere out in the woods. Police sirens warbled and rubber squealed, somewhere in the town down the road. He couldn't remember the name of it. Couldn't remember the name of the bar he'd played, either. "Ain't nobody on earth badder than a bluesman," he said.

"The stone truth," said the soloist.

"It is, for now," said the bluesman. In the old days he'd remembered everything—every show, every note, every step—but those days and those people were gone. Used to be he'd play for laborers, farmhands, field workers. Workingmen. Now it was just shitkickers who thought it was bluegrass night or yuppies who wanted an authentic juke-joint experience, encouraged to venture out of the city limits by the new cell towers that had sprung up along the interstate. "But there's less of us every day. Soon we'll all be gone, an' you'll have to find something badder to take our place."

"Sooner than you think," said the soloist. "I already found it. It just hasn't grown into its badness yet."

"I thought that was the kind of thing you liked. New kinds of badness."

"I do," said the soloist, "but this time it's different."

"I thought every time was different."

"Not really."

The bluesman looked at him, but the soloist wasn't going to say any more. "Well, you need my help, you know where to find me."

"Thanks, Jack, I appreciate it," said the soloist. "But I think this new badness is gonna find its way to you all by its ownself."

"What kind of a badness we talking about?"

"Rock'n'roll badness."

The bluesman blinked slowly. "You serious?"

"Is cancer of the bowels serious?"

He snorted. "Them rock stars talk big, but there ain't a one of them that's really, truly bad. If passing out drunk in the lobby of a five-star hotel is the worst it gets, I'd say you got bigger troubles than you know."

The shadow-faced soloist seemed to smile again.

"Trust me, them rock'n'roll boys ain't nothing to concern yourself over."

"You're right, Jack, they aren't," said the soloist. "But this one's a girl."

— GIRLHOOD OF A GUITAR FIEND —

1. Rock Star Barbie

For Clarice Marnier's tenth birthday, her mother bought her a Funtime Barbie in a pink dress with a pink Barbie House and a pink Barbie Convertible.

Funtime Barbie languished in her pink dress next to the pink house and the pink convertible until Clarice, left to her own devices in the Macy's toy department, found a Rock Star Barbie accessory kit hanging amongst the He-Man and Transformers displays.

"I'm not buying you that."

Amy Marnier was still wearing her uniform, although she'd put her sidearm and her badge into her purse since coming off duty. She folded away the Egyptian cotton towel she had been inspecting and turned to frown down at her daughter. "You haven't even taken Barbie out of her box."

"That's because she's pink," said Clarice.

Clarice's mother looked at the coveted accessory pack. "Rock Star Barbie is pink, too."

"Yes," said Clarice, "but she has a guitar."

"You don't ever play with the Barbie you have. I'm not buying you another one."

"Fine," said Clarice. "Then I'll just have to steal it."

When they got home, Clarice ran upstairs to her bedroom and opened the Rock Star Barbie kit. She tore Funtime Barbie out of her box, threw the glittery pink frock into a corner and dressed the doll in her new plastic jacket and skirt. She strapped the guitar onto the doll and leaned it up against the convertible.

It was still awfully pink.

At midnight, Clarice sneaked downstairs and stole into the kitchen. She pulled a chair up to the cabinet and climbed onto the alcove where the toaster and the kettle sat, reached up over her head, and drew her father's model airplane kit down from its shelf. Then she set to work.

Clarice carefully coated Rock Star Barbie's pink vinyl skirt and jacket with black enamel. Barbie's guitar got an even more careful coat of black. She put silver on the strings and the input jack, gold on the tone and volume knobs, white on the tuning machines. There was no matte black for the amplifier, so Clarice made it brown. She cut Rock Star Barbie's hair with a pair of manicure scissors.

Amy was furious. Clarice could have slipped and fallen and broken her neck while climbing onto that cupboard. Ray Marnier muttered and grumbled because Clarice had used up all of his paint. They sent Clarice to her room.

That was fine with Clarice; she'd been planning to spend the day playing with her newly renovated Rock Star Barbie.

At the end of the week, Clarice issued an ultimatum to her parents: she wanted a guitar for Christmas.

2. Hendrix is Dead

Mr. Peabody was a portly, balding, bearded man who taught clarinet and saxophone at the local high school. He also gave private guitar and piano lessons from his home. A friend of the family had recommended him to the Marniers.

"Peabody?" Clarice said, upon first introductions. "For real?"

"*Mister* Peabody," he replied.

"Okay, Mister Peabody," said Clarice. "Teach me to play the guitar."

In her first lesson, Peabody taught her the anatomy of the guitar. Clarice knew it already–she had read everything she could find about guitars and music during the interminable months she had waited for Christmas. Peabody then proceeded to teach her a simple three-chord song, "Little Brown Jug." He insisted that she sing as she strummed.

"You sing," she replied. "I'm here to learn guitar."

He sent her home with instructions to practice the chords and to learn the words that went with them.

When Clarice returned the following week she had tried to learn an additional fifteen chord shapes, and she was upset that her fingers refused to form them correctly. Peabody told her that she couldn't learn everything at once; he would make sure that she progressed at an appropriate rate. "What about your homework?"

"What homework?"

"'Little Brown Jug.'"

"Oh, that," she said.

Clarice played the whole song through without error, but she claimed to have forgotten the lyrics. Peabody made her hum.

Clarice improved quickly. Soon she could finger every one of those eighteen chords quickly and clearly, and she was learning more all the time. Peabody forced her to sing by refusing to let the lesson progress until she complied.

"I'm not interested in singing," Clarice complained.

"You have a nice voice."

"I don't care," she said.

"I do."

"Jimmy Page doesn't sing."

"Bob Dylan does."

"Yeah, as badly as he plays the guitar."

"Eric Clapton sings."

"Most people wish he wouldn't."

"Jimi Hendrix used to sing."

"I'm not Jimi Hendrix."

"But you could be," said Peabody.

"Hendrix is dead," she said. "I'm Clarice Marnier."

Clarice started going for lessons twice a week. Peabody taught her to read music, and she learned a finger-picking piece based around the three natural notes that could be played on the high E string in the third position. There were no lyrics for the note-picking piece. Clarice returned the following week knowing every note on every string, all the way down the fret board.

Peabody gave Clarice more and more difficult classical pieces to learn. His praise of Clarice's progress went from grudging to effusive.

At school, Clarice's grades began to drop. She was spending all her class time thinking about playing the guitar, imagining chord shapes and right-hand patterns, dreaming about what it would be like to play an electric. She stopped doing her homework altogether.

Clarice's father broached the subject tactfully: "If your grades don't improve, I'm taking away the guitar."

"I'd like to see you try," she replied.

Ray looked at his wife, who squelched a smile and frowned. "Good grades are important, Clarice," she said. "You want to get into college, don't you?"

"I want to play the guitar."

"You can play the guitar and go to college," said her father.

"If I have to."

"I want to see your grades improve," said Clarice's mother, "or there'll be trouble."

Clarice's grades did not improve. Her parents didn't take away the guitar, but they did terminate Clarice's tuition under Mr. Peabody before she moved up to junior high. That was fine with Clarice; the lessons had been eating into her practice time.

3. Volcano High

After Clarice had ceased taking lessons from Mr. Peabody her grades improved–not because she had more time to devote to schoolwork, but because she began to get over the fact that *she had a guitar.*

Once the knowledge that she could play became implicit, the delight of it ceased to occupy all of her attentive resources. Clarice's grades returned to their previous levels, then exceeded them. She never took less than As for English and Mathematics, and it was Bs and above for everything else. Her parents were so pleased that they allowed her to spend as much time in her room with her guitar as she liked. They did not seem to care that Clarice's playmates were dwindling in number, and neither did Clarice.

She was saving up for an electric guitar.

Junior high was a new environment. A new place, new classmates, new subjects, new opportunities. The school offered students the option of learning an instrument, and Clarice jumped at the chance. They did not offer guitar or piano, so, after careful consideration, Clarice chose the trumpet. She claimed that this was because it "had balls". Another important consideration was that it was a relatively small instrument that would not take up much of the space in her bedroom that she was saving for new guitars.

Clarice could already read music, so she progressed quickly on her new instrument and she was made first trumpet in the junior band. She was the best player in the ensemble, and everyone knew it. She was also the only girl who played a brass instrument.

Clarice preferred to joke around with the trumpet boys and the fat kid who played the tuba, rather than giggling with the flute girls or muttering amongst the mixed crowd of clarinetists. This developed into a fierce enmity and, before long, the giggling and muttering—and hissing and snarling—was almost exclusively about the topic of Clarice Marnier. But Clarice wasn't interested in feuds. She was interested in music, and only music.

Clarice's mother finally became worried that she was fixating a little too much on music, but she knew that forbidding Clarice from playing would do no good. After some careful thought she braced Clarice at the kitchen table before her pre-dinner guitar practice.

"Honey, there are some important things we need to discuss."

Clarice looked up from the sheet music she was eating over and swallowed her mouthful of sandwich. "Yeah, Mom, I know where babies come from."

"No, Clarice, this is about being healthy—"

"It's okay, Mom. This is California. They taught us about birth control already." She took another bite of her sandwich and looked down at the music again.

"Clarice, listen to me."

She sighed, swallowed her mouthful and looked up again. "I promise not to do any drugs?"

"Clarice."

"All right, Mom, just spit it out already."

Clarice's mother took a deep breath. "It's important that a young lady be able to take care of herself."

"Yeeees…?"

"And I want you to get some exercise, too."

"Aaaandd…?"

"I want you to start coming to jujutsu with me."

Clarice looked down at the music again. "Sounds okay."

It took a bit more wrangling, but they quickly arrived at a deal: Clarice would go to jujutsu once a week, provided that she was allowed to stay up late on that night to make up the lost practice time.

4. Ride the Lightning

Clarice continued to save for her electric guitar.

She checked out every secondhand music store, pawn shop, and junk dealer she could find, looking for the best instrument she could get for the best price. She spent hours poring over price guides and technical specs, trying out different rigs, and generally annoying the shit out of every salesman in every music shop within bussing distance of her parents' house in Los Angeles County.

Finally, she found what she wanted: a scratched-up, blue Ibanez. The paintwork was damaged, but the electrics and the neck were in perfect shape. Clarice visited it in the pawn shop in Inglewood every fortnight until she had enough cash to buy it.

For an extra twenty bucks the clerk threw in a thirty watt Marshall amp that he had in the window, muttering that he was pleased to have finally gotten rid of the instrument–and Clarice. The amp was worth about two hundred.

Once Clarice had the Ibanez she quit playing the trumpet. "I don't have time anymore," she told the heartbroken conductor. "I'm joining a rock band."

— ON THE BANDWAGON —

1. Stalin's Mo

The first band Clarice joined was called Stalin's Mo.

The auditions were held in a warehouse. The front office was closed up on the weekend, but the door to the loading bay was rolled up. A wiry, olive-skinned guy in a Pearl Jam T-shirt was sitting on the concrete apron beside the parked delivery trucks.

Clarice got out of the car and unloaded her guitar case and a tote bag full of FX pedals. Her father waited in the car with the amp.

The olive-skinned guy got up and shook his curly black hair out of his eyes.

"Who're you?" he asked.

"Clarice," said Clarice.

"And you're here to...audition?"

"What does it look like?"

"You're a guitarist?"

Clarice looked down at the guitar case in her left hand, then looked up again. "I play the sousaphone."

The olive-skinned guy introduced himself as "Jofe". He was the vocalist. They rode the conveyor belt to the upper floor of the warehouse, where the band had set up in a cleared space amidst the towers of precariously stacked boxes. It was dark and dusty and stiflingly hot. The other members of Stalin's Mo were clustered around five buckets containing ice and beer.

Jofe introduced the band to Clarice. Kim, the lead guitarist, was lanky and long-haired. He gave her a limp handshake. Colin, the drummer, was short, stocky, and equally long-haired. He tried to shake her hand more vigorously, but the sweat on his palms made it difficult for either of them to get a decent grip. Colin was the one who hauled boxes in the warehouse during the day. The bassist, Samuels, was a tall and overweight guy with short-cropped blond hair. He shook her hand firmly and said "Pleased to meet ya. How old are you?"

"Sixteen," said Clarice. Samuels looked about eighteen, and she judged the others to be upward of twenty-one.

"You been in a band before?" asked Jofe.

"No."

"Well," said Samuels, "are you any good?"

"Yes," said Clarice. She knelt down and opened her guitar case. "Are we going to play or what?"

The audition was pretty straight-forward. The band would start to play a song and Clarice was expected to fill out the guitar rhythms.

"Fake it if you gotta," instructed Kim. "If you don't know the song, make up whatever you want…just stay on the beat and in key."

Clarice knew most of the songs, and she had little difficulty working out the ones that she didn't. Jofe had a talent for squishing the vocals from any song in the band's repertoire into his single octave, but he could certainly belt it out inside that limited range. Colin could keep time; Kim couldn't. Samuels was pretty decent.

Clarice had played in the school band before, with forty other kids and a conductor. This was...better.

Way better.

After about forty-five minutes, Jofe called an end to the audition.

"She can play," said Kim.

"Can we keep her?" said Colin.

"Does she want to stay?" asked Samuels.

"Call me," said Clarice.

In the car, her father looked up from the comics pages of the Saturday paper and asked, "How was it?"

"There's no *it*," said Clarice. "They were okay. *I* was awesome."

2. Gig

The regular place where Stalin's Mo used to play before the departure of Clarice's predecessor had replaced them with another band. It was difficult to find a new gig on short notice, but Clarice was keen, and she took matters into her own hands. She called up two dozen small venues before she was able to get them a fill-in slot on a Tuesday night in a small club somewhere deep in the Valley. It was called the Hip Case.

The Hip Case was a small, freestanding building adjacent to a strip mall with a capacity of maybe fifty. It had two rooms and two bars: one full of benches and tables, the other set up with couches and chairs and a small dais. Both rooms smelled of alcohol and varnish. The signboard advertised "Live Music," but did not name the band. Clarice didn't care. She was there for stage experience, not exposure.

Setup and sound check took about fifteen minutes. They had more than an hour to kill, so the band ordered some pitchers of beer, which the barman said were on the house. He did not ask any of them, even Clarice, for ID. The boys guzzled the first pitcher in less than a minute. Clarice drank water.

More patrons started to trickle in, but it was going to be a quiet night: it was 100F outside, and people were staying home by their air conditioners.

When it was time, Stalin's Mo staggered into the back room to tune up again.

Clarice and Kim checked their instruments. Samuels seemed more intent on finishing the last pitcher of beer—which he'd brought with him—than he did on getting his bass in tune. Colin bounced off the walls, twirling his drumsticks and panting. Jofe paced, hunched over, shaking his fist and leveling karate kicks at an empty keg. "We're gonna rock! We're gonna rock!"

Samuels looked up from his pitcher and his guitar. "Of course we're gonna rock," he said. "Stalin's Mo and their new guitar chick."

"Rhythm guitarist," said Clarice.

"Rhythm-guitar chick."

"I don't see how being a chick enters into it."

Jofe stepped between them. "All right! Are we ready?"

"Yeah!" said Kim.

"All right!" said Colin.

"Yea, verily, my brother, we are ready to bring forth the rock and the roll," said Samuels.

"Then why the hell are we standing around talking?" said Clarice.

The room was pretty full when Stalin's Mo took the stage. About half of the patrons looked up when the piped music stopped and the stage lights came on. Then they went on with whatever they had been doing. Nobody clapped or cheered.

Jofe stepped up to the mic. The guitarists plugged in and Colin sat down behind the drums. Jofe looked over his right shoulder at Kim and Colin, over his left at Samuels and Clarice. He gave

Clarice a thumbs-up. Clarice rolled her eyes and gestured for him to hurry up.

Jofe turned back to the audience and pumped his right hand over his head. On the fifth oscillation of his fist the band came in with the first blistering bars of "Whole Lotta Love."

It went off pretty well. Jofe screamed and wailed his way through as best he could. Colin pounded out the beat and even made an attempt at the drum solo. Samuels shook and stomped around the stage like a pro. Kim managed to hit every note on the solo, although he couldn't quite keep it in time. Clarice stood in her corner and played her part.

The audience applauded politely when the song was done.

"Hello!" said Jofe. "We are Stalin's Mo, and we are here to rock your world!"

More polite applause.

"And please welcome our new rhythm-guitar chick, in her debut performance, the beautiful and rockin' Clarice Marnier!"

The applause was a little louder. People looked around to see the beautiful and rockin' Clarice Marnier: a slim sixteen-year-old girl with short auburn hair and a guitar. Clarice inclined her head curtly. The audience went back to their conversations.

The band played on; classic rock fare with a few grunge or '80s rock hits for good measure: ZZ Top, Deep Purple, AC/DC, Alice in Chains, Midnight Oil, The Rolling Stones, The Beatles, Chuck Berry.

Clarice hung back and kept her head down. Her biggest difficulty was finding a way to stay in time while Kim joined her on rhythm. Clarice just tried to play louder and hoped his faulty riffage would fall in with her.

They played well. The crowd clapped when they left the stage. It wasn't a standing ovation, but they'd enjoyed the show in an absent-minded sort of way.

It was a start.

3. Enter the Motherfucker

Stalin's Mo started to wear on Clarice's patience before long.

Jofe introduced her as "Clarice the guitar chick" at every gig, although she repeatedly asked him not to. The others were frustratingly slow to learn new songs, not to mention reluctant.

The band had won a number of regular paying gigs at a few small venues around LA. They didn't make a whole lot of money, even before they split it amongst themselves, but it added up. Clarice saved every cent. It was the first money she had made as a musician and she felt that it should be spent accordingly. Six months later she found herself in a guitar shop with a fat roll of bills in her pocket and the need to buy something.

It was big and black and had seven strings, and she knew it was hers as soon as she saw it.

The salesman gave her a skeptical look when she asked him to take it down off the top rack so she could look at it. "That big ol' seven-stringed motherfucker?" he asked.

"The seven-stringed motherfucker."

The salesman reluctantly handed it to her. Clarice sighted down the neck. Turned it over and looked at the back. Hefted it in her hands. "Got an amp?" she asked. "I want to try it out."

"I think it's kind of big for you."

"You have an amp or not?"

The salesman shrugged again and led her to a small glassed-off room at the back of the store. The room contained a couple of stools, some amplifiers, and a mess of cables and FX pedals. Clarice sat down and put the guitar over her knee.

The salesman handed her a cable and she jacked in. He turned on an amp.

Clarice found a plectrum and ran it over the strings slowly, listening to the tuning.

"Thing with a seven-string is," said the salesman, "it has an extra wide neck."

"Yes," said Clarice, tuning the low E string down to a D. "That would be on account of the seventh string."

She dropped the bottom string from A to B, but it wouldn't hold the note. She returned it to A and made a mental note that she'd need a heavier gauge string for it.

"That's right," said the salesman. "That extra wide neck means you need longer fingers to play it."

Satisfied with the tuning, Clarice turned up the volume knob and toed the distortion pedal. Feedback whined. She raised the plectrum. "Your point is?"

"And, well. You're a girl. Not that I doubt your chops, or anything, but...you got girl-sized hands."

"You don't think I can play this guitar because I have girl hands?"

The salesman looked at her hands mournfully. "Not that I doubt your chops, or anything."

Clarice spun the volume up to full and tore a barrage of chords out of the guitar; a massive, palm-muted riff sprinkled with artificial harmonics, like tiny pieces of broken glass glittering amongst shards of exploded asphalt. She eased off and played something smooth and sweet, soaring from the middle range of the guitar up to the highest it would go. Then she slashed down to the depths of the seventh string and opened up another fusillade.

The salesman stared at her.

She muted the strings abruptly and spun the volume knobs down to zero. "How much?"

"Huh?"

"How much?"

"Uh, nine hundred."

"I can give you six."

"Uh..."

"I want this motherfucker," said Clarice. "Six-fifty."

"Uh," said the salesman, "seven is the lowest I can go."

"Okay," said Clarice, "but only if you throw in a hard case."

"Uh. Okay."

Clarice had to make do with a nylon gig-bag; the store didn't have a hard case big enough to accommodate the guitar. The instrument needed a name, she thought.

After a moment's reflection, Clarice realized that it already had one.

4. Mean Tambourine

Clarice never took The Motherfucker with her to Stalin's Mo rehearsals or gigs. She didn't even tell them about it. It was For Special.

She played about five more gigs with them before Jofe asked her to do backing vocals on a new song the band was learning, "Dazed and Confused."

"Would you like me to bang a tambourine as well?" she asked.

"Uh, not on Dazed," said Jofe. "Maybe we can find another song with tambourine for you, though."

"Well, you can make tambourines and backing vocals part of the audition while you look for a new rhythm guitarist," said Clarice.

5. Ignition Corps

Clarice fell in with a new band, the Groulx. Groulx specialized in party songs with lyrics that rhymed hipster slang with meaningless syllables, but it was original material and they allowed her to play leads when she wanted them. They weren't very good, and they didn't get many gigs, but it was the soap opera that developed around the disintegrating relationship between the keyboardist and the lead singer that proved the final straw. When it spilled onstage during a gig, Clarice walked off and never spoke to them again.

Her next move was obvious: Clarice wanted her own band, and she wanted it before she'd graduated from high school. There was no time to waste.

Finding a name for the project was easy. She'd known it was going to be called Ignition Corps since she had watched her mother hotwire a rental car after losing the keys down a truck stop culvert on a family road trip years prior. Finding players was a bit more difficult.

Clarice posted ads in all the music stores in bussing distance of her house. These mostly yielded replies from thirteen-year-old girls who wanted to be pop stars or band geeks who thought the time was right for the rock'n'roll oboe. After a solid week of this, she decided that she was going to need some help. It took another week before she conceded that she only knew one person who might be of any assistance.

Samuels told her that Stalin's Mo was still going. They had a new rhythm guitarist who sang backup. They had their material down pretty well and they didn't rehearse often; they weren't learning any new songs. Samuels told her that he thought that what she'd said about the tambourine was pretty funny.

"I didn't hear you laughing at the time," said Clarice.

"Hell," he said, "I'd lost my job at Denny's. Stalin's Mo was all the income I had."

"And now?"

"Now, I work at Burger King."

"You want to be in my new band?"

"Your band?"

"Yeah."

"Uh, okay. Sure."

Samuels knew some other musicians and he introduced Clarice around, but the only ones she judged good enough to join the band were guitarists who refused to play rhythm behind a girl. Clarice decided that she didn't need a rhythm guitarist, but she did need a drummer and a singer.

They put up new ads that specified Ignition Corps was a HEAVY METAL band in spiky bold letters. Clarice put Samuels' name and number on the bottom. The new flyer yielded immediate results.

Alan Lo was a tall guy with a Hong Kong British accent. He was in his early thirties, substantially older than Clarice and Samuels. He was adept on the piano and the violin, but percussion was his true love. By day, Alan was a lawyer.

Brenda Jacobs was a six-foot college girl, buck-toothed and big-hipped. She had a honeyed voice that could drip sweet and clear or clotted and crystalline.

Ignition Corps was ready for their marching orders. Now all they needed to do was write some songs.

6. Priorities

Clarice wanted to rehearse every night, but the others thought two nights a week was plenty. Some dickering ensued; Clarice agreed to two rehearsals for the first couple of weeks, then three if it seemed to be working out.

Ignition Corps spent the first two rehearsals in Alan's garage playing rock standards: Black Sabbath, AC/DC, Metallica, Cream. They did some Blackhearts, some Banshees, some Pat Benatar, some Lita Ford songs to get Brenda's vocals working, but Clarice was very pleased with the way she interpreted male singers. They'd all played the songs before in other bands and nobody had a lot of difficulty with any of it.

Clarice warmed up the third Ignition Corps rehearsal with a couple of covers, then, without warning, she spun up the volume and launched into some free-form riffing.

"Let's see what you boys and girls can do," she said.

Alan had no trouble keeping up, changing time signatures and tempos whenever Clarice asked. Samuels proved better able to handle Clarice's key switches and tempo changes than she'd expected—he'd been practicing, although he denied it. Brenda took a back seat during the jam sessions, singing wordlessly or adapting bits of other songs the band had practiced to the music. It was good.

After the rehearsal, Clarice pulled Brenda aside. "We need to get together and talk about some lyrics," she said.

"Sure," said Brenda. "I can do lyrics."

Clarice had about a dozen songs written carefully in a small black notebook, alongside riffs and solo ideas. She hadn't considered that Brenda would want to write.

"Me, too."

Brenda scowled. "I thought you played the guitar."

Clarice gave it some thought, and decided that her first priority was, indeed, playing the guitar. Her second priority was to get the band up and running. It had taken her a lot of effort to find three good musicians; she didn't want to ruin it over this. She was already convinced that they had what it took.

Brenda, she decided, could write the songs. At least to start with.

— LEGION OF THE DAMNED —

1. Whammy Cake

Clarice's parents arranged a surprise party for her eighteenth birthday.

Clarice herself was not aware of the date when she came down to the darkened living room, after her regular afternoon practice session, to find out where dinner was. As she stepped off the bottom step and reached for the light switch, a dozen of her former schoolmates jumped out from behind the furniture and yelled, "Surprise!"

They gave her presents. They played rock'n'roll music on a jukebox filled with many of the same CDs that Clarice had up in her bedroom. Snacks and sweets and sodas and punch were served. Pizzas were delivered. Clarice blew out the candles on the huge, guitar-shaped cake her mother had baked for her. Clarice assumed it was a guitar, at any rate–it might have been a tennis racquet. Amy even changed out of uniform for the occasion, and Ray put on shoes.

Clarice wandered amongst the proceedings with a slightly bewildered air. She chatted to anyone who approached her and snacked on all the foods laid out–she had, after all, come downstairs because she was hungry. Otherwise, she'd have stayed upstairs with her guitar all night. At her mother's insistence, she opened all of the presents. Then everyone went home.

When the last of them was gone Clarice started heading upstairs, but her father called her back.

"It's past midnight," he said. "Birthday treatment no longer applies. Stay and help me straighten up."

Clarice sighed. "All right."

Ray called his wife out of the kitchen. "Amy, don't worry about the cleaning," he said. "We got it covered."

"Thanks, Ray." Amy took off her apron, which had a faded portrait of Dirty Harry on it. She kissed her husband on the chin, then her daughter on the forehead. "Happy birthday, honey," she said, and went up to bed.

Clarice found a big, black Hefty bag and started collecting the plastic cups and paper plates that had been left on the tables, the sofas, in the corners, on the mantelpiece, under the sideboards...

"Your mother's upset with you," said Ray.

"Why?" said Clarice. "I didn't even punch anyone."

"Those guests are your friends," he replied, leaning against the doorframe, with a dustpan and a brush hanging loosely from one hand.

"I guess."

"You guess."

"I went to school with them," said Clarice. "That's all. I've barely seen any of them since graduation."

"That's because you don't call them," said Ray.

"They can call me, they want to see me."

"They have been," he said. "But you're never here. You're always off with your band."

Clarice looked up. "Sure they have," she said.

"Well, maybe not all of them," he said. "That's not the point."

"I guess," said Clarice, resuming her mission to locate and eliminate any party waste products that might be hiding from her. "So, Mom's upset because I don't see my school friends anymore?"

"Partly," said Ray. "And partly because you did not seem very happy when everyone yelled 'Surprise!'"

"I got a fright," Clarice lied. "I don't like surprises."

"That's what I told her."

"What did she say?"

Ray shrugged and grunted, in perfect imitation of his wife. Clarice nodded.

Ray came away from the doorway and started brushing the crumbs off the coffee table. They continued straightening the room quietly for a few minutes. When all the garbage was put away and the surfaces had been wiped clean, Ray said, "Okay, that'll do. You can sweep out the kitchen and do the dishes tomorrow."

"Goodnight, Dad," said Clarice, wiping her hands on her jeans and heading for the stairs.

As she got to the first landing, he called her name: "Clari?"

"Yes?" she said, irritated that he had shortened it. Irritated with the whole evening. Irritated that her parents were starting to interfere with her life, now that she was finally getting it headed in the right direction.

"We should have invited your band. Ignition, uh, Core. Corps."

"The P is silent, but whatever. I don't mind." It hadn't even occurred to her to invite the band. She would have enjoyed their company, she supposed, but she didn't think they would have appreciated being stuck in a house full of teenagers barely out of high school, drinking soda and eating microwave snacks.

"I'm sorry," he said. "I should have thought."

"Don't be sorry," said Clarice. "I'm not."

She went upstairs, moved toward her room...then veered off toward her parents' bedroom and inched open the door.

"Mom?"

"Clarice?" Amy was wide awake. She did not seem angry, but she was *awake*. After years and years of long nights and late shifts, Amy Marnier had the ability to fall asleep at will.

"Thanks for the party, Mom," said Clarice. "I had a good time."

"It's your eighteenth birthday, Clarice," said Amy, sitting up in bed. "I was beginning to think you'd forgotten it altogether."

"I didn't want to make a thing of it."

"Well, so long as you enjoyed it."

"I did. And the guitar cake was great."

"It was a tennis racquet," said Amy.

"Tennis racquets don't have whammy bars," said Clarice

Amy grinned. "I knew I should've left the whammy thing off."

"Goodnight, Mom."

"'Night."

Ray was still downstairs when she went back to her room. She could hear the cookware rattling and dishwater splashing.

She slipped on her flannelette pajamas and set her alarm for 6 a.m. The party had cost her hours of practice time and she would have to make it up before breakfast every day that week.

2. Hitting the Smalltime

Clarice barely even noticed when her finals were done. Her SATs were excellent; she had her choice of college. Clarice went for UCLA, so she'd be close to her band. She didn't even consider a different school. She wanted to stay in LA. Moving would take a lot of time and effort, and she resented anything that distracted her from her music.

First semester at college was good. Nobody cared if she skipped lectures so long as she turned in her assignments and showed up for finals. She didn't hang around on campus. Any new friends

Clarice made were accidental–she certainly didn't want any. She already had a band and a growing brace of guitars.

Summer came, and Clarice threw every spare moment she had into Ignition Corps, only taking time out to work her job stacking shelves in a supermarket and to attend a single jujutsu class each week.

Ignition Corps started out playing small venues and pubs, sharing the bill with five other small bands no one had ever heard of, all trying to make it to the small time. It was harder to make money playing original material. Some of the venues split the tiny amount of money they made from the cover charge amongst the bands; some paid only in free beer. Some of those wouldn't give Clarice her beer because she was well underage. Ignition Corps did not play any of those venues twice, even though Clarice seldom finished any beers she was given.

"We're professionals," she told the band. "We don't play for free."

3. Nuggets of Wisdom

It was after their twelfth live performance and Ignition Corps were loafing around amongst the crowd most of whom had arrived after the band had played their set. They were halfway through their third pitcher and watching the third act leave the stage when Alan cleared his throat and prepared to make a pronouncement.

"Something go down the wrong way, buddy?" interjected Samuels. "I think you need another drink."

Alan waved him away. "This band," he said, his diction perfect despite the fact he had consumed half a bottle of vodka in addition to his share of the free beer, "is really gonna go somewhere."

"I'd be surprised if we could get halfway to San Diego without filling up the gas." Samuels owned a beat-up old VW van, and was thus responsible for hauling the band and their equipment between venues.

"No, I mean it," Alan said. "I've been in lots of bands, but this is the first one I ever thought would go the distance."

"Honey, you're a lawyer," said Brenda. "You got a good job and buckets of money. You don't have to dream about becoming a rock star to get a shot at the good life."

"Exactly," said Alan. "I don't need to delude myself about our chances. But I believe that we–Ignition Corps–could become full-fledged rock gods, given the right opportunities."

"Given enough free beer, I might come to believe I was twenty feet tall and could pick gold nuggets out of my butthole," said Samuels, "but, come the morning? I ain't gonna be but six-nothing with a sore ass."

"Back me up, Clarice," said Alan. "I know you believe it."

Clarice was nursing her second beer and watching a roadie setting up the stage for the main act. She was always careful about how much she drank. She didn't want to overdo it. Didn't want to show weakness in front of her band. "Sure."

"See? We can do it."

"Because Clarice said so?" said Samuels.

"Because Clarice, period."

"Oh?" said Brenda. "Is that so?"

"Look," said Alan. "You, me, and Samuels? We're all pretty good players. We sound good and we look good—"

"I think you're real pretty, too," said Samuels.

Alan continued with barely a pause. "We're good, but that doesn't set us apart from the thousands of other bands that are out there, paying their dues."

"I thought we were all set for the big time," said Samuels.

"We are, because we have something no other band has: Miss Badass herself on guitar."

Brenda, Alan and Samuels all turned to look at Clarice. She was still watching the roadie. They had played with the next band before; the roadie looked an awful lot like their drummer. Clarice supposed that the rest of the band were in the staff toilets, doing their hair.

"We're not the only band with a chick guitarist," said Samuels.

"She's not just a chick guitarist," said Alan. "She's really fucking good."

"She is, huh?"

"Come on, you know it. We're good, but Clarice is special."

"Huh," sniffed Brenda. "Speak for yourself."

"Okay, maybe we are special," allowed Alan, "but Clarice here is really fucking special."

"She's too young for you, dude," said Samuels.

"I'm a lawyer. I already have six girlfriends," said Alan.

"Strippers don't count."

"They do if they tip you."

"That was a vision I could've done without."

Brenda cleared her throat loudly. "There are ladies present."

"Oh, yeah," said Samuels. "Sorry, Clarice."

"Hey, fuck you," replied Brenda.

"Anyway, I'm serious," said Alan. "Clarice is amazing."

"Don't hold back on the praise there, Alan," said Brenda.

"I'm holding back, too," said Samuels, "but sooner or later, I'm gonna have to go take a dump the size of a snare drum."

The roadie had finished setting up the stage and the piped music went off. Clarice drained her beer and put the empty glass down on the table. "We've seen these guys before," she said. "They suck." She stood up.

The others rose.

"I meant what I said," said Alan.

"So did I," said Samuels. He got up and shambled off toward the men's.

Brenda shook her head. Alan turned to Clarice and looked her right in the eye. "Well?" He stifled a small hiccup. "What do you say to all that?"

Clarice stared right back at him. "I think you're underestimating me," she said. She turned and headed for the exit.

4. Cutting Demos/Pulling Teeth

College started up again. Clarice was enrolled in English, Music, History and Mathematics. Music and English required very little attention or effort. History took some study—names and dates did not stick in Clarice's head as well as chords and scales. She took the mathematics because it was easy and because it pleased her father. He said it was a pathway into any of the scientific or engineering disciplines, which he thought she would be good at. They both knew that she didn't have the temperament to be an actuary like himself.

Ignition Corps started to gain a bit of local recognition. They played two regular gigs a week in the headline slot. Clarice decided it was time to cut a demo.

They picked their five best songs and booked some studio time. Clarice cancelled all of Ignition Corps's gigs and scheduled a rehearsal for every night of the two following weeks. She wanted the band to be able to play every song note-perfect when they got into the studio.

Alan fronted most of the money for the studio, but Clarice insisted that all members contribute something.

The band spent one day recording each song. Clarice and Alan spent two further days mixing and mastering it. She would have liked more time to lay down some extra guitar tracks and smooth out some of the kinks in the production, but money was running low and Brenda actually wanted time to study for her finals.

Clarice contented herself in the knowledge that she could re-record the songs later, if the EP got them where they wanted to go.

A graphic designer Alan was seeing helped them out with cover art. Clarice sent the EP to every alternative or college radio station in California and its adjacent states. One of them, she was sure, would even listen to it.

None of it worked. Ignition Corps remained one of about a dozen acts that the locals knew by name, but who never achieved the velocity required to escape the local scene. Clarice booked the band in for three, sometimes four gigs a week. She played harder and harder each night. She played with fury and bravado. She played until the band couldn't keep up and she was left to shred, unaccompanied. Nobody seemed to notice.

5. A Case of the Mundays

Clarice was coming down from the stage with sweat plastering her hair to her face and blood drying on her fingers when the man stepped in front of her, quite deliberately blocking her way.

He was wearing a black Bestial Warlust T-shirt and jeans. Scuffed black boots. He was tall and lean, with long red hair and big, dark eyes. A metal-head. She couldn't tell his age. He looked up at her and smiled.

"Get the fuck out of my way," she said, wishing that, just once, they could play a venue with an actual backstage.

"Gimme a minute," he said. He had an American accent that was so neutral he was probably a Canadian. Despite his appearance, he sounded like a TV news anchor. "I promise it'll be worth your time."

"I doubt it," said Clarice.

The red-haired man laughed and extended his right hand toward her. "I'm Rex Munday," he said. "Nice to meet you."

She took a slow, suspicious step down toward him. Rex Munday. The name was familiar. And the face, somehow.

"Rex Munday," she said, grabbing his hand and giving him a cartilage-popping handshake. "Clarice Marnier."

Rex Munday. She knew the name. He was the frontman for the DreadLords, a second-string metal band that were still hanging on to some minor success from the late '80s.

"How you doing, Clarice Marnier?"

"Very well, thank you, Rex Munday," she said.

Clarice had never had much regard for the DreadLords. They could play, and they went at it like they believed in it, but the most interesting thing about their material was the unintentionally hilarious lyrics. Clarice was pretty sure that the man who had accosted her was principally responsible for them.

"Go stash your gear and clean up," he said. "I'll wait."

"You don't have to." Finally, she'd worked out why his accent continued to confound her: she had always thought the DreadLords were British.

"Sure, I do. I got a proposition for you."

"A proposition," said Clarice.

"A proposition you'll like," he said.

6. DreadLords' Daughter

There was never any question that the members of Ignition Corps would drop what they were doing to tour in support of the DreadLords. Samuels quit his job at Burger King. Clarice left hers at the supermarket. She and Brenda deferred their semesters at college. Alan demanded–and received–twelve weeks of unpaid leave from his firm, even though he was being considered for partner status.

"We're going full-on for these shows," said Clarice. "The DreadLords' fans want metal, and that's what we're gonna fuckin' give them."

"No big ask. What else?" asked Samuels.

"We're going to get ourselves some wardrobe," said Clarice.

Brenda was all too happy to squeeze into a black leather mini and a halter top, fishnets and fuck-me boots. When Samuels told her that she needed a whip, she punched him hard enough to leave a bruise. He told her that he usually had to pay for that kind of treatment.

Samuels outfitted himself with some cheap pleather pants, army boots and a studded collar. Clarice went for jeans, boots, and black tank tops.

"What about me?" said Alan.

Clarice looked him up and down. "You're the drummer," she said. "Just make sure you remember to wear pants."

The DreadLords tour was set to spider across twenty-five states over three months. They played halls and clubs, up to a thousand warm bodies a gig. They weren't arena shows, but it was a big step above the pubs and clubs Ignition Corps usually serviced. None of the dates sold out but the venues were pretty full. All of them had proper backstage areas. Some of them even had dressing rooms.

The DreadLords did their thing: two-hour sets covering all of their different "periods," but heavy on their older stuff. No one ever got less than they expected.

Ignition Corps thrived on the large crowds, cramming every second of their meager fifty minutes on stage with blistering rock, barely taking the time to introduce themselves or name their songs. The crowds loved them. The DreadLords loved them, too. Rex Munday told Clarice that they'd never come on stage to audiences as hot-in-the-pants ready for them as they had with Ignition Corps to warm them up.

Clarice thanked him. "I always wanted a career as a crowd warmer."

Munday clapped her on the shoulder and winked. "Warming up is fine," he said. "Just try not to burn them out before I get on stage."

Clarice smiled and laughed and stomped away to sulk in the ancient bus the DreadLords' touring company had hired to haul her band and their gear around in.

The first week of the tour went fine. Ignition Corps was in good spirits. They hung out with the DreadLords, drank and partied and generally went wild. Clarice did her best to make sure that they never went too far off the rails. They were living like rock stars, but they did not have the big money or the clout of celebrity to get them out of bad trouble.

The second week was the same, but less so. Boredom started to set in as they rattled down endless roadways and sat around in anonymous motel rooms. They took to fighting amongst themselves just to stay entertained. Clarice stamped out any such arguments as quickly as they arose. No single member of Ignition Corps had the stones to start a fight with her, but they would sit together and stew in resentment at their common enemy.

Clarice was the only one who never got bored. She just went on as usual, maintaining her practice regimen as best she could. She sat alone with her instrument for hours on end, day after day, no matter how late the previous night's gig had gone or how hard they had partied afterwards.

In the sixth week, the band came to her as a group to air their grievances.

"What you're saying," said Clarice, "is that you think I should drink more, I should let you get arrested, and that I spend my spare time sitting around on the tour bus bitching instead of practicing and writing?"

"We just want to have a little fun, Clarice," said Samuels. "Loosen up a little. You're the youngest and you're acting like you're our fuckin' mother."

Clarice cocked her head left. Right. Squinted at him. "Your mother?"

"Yes, Ma."

"Well," she said, stepping right up Samuels, "if that's the case, I guess you better start calling me Mommie Dearest."

She sank her fist into Samuels's amply padded belly. He took a step back, trying to regain his balance, gagging as he tried to suck in some air to replace the breath that had exploded from his lungs. Brenda caught him and steadied him.

"Next time, I'll make you bleed."

Brenda and Alan stared at her mutely. Samuels hung between them, coughing and looking at Clarice's tennis shoes.

"This is my band and I'll run it how I want," she said. "If you don't fuckin' like it, you're free to leave."

The band sulked for the remainder of the tour, each member going off by him or herself between gigs. Samuels would drink. Alan would talk lawyer talk on his cell phone. Brenda hooked up with one of the DreadLords' roadies. Clarice practiced the guitar and kept herself fit and read books. It did not bother her that morale was in the toilet and she was the cause: the band was playing more furiously than ever, and they were staying out of trouble.

Something good was on the horizon, she just knew it.

7. Lawyers, Guns, and Money

They were playing Jackson, Mississippi, and there were three more dates left before the tour was over. Clarice sat near the stinking lake that stood in the property adjacent to the motel, practicing scales on her old spike-bodied Ibanez. The notes rang tinny on the unplugged guitar.

Munday stood watching her through his Oakley shades for a good minute before she acknowledged him. "Hey."

"Hey." Everyone was sweating profusely in the hot, heavy air. Munday was no exception, although he was far too self-possessed to show any discomfort.

Clarice went back to her scales.

"You play pretty good."

"Thanks," said Clarice, without looking up.

"Very good."

"Thanks," she said again.

"Very, very good."

"Thanks, Rex."

He didn't look like he was going anywhere.

"Is that all you came here to say?"

"Well," said Munday, grinning, "I was gonna introduce you to the guy from the record company who's been asking for you, but if you're too busy with F minor in the Aeolian mode, I can always send him away again."

It was almost as hot inside Clarice's and Brenda's motel room as it had been out by the lake. The fan only worked at its slowest setting and the wonkily spinning blades didn't seem to be cooling the room so much as redistributing the odors that emanated from the flooded bathroom. Samuels's and Alan's room was even worse.

The guy from Marchind Records was slim, young, and slick-haired. It looked like he'd been sharply dressed when he flew in from LA, but ten minutes in the humid Mississippi heat had left him looking as sodden and itchy as the rest of them. He introduced himself as Hoben Rhys.

"Love your work," he said. His accent, Clarice thought, was Australian. "You guys were great last night."

"You were there?" said Clarice.

"Uh, no," said Rhys, "but we got a tipoff from one of our local spotters who specializes in the genre."

"Which genre?"

"The rock genre, of course," said Rhys, puzzled and patronizing at once.

"Oh," said Clarice. "Of course."

"Anyway, he was so impressed that I flew out to see you personally. I want to sign you guys before someone else snaps you up."

"Let me see the contract."

"I'm A&R," said Hoben Rhys. "Lawyers do the contracts."

"So what am I supposed to sign?"

"What I have for you is a deal memo."

"A what?"

"It's a letter of intent. It affirms that you will sign with Marchind Records."

"But it's not a contract?"

"No, it's a letter of intent."

"If it's not a contract, why should I bother signing it?"

"You have to sign it before Marchind can deliver a contract."

"And when will that be?"

"We'll have to hammer one out with your lawyers in LA."

"My drummer is my lawyer," said Clarice.

Rhys paused, grinned, and laughed a clear, ringing laugh that echoed with sincerity. "A drummer joke," he said. "I love it. Is your bassist your physician?"

"Alan passed the California bar," said Clarice.

"It's true," said Munday.

"Does he work in the music industry?" asked Rhys.

"He's in a band, isn't he?"

Rhys laughed again. He took a large envelope from his briefcase, clipped a business card he took from a small aluminum holder onto it, and handed it to Clarice with a flourish. "Sign this and send it back to me ASAP. Then, when you get home to LA, find yourself a real lawyer and call me."

"I—"

"You have my home number, my office number, my cell phone, and my pager. We'll meet, the lawyers will sort it out, Ignition Corps will get rich and famous, Marchind will make money..."

"And Clarice," said Munday, eyes twinkling, "will continue to play the guitar."

8. Deal Memo

"What it is," said Alan, "is a binding statement that says we will sign with Marchind Records and no one else."

"But they're offering us a record deal," said Brenda, "and no one else is."

"I heard of these things before," said Samuels. "Everybody does them. There's nothing to worry about."

"I still don't like it," said Alan. "This 'memo' never expires."

"They never do," said Samuels.

"I wish we had a manager," said Brenda.

"They wouldn't have bothered if they didn't want to give us a contract," said Clarice.

"Yeah," said Alan, "but this means that if we don't like the contract they offer, we can't go anywhere else. Ever."

"And if we don't sign the memo?" asked Clarice.

"No contract at all," said Samuels.

"Whatever company we end up with, we're going to have to sign one of these before we get a contract, right?"

"I guess."

"Then we have to do it."

"I still don't like it," said Alan.

"Neither do I," said Clarice, "but it's a choice between an unfavorable deal or nothing."

"All right," said Alan. "But–as a lawyer and as a musician–I still don't like it."

"You're in the record biz now," said Samuels. "Get used to it."

9. Screwing the Pooch

"Marchind Records. Hoben Rhys speaking."

"Rhys, it's Clarice Marnier from Ignition Corps."

"Clarice! What can I do for you?"

"We're back in LA. You've got a record contract for me."

"Yes, indeed."

"Let me read you my new lawyer's details..."

"Oh, don't worry about that just yet. When can I meet with you?"

"I'm free tomorrow night, but I don't know about the others."

"Just you. It's your band, right?"

"Yes."

"Okay, just you and me. Tomorrow night. Do you know Bernadi's?"

"No."

"It's in the phone book. I'll make a reservation for eight."

"Eight at Bernadi's."

"Dress nice."

Clarice wore black slacks, a white blouse and a too-large black suit jacket she borrowed from her father. Her footwear collection consisted exclusively of boots and various types of sports shoes, so Amy had to take her out to buy some low-heeled pumps. Clarice wore them for the whole afternoon before discarding them in favor of spit-polished army boots.

"These boots are made for walking," she said. "Women's shoes aren't."

Bernadi's was a small place on Rodeo Drive with an elaborate Spanish exterior. The interior was done up in brass and brown leather. Baroque lamps grew off the scrollwork on the wood-paneled walls, shedding a diffuse orange light throughout the dining room.

Rhys was late. Clarice sat at the bar stewing and drinking imported beer for twenty minutes until Rhys showed up. He looked altogether less rumpled and considerably greasier than he had out in Mississippi.

Clarice wondered briefly why Marchind Records had seen fit to fly him out to Jackson so urgently. Were other companies really hustling to sign them? Or was it just that he was a jet-setting music industry maggot with a budget that could be freely spent on anything at all, so long as none of it fell into a musician's pocket?

The maître d' showed them to their table. It was low and round, covered with heavy white linen and set with chunky silver cutlery. A small candle floated in a yellow glass bowl amongst the crystal glassware.

Rhys made small talk until a waiter brought them menus and took their drink orders. Rhys ordered a bottle of expensive wine that Clarice had never heard of. She ordered a six-pack of Schlitz, just to see what the waiter would do.

"That is not on the menu."

"Then get your ass to the convenience store on the corner."

The waiter looked at Rhys, who shrugged and smiled. Clarice glared at the waiter until he went away.

Rhys talked endlessly about the big name acts he had worked with, citing sales figures and production costs, sharing amusing anecdotes about the poor business acumen demonstrated by exponents of the suddenly departed grunge scene.

The waiter arrived with Rhys's glass of Pinot and a glass flagon of Schlitz for Clarice. Clarice sent hers back. "I want them all at once, still sealed, in the plastic ring holder," she said. "And take away the glass."

The waiter did as he was told.

Rhys continued rambling until the waiter brought Clarice a fresh six-pack and asked if they were ready to order. Rhys ordered lobster in lychee and rosemary sauce. Clarice ordered a New York Strip, medium, with fries and a bottle of ketchup.

"Make it a big one," she said. "If I see more plate than steak, I'm gonna be upset."

Rhys found all of this mildly amusing.

Clarice drank the Schlitz and ate the bread rolls and pretended to listen to Rhys's stories. It seemed that her involvement in the conversation was not required. It was not until the food arrived that he turned the conversation to Ignition Corps and Clarice's career.

"You're going to go all the way," he said. "I know it. You have that look about you."

His timing was impeccable: he waited until Clarice had just put food in her mouth before pausing to let her speak, watched her chew for a moment, then continued before she could swallow and answer.

"You have the look. You have a great figure and a nice face. Not a gorgeous face, I admit, but you got attitude to make up for it. Bit of makeup and Michelle's your Auntie."

She swallowed a half-chewed mouthful quickly, but not quickly enough.

"I guess you're a bit more...athletic...than most other singers... but..."

Clarice put down the knife and fork. "I don't sing. I play the guitar."

"Your image is important."

"I'm not selling my body," said Clarice, "I'm selling music."

"You're selling whatever it is that kids will buy," he said. "Ignition Corps is fronted by two women; your market is girls."

"L7 sells to everyone. Veruca Salt. Juliana—"

"They were the sideshow at the carnival of grunge, and that carnival left town." Rhys looked at Clarice's boots. "We can't put you in a music video dressed like a truck driver."

"I don't think you—"

"No, Clarice, I understand perfectly well. 'Alternative' music belongs to us now. We bought it, and now we're the ones who have to sell it back to the kids...and believe me, we know how to sell. That's why we're still in control. That's why grunge is gone and we're still here."

"You still need musicians to write music for you to sell."

"Actually, no. We don't. And we're going to have even less use for musicians going forward; just you watch. In the meantime, we can still make money from your stuff, but...you need us more than we need you, and you know it."

"That's—"

"The truth. Clarice, if you want a career as a musician you have to sell records, and you can't sell records without making a deal with a record company."

"So why bring me here?" said Clarice. She'd given up on her meal altogether. "I said I'd sign your damn contract. What more can you want from me?"

"You know what I want?" said Rhys.

"What?"

"What I want is to see you play the guitar."

That gave her pause. "It can be arranged," she said. "I'm not booking any gigs until I know when we have some studio time, but—"

"What I want," said Rhys, "is to see you play the guitar. Naked."

Clarice gave him a flat, expressionless stare.

"What I want is to see you play the guitar, naked," said Rhys, "and then I want to bend you over a 200 watt Marshall and spank that cute little ass of yours. And then…"

"What I would like," said Clarice, "is to watch you bleed out in an alley–but I'm far too polite to ever bring something like that up at the dinner table."

"What I would like," said Rhys, "is for you to smile and say, 'Sure, Mister Rhys, whatever you want. I'll do anything for a record deal.'"

"You son of a—"

"You got to play the game, Clarice," said Rhys. "You got to make the record man happy, if you want him to…invest…in you. It's going to take a lot of marketing dollars to make rain in next year's climate, and I can promise you it's not going to get any easier for you than this."

"If you're looking for a novelty act and a quick fuck, you're looking in the wrong place," said Clarice. "But if you're looking for some grievous bodily harm you're sure going about it the right way."

"You signed the deal memo," said Rhys, smiling sweetly. "You do what I want, or Ignition Corps will never see a contract from me or from anyone."

"I'll deal with that—"

"I can also arrange to have you, personally, blacklisted by every record label in the country. You'll never get another chance, even if you put together a new outfit."

"I'll—"

"Start your own label? You won't get distribution. You play it my way, or your career is over already."

"We'll see about that, motherfucker," said Clarice, upsetting her chair as she stood up.

"We will indeed," said Rhys.

— BLOODY WATERS —

1. Going Down Swinging

Clarice did not furnish Ignition Corps with every last detail of her dinner with Rhys, but she did give them the worst of it: he was not going to give them a contract and wouldn't release them to sign with someone else.

"And you managed to get us blacklisted?" said Samuels.

"Not you guys," said Clarice. "Just me."

"You killed our deal with Marchind and you wiped out all of our chances of getting another one," said Brenda.

"That's correct," said Clarice.

"Shit," said Alan.

"I'm not going to say I'm sorry," said Clarice. "Because I'm not."

"Shit, girl," said Brenda. "All he did was make a pass at you. If you'd just said 'no, thank you,' he might just have laughed it off."

"I don't know about that," said Clarice.

"Okay, so maybe he wouldn't have given us a contract," said Samuels. "I can accept that. But if you'd been polite, he might have cut us loose—"

"Why would he bother?" said Alan. "There's no percentage in it for him."

"Because it's the right thing to do?"

"I told you that signing that deal memo was a bad fucking idea."

"Well," said Clarice, "it's too late now."

"So are what we gonna do?" asked Brenda.

"Same as before," said Clarice. "We play. If we can attract a label who'll offer Marchind a big enough sum to release us, I'm sure someone will step on Rhys and his grudge."

"Yeah, like that's gonna happen," said Samuels.

"What about this blacklisting thing?" asked Brenda.

"I think it was just a mindfuck. But even if it's true, I sure as hell ain't going down without a fight."

So they went about their business, same as before the DreadLords' tour. But it became harder, not easier, for them to book shows. The CDs they mailed out to radio stations and record companies started coming back unopened. The mainstream music press wouldn't speak to them, and the street press had lost interest.

"Did you speak to Munday?" asked Samuels.

"No," said Clarice. "He's in the Caymans, I think."

"Surely he can help us?"

"You don't think he's done enough for us already? Now we're gonna interrupt his holiday and ask for more favors?"

"Yes?"

"No."

The band started to screw up onstage. Samuels showed up drunk. Brenda stopped trying for the high notes. Alan hit the skins with perfect precision, but without passion. Clarice played harder and harder to make up for the deficit, but it wasn't enough.

"Fuck it," said Samuels. "Ignition Corps is done for."

"You're throwing in the towel?"

"Yeah," said Samuels.

"I think it's time we all moved on," said Brenda. "We might get somewhere if we split into other bands..."

"So long as I'm not in them," said Clarice.

"Yes," said Alan. "I'm afraid so."

"You're right, of course," said Clarice, "but I'm disappointed."

"Clarice, honey, someone like you is always gonna be disappointed," said Brenda.

"You expect others to be as dedicated, as committed as you," said Alan, "but people just aren't."

"'People' are weak," said Clarice.

"Yes," said Alan.

"Present company most certainly included," said Clarice. "All right. Ignition Corps is done. You're all dismissed."

2. In Session

Clarice went back to school and slogged through her degree. She joined other rock bands: some good, some bad. Tom's Dog, the Gunhawks, Squiddly Dee, the Bitches Three, Mucous Membrane. She played the blues with the Turkos, ska with the Burntboys, reggae with the Bread Monkeys. The bands in that small college scene shared players amongst themselves and Clarice cycled through all of them.

None of those bands copped regular gigs or support slots. None of the demos they cut got played. Nothing she did made any kind of ripple.

She had one semester of college left when Rex Munday called her up.

"Clarice," he said. "Mondrian just walked out on us, and I need someone to finish the guitars for the new album. You want to do it?"

"You sure you want me? I'm supposed to be blacklisted. Nobody will sign me to shit."

"Yeah, I heard about that," Munday replied, "but the DreadLords already have a contract. Nobody can stop us from hiring on a session guitarist...even if it's you."

"You really don't have to do this for me, Rex."

"Clarice, I'm asking you for help. What do you say? Worst case, you've made some money and you got your name on a real album. Best case...well, we'll see."

"What the hell," said Clarice. "Sure."

The album was pretty much done, except for the lead guitars. Clarice put in all of the free time she had and, when that wasn't enough, she started cutting classes to be in the studio.

The rhythm guitar Munday had laid down was pretty basic. Most songs only had a couple of riffs and an intro over the drum and bass and behind the vocals. Clarice added more rhythm, a sprinkling of licks and flourishes, and a solo to each song. Munday sat in the sessions, occasionally changing or adding a vocal line to go with the new guitars, but he never touched an instrument himself or interfered with Clarice's work. The engineer and the producer let her observe the mixing and mastering and answered all of her millions of questions about the process.

Clarice finished her finals while the album was being pressed. Cover art was commissioned. The track order was finalized. The DreadLords' PR people got them plenty of small interviews in the mainstream rock press and a lot of column space in the metal 'zines. They asked endless questions about Mondrian's departure. Nobody asked about Clarice.

Since she was not an official member of the band, Clarice stayed out of the publicity altogether, though she did join the band onstage when they played their pre-launch gigs. Playing with the DreadLords was easy; she'd watched them a million times when she'd been on the road with them. The music was simpler than her own material, and—with Munday playing rhythm—all she had to think about was the leads.

Clarice did not appear in any of the music videos or on any of the photographs inside the album sleeve, although her name did appear beside "Additional Guitars" at the bottom of the credits page.

When the album, *Satan Says Do THIS*, shipped to the public, a couple of radio stations picked up the first single. "Rock'n'die, Baby" wandered into the top 20 of the metal charts for a few weeks. After nine weeks the album went gold. Established DreadLords fans grumbled about Mondrian's absence, but they bought the disk anyway. New listeners started picking it up as well, liking the spruced-up sound.

Sales picked up for the second single, "Hardwired Evil." The album went gold again and the DreadLords asked Clarice to join them as a permanent member. She kept her reservations to herself and agreed. The DreadLords were still firmly entrenched in the subgenre that Clarice privately thought of as Big Stupid Metal, but they were competent and dedicated, they got regular gigs with decent-sized audiences, they had a record deal, and, most importantly, they let her play however she liked. It sure as hell beat stacking shelves in a supermarket.

Clarice didn't see the DreadLords as a permanent situation, but for the first time she felt like a professional. Her job was to perform and to record music, and she was paid nicely for her trouble. It wasn't really her band or her music, but, if she could build enough of a following with the DreadLords...

Well, she told herself, let's not sacrifice any chickens before they hatch.

The DreadLords booked a tour schedule that was just as punishing as the one that Ignition Corps had supported them on. Munday personally scouted local acts to support them in each destination, and all of them, without exception, proved to be abominable. Clarice wondered exactly how he had come to hire Ignition Corps on his previous outing.

The DreadLords were an affable bunch of guys, and they took good care of Clarice, treating her like a favored niece. They tried not to swear or fart or belch in her presence, they held doors for her, they let her have her own hotel room and they rigged a curtain inside the tour bus for her personal area. No one made a pass.

Clarice watched their antics with amusement; she knew how they usually behaved. "This isn't necessary," she told them on the first day of the tour.

"You're a sweet young girl. You don't want to be corrupted by a bunch of disgusting old men like us," said Antonovic, the DreadLords' bassist.

"Oh, bullshit," said Clarice. "I can out cuss and outfight every fucking one of you—one at a time or all at once."

They laughed. They kept on holding doors for her. She kept on cursing at them. It became a game.

The tour went more easily than it had when Ignition Corps had been around. The DreadLords fought amongst themselves occasionally, but it never got nasty—the boys were so accustomed to being in each other's presence that they'd already argued through every variation of every gripe to the point where they already knew how every disagreement would end.

Clarice had no responsibilities other than to show up on stage and to hit the right notes at the right time. Unlike her tour with Ignition Corps—which had lasted forever—this tour passed in a haze. When it was done, she it felt as if she'd driven down one very long road, stayed in one cheap motel, and played one extended gig.

After the tour, the DreadLords took a break. The album was gold and still selling reasonably well. Clarice found herself a new apartment in West Hollywood, bought herself a car, and still had a sliver of DreadLords money left over. She got back into jujutsu and practiced the guitar all day, every day. She did not perform or go out. She went unrecognized in the street.

Clarice had been in a spell since Ignition Corps had disbanded, and she knew it. It was like living in a dream, but she couldn't figure out if it was a good one or a bad one.

3. Ménage à Trois

A month after the end of the Satan Says tour, Munday called up Clarice and arranged to meet with her in a restaurant on Rodeo Drive somewhere. She took down the time and the address and stuck it on her fridge with a skull-shaped magnet. It was not until she arrived that she realized that she'd been there before.

She wasn't dressed for Bernadi's. Didn't give a shit. She didn't have to impress anyone, and God help any maître d' that refused her entry.

The maître d' didn't look at her twice when she walked in wearing ripped jeans and a faded Primus T-shirt. Rex was waiting for her at a window table, dressed in much the same way. His T-shirt said "Sadistik Exekution."

"Am I late?" she asked.

"Nope," said Munday. "I was early. Sit down, I'll find a waiter." He seemed pleased to see her, but there was a concern in his voice she had never heard before.

Rex ordered wine; Clarice asked for water. The waiter left them with menus. Clarice wasn't sure if he was the one who had previously served her Schlitz.

"I'll get right to the point," said Rex. "Otherwise, it's gonna spoil both our meals."

"Go ahead," said Clarice.

"Mondrian's back," said Rex.

"That's gonna be a problem," said Clarice.

"I don't much want him back," said Rex. "He's always been an asshole and he's never been much good...but he's also been one of my closest friends."

"Especially now that the DreadLords are making money again?"

"Right."

"I see where this is going," said Clarice.

"He went to the record company and they signed him back before they spoke to me," said Rex.

"I see."

"I said, 'okay, so we're a three-guitar band, now?'"

"And the record company said 'no'?"

"The record company said 'no'," said Rex.

"So, I'm out."

"Yes."

Clarice nodded.

Munday sighed. "Clarice, we haven't been this popular for ten years, and it's entirely your doing. We all know it."

"Thanks, Rex."

"We all know it, but Mondrian doesn't want you around and neither does the record company."

"Did Mondrian approach your label, or did they come to him?"

"I don't know," said Rex. "Everybody has been really cagey about the whole deal."

Clarice smiled slowly. "So Rhys *did* have me blacklisted, after all."

"Sure looks that way." Munday sounded glum.

Clarice could feel the blood pulsing through her. Her heart pumped a slow, measured beat. There was no adrenaline rush, no increase in her respiration, no physical reaction at all to signify her return to full consciousness. No anger or fear or hatred. Just a wakening.

Her enemy was real.

It was the best news she'd had since Munday had invited her band to support him on tour.

A real enemy. That was something she could fight.

"Thanks for giving it to me straight, Rex," said Clarice. "Let's order. I'm hungry."

She let Rex pay for the meal and wished him and the new-old DreadLords the best of luck. He apologized to her for not having done more for her and wished her luck in return. She didn't really hear any of it.

It was time to start a new band.

4. Johnny Chernow

Clarice started going to see bands on the local circuit. Any band, any genre, any time, any venue. Anywhere in LA. Here and there she found a musician that she wanted for her new band, but she did not approach any of them. She needed something else–some catalyst–if this was going to come together properly. She didn't know what it was, but she knew it was out there. Knew it as surely as her fingers made their chords.

Clarice found the Razorbacks playing grunge covers on a tiny stage on the second floor of a huge nightclub on Santa Monica Boulevard. The bassist was good–probably had some kind of jazz background–but a bit stiff. The drummer was talented but lacked the mad-eyed wildness Clarice was looking for. And then there was the front man, who introduced himself as Johnny Chernow.

Johnny was about Clarice's age. Tall, broad-shouldered, with long blond hair and friendly blue eyes. He wore black jeans, a black T-shirt and a pair of outrageously buckle-encrusted motorcycle boots.

Johnny was good. Damn good. He could switch from rhythm to leads without pause, making the music his own on both guitar and vocals, referencing the original artists without copying or kissing ass. Clarice was impressed.

There wasn't much of a crowd for the Razorbacks. The rock scene had really ebbed since Kurt Cobain had eaten his shotgun, and most of the club's patrons had come to dance to the saccharine-pop that was playing on the dance floor on the ground level.

When it was plain that nobody gave much of a shit what they played, Johnny Chernow took a moment to address the crowd. "All right," he said. "The good people who run this fine establishment have employed us to play covers, but this show is for you ladies and gentlemen, not for them. You know all these songs already and you seem to be a bit bored with them, so I gotta ask: are any of you folks interested in hearing something new?" He spoke with good humor, but there was a hint of desperation in his voice.

The crowd didn't provide much of a reaction, just confused mutters and a rising tide of inattentive chitchat.

Clarice, sitting at a table by herself at the back of the room, said "Yes."

"All those in favor, yell out," said Johnny Chernow.

"Yes," said Clarice, raising her voice until–just barely–it cut through the hubbub.

"All right!" said Johnny Chernow. "By popular demand, some Razorbacks originals. Can I get a 'yeah!?'"

He didn't get much of a yeah, but they went for it anyway. It was like watching a completely different band.

Johnny slashed out big, crunching riffs and sharp, focused solos. He let the drums and the bass have their space, but there was no question it was his show. He switched to a steel-string and played a bluesy slide-guitar bridge. He drew out some Middle Eastern sounding lines while the rhythm section kicked up a jungle beat that Clarice couldn't quite identify. And they made it sound good.

She hated to admit it, but the Razorbacks were better than Ignition Corps had ever been. It was a shame she was going to have to destroy them.

Johnny Chernow was the real deal. Easily the best guitarist she'd seen in her rounds: agile, precise, and soulful. But it wasn't his guitar work that impressed her, as much as his voice.

Johnny preferred to sing low, but he could hit the higher registers if he wanted. He could do smooth, he could do rough. He could scream and growl and croon and howl. He could invoke any other vocalist he wanted, every croak and crack and imperfection, every trademark yelp or wail, cry or roar. He had a voice, and he knew how to use it.

The Razorbacks finished their set to a smattering of applause. They thanked the audience and came down off the stage, carrying their unplugged instruments. Clarice got up and moved to intercept them as they negotiated their way through the clot of tables. The bassist and the drummer filed past her, oblivious, but Johnny, who had watched her threading her way toward them, stopped and waited for Clarice to draw level.

"I help you, Miss?" he said. He had his guitar at port arms.

"Yes, you can," said Clarice. "Come find me in the foyer when you're done packing up."

Johnny looked her over expressionlessly. He was a good five inches taller than she was. After a moment he smiled, said "Yes, ma'am," and turned and headed after his band before she could retort.

Twenty minutes later Johnny walked into the lobby, empty-handed. His hair was tied back, and he was wearing a leather jacket over a fresh T-shirt, but he still smelled of the stage. "What can I do for you?" he asked.

"My name is Clarice Marnier," she said.

"Oh, yeah," he said, shaking her hand. His grip was warm and strong. "You did the guitars on the DreadLords' last album. I heard about you."

"Nothing good, I hope."

"Nothing good at all," he said, grinning.

"Well, I'm not with them anymore."

"I heard that, too. They got Trevor Mondrian back."

"Where he belongs."

"I think it's to the detriment of the band, but I guess you're right."

Clarice just stood there, looking at him with a disconcerting intensity.

"Funny, though..." he said. "I always thought they were part of the New Wave of British Metal. I had no idea they were from LA. "

"Before I met them, so did I."

"Anyway, Miss Marnier, how can I help you?"

"I'm starting a new band," she said. "I need a singer."

He did not seem taken aback. "You don't know anything about me."

"Describe yourself in thirty words or less."

"Uh, oh. Okay." He shrugged. "Johnny Chernow. Twenty-two, college graduate. I work for a temping company doing office shit and I play in a band called the Razorbacks. My hobbies are tennis, old horror movies, black magic, and saving homeless kittens. How many words was that?"

"Enough," said Clarice. "You'll do."

"Really?"

"Really."

"I lied about the kittens."

"I know," said Clarice.

"So, I'm your new singer now?"

"Yes," said Clarice, leering. "And I'm pretty sure I can find some other uses for you as well."

It was the last time the Razorbacks ever played together.

5. Blood on the Water

Once she had her catalyst it did not take long for the rest of the band to fall into place.

Johnny knew a session bassist named Enrique Pizarro who played with metronomic precision and blinding speed. He could pluck, pick, or slap with equal facility, and he never needed to be prompted as to which key they were playing in.

Enrique didn't say much, even for a bassist. Once he had introduced himself–"I'm Enrique, I play the bass,"–Clarice heard nothing but grunts and monosyllables from him unless he was ordering drinks at a bar. "Eight shots of Cuervo. Leave the bottle."

Clarice found Mia Beresford in an all-girl thrash-punk outfit, playing a fifteen-minute set amongst five other bands in a tiny bar somewhere out near LAX. The band was forgettable, but perhaps that was because the other instruments were so hard to hear over Beresford's vehement drumming. After their set, it took five bouncers to drag her bodily out from behind the drum kit.

Beresford had moved to LA as soon as she'd graduated high school. She worked on the killing floor in an abattoir by day. By night she played drums in three different bands. She would not allow anyone to address her by her first name.

Clarice rented a small hall in the youth center near where she lived and set up a jam session for the four of them. No warmup. She just plugged in and cut loose and demanded they join in.

Clarice hadn't really wanted a rhythm guitarist, but Johnny was too good to pass up. He brought new ideas to music that complemented Clarice's work without competing with it, slotting in smoothly and seamlessly, enervating her leads without diverting attention from them.

It all worked beautifully. Clarice's chemistry with Johnny was undeniable, and Enrique and Beresford seemed to cohere equally well as a rhythm unit. They had an intuitive understanding and, while Clarice was most definitely in charge of the proceedings, each musician got their chance at being the sun around which the other players orbited. All of them shone in the role.

After the jam session Clarice opened a case of Sierra Nevada and passed bottles to everyone.

"Congratulations," she said, using the inside of her forearm to twist the top off her bottle. "We are *fucking awesome.*"

"Hey, that's not bad," said Johnny, opening his beer with his fingers, "but I can't see a record company signing us with a name like that."

"A name like what?" mumbled Beresford. She spat out a bottle cap.

"Like 'Fucking Awesome'," said Enrique, still struggling to open his own beer.

Beresford took it away from him, smashed the top of it off on the side of a table, and handed it back. "That's a fucking awesome name for a band," she said.

"I don't think it's hardcore enough," said Clarice.

"The Skullfuckers," suggested Beresford.

"No," said Clarice. "Come on. What do we want in the name?"

"I always wanted to be in a band called 'Red Jack,'" said Johnny.

"Good reference," said Clarice, "but no."

"I guess." Johnny sounded a bit disappointed.

"I want something that invokes the blues," said Clarice. "But I want something that's forward-looking, too. And it has to sound hard ass."

"'Robert's Johnson,'" said Johnny.

"Too lame."

"'Hooker's Asshole?'" said Beresford.

"Too stupid."

"'Black and Blue'?" said Enrique.

"Sounds like a soccer team."

"I don't hear any suggestions from you, Marnier," said Beresford.

"Fine," said Clarice. "The band is now officially called 'Bloody Waters.'"

"You just think of that now?" said Enrique, after a brief silence. "Or were you saving it up?"

"Just now."

"I like it," said Beresford.

"Good for you," said Clarice.

"Okay, what next?" said Johnny.

"First, we need some songs," said Clarice. "From the way today went, that shouldn't take long." She turned to Johnny. "The vocals are all yours, but I'm writing the lyrics. Is this going to be a problem?"

"Are they gonna be like...DreadLords lyrics?"

"Absolutely not."

Johnny grinned. "Okay, sure. What's second?"

Clarice hesitated for a moment. This was the hard sell.

They were a winning unit. She knew it already, and they did, too. But Clarice's past was a liability. She needed to put some space between herself and Ignition Corps and the record companies and Hoben Rhys if they were going to have any chance at success.

"Second thing," said Clarice, "is a fresh start in a new scene. No old band buddies, no old fans, no old enemies..."

"What you're saying is, we got to pull up our socks and wash behind our ears?"

"What I'm saying is, we're moving to San Francisco."

6. San Fran

In the end, they went for it.

Johnny didn't have much of anything in LA. Enrique and Beresford were dirt poor, barely scraping by, and they weren't really getting anywhere in their current situations. Clarice offered to pay everybody's moving costs and that was that.

The plan was to come in low and hard and fast, under the radar. To get so big so quickly that the record companies would have to give them a record deal or risk seeing San Francisco Bay run red. Bloody Waters would secure a record deal or provoke the apocalypse–and then they'd play the Four Horsemen out of the sky.

It might have worked, too, if they'd been a year earlier.

Even at the end of the grunge revolution it might have been possible for an unknown band to force its way into the limelight, if they were good enough and dedicated enough. But Cobain was dead, the '90s were aging, and there wasn't much limelight left.

Bloody Waters certainly made an impact. They blew away the small shows they played in their first week. They were promoted to headline billing in the following weeks, and they blew those out as well. The street press got interested, and Johnny–whom Clarice had appointed as the band's spokesman–fielded a number of interviews. Clarice herself kept a low profile. She avoided the press, and Johnny was under instructions not to give out her full name in any interviews. She told him she was thinking about wearing a mask on stage. Or a paper bag.

"Like Buckethead?" he had asked, as innocently as he could. That was the end of that idea.

She was a strange girl, but Johnny liked her. He liked her unrelenting intensity, her refusal to compromise, her bluntness, her ferocious intellect. The rest...the rest of it puzzled him, and she offered no explanation. He thought she was destined to be a single-name celebrity: like Madonna or a Prince, in army boots and brass knuckles.

Clarice wasn't as angry as he had expected when her name leaked out. She swore and looked away and actually seemed to retreat a little. "It was going to happen eventually," she said. "I guess we'll see what happens now."

Johnny didn't understand what magic her name was supposed to invoke, but as far as he could tell nothing happened. A whole lot of nothing, in fact. Interviews dried up, press coverage went away, the buzz died off. San Francisco may as well have been the Kalahari Desert, as far as Bloody Waters was concerned.

Johnny didn't understand it, but he was certain Clarice did.

7. Drastic Measures

A thunderstorm rolled in off the Bay. Gale force winds shook the city. Hailstones the size of throwing stars exploded against its towers. Lightning clawed the sky, and the thunder bellowed its hate.

Clarice had been working the 100-pound punching bag strung up in the living room of her apartment for forty solid minutes before Johnny ambled in from the bedroom in his boxer shorts and motorcycle boots. He sat down on the couch and watched Clarice continue to brutalize the bag.

"You gonna tell me what's going on, exactly?"

"Same. Old. Shit," she said, slamming a fist into the bag with every syllable.

"And that shit is...?"

"Some things I never told you," she said. She loosed a final flurry of punches and elbows and knees at the bag and turned away from it abruptly, leaving it swinging and spinning on its chain.

He waited for her to collect herself.

"The short version," she said, shaking her hands free of the binding tape. "Back in the day, I messed with the wrong record exec, and I've been blacklisted."

"Blacklisted?"

"From getting any kind of record deal."

"How...wide...is this blacklisting?"

Clarice sat down on the floor and started rolling up the tape. The bag swung slowly behind her, twisting on its creaking chain.

"Don't know," she said. "California, looks like. Probably all of North America."

"You could go overseas. Europe, Canada..."

"I'm an American," said Clarice. "That's not fucking good enough."

"So, what are we gonna do about it?"

Clarice stood up. She flexed her fingers, her knees. Clenched her fists. "Something drastic."

"How drastic?"

"Drastic," she said.

"Can I make a suggestion?" asked Johnny, folding his arms and cocking his head.

"You can," she said, "but if it's lame, I'm going to hit you."

"Well," he said, "you remember I said I was into black magic?"

— GET THEE BEFORE ME —

1. Patron of the Dark Arts

Clarice rented a small house near the beach in Malibu while Johnny returned to Los Angeles to retrieve his library of occult literature from storage. He loaded it all up into the back of his El Camino and drove up to meet her the following day.

Johnny took over the living room and the downstairs bedroom of the beach house for his necromanteion and buried his head in the books. He found about a dozen different spells for summoning the Devil pretty quickly, but none of them looked very easy to pull off.

Clarice had agreed to Johnny's idea without a moment's hesitation, but he wasn't entirely certain why. Perhaps she was humoring him. Perhaps she was curious. Perhaps it just seemed like a rock'n'roll thing to do. But, as long as she appeared to be taking it seriously, he had to as well. At the very least, it was an excuse for a holiday at the beach. Not that Johnny got to see very much of it.

Three days into his preparations, the singer started to feel like he was being set up for a practical joke.

"Why would you say that?" asked Clarice.

"Because you don't seem very concerned about how this is gonna turn out."

"Why should I be? It'll turn out fine." They were standing on the back porch. Clarice was barefoot, carrying a towel, ready to walk to the beach. Johnny stayed in the shade of the veranda. He burned easily.

"Because...because I'd have to be seriously messed up to actually think I could do this, right?"

"Not any more messed up than I am."

"Even if you don't think I'm messed up, and I do pull this off... the Devil is way scarier than a psycho boyfriend."

"I don't believe you're a psycho."

"I'm not," he replied. "Do you believe in the Devil?"

"I'm not religious," said Clarice.

"You don't believe in a God, then, either?"

"Let's just say I'm agnostic," said Clarice. She hesitated. "But I don't see how that matters."

"Right now, it matters."

"I'm keeping an open mind. But even if I did have evidence one way or the other, why should it change how I live my life?"

"Really?"

"Say I saw an angel. What then? Do I become a priest? Fuck that—I'm a musician."

"If you saw an angel, surely that would make you think there's a heaven? And then you'd want to go there. And that means being good and playing by the rules."

"Bullshit." Clarice adjusted her sunglasses and pulled the peak of her cap lower. "I don't care how the universe runs itself—I'm going to think for myself. I may not have an opinion about God and the Devil, but I do believe in free will. I live for me, not for... whatever." Clarice waved a hand in the air. "Otherwise, what's the point?"

"Some might say that's precisely the point."

"What is?" Clarice was getting impatient.

"To test your faith."

"I have faith in myself. Any deity who wants more than that can go fuck itself." She turned and started walking toward the beach.

"So, you think it's a waste of time, trying to work out how to summon the Devil?"

"I didn't say that." Clarice didn't look back. She pushed open the gate and was gone.

On the sixth day of their Malibu sojourn, Johnny walked down to the beach holding a sheaf of notes and blinking in the sunlight. "I think this is the one," he said.

Clarice was lying on a towel reading a Joe Lansdale thriller. She was wearing a black one-piece and a pair of mirrored shades. The towel was also black. She looked lean and tanned and relaxed and dangerous and altogether fine, Johnny thought.

"The one what?" Clarice didn't look up from the novel.

"The spell."

"Oh?" Clarice tried to sound disinterested, but she got a kick out of all the old books with the text in Latin and Hebrew. Didn't hurt that this was the first holiday she had taken since she was in high school, either. She was surprised at how much she enjoyed having time to sit on the beach and swim in the sea and jog along the esplanade. And practice the guitar, of course, but that didn't count as work. Work was organizing gigs, accommodation, transport, publicity, rehearsals.

It was nice to spend time alone with Johnny, too.

"Yeah," said Johnny. "This is the spell. The syntax is nice and clear, it doesn't require any fancy ingredients, and the incantation is in modern English."

"Great," said Clarice, lowering the novel and turning her head to look at him, "so when are you gonna try it out?"

"Now?"

"Now is good."

"Come on inside," said Johnny. "I've already laid down the pentagram and I can be ready to go in about ten minutes."

"Okay," said Clarice. She tucked the book under her arm and stood up. "Have you thought about what you're going to do if... you know." She couldn't quite bring herself to say it. She would feel ridiculous, and then she would laugh, and then Johnny would feel stupid, too, and that would ruin the whole idea. And Clarice liked the idea.

"If somebody actually shows up?"

"Right."

"I have some ideas," said Johnny, "but you're right: we should talk about it first. You have a plan?"

"The plan is, we ask for a record deal," said Clarice.

"You know the terms, right?"

Clarice scowled. "I'm not selling my soul. Not to the Lord of Darkness, not to Hoben Rhys, not to anyone. And you better not think about offering yours."

"I think we're getting in line for Hell just by casting the spell," said Johnny. "Just by being in the music business. Does it really make a difference if we sign ourselves away a little earlier?"

"Yes, it does," said Clarice. "I'll deal with Hell when the time comes, if I have to."

"So how are we going to pay for this?"

"I'll figure out something."

They went inside. Johnny tuned the radio to a local classic rock station and set about marking out the rest of the spell on the slate floor. Clarice went into the kitchen for a can of Coke and a sandwich.

When she emerged, the curtains were closed and the blinds drawn. There were three pentagrams painted on the floor. Johnny stood wiping the paint off his hands with a piece of paper towel.

"You stand in that one," he said, pointing at one of the two smaller pentagrams that he had positioned across the room from the large one. "I'll be in this one." Curved lines strung with strange symbols connected all three circles. "If the spell works, Satan will be in the big one."

"Okay," said Clarice. She stepped into her pentagram and took a sip from her can of soda.

Johnny laid down the candles and then went around lighting them with the flame-wand that had been clipped to the gas stovetop. When they were all lit, he stood up and surveyed his handiwork.

"Are you ready?" asked Clarice.

"Yes. Are you?"

"Yup."

"Aren't you going to put some clothes on?"

"Why?"

"Well, I dunno. Do you think swimwear is appropriate?"

"What's appropriate? A red robe? An Ozzie T-shirt?"

"Clarice, this is business."

"We're rock stars. No one is going to take us seriously if we look like we work in an office."

"Will you at least put down the soda?"

Clarice drained the can in three big gulps, crushed it in her fist, and turfed it in the direction of the kitchenette. "Are you going to cast your damn spell already?"

"Yes," said Johnny. He walked over to the radio and switched it off, then returned to his pentagram. Clarice checked that both her feet were still inside her own, took off her sunglasses, and folded her arms.

Johnny took a deep breath, looked at the sheet of paper that he'd copied the incantation onto, and spoke:

"Great Lord Satan, I call upon thee to manifest thyself in the space I have marked. King of the Darkness, I bind you to this circle by your dread symbols and by my own."

He spoke with confidence, but the wood paneling dampened his voice too much to let the words ring.

"While contained in this circle, your Dread Majesty is constrained from doing harm to me and mine; by might or by sorcery or by any agency external to yourself. I bind you with the power of all the sages and sorcerers who have laid this very enchantment before me in ages past; I bind you with the power of all the magicians and conjurers who will lay this enchantment yet, in the ages yet to come; I bind you now, in this age, in this moment, with my own will.

"I bind you until Armageddon falls or I speak your release. I command and abjure thee, Lucifer, your Black Highness, Warden of Hell: come forth."

In the quiet following the invocation the sounds of the beach filtered into the house: the sea rushing in to the shore and receding, palm trees rustling and shivering in the breeze. A car rumbled down the gravel track on the property next door. A rollerblader skated by on the esplanade. A seagull cried for scraps.

The refrigerator cycled on. The darkened house smelled of pine needles, suntan lotion and dust.

The main pentagram stood empty.

Clarice looked at Johnny. He turned to regard her, expressionless. His shoulders fell. Clarice shrugged and looked away.

"Ahem."

Johnny raised his head and squinted. Clarice looked at him, then followed his gaze across to the main pentagram.

The air above the painted lines seemed to be smudged. A gap in the blinds behind the pentagram cast a narrow blade of bright sunlight across the room, making it difficult to discern any details of the dark shape that stood there—if there was, in fact, anything there at all.

"Ahem," said the smudge, a little more loudly. It wasn't any more distinct than before, but it seemed bigger. It looked, she decided, as if someone with extremely large, dirty hands had left a six-foot tall fingerprint on the air.

"Oh." Clarice addressed the fingerprint. "Was that supposed to be a dramatic entrance?"

"It's only dramatic if you don't expect it," said the Devil. "I quit doing smoke and thunder in the sixteenth century." His voice was male. Deep, but not unusually so. A neutral American accent. Unremarkable.

"I'm Johnny Chernow," said Johnny. "This here is..."

"Hello, Clarice," said the Devil, doing a passable imitation of Sir Anthony Hopkins.

"Cute," snorted Clarice. "I've never heard that one before."

"So. Johnny. Clarice. What can I do for you?"

"I'm blacklisted from getting a record deal," said Clarice.

"I'm aware of the situation."

"Can you do anything about it?" asked Johnny.

"Of course I can do something about it," said the Devil, "but you should be asking me whether or not I *will*."

"Will you?" asked Clarice.

"Sure," said the Devil.

After a moment, Johnny said, "That's it?"

"That's what?"

"That's all it takes?"

"Pretty much," said the Devil. "Aside from the matter of payment, of course."

"Oh, uh, yes," said Johnny. "I forgot about that."

"Sure you did," said the Devil, good-naturedly. "Luckily for me, I didn't."

"What are you asking?" said Clarice.

"What do you think?"

"I couldn't possibly guess."

"Tell you what," said the Devil. There was something self-deprecating in his tone. "For today only, I'm gonna make you a special offer. Since only Clarice has been blacklisted, I'll be happy to fix you up for the cost of a single soul."

"I don't think so," said Clarice.

"Too bad," said the Devil. "I like you kids, I really do. I was looking forward to doing business with you, and I'd like nothing more than to see you achieve the success you deserve...but, you know, I am who I am. I'm not a patron of the arts. I need a soul, or it's 'thank you, goodbye'."

"Does it have to be Clarice's soul?" asked Johnny.

"Nope," said the Devil. "Not at all."

Clarice fixed Johnny with a glare. "I've already warned you," she said. "If you do this, Hell will seem like a vacation once I'm done with you."

"I wasn't going to offer my soul either," said Johnny. He turned to the fingerprint. "Can we sell you...someone else's?"

Clarice grinned.

"Lateral thinking," said the Devil. "I'm impressed."

"Is that a yes? Will you accept a third party...uh, fourth party... uh...somebody else's soul?"

"I will accept someone else's soul," said the Devil.

"Okay, cool," said Johnny, pleased with himself. He looked at Clarice, but she was still watching the fingerprint.

"What's the catch?" she asked.

"There's no catch. I'll accept any soul you deliver to me."

"But?"

"But...have you any idea how you're going to procure one?"

"What do you mean?"

"You have to forcibly separate it from its host body, contain it, process it, and package it before I can accept it. I can't just take it from whichever random schmuck you nominate."

"Oh," said Johnny. "That could be a problem."

"It's not an easy thing, to harvest a soul."

Johnny chewed the insides of his cheeks. "Shit."

After a few moments' silence, the Devil said, "Perhaps I could be persuaded to author an appropriate spell for you, Johnny. Since you're a sorcerer, and everything."

"Not much of one," said Johnny. "This is the first time I've done anything that actually worked."

"Don't be so hard on yourself," said the Devil. "This was a pretty good start, wasn't it?"

"I guess so."

"I can write you a one-off, easy-to-cast spell, tailored to the unwilling donor of your choice–no sweat."

"Really?" said Johnny.

"Of course," said the Devil. "I can help you with anything...for a price."

Clarice snorted softly. "Tell me you didn't see that coming," she said.

"Two souls?" said Johnny.

"Then you'll need two spells from me," said the Devil. "Do the math."

"Can't you just throw the second one in?" said Clarice.

"I'm already giving you a twofer."

"Shit."

"Maybe I can find the spell for myself," said Johnny.

The Devil sighed. "I was trying to encourage you," he said, "but we both know you're not up to it. It will take a good fifteen years of hard study before you can think about pulling off something like this, unassisted."

"I could find someone to help me..."

"Sure, you could," said the Devil. "And let's say you do find a sorcerer who can capture the soul for you. It'll be someone you trust to help you tear the soul out of some innocent. Someone you trust will allow you to keep the soul once you've liberated it."

"There are other options."

"Sure. You might try bargaining with one of my lieutenant demons. Or, you could approach an old pagan god. Petition for a Guardian Angel. Or, you know, just pray really, really hard..."

"What are you saying?" said Clarice.

"I'm saying that you're welcome to shop around–I won't be offended–but you won't find better terms than I'm offering you, and I can't promise that I'll be feeling this generous next time we speak."

"I don't believe you."

"That's your prerogative," said the Devil. "I am the Lord of Lies, these days." He sounded a little disgruntled about it. After a moment he brightened. "But I am prepared to guarantee that nothing I will say, for the remainder of this exchange, is a lie. If I speak you false you may have what you desire, free and gratis."

"That doesn't make this even one tiny bit easier," said Johnny.

"Oh, come on. Concentrate! I'm trying to help you guys out. I'll give you a really great deal, but if you can't figure out how to bargain for it properly then you just don't deserve it."

Johnny scratched his head. "If this spell is still going to cost me my soul, I may as well just buy the fucking record deal from you straight out and save myself all the trouble."

"No," said Clarice, "Listen to the man. The beast. The... whatever..."

"'The Devil'. Or 'Satan' or 'Lucifer', if you want something more personal. Or 'Sir', if that feels too familiar. I'm easy."

"Listen to Satan, here," said Clarice. "I don't think this spell will be as expensive as our record deal."

"What are you saying?"

"I'm saying, don't walk away without even asking him the price."

"Heh." The Devil sounded pleased, although it was difficult to discern his facial expression from his fingerprint. "You are a clever girl."

"All right," said Johnny. "What are you asking for the spell?"

"A favor," said the Devil.

"What kind of favor?" said Clarice.

"I don't have a specific one in mind," said the Devil. "That's why I called it 'a favor'."

"We could, say… sacrifice some chickens every now and again?" said Johnny.

"Don't be stupid."

"What kind of favor?" repeated Clarice.

"It won't be anything particularly horrible. Well short of murder, I think."

"We're going to have to murder someone to get a soul out of them, though," said Clarice, finally sounding a little bit troubled.

"No, no," said the Devil. "It's quite possible to live without a soul. Take any record executive, for example, and you will more than likely find a creature as devoid of a soul as your kitchen toaster."

"Funny you should mention record execs," said Clarice.

"Isn't it?" said the Devil.

"Okay," said Clarice. "A favor I can handle, but I'm telling you now…and I want this in the contract…I'm not going bear you any demon babies. I won't torture, maim, rape or kill. I will not cover any hair metal songs, either. That goes for Johnny, too."

"That works," said the Devil.

"Hey, what's wrong with hair metal?" said Johnny.

Nobody bothered to answer him. Eventually, Johnny looked at Clarice.

"Well, what do you think?"

"I think you're low on options," said the Devil. "Either you take this deal, or you'll have to go back to Hoben Rhys."

2. The Kosmik Kube

Clarice and Johnny drove back to LA and booked themselves into a room at a large hotel in Beverly Hills. As soon as the bellboy had opened the door to their room, Clarice pushed past him and Johnny and went straight to the phone. She left a message with Hoben Rhys' secretary at Marchind records.

Rhys rang back within the hour.

"Clarice, baby." Even the way he said her name was obscene.

"Rhys. I want to parley."

"No," he said. "What you want to do is surrender."

"Will you meet with me?"

"Of course. Somewhere private."

"All right."

"What are you wearing?"

"My boyfriend's Lakers T-shirt and my army boots," she lied.

"Ooh," said Rhys. "I like it. Hey, make sure you invite him along. He can watch."

"Funny," said Clarice, "I was going to suggest that myself."

"I'm surprised at you, Clarice, but I can't say I'm unhappy," said Rhys. "I'm warning you, though...if you've any funny business planned, I'll be highly upset."

"I promise you, Johnny won't lay a finger on you. How soon can we meet?"

"Tonight's good," he said. "I have a private appointment with a Swedish girl group at eight, but I can reschedule that. Shall we say seven?"

Clarice told him the name of the hotel and the room number.

"I hope you have a guitar with you," he said. Clarice didn't dignify that with a reply.

Rhys showed up at 7 p.m. sharp, hair slicked down, dark suit freshly pressed. He carried his briefcase and a large plastic supermarket bag. When Clarice opened the door he leered and entered without saying anything. She was wearing boots and Johnny's purple Lakers T-shirt, untucked, over a pair of faded blue jeans.

A fire-engine red Gibson SG was leaning against the sofa, jacked into a big 100 watt Fender amp. The rig was switched on. It filled the room with a low, menacing hum.

Johnny was standing in the kitchenette, setting a bottle of champagne into a bucket of ice. "Hi," he said, smiling. "You must be Mister Rhys."

"I am indeed."

Johnny produced a couple of champagne flutes. "You want a drink?"

"No, thank you," said Rhys. "I'd prefer to get straight to business."

"Right," said Clarice.

Rhys put down his briefcase and the supermarket bag, which contained a large bottle of vegetable oil, a can of dairy-whip, and some bulbous items Clarice could not see properly through the opaque plastic. "Right," said Rhys. "Shall we get started?"

"No point fucking around," said Clarice.

"None at all," said Rhys, smiling.

Clarice jackhammered a fist into Rhys's stomach. He doubled over, the wind whooshing out of him. Clarice spun him around and caught his neck in the crook of her elbow. She flexed her arm, squeezing the arteries on the side of his neck. Inside of five seconds Rhys went limp.

Clarice let go of him and stood away. The record exec slumped to the floor. Clarice rolled him onto his back, spread his arms, straightened his legs, and pulled his feet together. She pushed his tie out of the way and tore open his shirt. Buttons popped, fabric ripped. She undid his belt buckle and his fly. Then she rose and stepped back.

"Your turn," she said.

The spell the Devil had given to Johnny was printed in red-brown ink on a piece of copy paper. At first Johnny had thought the design was a cross, but closer inspection revealed it to be a net. He had cut it out and folded it into a cube with the text on the outside. Six facets, six words. A simple tab-and-slot arrangement held it together. It wasn't very big.

Johnny placed the paper cube on Rhys's belly, just below his navel. He stood up and moved to stand behind Rhys's head. "Hoben Rhys," he incanted, emphasizing each of the six words printed on the cube. "Your soul is hereby drawn from your flesh into this receptacle of power." He looked up at Clarice. "That's it."

"Did I blink or something?"

"Wasn't much to see, was there?"

"Are you sure you said it right?"

"Hard to fuck up something that simple, even for me."

"Did it work?"

"I assume so."

"Okay," said Clarice. She bent and retrieved the paper cube, inspected it closely. It did not seem any different than before. "Maybe you should have taped up the edges?"

"The instructions didn't say anything about tape."

"Okay," said Clarice. "Whatever." She tossed the cube up into the air, caught it lightly. "What would happen if I were to eat this little fucker?"

"You'll break the spell, and the soul would probably escape," said Johnny. "I think you got to be some kind of god before you can eat souls."

"Who says I'm not a god?"

"If it was up to me, sure, you would be."

"You're right. It's not up to you, it's up to me."

"You want to try it and see what happens?"

Clarice scowled and handed the cube back to him. "Smartass."

"You're the one who wanted to eat our payment."

Clarice bent down and grabbed the unconscious record exec by an ankle. "Don't open the champagne 'til I get back."

She dragged Rhys out of the hotel room by one leg and down the six flights of stairs to the ground floor, his head thudding softly on each step. There was no other traffic on the staircase, but the concierge at the front desk and the bellboy in the lobby gave her a pair of alarmed stares. Clarice stared back until they looked away.

She dragged Rhys out through the automatic doors, past the startled doorman and deposited the record-man, his bag of groceries, and his briefcase on the curb in front of the hotel. Clarice dropped to her haunches, grabbed him by the lapels and slapped him back to consciousness. "Rhys. Rhys. Rhys."

Rhys blinked awake. "Ugh," he said. "Clarice. Shit." He sat up, shook his head, looked around, trying to get his bearings. "What happened?"

"You just lost," said Clarice.

"What'd I lose?"

"Something you never had a use for anyway."

"The fuck are you talking about?" he said. He looked sad.

Clarice stood up and walked away.

Back in the room, Johnny popped the bottle of champagne, sprayed it all over the room–being careful not to get any near Clarice's guitar rig–and poured out a couple of glasses.

"You drink mine," said Clarice. "I hate champagne."

"I'd have thought," said Johnny, "you would be happy. You just won, and it couldn't have been easier."

"Nothing's ever easy," said Clarice. "Something isn't right."

3. The Devil His Due

The Devil wore an Armani suit for their second meeting. Inside of it, he was of average height and build. A pair of Caucasian hands protruded from the cuff-linked sleeves. A smaller, equally two-dimensional version of the black fingerprint they'd seen before served him as a face.

Johnny had placed the paper cube in the center of the big pentagram before the summoning. After pleasantries had been exchanged, the Devil extended his left hand and the cube leapt up into his open palm. He turned his hand over without bothering to examine it and the cube disappeared into his fist.

"Thank you very much," he said, opening his now-empty hand and lowering it to his side. "I'll see to your record contract forthwith."

"Thank you?" said Clarice.

"That's what polite people say when you give them something, Clarice."

"So, you're happy with the soul, then?"

"Why shouldn't I be?" asked the Devil. "Are you trying to rip me off?"

"No."

"Do you really believe you can cheat me?"

"I don't know," said Clarice. "Maybe I'm trying to find out."

"Maybe you are," said the Devil. "And maybe you're just losing your nerve."

"I'm not afraid of you."

"Of course not," said the Devil. "You have no reason to be."

"Well," cut in Johnny, "It's been a pleasure doing business with you."

"Likewise, I'm sure," said the Devil, affecting a British accent.

"Tell me," said Clarice. "What would you do if I were to step out of this pentagram?"

"Why don't you try it and see?"

"Clarice," said Johnny.

"I think I will."

"Clarice. Don't."

Clarice stepped out of her pentagram.

"No!" said Johnny, lurching as though he were going to stop her... but managing to check himself before he, too, was outside of his own pentagram.

The Devil stood in his, unmoving, his hands relaxed at his sides.

"Well? I'm waiting."

"For what?" asked the Devil.

"For you to do something."

"What kind of something?"

"Something to strike fear into my trembling mortal heart?"

"I told you," said the Devil, "there's no reason to be scared of me. Not today, anyway."

"Because," said Johnny, "He's still bound to the pentagram. The little ones are redundant. The big pentagram keeps him in, the little ones keep him out."

"Johnny," said the Devil, "Do you honestly believe that you can control where I can and cannot go by painting lines on the ground? That this is some kind of a metaphysical tennis match?"

"Yep."

The Devil sighed and shrugged. "Oh, well."

"If you can't be contained by lines on the ground, why don't you just step out of them?" asked Clarice.

Johnny shook his head. "Nonononono. Don't do this, Clarice."

"Courtesy," said the Devil. "Johnny asked me not to when he summoned me."

"But you could, if you wanted to?"

"Why should I? This transaction has been conducted to my satisfaction without me leaving the demarcated area. It makes everybody feel a bit more relaxed if I stay where I'm put."

"Too vulgar a display, huh?"

"You got that right."

"Can you say it in the voice?"

"Do I look like Linda Blair?"

"Point," said Clarice. "But I still don't believe you."

"I can't be contained. It's my documented function to be a free agent."

"Documented where?"

"Well, let's assume that I am the straight-ahead, Judeo-Christian Devil you've all heard so much about. Okay?"

"Okay, sure."

"Do you know where I had my first canonical appearance?"

"The Book of Job," said Johnny.

"Got it in one," said the Devil. "And what does Job say I'm supposed to do?"

"You're, like, a kind of special prosecutor..."

"It says that I am to go 'to and fro in the earth.'"

"That's not much of a job description," said Clarice.

The Devil shrugged. "It's enough. Or at least it was in those days. And it should be enough to answer your question."

"I don't get it," said Johnny.

"My job requires that I walk the earth," said the Devil. "Not only am I able to go everywhere, I'm *obliged* to—whether there are pentagrams set or KEEP OFF THE GRASS signs posted or not."

"What if I asked you to prove it?" said Clarice. "Would that be enough reason for you to leave the pentagram?"

"Why don't you try it and see?"

Johnny frowned. "Wait," he said. "If she does that, she's invited you out of the circle, and she's broken the spell."

"It's your spell," said the Devil. "Not hers. She doesn't have the Art to subvert it and she can't otherwise break it unless she physically interferes with the pentagram."

Johnny paused to consider. "That's true, I guess."

"So, Clarice," said the Devil. "Are you calling me out, or not?"

"Yes," said Clarice. "Step out of the circle."

"What's in it for me?"

"Nothing at all," said Clarice.

"Fair enough," said the Devil. He raised his right foot out of the five-sided chamber at the center of the pentagram and placed it into the bottom-most triangle, which pointed toward Clarice and Johnny.

Johnny started to take a step back, then realized where he was and stood firm in his personal pentagram.

"Clarice," said Johnny.

The Devil placed his left foot into the space between two of the triangles and the bounding circle of the pentagram.

"Johnny," said Clarice.

The Devil placed his right foot outside of the big pentagram.

"Clarice. Step back into your circle."

The Devil stepped completely out of his pentagram and turned smoothly toward Clarice.

"No," said Clarice.

The Devil took a slow step toward Clarice. Then another. Then another, and another, until he stood directly in front of her.

Clarice tried to look him in the eyes, but he had none. She cocked her head and opened her mouth, but she didn't manage to say anything.

The Devil placed a hand on each of her shoulders, leaned forward, and kissed her.

He withdrew, walked back to the center of the pentagram, and took a bow. "Would you care to dismiss me, Mister Chernow, or should I show myself out?"

It was not until the Devil was gone and Johnny had checked and rechecked the pentagram and its markings for errors–there weren't any–that he noticed the small black smudge on the end of Clarice's nose.

"What?" said Clarice.

"What do you mean, 'what?'" said Johnny, wiping away the print with his pocket handkerchief.

"I hope that's clean," said Clarice.

"That was extremely stupid," said Johnny.

"What?"

"Provoking the Devil."

"I provoked the Devil into kissing me on the nose," said Clarice. "If that's the worst he can do, we got nothing to be afraid of."

"That's not the worst he can do, and you damn well know it."

Clarice scowled.

Johnny exhaled slowly. "Hey," he said, smiling. "You know what? We got away with it."

"Remains to be seen whether our new associate comes through with his side of the bargain," said Clarice. She sat heavily on the sofa, which they had pushed back against a wall to make room for the pentagrams. An acoustic guitar leaned up against it.

"Oh, he'll come through," said Johnny.

"Yeah, I guess I know that, too," said Clarice. She grabbed the guitar and struck a chord.

"But you're still not satisfied."

"It was too easy."

"Okay, we discovered that the Devil can do whatever the fuck he likes, no matter what precautions we take," said Johnny. "But he got what he wanted and so did we. Does it really have to be more complicated than that?"

"Yes," said Clarice. "It does. It always is."

"Does it matter? Everyone's happy with what they got."

"For now," said Clarice. "But I know there's something I've overlooked."

— SELF-TITLED DEBUT —

1. Signed and Sealed

When Clarice returned to San Francisco with Johnny, she found a letter from NimHyde Records amongst the piles of bills and junk mail her neighbor in the next apartment had collected for her. The postmark on the letter showed that it had been mailed six days after she and Johnny had left San Fran–two days before she had met with Hoben Rhys to procure his soul for the Devil.

Clarice called around looking for a new lawyer. Then she rang NimHyde to inform them that her lawyer would be in touch. Then she rang Johnny and told him to inform the other members of the band.

Steve Heinman, their handler at NimHyde, was a tall, fat guy with a bald spot and a ponytail. Once the deal was signed and sealed, he told Clarice that his job was to oversee the recording and promotion of the band's albums and to act as an interface between the band's management and the record company.

"What you mean is, you're the one whose ass we have to kiss if we want to be paid," said Clarice.

"Ass-kissing does not appear to be one of your strong points," said Heinman.

"I prefer kicking them to kissing them."

"Sure, sure," said Heinman. "Understood."

"Good," replied Clarice. "Because, you know, yours is a pretty big target."

2. Inhuman Resources

Heinman's comment about the band's management did raise a very good point. Clarice had been handling most of that work herself, but she was keen to unload the responsibility now that she didn't have to worry about who she could trust.

The Rocks In Your Head Artist Management Company agreed to take them on, charging a fee for the manager they provided as well as a cut of the band's earnings. In exchange they delivered a bony, fast-talking forty-something named Stan Kranz.

"Hey-hey, glad to be working with you kids," said Kranz, shaking everyone's hands, smiling and nodding and not meeting anyone's eyes. He wore jeans, a designer T-shirt, and a Hugo Boss suit jacket. His earrings matched the frames of his photo-chromatic glasses.

"You believe this guy?" Beresford muttered to Enrique just loudly enough that everybody within fifty meters could hear it.

"We're not kids, we're musicians," Clarice replied. "And you're working for us, not with us."

Kranz laughed. "Ah, you got that rock'n'roll attitude down already. I can see you k...guys are gonna go all the way."

"That's not attitude, that's just how it is," said Clarice.

"You're the boss," said Kranz, making guns with his hands and pointing them both at Clarice.

Kranz was spineless, gutless, and heartless, but he had a way of weaseling whatever he needed out of you. Clarice decided that he was a good fit for the job.

3. Production

Clarice chose all the songs that would go on the album, worked out the track order, and led Bloody Waters into the studio with the whole operation planned with military precision. Even so, they were in the studio nine hours a day, five days a week, for two solid months; slaving under Clarice's direction as she rebuilt their songs from the ground up: cutting, tweaking, adjusting, reorganizing.

The record company assigned a quiet, competent guy named Connors to engineer the album. He didn't need direction, but he did what Clarice said, if she said it. Otherwise, he never spoke a word unless it was to ask a direct question. That was all good with Clarice. Every night she and Connors stayed back in the studio a further three or four hours, listening to the tapes, fiddling with the mix, experimenting with new guitar tones and additional tracks, planning the following day's session. Sometimes she made him work through the weekends with her. He was paid by the hour, so there were no complaints.

After the recording was done, Clarice and Connors spent a further month mastering the album. Finally satisfied with the music, she turned her attention to the cover art and flyer notes with just as much intensity. Clarice stood over the shoulders of the artists, designers, and copy editors who put together the cover and the leaf notes, making sure that the lyrics were quoted correctly, checking spelling and punctuation, making sure that every last detail was the way she wanted it.

"You've forgotten the thank-yous," said the layouts man, when she declared it ready for print.

"No," said Clarice. "We did this ourselves. Not even Satan gets a shout out."

4. Clipped Wings

Clarice selected the song "Shadow in the Valley" for the first Bloody Waters single: a crisp, hard-but-not-ultra-heavy song. Aside from the mutating chorus, it was a pretty straight-ahead rocker.

NimHyde assigned a director named Gerald Stroman to shoot a video for the band. The budget they fronted was pretty generous, considering that Bloody Waters was a new band with no market presence whatsoever. Clarice insisted on meeting with Stroman immediately.

"What are your ideas for the clip?" she said.

"I have lots of ideas," said Stroman. "Don't concern yourself. Just show up when I tell you and I'll whip up something good."

"Don't concern myself?"

Kranz cut in before Clarice could finish. "Mister Stroman here will be more than happy to listen to your ideas," he said, "so long as you are prepared to listen to his."

"If he had any ideas he would have told me instead of giving me a line of bullshit."

"I—" said Stroman, but Clarice had not finished.

"'Shadow in the Valley' has a distinct story that progresses from verse to verse. It doesn't need any big new ideas."

"I was hired to bring my own vision to this, not to slavishly recreate somebody else's."

Kranz looked from one to the other, trying to decide whose side to be on. He chose the correct one. "This is Clarice's song."

"Her song, my video."

"Okay," said Clarice, surprising everyone. "Okay, I see where you're coming from."

They stood and looked at her, expectant and a little stunned.

"If this was a boy-meets-girl song, or an I-feel-so-whatever song, or a let's-have-a-party song, or a we're-a-rock-band-and-we-rock-so-let's-all-rock-out song, then fine. If I, the songwriter, couldn't come up with anything interesting, you, the director, might as well."

Stroman eyed her warily.

"Do you think my song fits into any of those categories?"

"Uh, no?"

"Well, in that case, you better fucking film what the song is about."

On the set they dressed up Johnny like some kind of mercenary biker and shot hours of him walking alone through a wasteland, which the crew had manufactured by filling a wrecking yard with truckloads of sand. The rest of the band appeared superimposed across the background. The wasteland scenes were intercut with footage of Clarice playing the leads, alone in a darkened studio. The camera zoomed in on her hands on the strings as the solos got intricate, then lurched back out as she slashed back into the rhythm.

Stroman let his assistant and cinematographer do most of the work while he sat in his fold-up chair, drinking out of his hip flask and scowling. Clarice didn't give a shit, and neither did NimHyde. The clip came in on schedule and within the budget. It proved popular on VH1.

Clarice refused to allow the record company to make too big a fuss over the album launch, preferring to put her energy into preparation for the tour. "Nobody's heard of us. It'd be obnoxious to pretend otherwise."

The single sold well, quickly shooting up to the top twenty on the alternative and indie charts–then the top five. The clip became a favorite on a number of hard-rock shows. Album sales were brisk, and the album went gold before they released the next single, "Butcherama".

"Butcherama" was a peculiar song about a BYO butcher franchise with organized crime connections. The lyrics and the music ran together as the song went along and the tempo changed, but there was no post-production magic–just tricky singing from Johnny and fancy guitar-work from Clarice.

The song was coolly received, but it slowly built until it hit the top ten on the rock charts, where it stayed. The lyrics aroused just enough controversy that people sought it out; the music proved just catchy enough to hook them into buying the album. The disk went gold again.

But Clarice didn't take any time out to celebrate. Bloody Waters was ready to hit the road.

— GUITAR MOJO —

1. Flowers and Skulls

Bloody Waters had finally quit the stage after three encores at their third sold-out show at Philadelphia's Sovereign Bank Arena, and the first thing Clarice had to say was, "Who the fuck sent the flowers?"

Beresford did not reply. She was already tongue-kissing a bottle of tequila.

"Not me, man," said Enrique, reaching for a quart of vodka.

Clarice turned her glare on Johnny. "You?"

"I know better than that."

"Well," said Clarice, "It's not fuckin' funny. Who did it?"

"Not me, man," said Enrique, in case Clarice had forgotten his earlier denial. Half the bottle of vodka was already gone.

"Wynokoff!"

From outside the dressing room came the sound of something heavy being dropped. And breaking into pieces. "Ow! Fuck! Shit! Ow!" the tour manager bellowed. "Fuck! Ow! Coming, Clarice! Fuck! Ow! Shit!"

The door swung open, and Terry Wynokoff limped in, dusting shards of broken glass off his jeans. "Yeah?" he asked. He was a big man: shaggy, thickening with middle age. His eyes were alarmingly intense. Terry had been touring with bands in one capacity or another since Clarice was in diapers.

"Did you leave these flowers here?"

"What?" Wynokoff spotted the flowers, already jammed into a garbage can. "Oh. Not me. Event staff delivered them." Before he had met Clarice, the only thing that had ever frightened him was the chestburster in the movie *Alien*.

"Morons."

"What's wrong with flowers?" slurred Beresford. "You allergic?"

"I'm not a fucking ballerina."

"How you even know they're for you?" asked Enrique.

Beresford fished them out of the trash. The lacy white package was festooned with pink ribbons. "You're right," she said, slowly. "I think they're for you, Rick."

Enrique spluttered. Beresford shoved the flowers at him, and he flapped his hands as if defending himself from a swarm of bees.

"Just get rid of them," Clarice told Wynokoff. "And, from now on, it's a rule: no flowers in the dressing room, unless they're growing out of a human skull."

They left the flowers in the room without looking at the note.

2. Swanning Around

The tour ended five months later, and Clarice declared it a success. They hadn't sold out every venue on every night, but these were big venues, and this was the first time the band had played outside of California. The crowds were just as big as those she'd played to with the DreadLords. Even Clarice was shocked by how quickly the band had grown from pariahs to a credible force in modern rock.

She was the only member of Bloody Waters who had been on a full tour before, but they'd coped with it much better than Ignition Corps. Clarice put it down to drugs and alcohol: Enrique and Beresford spent most of their off time passed out drunk, which pretty much left her and Johnny. They shared a room, and other things besides, but he gave her plenty of space and never, ever, lost his cool.

There had been a small rebellion once, when the liquor supplies ran out and Enrique and Beresford had insisted that it was more important they replenish the bar than to show up on time for the sound check. "On time," of course, meant "early" when Clarice was in charge. Clarice made them do pushups and go to bed sober after the show. The pair of them sulked all through the following morning until Wynokoff drove them to the liquor store. After that the matter was forgotten.

The tour was, indeed, a success. They had rapturous coverage in the print media and on radio in every region. Three different guitar magazines printed tablature for "Butcherama" and "Shadow in the Valley."

A few critics called Bloody Waters "guitar dinos:" throwbacks to some past era of rock that seemed to vary with the age of the critic in question, but the detractors were the minority. The consensus was that Bloody Waters was the real deal: original, clever, tight, innovative, and visceral as a Cuisinart full of offal.

Clarice seldom spoke in interviews, and Johnny was quickly identified as the face of the band in the mainstream media, but there was a rumbling undercurrent in the guitar subculture that she was the one to watch. Nobody had believed that she could actually play the music on their record until they saw it for themselves.

Clarice let the band take it easy once the tour was over while she formalized her plans for their second album. With one album and a year on the road, Bloody Waters was doing better than anybody could have expected, but the record company wasn't content, and neither was she.

Kranz and Heinman were perpetually wheedling the band about showing up at parties and events all over LA. Clarice refused to attend any of them, claiming she was too busy to swan around having her photo taken with minor celebrities and brownnosing corporate scumbags. She refused interviews and TV appearances.

"I just got home from the tour," she said. "It's too far to commute from San Fran."

Heinman reminded her that she was still receiving mail at her old apartment in LA and went on to mention that Johnny had been seen looking at houses in the Hollywood Hills. But Clarice wanted no part of the LA scene. When she finally, grudgingly accepted an invitation, it was for *Letterman* in New York.

3. Special Delivery

Johnny was helping Clarice set up her new apartment when the package arrived. After signing for it, Johnny carried the package into the living room, where Clarice was hauling a massive leather sofa into position.

"Special delivery," he said. He was covered in plaster residue and grease. His jeans were streaked with dust and perspiration.

Clarice looked up from the couch. She, too, was filthy, her T-shirt plastered to her with sweat, sticking to her in transparent patches wherever it lay close to her skin. She wiped her hair out of her eyes. "What's so special about it?"

"See for yourself."

Clarice walked over. "A guitar," she said, examining the triangular package.

"Well, there's a surprise."

"I didn't order any new guitars."

"Not this week," said Johnny.

The label on the package confirmed that it was, indeed, a guitar. The sender was named "A. Tuckson." It was addressed to Clarice Marnier, care of NimHyde Records.

Clarice took the box into the kitchen and laid it on a table that was still covered with newspaper. She cut open the box carefully. Inside, the guitar was wrapped in plastic. Clarice washed her hands in the sink and then tore open the thick plastic sheeting and the layers of bubble-wrap beneath it.

It was a black Jackson with a Floyd Rose whammy system. Two humbuckers. Flame decals.

"Used," said Johnny.

Clarice picked it up and inspected the scratches on the pickguard, the nicks in the finish. She sighted down the neck. "Very used," she said. "Needs new frets. And strings. I see rust on the pickups." She put the guitar down on the plastic and picked up the heavy box it had been shipped in. A small card slipped out.

It was a generic occasion card with the words "Best Wishes" printed on the front in flowing gold script. She opened it and read aloud the message. "Clarice, keep up the good work." She squinted. "It's signed 'Earl Tuckson.'"

"Earl Tuckson? I know that name," said Johnny.

"Is he a pawnshop owner?" said Clarice, giving the guitar a second distasteful inspection.

"Don't think so," said Johnny, shaking his head.

Clarice turned away from the table and headed back to the living room.

"Wait," said Johnny. "Arlo 'Earl' Tuckson. I *do* know who he is."

"Spit it out, already," said Clarice, pausing in the doorway. "The rest of this furniture still needs to be shifted."

"He was in, uh...shit. What were they called? Lion's Claw... Lion's...Court...yeah. Lion's Court."

"Oh," said Clarice. "I think I heard of them. Seventies hard rock band."

"A shitty Deep Purple clone. Earl Tuckson was the guitarist."

"You know any of their songs?"

"They did, uh... 'Black Gloves Girl?' Something like that?"

"Oh," said Clarice. "I know it."

"And?"

"And it's what you said. Like a shitty Deep Purple knockoff."

Johnny gestured at the guitar on the table. "So what's with the guitar?"

"He's trying to pull a Clapton," said Clarice. "Honoring a peer by giving away one of his old guitars."

"Do you feel especially honored?"

"Yeah, sure," said Clarice. "This is the kind of thing that makes it all worthwhile."

"So, you're not going to call up Rolling Stone and gush about it?"

"I don't think so."

The guitar went into storage with Clarice's other old guitars–not as an homage to Tuckson, but out of respect for the instrument itself. She figured that it deserved a dignified retirement after a lifetime of abuse and neglect.

Clarice did not think about Earl Tuckson again until he showed up at the signing.

4. Snotball and the Fatman

The Hollywood Virgin Megastore had set up the tables for the Bloody Waters signing just inside the main doors. Clarice sat facing the entrance with Johnny on her right. Enrique and Beresford's table sat at a right angle to theirs, facing the cash registers. The queue wound out through the doors, across the mezzanine, down the escalators and out to the street.

Clarice had a stack of 8x10 photographs by her left hand, a silver marking pen in her right hand, a crick in her neck, and the desire to head-butt someone to within an inch of death. Johnny seemed like a particularly good candidate: showing no signs of discomfort, he chatted easily with the most obnoxious fans, putting his signature beneath Clarice's and sending them on to Enrique without a flicker in his smile.

"I don't do interviews because I hate coming to this miserable city," Clarice told a teenage boy that was leaning over the desk, his stomach jiggling like a beach ball half-filled with Jell-O. He was sweating profusely in his Bloody Waters T-shirt, and he smelled as though he had been doing so for a number of weeks. A bubble of snot nestled in his left nostril, ready to burst at any moment. "But we are gonna be on *Letterman* later this week."

"That's so cool," said the Snotball Kid.

She signed the photograph and pushed it across the table to him. "Thanks for your support. Go blow your nose." She looked over his shoulder at the next person in line. "Hello," she said, making a small and ineffectual attempt at a smile. "Nice to meet you."

The Snotball Kid shuffled across to talk to Johnny as the next loser moved to the front of Clarice's line. He was a tall, fat man with long, curly brown hair showing grey at the roots. He wore pants, a black T-shirt, mirrored sunglasses, and a leather belt that was tooled with Native American designs.

"Hey, Clarice," he said, leaning down to shake her hand.

She didn't usually shake hands—it was a good way to get sick, or to injure her primary instruments—but she found herself shaking with the fat man before she realized it. He held her hand a moment too long, then put his hands on the table in front of her in a strangely self-conscious way. Like he wanted her to look at them.

"Lovely to meet you at last."

Clarice looked him in the sunglasses. "At last," she said, without inflection.

"I just wanted to stop by and, you know, give you a word of encouragement. You're a fabulous guitarist."

"Thanks."

The big man grinned knowingly. "No, I mean it. And, hey, I should know, right?" He had a southern accent, but he'd long since shed the folksy drawl. What remained was more California than Dixie, overlaid with a nasal, East Coast edge.

"Absolutely. You should know," she said, taking a photograph off the pile and uncapping the marker.

"So, anyway, I was going to call you, but, you know...the record company's red tape and all of that." Another knowing smile. "But I think we should get together some time. Just hang out, you know? Maybe jam a little."

"I'm sorry," said Clarice. "I'm kind of busy most days." She signed the photograph without addressing it and pushed it across to him. "Thanks for your support." She looked up at the skinny, buck-toothed girl in line behind him and said, "Hello. Nice to meet you."

The big man didn't move. The smile was gone from his face. "I don't think you understand," he said.

"I understand perfectly," said Clarice. "I don't have time to hang out with all my fans on an individual basis. Sorry." She looked up at the buck-toothed girl again and faked a fresh smile. "Hey there."

The girl stumbled forward, bounced off one of the big guy's meaty arms.

"I said, I don't think you understand." He picked his hands up off the table. Clarice thought he was going to shake them in her face. "Do you know who I *am*?"

"You're someone who's holding up a very long queue of my very patient fans."

The man leaned even further forward, completely blocking out Clarice's view of the buck-toothed girl.

"I," he said, "am Earl Tuckson." His breath smelled like Hawaiian pizza.

"And I," said Clarice, "am just about ready to pound your head through your asshole."

Johnny had dispatched the Snotball Kid and shifted across to see what the problem was. "Hi," he said to Tuckson, extending his hand. "I'm Johnny."

Tuckson turned his head slowly to look at Johnny. "Yes, I guess you are," he said, ignoring the proffered handshake.

"Mister Tuckson was just saying goodbye," said Clarice to Johnny. "He'd love to stay, but he thinks he hears his parole officer calling."

"I can see I've given you too much credit," said Tuckson, straightening up, but keeping his feet planted. "You didn't thank me for the flowers, I thought they got mislaid. Nothing about the guitar, I thought you were being humble. But the truth is, you're just a selfish little prima donna."

"Dude," said Johnny, rising and raising his hands in a peaceable gesture. The store rent-a-cops had finally noticed something amiss and were starting toward them. "Just relax. I'm sure–"

"Just fuck off already, will you?" said Clarice.

"This is gonna come back on you, I promise," replied Tuckson. He shambled off, glancing back over his shoulder and muttering to himself.

"Well," said Johnny, "that was kind of ugly."

"You want to see ugly," said Clarice, "you wait and see what I do to that inbreed's face, I ever see him again."

5. Mr. Mojo Falling

Tuckson threw the classified section of the *Philadelphia Times* down, unsettling the pile of bills and bank statements he had spread across the surface of his kitchen table. He got up and stomped over to the fridge.

The money he'd had made in the halcyon days when he had fronted Lion's Court was pretty much gone, and the session work that had been keeping him going was drying up. Rock'n'roll was on life support. Over-engineered puffery "performed" by dancing models was the dominating force in pop music. It was starting to look like he would need to find some kind of day job.

Tuckson hadn't worked any kind of day job since 1974.

He threw open the fridge door and looked inside. The remains of a two-week-old salad had the top shelf all to itself. Half a box of eggs and an empty container of takeout Chinese food occupied the second. The third was altogether bare. A single can of beer stood forlornly in the door beside a Coke bottle full of water. He grabbed the beer and kicked the door shut.

Tuckson took his beverage into the living room. He cleared a spot amongst the empty pizza boxes and old newspapers and sat heavily on the sofa. The couch barely groaned: the springs had long since had the life crushed out of them. Tuckson cracked open the beer and leaned back.

Thirty years in the music industry and look at him. Sitting in this shithole apartment, combing the classifieds for a menial job.

Everyone had been against him, right from the start. Lion's Court had managed a minor hit off each of their first two albums, but that was as close to success as he had ever come. What worked for other people just didn't work for him: when he was playing blues-rock, they called him a Clapton imitator five years behind the times. When he went through his psychedelic-Latin phase, he was a second-rate, hillbilly Santana. Alice Cooper had a soft-metal comeback hit in the '80s, but when Tuckson had tried it he was dismissed as a geriatric, a fuddy-duddy huffing and puffing along in the wake of Richie Sambora and Slash. Sambora and Slash: overrated egomaniacs nearly twenty years his junior. Even in the heyday of Lion's Court the critics said he wasn't as sharp as Page, wasn't as daring as Blackmore, wasn't as crazy as Nugent—if they said anything about him at all.

"Those fuckers," he said. He was Earl Tuckson, a musician with his own voice and his own abilities. Nobody ever talked about his sound, his innovations, about the generation of musicians he had inspired. "Fuckers." He leaned back and drained half the beer in three gulps.

Lion's Court had split up fifteen years ago, and none of his following three bands had lasted much beyond one album cycle each. He blamed the record company for that; they didn't push the albums hard enough. They didn't announce that he was in those bands: Earl Tuckson, Guitar Legend. He'd gone solo after that, putting out two albums with his own name on the sleeve, but they had followed his other work into the abyss of sales disaster.

He'd put it all on the table for the record company, told them what they needed to do to revitalize his career, but the execs were all young punks with MBAs. None of them knew about coming up hard. None of them knew music. They didn't remember what the radio played three weeks ago, let alone in the 1970s, when the airwaves were ruled from a Lion's Court. His contract was over, and they said they just couldn't afford to renew him.

Tuckson finished the beer, crushed the can in his hands, and threw it across the room. He had never been given the chance he deserved, goddamn it. That was all he needed: one chance. He was at the height of his powers. He'd never been better.

But nobody cared.

Tuckson looked at the clock on the wall, mentally adjusted for daylight savings, and nodded. It was time. He reached for the remote control, pointed it at the TV. Nothing happened. He swore, pulled the batteries out, and shook them. When he tried to put them back in they fell out again.

Swearing, Tuckson got up and turned on the TV. The tube crackled to life. He knelt in front of it and channel-surfed until he found what he was after: *The Late Show with David Letterman.*

Tuckson retreated to his chair, folded his arms, and sat back. He drummed his fingers while Letterman gave one of his lists, talked to some talentless Hollywood actors. Offered some light banter about the coming election.

"Come on, come on..."

Bloody Waters were on the side stage and ready to go when Letterman introduced them. Tuckson leaned in toward the thirty-centimeter screen to get a better view.

Clarice stood at the front of the stage, dead center, guitar strapped on, holding her empty hands out wide. Johnny stood behind her and to her right, Enrique on her left. Beresford raised her drumsticks and struck a short, infectious rhythm off the toms. Enrique joined her on the bass. On the third repetition, Johnny came in on guitar. Then Clarice put her hands on her instrument.

Clarice answered each stanza with a blistering lick, cutting right through the riffage and rhythm. When Johnny started to sing, she rolled strange harmonies against his voice and guitar, reinforced his vocals with slabs of color, answered his words with driving lead breaks. The song was called "King of the Cannibal Cyborg Mutants."

Tuckson listened to the lyrics. "Sci fi bullshit, Jesus Christ," he said. "It's rock'n'roll. Nobody wants to listen to a goddamn story."

There was no chorus. The band tore through another verse, and then Clarice kicked off her solo, hybrid-picking a spiky melody over Johnny's shimmering chords. She stomped off the distortion and gave it some naked overdrive from the amp, added some wahwah, and...and somehow the song mutated into something Tuckson had never heard before.

It felt like something had shut down inside his head. All of the faculties Tuckson developed in his life as a guitarist went off. He didn't know what key she was playing in. He didn't think about how she was fingering the chords, how she was striking the notes, didn't care to analyze the tone, the hardware, the signal chain. All Tuckson could hear was that music. That guitar.

Johnny's guitar restored the earlier rhythm. Clarice joined him, and they repeated the intro riffs while he sang the last verse. The rhythm section faded. Clarice played a short, mellow outro, and Bloody Waters stood in silence. Then, eventually, a strange kind of shell-shocked applause rose from the audience.

The show went to an ad break. When it returned, Letterman had Clarice and Johnny in the guest seats beside his panel. Coming off the stage, the host found her a lot more loquacious than she had been at prior interviews. Clarice answered his questions with her characteristic ferocity: harsh, articulate, and amusing; naming names and laying blame; criticizing or threatening anybody that she felt deserved it. It became one of the show's most notorious episodes, right alongside Madonna cussing and Drew Barrymore exposing herself.

Tuckson didn't hear a word of it. He just sat in his seat, seeing nothing, hearing nothing, that song still ringing in his ears.

When his brain came back on it was filled with certainty. He'd been right, after all. Clarice Marnier was it. She was the one. That ol' Guitar Mojo was hers, there was no doubting it.

He'd offered her his steel and she'd refused him, but he wasn't done yet, no sir. Now it was war. He had to show them that *he* had the mojo. *He* was the one.

Tuckson had paid his dues; he was done waiting for his turn. And now he had a plan.

6. Knees Up, Mother Brown

The show had gone well. They always did.

Capacity crowd. Three encores, standing ovation. Sales for the album had spiked again. Since the *Letterman* show, "King of the Cannibal Cyborg Mutants" was actually on the charts, even though it hadn't been released as a single. But that was old news, as far as Clarice was concerned. It was time to get back into the studio and record the new album.

Clarice was thinking about the new record as she led the band through the unfinished backstage corridors. One of the theatre's security goons opened the doors to the private alley that led around the back of the theatre. Clarice followed him out, Johnny one step behind. Enrique and Beresford staggered after them, sharing a bottle of vodka. A third guard closed the door once they were all outside. They stood there in the warm California night, breathing the filthy city air.

"Where's the fucking limo?" said Clarice.

"Not here," said Johnny.

"No shit," said Beresford.

"That useless bastard, Kranz," said Clarice. "If Wynokoff was running the show, the limo would have been here half an hour ago." Wynokoff had gone to see his family in Arizona after the big tour had finished, and Kranz was running their occasional gigs in his absence.

The concrete apron at the exit was lit by weak fluorescent tubes set on either side of the doors. Clarice looked down the length of the alley. She could barely see as far as the bend that led out to the main road. At the closed end of the laneway, all she could make out was an overflowing dumpster.

The guard raised the radio mic again, but he put it down without speaking when he heard the low rumble of a car engine. Headlights illuminated the far wall of the alley, and a large black vehicle slowly navigated the bend and pulled up in front of them. The back door cracked open, and Kranz's head popped out. He looked frightened and disheveled.

Clarice looked him up and down expressionlessly, arms folded.

"Um, sorry I'm late," said Kranz.

"So am I," said Clarice. She turned her head toward the band and said, "Get in the car."

Kranz opted to sit with the driver. Excuses or further apologies would only make Clarice angrier; best thing to do was to stay out of sight. He was shaken up as it was.

The fat guy with the mane of graying hair had been waiting for Kranz in the underground car park. Lying in wait, Jesus Christ. He'd known who Kranz was, called him by name. Kranz thought he would die on the spot.

The fat guy wanted backstage passes, of course. All Kranz had was his own security tag, but the guy was frighteningly persistent. He'd followed Kranz all the way to the limousine. Once Kranz was inside, that fat man had stood there staring for a full thirty seconds before stomping off.

But Clarice wouldn't care about any of that. Kranz had kept her waiting, and that just wasn't good enough.

Over the intercom, Johnny asked the driver to take them to a bar he knew somewhere off Santa Monica. The driver acceded.

Kranz leaned back in his seat and breathed out a long, long sigh. He would catch a cab from the bar. He couldn't wait to get home. The stalker was frightening enough, but having to deal Clarice when she was angry was another story altogether.

The pub was mostly empty and remarkably dark despite the neon around the main bar, which cast only a few meters of illumination. The overheads were masked for blacklight. Two couples were playing pool in the adjoining room, but otherwise it was quiet enough that they could hear the classical jazz piped through the PA.

Clarice and Johnny found a booth at the back of the main room. Enrique and Beresford joined them with armloads of drinks. Once they were settled, Clarice called them to order.

She laid out her ideas for the new record in detail, referring often to a notebook. Johnny liked the ideas, posited a few of his own—some of which Clarice noted down, some of which she dismissed immediately. He did not seem to mind either way. Enrique and Beresford drank and giggled and agreed with everything.

Earl Tuckson was sitting hunched on the seat in the second cubicle of the ladies' toilets. Every time someone entered, he would peek over the top of the stall to see if it was Clarice Marnier. If it wasn't, he would lock his door and hunch down again. He didn't want some innocent woman to find him there.

Tuckson had followed the limo all the way from the theatre. He'd sneaked in through the side room and had been hiding in his cubicle for more than an hour before Clarice pushed in through the doors. Tuckson ducked his head and prepared himself to leap if the door to his cubicle opened.

Clarice went for the end cubicle. Tuckson settled in to wait some more.

After a short while the toilet flushed. The door latch clicked. The door swung open.

Still sitting, Tuckson cracked his door and peeked out. If Clarice did not stop to wash her hands, he was going to jump out as she walked past and grab her from behind.

Clarice went to the center basin, directly in front of his cubicle, and turned on the tap.

Tuckson got up from the toilet seat.

—◖●◗—

Clarice put her hands under the faucet and looked around for a soap dispenser. Movement drew her eyes to the mirror–the door of the cubicle behind her was opening. She knew that the OCCUPIED latch had not been set when she went in there, and she was certain that no one had entered behind her.

Tuckson stepped up behind her and clapped his right hand on her shoulder. "Come quietly," he said. "I don't want to hurt you."

Clarice stepped right and spun left, looping her left arm under Tuckson's right and pivoting with her hips. She drove her right fist into his sternum, and he went back on his heels. Clarice turned and stepped again, locking Tuckson's elbow with her bent arm and using it to lever his face into the hand drier.

Tuckson squawked. Blood spurted from his nose. Clarice leaned forward, straightened Tuckson's arm, and turned it over. He bent double, and she drove a knee up into his face, grinding it into his already-broken nose. This time, his squawk was barely a wheeze.

Clarice used the arm lock to drive him to his knees. "Are we done yet?" she asked.

Tuckson raised his free hand to his face, vainly trying to staunch the flow of blood from his nose. He nodded without looking up.

"I think it's time you went home," said Clarice, "unless you'd like me to break something else."

7. Abducted Without Leave

After a month of rehearsals, Clarice had worked out what was going to be on the new album, but they still had two more shows booked before they could get back into recording mode. It was only another week, but Clarice felt herself becoming more irritable with every passing minute.

Clarice showed up late for sound check at the first gig. She walked into the main auditorium of the Luna Park with a guitar case in each hand and a look on her face that threatened death to anyone who looked at their watch.

"There you are," said Johnny. "I thought we were a couple of guitars short."

Kranz made himself as inconspicuous as he could beside the sound booth. Clarice put the cases down and grunted. She knelt down, opened a case and took out her newest toy, a brand new PRS.

"When did you get that?" asked Billy Wales, the guitar tech, coming over for a look.

"Today," Clarice told the guitar tech. "It's custom."

"You, uh, want me to set it up for you...?" Billy was tall and gangly and young and easily frightened, but he knew every solder point in every circuit in every bit of gear in the band's rig. He could play most of the music, too.

"'Custom' means that it was set up specifically for me by the shop."

"Oh." Billy looked like a kicked puppy.

Clarice softened. "You can play with it after the sound check. Now, get out of the way."

Billy backed away, grinning.

"All right, everyone, take your places."

Beresford sat down behind the drum kit. Johnny, who already had a guitar strapped on and plugged in, gave Clarice an odd look and stepped up to his mic. Clarice jacked her guitar into the pedal board, put one foot on her amp, and did something with her fingers to make a plectrum appear in her hand.

"Um, Clarice...?" said Johnny, slowly.

"What?"

"You notice anyone missing?"

She looked over to her right. Enrique wasn't in his place.

It was the first time he had ever seen her speechless.

Clarice turned to Beresford. "You know where he is?"

Beresford shrugged. "At home, I guess. Ain't seen him since Tuesday."

"Today is Friday."

Beresford shrugged.

"Well," said Clarice, her voice very, very quiet, "has anyone tried calling him?"

"Er, yeah," said Kranz, who was standing in the sound booth and looked as if he was ready to duck for cover. "There's, um, no answer."

"Well," said Clarice. "Somebody had better get down to his apartment and wake him from his drunken stupor–pronto."

Kranz was already halfway out the door with his car keys in his hand.

An hour later he came sprinting back in, his hair disarrayed, his Calvin Klein T-shirt stained with sweat. He was alone.

Johnny broke the silence. "Wasn't there?"

"Um, no. I got the super to open his apartment."

Clarice said nothing.

"You have any idea where he is?" Johnny asked Beresford.

"Uh, sleeping in a gutter somewhere?"

"Cancel the gig," said Clarice. "Call the police. I think Enrique's been kidnapped."

8. Punk in Drublic

The detective tugged at his yellow-spotted tie and let the elastic neckband snap it back up to his collar button. "Run this by me again," he said. "You think this old rock star abducted your bass player because you insulted him at a signing?"

"And I broke his nose," said Clarice. "But that was another time."

"Right," said the detective, rubbing a scabbed-over shaving cut on his jaw with sausage-shaped fingers.

"He tried to kidnap me."

"Okay…" The detective inspected his fingers, then wiped them on a memo that lay on his blotter. They left greasy grey marks on the paper. "He tried to abduct you, but you failed to report it?"

"I didn't feel like being charged with assault," said Clarice.

"Ah, yes," said the detective, laying his palms flat on the table. "Imagine the headlines."

Johnny shared a knowing smile with the detective. Clarice folded her arms and clenched her jaw.

"I still don't see what this has to do with your bassist."

"It's obvious," said Clarice. "Tuckson failed to kidnap me, so he took Enrique instead."

"There's no sign of any kind of struggle in Mister Pizarro's apartment. There's no ransom note."

"Tuckson doesn't want money."

"Then what *does* he want?" said the detective, drumming his fingers.

"Hell if I know. He's crazy as a loon."

"Correct me if I'm wrong, but Mister Enrique Pizarro is known to drink heavily, is he not?"

"Yes."

"Would you say that Mister Pizarro is an alcoholic?"

"He's a musician," said Johnny.

"This is all beside the point," said Clarice. "I've lost my bassist and I want him back."

"You thought about where you might have left him?" said the detective.

"Very funny."

"Seriously: when did you last see Mister Pizarro?"

"Mia Beresford last saw him on Tuesday."

"Where is Miss Beresford?"

"We thought it would be better if she didn't come."

"I see. And where did she see Mister Pizarro?"

"They shared a cab to somewhere after rehearsal."

"Where?"

"She doesn't recall," said Clarice. "She was drunk."

The detective shook his head. "I don't see it, kids. Your suspect has no motive. All you have to go on is two unreported past incidents which had nothing to do with the missing person."

Clarice rose to her feet and leaned over the desk. "So, what are you saying?"

The detective stared straight through her. "I'm saying I'll file the report, but if I were you I'd keep checking the drunk tanks. I'm sure someone will pick him up on vagrancy or D&D before much longer."

9. Grievous Bodily Harm

When they got back to Clarice's place, they found a dog-eared piece of notepaper with her initials written on the back in flowing cursive shoved under the door.

"Shit," said Clarice. "I forgot that he knows where I live." She bent down to pick it up.

"What's it say?" asked Johnny, perching on the arm of the couch.

"He's waiting for us at…sounds like a high school gymnasium. He says no cops. 'Bring your best guitar.'"

"A school gym?"

"Summer vacation," said Clarice. "I guess it's not being used."

"Should we call the cops?"

"You saw how much help they were."

"Well, now we have evidence."

"I can deal with Tuckson without their help."

"Clarice, Tuckson is dangerous."

"I don't think he is. He wants a guitar showdown, not a shootout."

Johnny rubbed his eyes. "What is wrong with this guy?"

"Who cares?" said Clarice. "I just want my bassist back."

Johnny raised an eyebrow. "That's all?"

"Well," said Clarice, "if I have to administer some grievous bodily harm, I guess it'll just be too bad."

10. Finger Speed

Tuckson watched the car bounce onto the gravel driveway and wind its way toward the gym on the blue-grey screens of the security system.

The vehicle stopped, and Clarice got out on the driver's side. Johnny opened the passenger door. Tuckson had expected her to bring that blond-haired cocksucker with her.

Clarice popped the trunk and pulled out an oversized guitar case—that monstrous seven-string of hers. He had expected that, too.

Tuckson had been sitting there, staring at the security monitors, for two days straight, subsisting on candy and soda from the vending machines. He'd maxed out his remaining credit card renting the gym and all the video gear, but Tuckson had never doubted that they'd show up. There were higher powers at work. Fate. Destiny. The Guitar Mojo itself.

His knees cracked as he rose from his chair and walked over to where his Best Girl stood in her stand. The polished floorboards creaked with every step. Tuckson slipped the strap over his shoulders, plugged her in, and moved into position.

It wouldn't be long now.

The gym smelled of sweat, floor polish, and dust. Darkness swallowed the wedge of light from outside as the door swung closed behind them.

"Switch on the fucking lights, Tuckson," said Clarice.

A sharp hum cut through the heavy darkness: a guitar amp being powered on. Lights came on over the stage at the far end of the hall. Tuckson's bulky silhouette stood there, posed: legs apart, hands by his sides, head down, a Les Paul special hanging from his shoulders.

"Oh, for Christ's sake," said Clarice.

Tuckson slowly raised his head and struck an E5, filling the gym with an ominous growl. He let it ring while he waddled sideways to the side of the stage and then fumbled with a switch.

The fluorescent tubes in the ceiling flickered uncertainly and came on. Tuckson stood on the stage with two large amplifiers and a morass of guitar FX pedals, ringed by stage lights and video cameras. He was wearing leather pants, black-lacquered shoes, and a black silk shirt. He had about a week's beard on his cheeks. Clarice could smell him all the way across the hall.

Enrique was bound to a chair at the foot of the stage. His mouth was taped shut, and a dozen sticks of what looked like dynamite were secured to his scrawny chest. Fuse wire led from the blasting caps across the floor and up onto the stage.

"Your bass player is wired to my channel switch," said Tuckson. His voice was wetter and more nasal than Clarice remembered. "Put a foot wrong and I'll put my foot *down*."

"I get the picture," said Clarice, approaching the stage slowly. Johnny was close behind. "What do you want?"

"I want to prove that I'm the best." Tuckson's face was still swollen and bruised from his last encounter with Clarice. His nose hadn't set properly. She doubted he had health insurance.

"The best what?"

"The best guitarist. In the world."

"Oooh... kay," said Clarice. "How do you propose to do that?"

"On camera," said Tuckson, turning down the volume on his guitar. The hum of the amplifier faded.

"So, why do you need me?"

"For reference. Right now, everyone thinks you're the best there is. I have to prove I'm better."

"How are you going to prove something like that?"

"We can measure it right off the tapes."

"What exactly are you going to measure?"

"Speed."

"As in...amphetamines?"

"No!" roared Tuckson, suddenly red-faced and angry. Blood started to trickle from his nose. "Finger speed. How many notes you can play in a set period of time–with melody." He wiped off the blood from his upper lip with one of his sleeves.

"You want a shredding duel?" she said. Johnny waggled his eyebrows.

"Yes," replied Tuckson.

"All right," said Clarice. "Then what? You'll let us go?"

"Yes."

"If we go straight to the cops, your video will be evidence against you."

"Doesn't matter; I'll have proved my point. I'll have it by then."

Clarice looked at Johnny with exasperation. He shrugged. She looked back at Tuckson. "You'll have what?"

"There is a certain...power...that comes with being the best. A mojo," said Tuckson.

"A guitar mojo?"

"*The* Guitar Mojo."

"Okay, now you're really starting to creep me out."

"You can laugh all you want, but you know it's real...because right now it belongs to you."

"And you want it for yourself."

"It has to move on; that's its nature. All through this century—since the blues emerged and especially since rock'n'roll—every era has had its singular guitarist."

"Uh huh?"

"Son House. Robert Johnson. Chuck Berry. Jimi Hendrix. Clapton. Page. Van Halen. Satriani. Vaughn. For a while, at least, every one of them had the power of the Guitar Mojo."

"And how exactly did I become queen? Who did I take it from?"

"I don't know. Maybe no one. I don't think it has to have an embodiment if there's no appropriate vessel."

"You've really put a lot of thought into this," said Clarice.

"Exactly what kind of mojo we talking?" asked Johnny.

"Nobody was talking to you, asshole," said Tuckson.

"Never mind, Johnny," said Clarice. "It's just a bunch of hippy bullshit."

"It's power. Real, true, genuine, magical power."

"Like...spoon-bending?"

Tuckson didn't skip a beat. "It's the power of the Guitar. It's influence, it's fame, it's *presence*. It's luck."

"Seems to me that a whole lot of the previous recipients lucked into tragedy or untimely deaths," observed Clarice.

"The Guitar Mojo doesn't prevent you from fucking up," said Tuckson. "It doesn't prevent mistakes or plain old misfortune. Maybe it even encourages it."

"Sounds like a gyp to me," said Clarice. "It makes you a better guitarist, but you already have to be the best before you can have it? And then it fucks you? This kind of magic, I can do without."

"If that's how you see it, you should be happy that you're about to lose it."

"Can't I just sign it over or something?"

"No."

Clarice didn't like the look on Tuckson's face when he said that.

"All right," she said. "Fine. Let's get this over with." She shrugged off her jacket, walked up to the lip of the stage, hefted the guitar case onto the boards, and vaulted up.

Tuckson moved his foot closer to the switch he had rigged to the detonator. "No funny business."

"Oh, please." She opened her case, strapped on The Motherfucker, and stepped into the semicircle of video cameras and stage lights. They seemed to crowd around the pair of guitarists, like children watching a schoolyard brawl.

Tuckson looked warily at Johnny. "You, back away."

"Sure," said Johnny. He took a few steps away from the stage.

Clarice jacked in The Motherfucker, adjusted the way the strap fell across her shoulders, and put one foot on the low stool Tuckson had set out for her. "Okay."

"Sit down," said Tuckson.

"I'd rather stand." She spun the volume knob of The Motherfucker all the way down and turned on the second 300-watt Marshall.

"The cameras are aimed down at the stool."

"So move them."

Tuckson edged around behind the cameras angled on Clarice, using one foot to drag the detonator switch with him. Careful not to knock his treasured Les Paul on any of the equipment, he started moving the cameras and the lights, glancing nervously at Clarice all the while. She just smirked at him. Johnny stood quietly by, his thumbs hooked in his belt.

Eventually, Tuckson got the cameras adjusted. "Okay," he said. "Who goes first, you or me?"

Clarice considered for a moment. "You."

Tuckson sat down on his stool, hunched over his guitar. Turned up the volume. He found a pick, frowned. Suddenly his hands were moving. His right hand oscillated like a woodpecker hopped up on crystal meth, plucking and sweeping and tapping. The digits of his left hand struck with the speed and precision of a battery of sewing machines programmed to stitch in A melodic minor.

It wasn't a lot of fun to listen to. In fact, Clarice imagined that it was sort of what a migraine headache sounded like. But she couldn't help but be impressed with his technique. Tuckson was the fastest she'd ever seen or heard, there was no doubting it.

Eventually he let up. "Your turn," he said, letting go of the guitar and pushing the sweat-soaked curtain of hair away from his face with both hands.

Clarice turned down the volume and played C major in the third position, three times. Slowly. "Shit," she said. "I think you win."

Tuckson glowered at her. "No," he said. "You're not taking it seriously."

"If I won't get into the spirit of it, I'm obviously not good enough," she replied. "I concede your victory. Now can I have my bassist back, please?"

"No," said Tuckson. "Compete properly, or I will blow him up."

"You've got enough dynamite on him to blow up the entire school."

"I'm willing to do it," said Tuckson.

Clarice looked at him hard for a moment. She nodded, keeping her eyes locked on his. "All right. I believe you are." She tipped her head to the side and cracked her neck, raised her hands. Her left hand scissored up and down the fretboard in D minor, her right hand whirled and dove amongst the strings over the pickups. She played for about a minute, starting nice and bluesy and working her way up to a moderate shred. She never came close to the speed of Tuckson's amphetamine-woodpecker-sewing machine.

"I call that 'Napalm in the Nursery,'" she said.

"Very nice," said Tuckson. "Very evocative. But too slow."

"Well, to the victor go the spoils," said Clarice. "The mojo is yours. Thanks for the tea and biscuits, see you later." She took her foot off the stool and started to remove her guitar.

"SIT DOWN!" roared Tuckson, eyes popping, right foot rising threateningly over the detonator pedal.

Clarice clipped the strap back on. "I'm not going to sit," she said. "Remember?"

Tuckson was breathing hard through clenched teeth. A vein had risen over his right temple that looked like it was attempting to burrow down into his eye socket. His nose was bleeding again, but he hadn't noticed. "You're still. Not. Taking. This. Seriously." He took a deep breath. "I'll consider that. Your warmup. Now. Play your hardest, or..."

"Or what?"

"Or...boom."

"Boom?"

"BOOM!" Blood and spittle flew from his mouth. Tuckson paused and blinked, as though he'd actually startled himself.

"All right, all right." Clarice turned to her amplifier and switched it over to a clean channel. She adjusted the volume on The Motherfucker and flipped to the bridge pickup. She put one foot back on the stool. "You asked for it."

Clarice started with the woodpecker-sewing-machine-migraine solo Tuckson had played, note-for-note the same, but slower, with different emphasis. With feeling. Then she picked up the tempo, playing it through again. She took her foot off the stool and, still playing, took a step toward Tuckson. She incorporated passages from her Napalm Nursery solo, playing faster and faster.

Clarice took another step toward him. She was playing at a speed close to Tuckson's now. She looked right into his black-rimmed, red-marbled eyes and took another step. She played faster, matching his earlier speed.

Then she really started playing.

Tuckson's jaw swung open, and his shoulders slumped.

Clarice raised her guitar out of the way and kicked Tuckson's foot off the detonator switch. Her heel landed on his shoe with all of her bodyweight behind it. Feedback howled as Tuckson reared up out of his seat. Clarice used her forward motion and the weight of The Motherfucker to power her right elbow into his face. Tuckson made a choking sound and went over backward. His foot was broken, and blood was spurting out of what was left of his nose.

Clarice muted the shrilling feedback and turned off the amp, then put her guitar carefully back in its case. Tuckson was still lying on his back, moaning softly.

"You'd best stay right there," she said. Tuckson whimpered, and she didn't even bother to finish the threat. Instead, she bent to inspect the detonator switch.

"It's always the red wire," advised Johnny from the foot of the stage.

Clarice snorted.

The channel switch was a pretty simple device: ON or OFF. She couldn't see any extra cables or wires, so she doubted there was any kind of failsafe. Tuckson was not a demolitions expert any more than she was.

Clarice unplugged the foot switch. Nothing blew up. Johnny applauded.

"Cut that shit off of Enrique," she said. "There's a knife in my jacket."

Johnny went through her pockets until he found a nasty-looking five-inch butterfly knife. He looked at the knife, then up at Clarice.

Clarice looked back at him. "What?"

"Nothing," said Johnny, shaking his head. He opened the knife carefully and started working on Enrique.

"Shit."

Clarice jumped down off the stage. "What?"

"It's not dynamite."

The red tubes taped onto Enrique's harness were paper towel rolls, spray-painted red.

Clarice started to laugh.

Johnny drew the harness off the bassist and threw it aside. "You okay, Enrique?"

"Mmmfff!"

"Oh, sorry." Johnny reached out and pulled the tape off his face.

"Fuuuuuuuck!" Enrique tried to scream, but a hoarse croak was the best he could manage. He swallowed hard to stop himself from hyperventilating. "That fucking hurt, man."

"Sorry."

Johnny helped him to his feet.

"Let's go," said Clarice, hefting her guitar case. "We've wasted enough time here already."

"What do you want to do about Tuckson?" said Johnny, offering Clarice the folded-up knife carefully. The guitarist had managed to sit up and he was touching the side of his face woozily. A huge bruise was forming over his cheekbone and his beard was red with blood.

She pocketed the knife. "Nothing."

"I just learned some awesome new curse spells," said Johnny. "Can I try one of them out?"

"Nah, leave him alone," said Clarice, heading for the doors at the far end of the gym. "Poor fucker's miserable enough the way he is."

Johnny followed her out though the doors and into the sunlight, Enrique leaning on him and stumbling along. He could still hear Tuckson groaning inside.

Clarice popped the trunk and put her guitar inside. She slammed the lid and turned to Johnny, grinning. "What the fuck," she said. "Do you know anything that will give him hemorrhoids?"

— THE RIVERS RUN RED —

1. Underpants on the Outside

Bloody Waters had retreated to a rambling mansion out near Cape Cod to rehearse for the new album when Kranz called up about the comic book.

"Say that again?" Clarice was sitting cross-legged with her notebook computer on her lap, finalizing the lyrics for one of the songs for the new album. She had the phone tucked under her chin and continued to type with both hands.

"A guy from a comic book company wants to do some stories about the band," said Kranz, patiently. "He'll pay us to use the band's name and likeness, and NimHyde gets a deal on advertising in the company's books."

"A comic book," said Clarice. "They still make those?"

"Apparently."

"What are they gonna do stories about? Sitting around in the tour bus? Tinkering with our gear? Rehearsing until we fall over?"

"I don't think so," said Kranz, trying to sound amused but running low on patience. "It's going to be, like, *superheroes*, except with concerts and groupies."

"So the punchline of every issue is gonna be Enrique and Beresford throwing up on each other's capes?"

"Clarice, I don't know," said Kranz. "The guy obviously thinks he can do something interesting, or he wouldn't have approached us. It isn't much money, but it is free marketing. Can I just go ahead and authorize this?"

"No, you can fucking not just go ahead and authorize it," said Clarice. "I want to see what he plans to do with my likeness before I let him publish stories about me."

"I'll see what I can arrange," said Kranz, sounding tired.

"You do that." She hung up.

"I take it," said Johnny, sitting up in bed and pushing the hair out of his face, "that someone wants to do a comic book about us?"

"Yeah."

"You don't want your own comic?"

"I happen to like comics," said Clarice.

"But you couldn't tell Kranz that," said Johnny.

"Hell, no," said Clarice. "I don't want him getting any ideas. Next thing you know, he'll have us wearing our underpants on the outside and fighting crime."

2. By Bizarre Breasts

A week later, Bloody Waters was jamming on some new ideas in the dining room when Kranz came in, clutching a sheaf of pages. He threaded his way amongst the chairs and lamps, cables and crates, circumnavigated the huge dining table. It was starting to look like a *Blade Runner* set in there.

Johnny was singing, Clarice was slashing away and barking directions to the others. Enrique was bobbing slightly; Beresford was in a berserker frenzy. Kranz waited patiently until he had been noticed. Then he waited a few more minutes for Clarice to bring the proceedings to a halt.

"Yeah?" she said.

"Got some stuff from the comic book guys."

"Leave it on the table," said Clarice.

Kranz left it on the table amongst the piles of empty pizza boxes and assorted cans, bottles, glasses, tools, and spare parts.

An hour later, when Clarice declared the jam session over, the band gathered around the big table for some refreshment.

Enrique drained two beers before Clarice had the cap off her bottle of water. Beresford crammed almost an entire slice of cold pizza into her mouth and started pouring vodka down her throat before she had even started to chew. Johnny popped the top off a beer and reached for a box of pretzels.

"That was good stuff, guys," said Clarice. "I think there are two different songs in there."

Enrique carefully put down his third and fourth beers and reached for the pizza box. "'ey," he said to Beresford, "leave some for me."

"No," said Beresford, her mouth full of half-chewed food. "You'll microwave it."

"Cold pizza is better hot."

Beresford grabbed the box. Enrique pulled it toward him.

"This," said Clarice, "is why I never want children."

The grease-sodden cardboard tore wetly, and pizza went everywhere. Enrique howled. Beresford scooped as much as she could up off the floor and danced away with it.

One slice had landed on the table. Enrique picked it up sullenly. It was stuck to a piece of paper. Enrique peeled the paper away and inspected the slice, then the piece of paper.

It was a black and white sketch of a hugely muscled, dark-haired man holding a bass guitar with a chainsaw attachment, framed by a triangular splotch of cheese oil. "Hey, cool, man."

"What?" said Clarice.

"This slice has no anchovies on it."

Clarice glanced from the pizza to the sketch. "Gimme that."

Clarice found the rest of the sheaf of clipped fax paper and found a chair to sit on. Aside from the page Enrique and Beresford had pizza-ed, the rest of it was clean.

Johnny came to join her. "What you got there?"

"The comic book stuff."

In the kitchen, Enrique bellowed at the top of his lungs.

Clarice looked up from the editor's introductory letter in time to see Beresford bolt down the corridor, laughing madly, her arms wrapped around the microwave oven. Enrique was close behind, still bellowing. He stepped on the trailing power cord, and they both went down in a heap. Moments later, the microwave exploded in a shower of broken glass and plastic.

Silence fell. Enrique and Beresford looked at each other. Then at the remains of the microwave. Then at each other.

Enrique started bellowing again, and Beresford scrambled away, laughing.

Clarice shook her head and returned her attention to the sheaf of fax paper, sorting the artwork out of the way and checking that the text pages were in order. Johnny looked away from Enrique and Beresford.

"How's the script?"

"Not so many exclamation marks as I expected."

"What's the story about?"

"Evil aliens impersonate a bunch of groupies."

"It's never good aliens, is it?" said Johnny.

"Maybe that's the twist ending," said Clarice.

Enrique returned with his slice of cold, un-microwaved slice precariously perched on a floppy paper plate, two beer bottles in his other hand. Beresford sauntered back in after him, swinging a bottle of vodka. Enrique refused to look at her, even when she put her chin on his shoulder. She was grinning like a Cheshire Cat. Enrique grunted sourly and shrugged her away.

Beresford turned her attention to Clarice and Johnny. "This is our comic book?"

"If I approve it, yeah," said Clarice.

"I wanna be in a comic book," said Enrique, brightening.

"Good," said Clarice, absently. She handed Enrique the page with the pizza mark on it, which she had kept separate from the rest of the documents. "This is supposed to be you."

"Hey, cool," said Enrique, looking at the page. "I have Vibrato/ Destructo powers."

"What's the chainsaw for?" said Beresford.

"Sawing things up."

"Why can't you just Vibrato/Destruct them?"

"Because the chainsaw is more badass."

"Ha!" said Beresford. "What are my powers?"

Clarice handed her the character sketch section without looking up from the script.

Beresford found her page and held it up proudly. It showed a girl in a shredded shirt pounding away on an oversized drum kit, all wild hair and mad eyes. Stormclouds gathered behind her; electricity arced between her drumsticks. "My power is Thunder of Drums and my weapon is Boots of Stomping," she said. "I kick ass."

"What about me?" asked Johnny. The comic guys had made him a bare-chested Viking warrior. He was striking a kung fu pose and firing a grenade from an M203 that was strapped to his guitar. "Johnny Chernow: ex-Delta Force Martial Arts Expert," he said, sounding glum. "I guess that means no superpowers." He flipped to the last page. "This one is you, Clarice."

Clarice's stand-in was dressed in leather pants, spike-heeled boots, and a bikini top. She had short hair, legs that were three times as long as her torso, a waist that was as narrow as her ankles, and breasts that were wider across than her shoulders.

"Clarice Marnier: Telepathy, Precision Cutting Guitar," said Johnny.

Clarice scowled.

"I guess that's kind of lame."

"Get Kranz in here," said Clarice. They knew exactly what that meant.

"'ey, I want to be in a comic book!" said Enrique.

"I want my Boots of Stomping," said Beresford.

"Sorry," said Clarice, "but this comic book is hereby dead in the water."

"Glub glub glub," said Johnny, pretending to drown.

3. Grist for the Millner

Bloody Waters went into the studio as soon as they got back to San Francisco. They managed almost two weeks uninterrupted before Clarice found out that she'd been mentioned in Gabrielle Millner's interview on the *Oprah Winfrey Show*.

Millner was a pop diva, although Clarice wasn't sure which one. Apparently, she'd used Millner as an example in her rant about the music industry during her *Letterman* appearance, but she'd pretty much chosen her name at random. Clarice couldn't even remember what point she'd been trying to make; she hadn't bothered to watch the show when it aired.

Kranz, Clarice, and Johnny took the tape of Millner's appearance into a conference room and watched it from the beginning.

Oprah questioned Millner about her impoverished childhood, about how she had worked three jobs to pay for her singing lessons, about her talent contest victories and subsequent rise to fame.

"I guess I was lucky," said Millner. "Obviously, I had talent, but I got some breaks, and I made the most of them."

Oprah maneuvered Millner into talking about what lessons she had to share with other women.

"Be true to yourself," said Millner. "Follow your dream, whatever it is. Find a role model—and I don't mean me. There's someone to look up to, no matter what you want to do with your life. I mean, look at Clarice Marnier..."

Oprah didn't know who Clarice Marnier was.

"Clarice, from the...you know...rock band? Bloody Waters?"

Oprah still didn't know, so she let Millner continue without comment.

"Clarice is a great role model. She wanted to be a guitar hero, and look at her! Even though rock'n'roll is like, twenty years dead, she's still doing it. She's successful, and she made it with nothing but pure determination. If she can do it, you can, too!"

"That was really nice of Millner," said Kranz. "After what you said about her..."

Clarice gave him a look that shut him up immediately. The interview concluded, and Clarice stopped the tape.

"I don't see what was so bad about that."

"Don't bullshit me, Kranz, you know exactly what she just said."

"I...it still didn't seem all that bad..."

"That's why she said it."

"So what are you going to do about it?" asked Johnny.

"Nothing," said Clarice. "Not a thing. Not yet."

4. Afterdog/Underparty

The recording of Bloody Waters' second album, *DIY Hemispherectomy*, proceeded apace. When Clarice was satisfied with the structure and texture of all the songs, she let the rest of the band have some time off. Meanwhile, she spent her days closeted with Connors, mixing and tweaking, adding or subtracting new leads, tinkering with the solos.

Hemispherectomy was almost a wrap when the MTV Music Award nominations were announced. Bloody Waters' "Butcherama" video was nominated for Best Rock Video. Gabrielle Millner's "Love Forever" was up for Best Female Video.

Clarice wore a pair of faded jeans, snakeskin boots, a black T-shirt, and a short, black jacket to the awards ceremony. Johnny wore tails and a top hat; Enrique went for a James Bond casino ensemble. Beresford wore a white, off-the-shoulder evening gown and dyed camouflage patterns into her hair for the occasion. Kranz and Stroman wore suits.

They arrived at the allotted time. Clarice led them so briskly down the red carpet that it seemed she was going to blitz through the party ahead of them: a wild-haired folk-rock prodigy and his retinue of bongo players and nutritionists. When the prodigy turned to stare over his shoulder in alarm, Clarice slowed her charge to a saunter.

"Always wanted to do that," she said to Johnny. A nasty smile settled on her face.

Inside the reception hall, Enrique and Beresford went straight for the bar. Kranz went off to schmooze with some corporates and other managers. Stroman found a knot of beret-wearing video-clip directors and disappeared into their midst. Clarice stalked amongst the guests, Johnny trailing behind her like a porter.

Gabrielle Millner stood in a clique of her own, talking to a supermodel, an actress, and an overweight executive in a tailored suit. She flashed Clarice a dazzling smile and waltzed off to the cloakroom.

"Well, she's seen you now," said Johnny.

"And I've seen her."

"You're not gonna do anything?"

"No," said Clarice. "Too many press people here."

"But you're gonna do something. I can tell."

"She's hosting an afterparty. We'll see her there."

"Should I be surprised that we're even invited?"

"We're not."

"Ah."

Kranz and Stroman sat with Bloody Waters through the ceremony. They listened to odious industry fixtures reading scripted jokes from a teleprompter; they watched bedazzled singers gush their thank-yous; they witnessed half a dozen inoffensive pop acts lip sync their stuff on the second stage. It went on for hours.

Best Female Clip came up before Best Rock Video. The host, an aging (and swelling) second-string Motown songstress, called the nominees and showed snippets of the various artists' clips. Millner's showed the diva walking on a beach at sunset looking melancholy, intercut with footage of her beside a lake full of swans, swooning in the presence of a male model in an open-fronted shirt. Other nominated clips showed a cartoon world inhabited by singing animals, a starlet in an open-topped convertible waving an accusing finger at a no-good (but handsome) boyfriend, and an elaborately choreographed chorus line.

The no-good boyfriend clip won. Clarice could not see where Millner was seated, but she imagined the diva's reaction would be sportsmanlike and unconvincing.

There were several nominees for Best Rock Clip, which was presented by a 1980s teen movie star. Clarice did not think her chances were good—"Butcherama" was a difficult song, and the video had been shot on a comparatively small budget—but stranger things had happened. The other Best Rock Clip nominees showed skinny men in leather pants playing agonized guitar solos in a junkyard, spike-haired designer punks in baggy pants jumping around in a skate park, and an emaciated goth lord being welded into the machinery of a horror-movie factory.

The skater-punks won; the goth lord would probably take Best Special Effects. "Ah, shit," said Clarice.

Johnny shrugged. "Next time," he said.

"No," said Clarice. "Award ceremonies are lame. I'm never doing this again." She never did.

Kranz went home after the final awards had been given out. Stroman went off with his director friends. Enrique and Beresford forced their way into the closest bar, jam-packed as it was. Clarice and Johnny headed for Millner's party.

Millner had rented an entire hotel for her shindig. Clarice and Johnny arrived too late to hear Millner's teary-eyed and long-winded address to Ursula McIntosh, the woman who had pipped her for the Best Female Clip.

Dance music pulsed at a huge volume out of the windows of the place. It was even louder in the lobby, where the five different songs playing in the downstairs rooms railed against each other. Clarice and Johnny moved through the noise and smoke and strobing, shimmering lights. Pop stars and their hangers-on were partying it up, drinking and smoking and snorting...but mostly preening.

Millner was upon them immediately, coming out of nowhere, her teeth glistening more brightly than the diamonds in her ears. She had changed her outfit since the ceremony to something lower cut, but less glittery. "Clarice! Johnny! How lovely to see you here! I had no idea you were coming."

"We're gate-crashing," said Clarice.

"Well," said Millner, "I feel privileged to have had my party gate-crashed by the likes of you. In fact, you have my full permission to crash any of my functions, any time you like."

Clarice scowled at her. Millner was smarter than she looked.

"Do make yourselves at home," said Millner in an unconscious and awful faux-British accent. She looked over her shoulder and did a double-take. "Oh, good heavens…Cecelia!" Millner swept on toward Cecelia with her arms wide.

"Huh," said Johnny.

"She'll be back," said Clarice. "She just needs some time to prepare what she's going to say."

"Right."

"C'mon, let's go eat some of Millner's food."

An hour later the party was starting to wind down. The crowds had thinned, the music had softened, and the amount of radiant body heat had fallen. When Clarice saw Millner gliding over, she scoffed the last of the mini-quiches she had been working on and smiled. Johnny drank his beer.

"Are you enjoying yourself, Clarice? Johnny?"

"Of course," said Johnny. "Great party."

"Food's okay," said Clarice.

Millner sighed and smiled. "I was really sad you didn't win your category," she said. "I thought your song was by far the best." Her eyes opened wider. "In your genre, you know."

"I noticed you had a disappointment, yourself."

Millner smiled insincerely. "Oh, but Ursula deserved to win. She has such a *huge* talent, you know? And she's been on the scene for simply *ages*."

"Right," said Clarice. "They wanted to recognize her before she gets any fatter and people forget who she is."

"Oh, Clarice," said Millner. "You say the wickedest things."

"I was raised badly."

"Well, you are a rock star."

"Uh huh?"

"Oh, I didn't mean it that way—"

"It's okay, Millner, we both know how it is. Pop stars are like butterflies: a couple of weeks in the sun and then they die beautiful. Rock musicians go on forever, just getting uglier and more obnoxious."

"That's not really true, Clarice," said Millner. "Some pop stars last...and lots of rockers die awfully young."

"Everybody dies, Millner," said Clarice. "It's a question of who gets to be remembered."

"Who wants to be a dinosaur, anyway?"

Clarice's grin widened. "Hey, did you see that movie, *Jurassic Park?*"

"Yes...?" said Millner. Johnny knew the contest was already over.

"You know those little mosquitoes trapped in the amber?"

"...yes...?"

"Well, those are pop stars. Parasites with a bellyful of dino blood, trapped in fossilized tree shit."

"Oh, Clarice. You have such a...vivid...imagination."

"And you have no imagination at all," said Clarice.

"Anyway," said Johnny, "thanks for having us, Gabrielle. Awesome party. Lovely to see you." He shook Millner's hand and kissed her on the cheek.

Millner turned to Clarice and smiled beatifically, spreading her arms and moving in for a hug. She walked straight into the open palm of Clarice's left hand, which had somehow materialized between them at the end of Clarice's extended arm. "Thanks, Millner," said Clarice. "You were swell. See you around."

Clarice turned and walked away. Johnny gave Millner a shrug and a wink as he turned to follow Clarice out into the night.

5. TPB

DIY Hemispherectomy hit the racks six weeks later. It sold solidly at launch, and it kept selling well after. The first single, "Cross My Heart and Hope You Die," went to number two on Billboard's alternative countdown. The second single, the thrashy "Hate

You All," went all the way. The album went gold twice in quick succession.

Bloody Waters were not in the heavyweight division yet, but they had name recognition and a growing legion of followers all around the world. For this album tour they were going to hit Europe, Japan, Oceania, and Brazil.

They were signing in an independent record store when they first saw the book.

It was a paperback collection of a monthly comic book called *Rock Babes in Space*. It was sort of *Josie and the Pussycats* combined with *Baywatch* and X-Files. One of the stories was about a group of evil aliens attempting to conquer the world by masquerading as a rock outfit called Red Rivers. The character designs that they'd seen for the Bloody Waters comic book had been used for the Red Rivers characters. The plot was nonsensical, but the Red Rivers scenes crackled on the page: super-villain plotting included, the writer had captured the internal dynamics of the band beautifully.

The fan who presented the book to Clarice to sign told her that the monthly comic book had been cancelled before a second paperback collection could be published, and the first one had gone out of print. This, combined with Bloody Waters' growing fame, had made the book something of a collector's item.

Kranz asked Clarice if she wanted to sue.

"What the hell for?" said Clarice. "Satire was still legal, last time I checked."

"There's a difference between satire and defamation."

"Waste of time and effort," said Clarice. "Besides, I like being a comic book villain."

THE WICCAN WITCH
— OF THE MIDWEST —

1. Gathering Moss

The *Rolling Stone* feature opened with a list of names: Eric, Jimi, Carlos, Jimmy, Joe, Steve, Eddie, Stevie, Clarice. Which of these is not like the others?

None of them, the author concluded. They were all masters, virtuosos; unique and unmatchable. That was all that mattered, right? The author was more than certain that Bloody Waters' Witchy Guitar Woman could stand amongst that august company, regardless of her gender.

Clarice was furious. "I'm not a witch," she replied to a rival publication. "It may have taken a pact with the Devil to get a record deal, but I learned to play the hard way. Nobody ever cut me any breaks."

Rolling Stone ran an edited version of her response under the headline: "Voodoo Chick (Slight Return)."

2. Whale Thongs

When her fifteen-year-old niece Sasha came down with the flu, Jermaine Ophelia "Brightstar" Dean packed up her amulets and powders and crystals into a large hemp carry-bag and took the Greyhound up to her sister Marlene's house in Columbus. It took three cups of herbal tea and a full hour of wheedling and bullying before Marlene finally agreed to let her sister treat Sasha.

Sasha was sitting up in her bed with an Iain Banks novel in one hand and a box of tissues in the other. Her nose was red, and her hair was stringy and moist. The blinds were drawn, the bedside lamp was on, and the stereo was emitting obnoxious rock'n'roll music at a moderate volume: Sasha had both Bloody Waters albums cycling continuously.

"Sasha?" said Jermaine.

"Dthermaine?"

"Please, call me Auntie Brightstar," said Jermaine, moving into the room. "How are you doing?"

"Thick ath a dog," said Sasha, frowning down at her book.

"We'll see what we can do about that," said Jermaine, bustling closer and opening her bag.

"Oh, Chritht," said Sasha, closing the book on one finger and looking up. "Will it take long?"

"Not really," said Jermaine, "but you'll have to turn off the music. I don't think this noise is conducive to wellness. I have a CD with some forest sounds and whale songs that will be much better for you."

"Whale thongs?"

"Whale songs."

"I don't think tho." Sasha picked up her book again. "Thee you later, Auntie Brightthtar."

"I'm sorry?"

Sasha did not look up from her book. "I thaid, thee you later."

"Fine." Jermaine snapped her bag shut and forced a smile. "Hope you get better soon. Goddess willing."

As she turned to leave, something on Sasha's desk caught her eye. Lying amongst the menagerie of furry animals was the current issue of *Rolling Stone*. Clarice stood against a burning sea with a guitar slung behind her, staring angrily out of the cover. 'Bloody Waters' Witchy Guitar Woman speaks out!' it said.

"Thee you later, Auntie Brightthtar," said Sasha, looking up from her book. "Thankth for coming by."

Jermaine smiled and bobbed her head and stalked out of the room.

The issue of *Rolling Stone* was still on the newsstand at the bus station.

3. The Evelyn McInnes Show

Against her better judgment, Clarice accepted the invitation to appear on Evelyn McInnes's talk show.

"No stunts," Kranz had promised. "No parents, no church groups, no jilted exes. Just you and the music and the issues."

Clarice went into the studio expecting to be bored, but the minute she stepped onto the sound stage she realized that she might actually be able to have some fun with this.

Evelyn was not even halfway through her introduction when Clarice barged in, Johnny trailing two steps behind.

"Oh, hello!"

"Hi, Evelyn."

It took Evelyn two beats to find her new mark and reword her intro, by which time Clarice and Johnny had already draped themselves all over the plush velvet sofa while the director scrambled to get the cameras realigned. Neither of them had submitted themselves to makeup, and they looked more than a little unkempt in their black T-shirts and jeans. Clarice smiled a nasty half-smile when a camera finally did dolly in toward her.

Evelyn asked where the rest of the band was.

"Don't worry about them," said Clarice, putting one sneakered foot up on the coffee table. "They're sacrificing some chickens in preparation for our musical number."

Johnny smiled and nodded.

Evelyn laughed haltingly. "Oh, haha! Rock and roll humor."

"Of course," Clarice grinned. "If we let them do the chickens, they'd screw it up."

Johnny smiled and nodded.

Evelyn's mouth opened and closed twice. The studio audience sat quietly in their seats, blinking furiously.

Evelyn was going to have to roll with these two, however weird and obstreperous they were. She could do that. She was a professional. "Clarice, you play the guitar like nobody's business, you write all of the Bloody Waters songs, you're outspoken on any number of issues and affairs. Tell me, how does it feel to be an emerging role model for—"

Clarice jumped on that immediately: "I'm not interested in being any kind of role model. I'm interested in making music, period. It's great that people listen to what I do, but, so long as they keep listening, I don't give a rat's ass if they actually like me."

The audience wasn't digging it. No one yelled, "Right on, sister!" or "You go, girl!" They just sat there looking at each other, muttering expressions of confusion.

"But Clarice, you must understand that you are a role model, just by virtue of your fame. Surely, you feel responsible for..."

"Responsible? I'm a freakin' *rock star.*"

Johnny grinned.

Evelyn tried a different tack. "Okay, so, tell us about what hardships you had to endure, what prejudices you had to break down in order to get where you are as a woman of rock?"

Clarice shrugged. "I paid my dues, same as everyone else."

"But surely it wasn't easy?"

"No, it wasn't easy," said Clarice. "But what's the point whining about it now? I made it and here we are."

"Yes, but…" Evelyn looked away, sighed through her teeth. More ego stroking was in order. "You are the first woman to become a guitar hero of such stature. Why has there never been one before you?"

Clarice shrugged. "A lot more guys play the guitar than girls, so they get more competitive about who has better chops."

"Ah ha! And why is that, do you think?"

"They're compensating? I'm not a man, how the hell would I know?"

"It must have been difficult to be taken seriously."

"Well, sure, there's the occasional heckler, or whatever, but the truth is that most guys love to see a woman playing the guitar."

"Do you think they feel…threatened?"

"Only when they see that you're better than them," said Clarice, grinning like a steel trap, "and by then it's too late."

Evelyn was unable to elicit anything deeper or more meaningful from them. What were the themes of their music? "Love and sex and drugs and dancing all night long." Why was their music so dark? "It's a rough world out there." Was it true that Clarice and Johnny were a couple? "Yes, but it's none of your business."

Johnny just smiled and nodded at whatever Clarice said. He didn't seem like a psychopath, and he was also quite handsome, so Evelyn pitched him a couple of questions. Perhaps the audience would like him better.

"Ask Clarice," he replied. "She's more interesting than I am."

The pair of them clearly held the entire proceedings in contempt, and it was starting to piss Evelyn off. She called a commercial break and announced that when they returned, Bloody Waters would perform one of their songs.

As soon as the cameras were off, Clarice and Johnny were out of their seats. They went straight to the side stage without saying a word to Evelyn. Enrique and Beresford joined them, and Clarice got everyone into place with a few terse orders. Roadies and crew scattered as the band took up position. Billy brought Clarice her big, black seven-string and Johnny a green Telecaster.

Evelyn had never seen anything like it. She could hardly believe these were the same snide and intractable egomaniacs, standing on the stage waiting quietly for their cue.

Clarice started "Davey Jones' Locker" with an insidious, tinkly little riff. Enrique and Beresford rumbled in, low and hard. Then Johnny's guitar cut in. He leaned into the mic and crooned about a passenger liner leaving its moorings. In the depths below, Davey Jones stirred and woke.

Clarice, stalking up and down the stage, answered each repetition of Johnny's riff with a series of ever-crazier licks. When he sang the verses, she tremolo-picked the same chords as he played, finding the most unlikely voicings for each of them. The walls of the soundstage vibrated in sympathy.

Storm clouds gathered, Davey Jones opened his locker and ascended into the black waters. The plectrum rippled amongst Clarice's fingers as she tapped a lead break with her right hand.

Johnny spread his arms and clenched his fists. The boat broke apart, and the seething waters claimed the passengers' lives. Beresford's drums crashed, Enrique's bass juddered, Johnny's guitar rolled and roared. Clarice hit the solo, using a whammy pedal and massive reverb to draw a spiraling melody down, down, down as low as the seven-string could take it.

The storm abated. Corpses rose to the surface, swirling slowly amongst the wreckage of the boat. Seagulls lit for carrion. The doors closed on those few that were granted a place in Davey Jones' locker.

Johnny's guitar faded, the bass calmed, the drums slowed. Clarice picked out the opening riff one more time and took her hands off the guitar.

The walls stopped shaking.

The audience applauded politely. Evelyn announced another break. Enrique and Beresford stumbled off into the wings, while Clarice and Johnny headed back to the main stage to continue the interview.

When the ad break was over, Evelyn stepped between them and the camera and said, "Now we have a special guest who would like to converse with you."

Clarice sighed. "It's not another angry diva, is it?"

Evelyn smiled and shook her head. Whitney, Toni, and Gabrielle had declined the invitation, and Celine and Mariah were on tour overseas. "Oh no," she said. "This is somebody quite different." Evelyn grinned. There was no way they were ready for this one.

"Everyone, please welcome Jermaine Ophelia 'Brightstar' Dean!"

Jermaine wore a green dress woven with Celtic patterns and a dark shawl spangled with a stylized zodiac. Dozens of bracelets clattered on her left wrist, and an ankh hung around her neck. Her feet were bare.

The audience applauded loudly–Jermaine's appearance marked her as entertaining. Clarice looked her up and down, frowning. She looked at Johnny, who shrugged. She shook her head. Jermaine flushed scarlet and started to sputter.

Evelyn somehow managed to get Jermaine into her seat. "All right, ladies, go ahead," she said, and got out of the way.

Jermaine puffed herself up, but Clarice spoke first. "Let me guess," she said. "You are...a...a flower child?"

"I...am a witch," said Jermaine.

"Oh," said Clarice. "That's...lovely."

Johnny smiled and nodded with a bit more vigor than he had previously.

Jermaine blinked. Her mouth opened and closed a few times.

"Well, sister, do you have something to say to me?"

"Yes," said Jermaine, straightening in her seat. "I want you to take back the vilifying remarks you made about the Wiccan faith in *Rolling Stone* magazine."

Someone in the audience said, "Yeah!" Several people echoed him.

"They called me a witch," said Clarice, as reasonably as she could manage. "I'm not a witch."

"The way you said it, you said that Wiccans are devil worshippers."

"I didn't say a thing about Wicca."

"You implied that Wiccans are Satanists."

"I didn't even mention Wicca."

"The Devil is a patriarchal symbol of a monotheistic and culturally imperialistic…"

Clarice folded her arms and looked at the ceiling. Jermaine's tirade continued.

Evelyn cut in: "Perhaps you should explain to us a bit about your faith, Jermaine."

Jermaine smiled hugely. "Wicca is a pagan faith, or, more correctly, a neo-pagan faith—"

"The Readers' Digest version, please," said Clarice.

Jermaine glared at her.

"We'd really love to hear it," coaxed Evelyn.

Jermaine harrumphed. "We worship nature, as embodied by The Goddess and The God. We are a polytheistic, environment-loving religion. We practice magicke, but we are not Satanists. You have to be a Christian to believe in the Devil."

"What do you believe in?"

"We choose our gods from amongst the old pagan religions," said Jermaine. "Greek, Roman, Egyptian, African…"

"Sounds like kind of an ass-backwards approach to faith, you ask me," said Clarice. "You pick your religion, then you pick your gods?"

"We are a progressive, modern—"

"You're into crystals and spells and the outdoors."

"I don't know what your problem is. We're totally benign. Our credo is 'harm not.'"

"You don't understand," said Clarice, shaking her head. "Religion isn't about being nice. It's about missionaries and crusades and inquisitions and dogma."

"Not to mention acquiring wealth," added Johnny, brightly.

"You...judgmental...goddamn..."

The studio audience rumbled epithets at both antagonists.

"Ladies, ladies, please," said Evelyn, ignoring Johnny, "Let's try not to insult each other personally. Jermaine, you were raising a point about the remarks Clarice made in Rolling Stone?"

"Yes! Yes." Jermaine bit off every word. "I think it was wrong for Clarice to imply that all witches are Satanists."

"Sure," said Clarice. "And I think it was wrong for Jermaine to suggest that all witches are Wiccans."

4. Razorblade Moon

Bloody Waters went into the studio with Connors to record their third album. Since *Bloody Waters* and *DIY Hemispherectomy* were both still selling well, Heinman actually tried not to impede their progress. Not only did he stay out of their way, but he actually assisted them in resolving the usual disputes that arose regarding the cover art, video clips, singles and press.

It was not quite nine months after Bloody Waters' appearance on *The Evelyn McInnes Show* that *Razorblade Moon* was released. The album cover sported a picture of a devil cutting open the sky with a razor-edged crescent moon. The last track on the album was called "The Wiccan Witch of the Midwest."

5. Coven and Cabal

Jermaine's coven agreed to cast some rituals to protect themselves from the malignant influence of Bloody Waters' music, but Jermaine wanted to do something more direct. She wanted to work some magic directly on the band and particularly on Clarice Marnier.

The coven did not perceive the rock star as a serious threat, but Jermaine knew better. She argued and badgered them until they held a formal vote. The motion was denied, seventeen to two. Muriel Trask was Jermaine's single ally.

After the moot was over, Muriel approached her privately. She thought they should make it a mission. Take the battle to the enemy. Muriel had found Wicca through her ex-husband, whose coven had been made up of personnel serving at the US Army base in Aberdeen.

The two of them spent a full week putting the operation together. Muriel acquired the band's touring schedule and finagled information about the band's retinue, transport, accommodations, and security. Jermaine consulted her calendar and grimoires, drew up a list of correspondences, and scripted the spell invocations.

Their primary mission was to deliver the spell to Clarice Marnier. It would be a healing spell, Jermaine decided, to rid the guitarist of whatever evil she harbored. They would also need spells for stealth, courage, and protection against hostile magic. Jermaine was convinced that the rock star was a Satanic witch who probably had Dark Powers at her disposal.

Muriel did not agree. "The Devil is part of monotheist dogma, and therefore does not exist," she said. "How can he grant Clarice powers?"

"Better to be safe than sorry," said Jermaine.

6. Operation Tour Bus

Jermaine and Muriel planned the operation around Bloody Waters' show at the Richfield Coliseum. It was a Thursday, which was a good day for spirituality and healing magic. The waning moon would be in Aries, the ideal time for spells involving authority, spiritual conversion, and the healing of ailments to the face, head, and brain.

On the morning of the selected day, the two witches caught the Greyhound bus to Cleveland. Muriel insisted they wear black jumpsuits over the purple and yellow garments that Jermaine had picked out for protection and confidence.

"Gods can see through fabric," she said, "security guards can't."

Jermaine wore alligator teeth and an Eye of Horus around her neck for protection; Muriel wore a simple pentagram. They filled their belt pouches with lilac, aloe, incense, and salt. Jermaine carried the magical paraphernalia; Muriel carried all of the infiltration gear.

They spent the afternoon hanging around on Euclid Avenue, hopping from espresso bar to espresso bar, window shopping and going over the spell rites. After a quick dinner, they took a commuter bus out to Richfield. Jermaine and Muriel alighted about three blocks from the band's motel.

Richfield seemed particularly quiet as evening descended. There were no lights in any of the squat, single-story buildings they passed. No stores were open. No pedestrians were on the sidewalks. Even the streetlamps were dead. A breeze ruffled their hair. Their shoes clumped softly on the sidewalks.

Jermaine and Muriel rounded a corner, and the motel came into view.

The NO/VACANCY sign was unlit. All the rooms were dark. They skirted Reception, which appeared to be closed. There were no guests about.

Jermaine stumbled on a loose paving stone. Muriel shushed her grumbling; darkness favored their mission. Jermaine changed her tune immediately: "Our spells are wooorkiiiing," she sang. "Goddess be praaaaiiiised!"

Muriel shushed her again.

There was one guard in the main courtyard: a fat guy in a cheap, blue nylon jacket with the security company's logo on the back. He occasionally limped up and down the three-quarters-empty car park to shine his torch around, but he spent most of his time leaning against the wall beside the ice machine, smoking and drinking coffee from his thermos. Both of the parking lot spotlights were out.

"Are you sure this is the place?" hissed Jermaine.

"Yes."

"Well, where the hell's the tour bus?"

"There's an open area behind the building."

"Are you sure the show wasn't cancelled?"

"It was in today's paper."

"I told you we should have gone to the stadium."

"I told you we should have scouted this out in advance."

"Well, we're here now."

The Wiccans went around the block so they could approach the motel from a less conspicuous angle. They slipped into the courtyard while the guard wasn't looking, then scooted down the perimeter fence until the main block of rooms blocked them from his view.

A six-foot chain-link gate barred their access to the open area behind the motel. They could see the tour bus through it. Muriel shone her light on the gate's bar. "Oh."

"What?"

"The lock's already been cut."

"How?"

"I don't know. Help me get this open."

Muriel and Jermaine hauled on the gate. It scraped a few inches through the dirt. "Pull!" hissed Muriel.

Their combined efforts got it another two feet open. They slipped through.

The area behind the motel was twenty feet wide and as long as the main building. It smelled of rubber and mildew and wet soil. In the darkness, Jermaine could make out the shapes of worn-out tires, a mattress, a felled tree, and a stack of broken TVs. A large set of tire tracks in the bare dirt led to the tour bus itself.

"Door's open," said Muriel. There was no movement, no light coming from the bus. "Let's do it."

Jermaine nodded grimly and pulled an *athame* dagger from her tote-bag. Incanting under her breath, she used the wavy blade to scrape a circle in the dirt all the way around the bus.

When the circle was complete, she and Muriel stepped over its border and climbed up into the bus. The metal step gave slightly beneath their weight, groaning softly. The leather of their shoes creaked.

The bus was an ordinary coach with some of the seats removed for legroom and stowage space. The back of it was filled with stage equipment: guitars, amplifiers, drums, stands, cables, sound boards, all strapped down and secured for transport. There was nobody present.

They stood there, listening to their own breathing and the humming of the bar fridge, which was powered by the bus's battery.

"I don't like it," said Jermaine.

"The concert won't even start for another half hour," said Muriel. "We'll be fine. Let's just get this done."

"Shouldn't the bus be at the theatre?" asked Jermaine, belatedly figuring out the hole in their plan. "Looks like all their gear is in here."

"Well, it's here," said Muriel. "So I guess we got lucky. Do the spell."

Jermaine squatted down in the aisle and assembled her portable altar from three sections of polished wood. She oriented it toward the east and lit three squat beeswax candles. Then she stood up again and began the incantation.

"Lady of Day, Mistress of Night, heed the calls of your daughters. Silvered Moon Woman, observe how we lay this Circle of Power." She took a long breath. "Father, Great Hunter, hear us. Laughing Man, guard our Circle."

Jermaine presented some incense over the altar. They added salt to the water in their canteens and presented those, too.

"Circle, be thou cast. As we have walked thine perimeter, so do you contain our power. Set us apart from this world of man, apart from the domain of spirit. Set us between the worlds, that we may work our magickes."

Jermaine saluted to the east with the *athame*. "We call to you, Gods and Goddesses: heed our cries; aid us in our rites. We call to you, Anotchi. We call to you, Apa. Great Goddesses, lend us your powers of healing, of purifying. We call to you, Mars, God of War. Give us the strength to face those who would bring ruination upon us."

"Now, that is more like it." The voice was strong, female. Resonant. A beam of light fell upon them. Jermaine shaded her eyes and stepped back from it. Muriel squinted and bunched her fists.

"Absolutely," said a second voice. This one was softer, deeper. Male. "Not every day somebody accuses you of plotting ruination."

"I don't think I've actually heard anybody say that word out loud before. 'Ruination.'"

"It's a good one, isn't it?"

The light grew brighter as the source approached. Footsteps came with it.

Clarice Marnier and Johnny Chernow stopped about ten feet away from them. Johnny smiled pleasantly; Clarice did not.

"Put the knife down, please," said Clarice.

Jermaine carefully put the *athame* on ground, blinking at the loss of her night-vision. "What are you doing here?" she demanded.

"It's our tour bus, we're allowed to be here," said Clarice. "What are you doing here, and why are you dressed like...fat, little... ninjas?"

"Nothing," spluttered Jermaine.

"Why aren't you on stage?" asked Muriel.

"The city of Cleveland and, in fact, all of Cuyahoga County, is blacked out tonight." She said. "An ice storm up north has fritzed up the power station."

"I told you the darkness was bad," Jermaine accused Muriel.

"*You* praised the Goddess for it."

"Come now, ladies," said Clarice, shining the torch in their eyes again. "I don't want to listen to anybody argue, unless they are arguing with me."

Jermaine was happy to oblige. "We're on to you, Clarice."

"On to me?"

"We know you're a Satanic witch."

"I am?"

"Yes.

Clarice looked at Johnny. "Do you recognize either of these two ladies?"

"The...larger...one was on *The Evelyn McInnes Show* with us," said Johnny. "I don't think I've seen the smaller, ferrety-looking one before, but I'm gonna guess that she's also a witch."

"A different kind of witch than she is," spat Jermaine, pointing a finger at Clarice. "Devil whore."

"Okay, okay, I admit it," said Clarice. "There has been some deviltry going on around here, and there are, indeed, three witches present on this bus."

"We're not scared of you, Clarice Marnier," said Jermaine. "It's two against one, and we're already warded against your magickes."

"I'm not a witch," said Clarice. "I just play the gee-tar."

"Perhaps it would have been clearer if you'd said 'two witches and a warlock,'" said Johnny, helpfully.

"'Warlock' is a misnomer," said Jermaine, fixing her gaze on Johnny. "It means 'traitor to the faith.'"

"Exactly," Johnny replied. "I was raised Catholic."

"It's not the same thing."

"I still prefer it." Johnny shrugged apologetically. "'Warlock' feels more manly."

Clarice sighed and shook her head. "I don't suppose you girls are willing to just pack up your shit and get off my tour bus?"

Muriel looked ready to capitulate, but Jermaine said, "Not until we've settled our differences—one way or the other."

"Okay, fine," said Clarice.

"What's on the menu, Clarice?" asked Johnny.

"Can you do frogs legs?"

"I'll give it a go," said Johnny, doubtfully. He shut his eyes, murmured some words, and looked down. His eyes glowed red through his eyelids

Jermaine and Muriel became smaller and greener.

"Holy shit. That actually worked!" Johnny seemed as alarmed as he was pleased.

Clarice squinted. "Are they...is that actually them?"

"Yep."

"Well, hell."

The frogs ribbited.

"Hey, do you know what frogs' legs are called?" asked Clarice.

"How do you mean?"

Jermaine and Muriel hopped about confusedly.

"In French, I mean. Snails are 'escargot,' but I don't know what frogs' legs are called."

"Dunno either, but they're good," said Johnny. He bent down and caught the frogs, one in each hand, with the ease of many long years of practice. "You ever try them?"

"Nope," said Clarice, "but I heard they taste like Wiccan."

— STORMY MUNDAY —

1. Razorblade Moon

J ohnny lifted the curse on the Wiccans the following morning and Clarice, turned the two frightened, confused, and embarrassed witches loose on the streets of Cleveland at about 6:30 a.m. She handed them each a bundle of their clothing, which had fallen off them when Johnny had set the curse.

Johnny shrugged and smiled apologetically and rushed to catch up with Clarice, who was already walking away. One of the witches–the fat one–yelled something at his back. That was the last trouble Bloody Waters had from the Greater Wiccan Community, or the Lesser Wiccan Community, or even the company that sold the Midwestern Wiccan Association's promotional coffee mugs. Clarice kept Jermaine's dagger as a trophy.

The *Razorblade Moon* tour continued, and ticket sales remained strong. Audiences seemed no less appreciative than before, but the album had barely made gold and none of the singles were on the charts.

"I don't understand it. The album is better than the previous two," said Clarice.

"Me neither," said Kranz, who could be relied upon to agree with anything Clarice said. "There's no explanation for it."

"Of course there's an explanation," said Johnny. "Rock'n'roll is out of fashion. It's gonna slump further before the curve turns."

"What, really?" Kranz affected disbelief.

"A lot of big rock bands have split up in the last couple years," said Johnny. "Faith No More, Soundgarden...it's difficult for everyone right now."

"We're not everyone," muttered Clarice, but that was the end of the argument.

Audiences were down and spirits were low by the end of the tour, so Clarice decided that it was time for a break. She ordered each of the respective band members to go on holiday.

"Me included?" said Johnny.

"Of course, you included."

Johnny just looked at her.

"What?"

"Do I get to hang out with my girlfriend while I'm on this mandatory vacation, or are you sending me away?"

"I hadn't thought about it that way."

"I know."

She could tell he was unhappy. "Uh, yeah," she said, "I guess you can hang around if you want."

It wasn't an apology, but she did look a little mortified. That seemed to be good enough for Johnny.

"Enrique and Beresford are going diving in Vanuatu. What are your plans?"

"Dunno," said Clarice. "I'm not good at vacations."

"Nothing to it," said Johnny. "I'll teach you all I know."

"I'm not a 'vacation' person," said Clarice.

In the end, Johnny arranged a number of short trips: the Grand Canyon, the Canadian Rockies, the Montreal Jazz Festival. Clarice went along on some of them, when she felt like it. If not, he went by himself. In between, they just bummed around in California, bouncing between LA and San Francisco.

Clarice went on doing her thing: practicing the guitar, staying fit. She wrote song lyrics. She taught herself to play the piano. She stayed as busy as ever, but the longer she was on holiday the more irritable she became.

When Rex Munday asked her to play on his first solo album it was as though the heavens had opened to her and the angels were lining up for guitar lessons.

2. Hating Munday

"All I know for sure is that it's called *Hating Munday*."

"You haven't written any songs yet?" said Clarice.

"Not one single note."

She and Rex were sitting in a Hollywood diner, eating pancakes and drinking coffee. Rex had already sorted out the legal and financial stuff. The deal was done; now all he needed to do was put the album together. Clarice had no idea how he had managed to pull it off.

"You have any material planned? Any demos?"

"Nope," he said. "I want every song to be a collaboration, ground up."

"Rex, it's a solo album."

"There's solo, and then there's solo," he said. "Let's plan some jam sessions and see what we come up with."

"Okay, sure."

"When are you free?"

"Now is good," said Clarice. "So is later. I'm supposed to be on holiday, and I'm dying for an excuse to quit."

They went directly from the diner to Rex's house in Burbank. Clarice had The Motherfucker with her, of course, and Rex produced a battered old Dobro. Clarice plugged The Motherfucker into a 60 watt Randall amp that Rex had lying about and dialed in some overdrive. It didn't take long to tune up.

"Okay," said Clarice, "this is your album, you go first."

"Sure," said Rex. He strummed a few open chords, fingered a slow sequence of power fifths. He nodded, changed up the rhythm, played it again. "Okay," he said, "there's the main riff."

Clarice played it back. "D minor," she said. She played a blues lick in the same key.

Rex banged out the riff again and started to hum. Clarice improvised some additional rhythm, and Rex subsided a bit while he listened.

"All right," he said, and began to sing in the smooth tenor he reserved for the occasional DreadLords acoustic ballad. Since Metallica had made a hit of "Nothing Else Matters," the DreadLords had decided that it was acceptable to lapse into something low key, so long as it didn't happen more than once per album.

"I woke up this morning," sang Rex, making it up as he went along (which meant borrowing from the greats), "Sat up in my bed. Had to do breakfast with Satan, had to earn my daily bread."

"Not bad," said Clarice. She raked an arpeggio, moved the cage up the fretboard, threw in a trill.

"Old Satan ordered deviled eggs, and coffee black as night. The waitress wrote his order down and ran away in fright."

Clarice improvised some more rhythm and spun up the volume a bit. She did not offer any further comment on Munday's lyrics.

"I'm not sure where to take the song from there," said Rex, strumming random chords in the key. "I'm thinking maybe we could have, like, a bunch of gangsters attack the place, and the Devil has to fight them. Or maybe ninjas."

"So the tone is gonna be a little less serious than your DreadLords stuff?" said Clarice, keeping a straight face.

"Right," said Rex, playing a slidey and mellow version of his main riff. "It's only rock'n'roll, after all."

"Sounds like fun. Who've you got on drums and bass?"

"That will change from song to song. I got a few different guys lined up: Les Claypool, Jason Newsted, Vinnie Paul, Melissa Auf der Maur, Neil Peart…"

"Jesus. Did anyone actually say 'no' to you?"

Rex gave it some thought, surprised by the question. "Arlo Tuckson was the only one," he said.

"Tuckson said no?"

"Yeah. You know him?"

"We've met," said Clarice.

"Well, if I'd known I would have called you. I had a bitch of a time tracking him down."

"He's a hard man to find."

"He sounded kind of lousy, now I think of it. I hope he's okay."

"Probably just got hemorrhoids or something," said Clarice. "Who else is in?"

"Tom Morello might be interested," said Rex, carefully. "Maybe I'll ask him to play lead on one or two tracks…if that's okay with you."

"It's your album, Rex. You don't have to ask my permission to do anything."

"I know," said Rex, chicken-picking an odd little melody over Clarice's gentle strumming, "but I want to have you on the record more than any of the others."

Clarice wasn't sure how to take that. Rex had his eyes closed; his attention appeared to be on the sounds coming from his guitar.

"Tell you what. If you're game, I'll give you lyrics for a couple of songs."

"Or, we could write one together," said Rex, suddenly delighted. He was now chicken-picking his syncopated little melody. Rex sweetened it with some natural harmonics. Clarice squinted at him.

He looked up. "What do you say?"

"Yeah, sure, we can try it." She knew she sounded doubtful. Clarice shook her head and answered his melody with a series of fat power chords.

"I'm sure it'll work," said Rex, his melody becoming more elaborate and strange. The slide was back on his pinkie finger, and he was using it to its full advantage. "I know you take pride in being difficult, but I think you and me get along just swell." He played a little solo, using his right hand to tap some notes on the neck during an elaborate hammer-on/pull-off motif, keeping the slide in there as well.

Clarice didn't reply. Her strumming slowed and she tipped her head, listening. Munday's solo picked up tempo and crescendoed. His eyes were closed, and his head was bobbing.

"Rex," she said, after a while. She had stopped playing altogether. "Rex."

Rex opened his eyes and looked up at her. "Yeah?"

"Where the hell did you learn to play like that?"

He muted the Dobro's strings abruptly. "Like what?"

"Like that!"

"Shit, I dunno."

"Rex, that was fucking awesome. Why have I never heard you play like that?"

"I don't play leads. That's Mondrian's job."

"That was better than anything Mondrian ever did."

Rex shrugged. "I like rhythm better."

"But...man. If you're that good, you should let people to hear it. You don't need Mondrian to do leads for the DreadLords."

"He's the one who started the band."

"You don't need my leads on this album, either. This is the perfect opportunity to showcase your own work. Show everyone what you can do without stepping on Mondrian's toes..."

"No, hon," said Rex. "This album isn't about stepping on toes, or showing my chops, or anything like that. It's about making some new music with my friends."

"That shouldn't stop you."

"Clarice, I'm a singer and a rhythm guitarist. That's who Rex Munday is, that's who Rex Munday's fans know and love."

"You don't think your fans want to hear how good you really are?"

"Not really, no," said Rex. "Not any more than they want to hear me talk about myself in the third person."

"You don't want your peers to know?"

Rex grinned and shook his head. "No, Clarice. I'm just a guy who plays in a rock band; I'm not *the* guy who plays in *the* rock band—which, by the way, is you, or soon will be. I don't want to be a guitar hero. I just want to be Rex Munday."

Clarice frowned and shook her head. "You know, Rex, you're a whole lot stranger than you let on," she said.

Rex grinned. "If by 'stranger' you mean 'shallower,' I gotta agree with you."

"All right, all right," said Clarice. "Enough chatter. We have songs to write."

"Right," said Rex. "So what do you think: gangsters or ninjas?"

"Gangsters, Rex. Gangsters all the way."

3. Soap Opera

It took months to finish recording *Hating Munday*, because Rex had to wait for the various guest artists to free up their schedules. Clarice played leads on about three-quarters of the album, and, in a surprisingly diplomatic turn, she managed to avoid co-writing the lyrics to any of the songs. She completely stayed away from the songs that had guest guitarists.

Johnny took it all in stride: he saw Clarice a few evenings a week, if he wasn't off on one of his trips. He did not complain that Clarice was working, although she had forbidden the rest of the band from doing so. Johnny just went on being Johnny.

"You're not jealous of the time I'm spending with Rex?" said Clarice.

"Nope," said Johnny.

"You're not concerned, or anything?"

"About what?"

"Like, maybe me and Rex are doing it?"

"Doing what?"

"*Johnny.*"

"No, Clarice, I'm not concerned that you're cheating on me."

"You don't mind that we aren't spending so much time together?"

"I'd like to spend more time with you," he replied, deadpan, "but I don't want to disturb your holiday."

"And you wouldn't be upset if I was fucking Rex?"

"I didn't say that."

"True. But...would you be?"

"I'd prefer it if you didn't," he said. "But if you want to, you will, and there's nothing I can do to stop you."

"If I did, what would you do?"

"I don't know. Probably nothing."

"Would you be upset?"

"Yes."

"Well," said Clarice, "I'm not sleeping with him."

"I know."

"Oh, so, now you're taking me for granted?"

"Look who's talking."

Clarice mulled that over for a few moments. "Fair enough." She thought about it a bit more. "How would you know if I was sleeping with Rex, anyway?"

Johnny smiled. "You'd just have told me straight up. It would have been 'Johnny, me and Rex are fucking,' not 'Johnny, are you jealous of the time I'm spending with Rex?'"

"I guess you got me there."

"I know that too."

4. Get Me Behind Thee

By the time *Hating Munday* finally shipped, Enrique and Beresford had returned from the South Pacific and Clarice was already planning the new Bloody Waters album. *Hating Munday* didn't get a huge marketing push and it sold accordingly: mainly to diehard DreadLords fans and more than a few Clarice Marnier completists. The best song, 'Get Me Behind Thee,' scraped into the Hottest 100 listener poll on an Australian radio station and blipped in the top fifty on the *Billboard* Modern Rock Chart for one week.

Most of the publicity Munday received concerned his association with Clarice. What was it like to record with her now? Was he proud of her? Did she really eat babies? Munday answered graciously and with good humor.

Clarice, on the other hand, was seldom asked about Rex Munday. When she was, the questions were snidely denigrating of Munday's back catalogue. Clarice answered them straight, refusing to rise to any bait she was offered.

But every so often, Clarice wondered how it was that Munday had learned to play the way he had in that first jam session...and just how good he really was.

— KISS OF THE GUITAR WOMAN —

1. Selling Out

When Stanley Kranz suggested that Bloody Waters make their fourth album "mellower, with less...you know... guitars," Clarice was actually rendered speechless.

Despite its lackluster sales, *Razorblade Moon* had been good for the band, and particularly good for Clarice. The music world was really starting to recognize her musicianship and songwriting chops, and she was getting a lot of column space. Her name, if not her photo, was on the cover of one guitar magazine or another every month, often in conjunction with the word "virtuoso."

"Say that again," said Clarice, when her powers of speech had finally returned.

"I think," said Kranz, smoothing the logo on the T-shirt he wore under his Armani jacket, "that the next album should be mellower."

"With less guitars," said Johnny, leaning back in his seat and crossing his boots at the ankles. "That's what you said, right?"

"Less, um, guitars," said Kranz. "Yeah."

"Oh-kay," said Clarice, stroking her neck with one finger and fixing her gaze on the ceiling.

"Well, you know, *Razorblade Moon* didn't sell so good, and I thought maybe we could try for a more...accessible...sound," Kranz said. "You know. I'm not asking you to sell out, or anything..."

"... but...?"

"But maybe a more recognizably indie sound would be more marketable."

"More indie?"

"You know, more...acoustic. More folky."

"This was...your idea?" said Johnny.

"Well, I was talking with Steve Heinman—"

"Yeah, I thought you might have been," said Clarice.

"It was his thought initially, but I fleshed it out some."

"Maybe you're right," said Clarice, speaking slowly. "Maybe we should write some...happier...stuff."

"We could even try for 'poignant,'" said Johnny.

"Poignant is great!" said Kranz. "Bloody Waters could record the next 'My Heart Will Go On.'"

Clarice and Johnny looked at each other.

On a roll, Kranz continued: "Clarice, let me ask you...can you sing?"

"No," said Clarice.

"Well, that doesn't matter. We have this technology now, we can..."

"No," said Clarice. "Johnny's the singer."

Kranz looked exasperated. He took a deep breath. "Well... Johnny's kind of voice isn't what's selling right now."

"You mean, he's not five guys whining in harmony?"

"I could try for that reedy Cali-punk thing, but it's harder than you'd think," said Johnny.

"I have confidence you can pull it off," said Kranz, beaming. "I know you have musicianship out the wazoo, but it's image that sells records in today's market."

"Whose image?"

"Well, *yours*, Clarice."

"I guess I do come off a bit 'in your face.'"

"You should be a Riot Grrl," suggested Johnny. "Get some tattoos, a belly-button ring."

Clarice shook her head. "I was thinking of something a bit more...I dunno. Demure. But sexy."

"Oh, yeah," said Kranz, "now you're talking. Forget the guitars; we'll get you into a bustier and hot pants, a couple of hours with the some make-up guys...you'll be the hottest thing on MTV this summer."

"That's it!" said Johnny. "This will be our summer album."

"It's what the kids want," said Clarice.

"Guys, I'm so pleased you've been open to my suggestions."

"Why would we fight with you, Stan?" said Clarice. "You're our manager; you've only got our best interests at heart."

"That's just swell," said Kranz. "I mean, I've been working in the business long enough to know that rock musicians are not all Satan-worshipping, drug-addled monsters, but sometimes, y'know...sometimes they are."

Johnny chuckled. Clarice exhaled through her nose.

"It's gonna be great," said Kranz. "We're gonna put out an amazing-ass album and we're gonna make a fortune. It's gonna sell out in minutes, I can just feel it."

"Those words again," said Johnny. "Selling out."

"But in a good way," said Kranz.

Clarice leaned forwards. "There is one thing."

"Shoot," said Kranz, making a gun with his right hand.

Clarice made a gun back. "You're fired."

Kranz sat frozen in his seat.

"Go on," said Johnny, gently. "Get the fuck out of here."

"If I see you again, I'll cut your heart out," said Clarice. "With a spanner."

2. Contract Lore

"You think this means our contract is in danger?" asked Clarice. She was sitting cross-legged on the sofa, unscrewing the lock nuts on the headstock of her favorite Flying V.

"Could be," said Johnny, putting his boots up on the glass-topped coffee table.

Clarice's living room had stark white walls. The carpet was gunmetal grey, and the furniture was black leather. A half dozen amplifiers stood amidst a morass of cables and effects pedals in the open area in front of the TV and stereo cabinet. There was nothing more decorative than a stack of old guitar magazines to be found anywhere in the room.

Clarice detuned the lowest string until she found the D she wanted. "How can our contract have expired?"

"The deal we made had no clause about how long our contract would last."

She struck a chord, tweaked a different machine head. "Fuck. I knew we missed something."

"Getting another contract shouldn't be difficult for us now," said Johnny.

"Well, sure," said Clarice, "but it's going to take time and effort and, before you know it, we're gonna be right back here again." She hit another chord, cocked her head to listen to it ring out.

"What are you going to do, pick a fight with Satan?"

"I would, if I thought it would help," she replied, "but I don't think he's the right person to pick on."

"Well, who is?"

"I think it's time I paid a visit to Steve Heinman."

3. Asking the Horse

Steve Heinman's office at NimHyde records was hung with glossy, framed photos of the best-selling artists he administered. Clarice didn't recognize many of them, but she was aware that a growing number of them were, in fact, models. Or film actors. Not a one of them appeared to play an instrument. Even so, every flat surface in Heinman's office was lined with gleaming music award trophies.

"Where's Johnny?" Heinman asked. Clarice was easier to deal with when he was around.

She ignored the question. "I just fired Stan Kranz."

"Stan?" Heinman ran a hand through his thinning hair, caught and held his ponytail, then put the hand back on the desk. "Good move. I think he was holding you back."

"He suggested Bloody Waters needed a new direction."

"Like?"

"Indie pop."

Heinman snorted and rolled his eyes. "What a ridiculous idea."

"Absolutely. Ridiculous idea," said Clarice. "He said it was yours."

"He did." Heinman didn't pitch it as a question.

"He did, and I believe him," said Clarice. "Kranz was too stupid to do 'ideas.'"

Heinman nodded and rolled on smoothly. "A change is as good as a holiday, Clarice," he said, "and *Razorblade Moon* really didn't sell all that well."

"I'm so tired of hearing that," said Clarice. "We're not outselling any of *these* characters," Clarice gestured at the posters on the walls, "but we're doing pretty good amongst other rock bands."

"True," said Heinman, "but rock is a niche market these days. You have to break out of that niche if you want to start making real money."

"Money's not—"

"You don't like money?"

"I do like money," said Clarice, "but I like music better, and I'm already rich and famous."

"So…you don't want any more money?"

"That's not what I said."

Heinman backed down. He'd dealt with his fair share of tantrums, but Clarice wasn't the type to start throwing things. He'd have preferred it if she was. "Well, those were just some ideas to consider. There are other ways to increase revenue."

"Sure."

"Now," said Heinman, "I take it you're coming to the NimHyde ball next week?"

"Nope."

"I want you to," said Heinman. "It's friendly ground, there'll be lots of media there, and I want to boost your mainstream profile."

"I'll think about it."

"Make sure you dress nice," said Heinman.

4. Popping the Weasels

Clarice wore a low-cut, strapless black dress with a pair of spit-polished combat boots to the ball. No jewelry. She had grudgingly spent some time in an expensive salon for the occasion, but her new hair cut was pretty close to her usual style: short, natural coloring, bangs on both sides. She wore no makeup other than the black lipstick Johnny had given her. Johnny wore a black suit with a black T-shirt and his most formal pair of motorcycle boots.

When Heinman saw the pair, he wheeled about ponderously and headed toward them like a boat on stormy seas, tacking between shoals of emaciated divas and gym-pumped pretty-boys, the bulge of his stomach filling his shirt as a wind fills the sails of a yacht.

Heinman shook Johnny's hand. "Johnny! Clarice! I didn't think you'd be here!" He offered Clarice his hand with the barest hesitation.

Clarice stepped past it and gave him a hug. When the look of surprise finally registered on his face, she planted a thick black kiss on his cheek. "Of course we're here," she said. "There's free booze."

"Easy, now," he said. "We're turning over a new leaf, right?"

"We're here to look pretty and get photographed," said Clarice. "Finding Jesus was never part of the deal."

Heinman grinned. "Well, I'm glad you're here. Mingle, mingle..." His head twitched around, as though he had heard his name called. "Will you excuse me?"

"Why, did you fart?" said Clarice.

Heinman laughed falsely, swung about, and tacked away in the direction of the mysterious dog-whistler.

"I need a drink," said Clarice.

"C'mon," said Johnny. "Let's mingle."

It was easy to discern who was who at the NimHyde ball. The stars were decked out by their patron designers or sports companies. The execs and agents looked underdressed; the lawyers and secretaries were the ones in the suits. Non-music industry guests wore tuxes or ball gowns. The press looked like winos.

Clarice set off with Johnny in tow, elbowing her way through the crowd, stalking the floor for someone to be seen with.

"Hey!"

An indignant man wearing cargo pants with a matching waistcoat had turned to address her. Four identically clad men stood near him, wrapped up in a conversation with somebody Clarice guessed to be a producer. A boy band. Judging by the ages of the 'boys,' they'd already begun their descent into addiction, depression, and failure.

"Hey, yourself," said Clarice.

"You spilled my drink." There was, indeed, a wet patch on the Boy's pants.

"I said 'excuse me.' You didn't move."

"Well," said the Boy, pushing out his hollow chest, "I think it's disgracefully rude to go shoving your way through a civilized party."

"Yeah, and I think it's disgraceful for a thirty-year-old man to pretend he's a teenager."

"I—"

"You're thirty years old, you sing like a eunuch, and you dance like a cheerleader." He stood there with his mouth flapping. Clarice made a shooing gesture. "You better go play with your little friends before they forget who you are and you can't make any new ones."

The Boy looked ready to cry.

Johnny frowned, put his hand on Clarice's shoulder. "I think you've gone too far, honey," he said. "Why don't you kiss and make up?"

Clarice sighed with as much fake remorse as she could muster. She looked the Boy in the eye and said, "Sorry, kid." She grabbed him by his hair and stuck her tongue into his open mouth. When she let him go, he lurched away and stumbled back to the other members of his group, rubbing the black lipstick off his face.

Clarice turned, grinning to Johnny. He just shook his head.

Clarice scanned the crowd. "Is that Gabrielle Millner over there? Let's go say hello."

"Uh, is that a good idea?"

Clarice grabbed him by the arm and hauled him after her.

Millner saw them coming. "Clarice! Johnny! How wonderful to see you!" Joy spilled from Millner's lips, and venom oozed from her pores.

"The pleasure is yours, as always," said Clarice.

"Lovely outfit you're wearing," said Millner, looking her up and down. Her gaze stopped at Clarice's boots. "Nice shoes."

"I like your outfit too," said Clarice. "Nice head."

"They're so...unexpected. And so...shiny..."

"So is your head."

Millner sighed and cast her eyes to the heavens. "Oh, Clarice, you're still so wicked. How come I never see you around?"

"Some of us work for a living, Gabrielle."

"Oh, Clarice," tittered Millner.

"Oh, Millner," said Clarice, "I thought you saved your warbling for the microphone."

"This is what I love about you," said Millner, "you have such a fabulous wit."

Millner swept her up in a hug. Clarice grimaced and planted a peck on her cheek. Cameras flashed.

Millner smiled triumphantly and danced away. "See you in the Weeklies, Clarice!" she said, eyes alight with malice.

When she turned to Johnny, he was grinning from ear to ear.

A shaven-haired man in baggy jeans, a tight grey Bitmap Brothers T-shirt, and a pair of sunglasses was lounging against the wall near the buffet tables, looking far too cool for the proceedings. He roused himself and came toward them. "Saw how you handled the Smurfs back there," he said. "And that Millner bimbo. Nice going."

"Thanks," said Clarice.

"Those idiots are poster children for everything that's wrong with the record industry."

"Sure."

"Their time is already done—they just don't know it yet."

"You didn't introduce yourself," said Clarice. She already knew what honorific he was going to offer with his name.

"Kevin Ziffleck," said the oracle. "Also known as DJ TroutSmack'd."

"Clarice Marnier."

"Johnny Chernow."

They shook hands.

"I'm a big fan," said Ziffleck, pretending that he'd heard of them.

Clarice smiled and batted her eyelashes. "Tell us about the future, DJ."

"The future isn't electric, it's electronic." He'd rehearsed this.

"Really?"

"The technology has never been so accessible. In ten minutes you can download all the software you need, and you can be writing music in twenty. It's the future."

"It's that easy?"

"Absolutely," said Ziffleck.

"So, like, how does it work?" asked Johnny. "I download the software, and then...?"

"Then you choose a period for your beat, add some sound effects, loop a couple of samples, and away you go," said Clarice.

"You got it," said Ziffleck. "The new musical geniuses are the ones behind the keyboard...but the keys aren't black and white."

"Wow," said Johnny.

Clarice put on a sad face. "I've tried to listen to electronica, but it just gives me a headache."

Ziffleck narrowed his eyes. "I thought you were producers."

"Oh, please," said Clarice.

"We're actually rock stars," said Johnny.

Ziffleck smirked. "Rock-luddites, huh? Feeling threatened by all the new technology?"

"I have a science degree–I like technology. I just don't like what you're doing with it," said Clarice.

"Because the music we make is non-traditional?"

Clarice stepped up to him. "No, because the music you make is boring. And so are you."

Ziffleck spluttered.

Johnny looked solemnly at Clarice. "Come now, darling, we're supposed to be on our best behavior."

Clarice sighed, rubbed her eyes, and said, "Shit, I'm sorry. I got carried away."

"You got a temper there, lady," said Ziffleck.

"*Mea culpa.*"

When Ziffleck grudgingly reached out to shake her hand, Clarice grabbed his fingers and swept them to her lips. She inspected the lipstick mark she had left on his hand, then let it go.

"*Enchanté,*" she said.

The DJ receded. Clarice turned to Johnny and opened her mouth to say something self-congratulatory, but a voice interjected.

"Excuse me. Excuse me? Are you Clarice Marnier?" A pair of enormous breasts was addressing Clarice.

The breasts were attached to a slight girl who looked about eighteen years old, although it was hard to tell through all the makeup. She was wearing capri pants and a bustier with day-glo camouflage patterns on it. Her hair was done up in pigtails.

"Yes," replied Clarice.

"Oh, like, wow!" the pop princess clapped with delight. "I'm, like, Melanie Lonegan!"

"Lovely to meet you, Melanie," said Clarice blandly.

"You're, like, that guitarist, right? In that band!"

"Bloody Waters, yeah." Clarice was surprised that Lonegan had even a vague idea of who she was.

"Yeah, that's it!" Melanie squinted up at Johnny. "And you're the singer!"

"Me?" said Johnny, looking around.

"Yes, you, silly! I recognize you from the video!"

"That was a body double," said Johnny. "I can't really dance like that."

Melanie covered her mouth and giggled. Johnny's eyes narrowed.

"Hey! You know what you should do?" said Melanie, addressing Clarice again.

"Shave my head and have my zip-code tattooed on my scalp?"

"No! Well, maybe. If you want to." Lonegan faltered, blinked, shook her head. "You should play on one of my songs!"

"You want me to record a song...with you?"

"Yes! I'll sing and you play the guitar. Just like Santana played on that Matchbox Twenty record!"

"I'm not sure I'm know what you mean," said Clarice. "Who's Santana?"

"Oh, I never heard of him either," said Melanie. "He must be new. But, you know, he looks kind of old, in the video." She blushed and covered her mouth. "Not that you look old, or anything."

Johnny was staring right at the girl. Clarice scowled at him, but he didn't appear to notice.

"Anyway, what do you say?" Melanie was actually jumping up and down.

"Firstly, Melanie," said Clarice, "that was Santana's song, on Santana's record. Secondly, I'm eighty years younger than Santana. And thirdly...I'm not Carlos Santana."

Melanie frowned, confused by all the arithmetic.

Clarice opened her mouth to deliver the *coup de grâce* when Johnny nudged her. She glanced at him, and he shook his head. She raised an eyebrow. Johnny inclined his head toward Lonegan, frowning intensely.

Clarice sighed and looked back at Melanie. "Tell you what," she said, "have your manager call Steve Heinman at NimHyde and he'll organize a time for us to brainstorm."

"I know Steve! He's my A&R rep!"

"Why am I not surprised to hear that?"

"Oh, I can't wait!" squealed Melanie, putting her arms around Clarice. "This is gonna be so good!"

Clarice shot a sour glance at Johnny. "It better be," she said. "It better be real good."

5. Kissed Off

"There's something about that girl that just isn't right," said Johnny. "She's more than just fake."

They were sitting in the hot tub on the deck out the back of Johnny's place up in the Hollywood Hills. Los Angeles glittered and burned below them. Above, the night sky was black and soft, the stars concealed by light-pollution and smog. Clarice's clothes were scattered around the patio. Johnny's were neatly folded and stacked by the side of the tub. His boots stood together, upright, behind his head.

"Well, duh," said Clarice.

Johnny took a swig from his beer. "I'm serious," he said. He turned around and carefully placed the bottle next to his boots. "She has a weird vibe."

"She has a *vibe*?"

"Definitely some occult trickery going on."

"Not much trickery there if you ask me."

"Clarice, there's something wrong with her, and somebody's gone to a lot of trouble to mask it."

"Should I have kissed her?" asked Clarice.

"No," said Johnny. "I think it's better that you didn't."

Clarice drank the last of her beer and put the bottle on the deck behind her. "Well, I guess we'll just have to see what happens. How long do we have to decide what to do to all the other people I kissed off?"

"Five days."

"Let's do them now."

"Who's first?"

"The guy from the boy band."

Johnny shut his eyes and visualized the Boy with the black lipstick marks Clarice had left on his face. "Okay, what do you want to happen to him?"

"I think a case of genital herpes would suit him nicely. It's not like he's ever going to spread it."

Johnny lowered his head and closed his eyes in concentration. His eyes glowed briefly through his eyelids. "Herpes," he said, and looked up. "Done. Next?"

"DJ Troutfucker."

"All right."

Clarice tipped her head back and stretched her legs out in front of her in the hot, bubbling water. "Can you make his hands shake when he goes to spin a record?"

"Situational palsy? No problem." Johnny shut his glowing eyes. "Done."

"Gabrielle Millner," said Clarice.

"Your favorite," said Johnny. "What do you want to give her for Christmas?"

"Syphilis," said Clarice, "And plenty of media coverage to go with it."

"Syphilis." Johnny grinned. "You're beautiful when you're diabolical, did you know that?"

"When am I ever not?"

"You're always beautiful."

"Diabolical, I meant."

"Uh, you're even more diabolical than you are beautiful," apologized Johnny. "What about Steve Heinman?"

Clarice smoothed back her hair while she considered it. "Let's come back to him," she said. "I want to see how Melanie Lonegan shakes out first."

6. Diabolus in Musica

Clarice took The Motherfucker to the session with Lonegan.

One of Lonegan's roadies unloaded the amp and a box of cables and FX pedals from Clarice's car, but she wouldn't let him touch the guitar. He followed Clarice and Johnny through the plushly carpeted corridors of the studio, pushing the gear on a hand trolley.

"I can't believe I'm saying it, but I'm starting to miss the old days," said Clarice. "This doesn't look like a studio; it looks like the offices of an advertising company."

"Doesn't smell like a studio either," said Johnny. "I swear I saw a no smoking sign on the door."

"You never smoked a cigarette in your life."

"Neither have you," replied Johnny.

"I'm not the one complaining about the fresh air."

The setup for Clarice and Melanie's jam session was more of a hall than a studio. A film crew had set up two cameras facing the dais and a dozen chairs were arranged in front on the floor. Lonegan was huddled up with her makeup team, wardrobe consultant, manager, publicist, and caterer. Heinman, standing on the periphery of Lonegan's group, was the only one who noticed Clarice and Johnny enter.

Clarice went right up to him. "What's all this? I thought we were just going to brainstorm." She considered that for a moment. "Although I guess a drizzle is about as good as I can expect in present company."

"We're recording this for posterity," said Heinman, beaming. "For the music video and the DVD extras."

Clarice just looked at him.

"Clarice, you know this is a stunt as well as I do."

"I knew this was your idea."

Heinman had no comeback. Clarice snorted and went over to the stage.

"Clarice!" Lonegan jumped up excitedly. A woman that Clarice assumed to be a director shouted something and cameras swiveled toward the stage.

Clarice pointed at the roadie who had brought in her gear. "You." She jabbed her finger at the amplifiers, keyboard, and drum kit that were set up on the dais. "Clear that shit out of the way and set up my gear."

Johnny, sitting quietly at the back of the room, smiled. She was on her worst behavior.

Clarice strapped on The Motherfucker. She raised her hands and a plectrum appeared in her fingers.

Lonegan watched her, wide-eyed.

"You still want to do this?" asked Clarice.

"Uh...yes?"

"Then get up here."

Lonegan joined her on the stage.

"Any ideas about what kind of song you wanna do?" said Clarice, stroking a couple of chords from the unplugged seven string. She adjusted the tuning minutely without looking at the headstock.

"Oh, yes!" said Lonegan, bouncing up onto the dais. "I have a song that I think would be just wonderful!"

"Oh." Clarice had some songs, too, although it seemed unlikely the record company would find 'I Was a Teenage Crack Whore' as funny as she did.

The roadie handed Clarice a cable and she jacked in her guitar. The amplifier popped and fizzed for a second until she muted the strings with an open hand. Clarice found a stool and sat. "Okay, lemme warm up and we'll see how it goes."

Clarice looked up at Johnny while she ran through some scales. He was still sitting at the back of the room, his head on his right fist, his eyes closed. Nobody paid him any mind.

Clarice looked at Lonegan. "You ready?"

"Ready!" said Lonegan. "You start off, then I'll come in."

"What's the song?"

"It's called 'Popsicle Heart.'"

"All right," said Clarice, making no effort to conceal her distaste. "Let's do this in E." She stood up, turned up the volume, stomped on a pedal, and cut the air with a string of furious power chords.

Lonegan stared at her, dumbfounded at the barrage of noise.

Clarice slowed, throttled back the volume, and looked across at Lonegan. "Go."

Lonegan blinked repeatedly.

Clarice waited, waited…then bent over the guitar, stomped on a different pedal, and launched into a blistering solo. After a minute of screeching, wailing leads, she subsided and looked to Lonegan again.

Lonegan remained silent.

Clarice muted the strings, spun the volume knob down to zero and took her hands off the guitar. "What do you think?" she said, deadpan.

"Um, that was…that was really amazing…but…could we try something a little…slower?"

"I can do slower." Clarice lowered her head, turned the volume up, and struck a low, funereal diminished-fifth progression.

"I don't know about that one either," said Lonegan. "I just…I don't think it's the right sound for 'Popsicle Heart.'"

"Well, I think it gives a sense of the futility of…of…having a heart that's got a wooden stick in it. I mean, that's got to hurt, right?"

Lonegan's brow knitted. "I hadn't thought about the stick," she said.

Heinman stepped in. "Maybe we should try something acoustic," he suggested. "You know, start this off at a more rootsy level."

Lonegan agreed enthusiastically.

Clarice looked at Johnny. His eyes were open now. Johnny indicated the exit with a small movement of his head.

"I didn't bring an acoustic with me," said Clarice.

"The studio has dozens," said Heinman.

"No," said Clarice, standing up and removing The Motherfucker's strap. "It has to be one of mine."

"Maybe it's time for a break," said Heinman. Clarice had played for less than three minutes. Lonegan hadn't sung a note.

"Call up Billy and ask him to bring over a steel string," Johnny told Heinman.

"Who?"

"Billy Wales, our guitar tech," said Johnny. "Nobody else is allowed to touch Clarice's gear. He has a key to Clarice's apartment. Terry Wynokoff has his number."

Heinman reached for his cell phone, annoyed.

Clarice grabbed Johnny by the elbow. "C'mon, let's go outside for a smoke."

"Those things will kill you," said Heinman. "And they're bad for your image."

"Same goes for cholesterol," said Clarice.

"Good one," said Johnny.

In the alleyway outside the musician's entrance, Clarice asked Johnny what was going on.

Johnny leaned against a wall and rubbed his eyes. "She's a demon."

Clarice blinked. "You're shitting me."

"I'm positive," said Johnny. "Melanie Lonegan is a succubus from Hell."

"She's possessed?"

"No, she's a succubus in human form."

"Jesus," said Clarice. "How can something that...insipid...be an agent of evil?"

"It's how she was programmed by her summoner. She has no choice."

"But...why?"

"I don't know," said Johnny. "But I do know that a demonic entity did not come to dominate the pop charts by accident."

"She's on the same label as us. The whole thing is a setup."

"Heinman?"

"He all but admitted it was his idea."

"So what are we gonna do about it?"

"First," said Clarice, "you're going send Lonegan back to Hell."

"I think I can do that. It'll take a few minutes," said Johnny. "What about Heinman?"

"We'll deal with him in private."

They went back into the studio. Clarice shouldered past the cameramen and picked up her guitar. Johnny returned to his chair at the back of the room. He sat on it backward with his hands clasped loosely in front of him.

Clarice jacked in, tweaked the settings on her amp, and stomped on a pedal. She strummed a chord; it rang clear and clean.

Lonegan looked up from her celery stick.

"Lonegan!" Clarice pointed at the microphone. "Enough bullshit. Get up here and sing."

Lonegan blinked, dropped the celery, and did as she was told.

Clarice played some open chords. She added a little overdrive and played a melody. "Too bluesy? You want some funk?" She threw on some wahwah. "Country?" Clarice put in some twang.

"Uh...can you do Santana-ey?"

Clarice sighed and bent to the amp again to dial up a bit of gain. She shook her head, sighed again, and put on her best Santana: high and sultry and sexy.

"That's it!"

"It'll sound better with some percussion."

Johnny closed his eyes. Clarice thought she could see them glow. His lips and his fingers were moving.

Thrilled, Lonegan bounced up to the microphone.

Clarice sighed. "Okay. Come in when I make the sign."

Lonegan beamed.

Clarice played about twelve bars of her best Carlos and waved at Lonegan.

Lonegan came in: "Oooh, hunky baby..."

They made it through the first verse without incident. Clarice played a lick and eased off to let Lonegan sing the chorus. The girl had pipes, it was true. She could hold key and she could stay in time. If she really was a succubus, she'd been well-programmed. Whoever had written the lyrics for her, though...

"Baby, baby, listen here, I've got something to say.

"When I say I love you, you frown and look away.

"Your heart is like a popsicle, it's hard and cold and sweet.

"Your heart is like a popsicle, it melts in the heat."

By the end of the second chorus Clarice couldn't take it anymore. She raised a foot to stomp on the distortion pedal and let loose a cluster-bomb of riffage, but a sudden weirdness in the air pre-empted her.

Johnny was sitting upright in his chair, hands raised before him, his open eyes bright as lasers and fixed directly on Lonegan.

The pop star's hands were the first things to change. They grew; fingers lengthening, nails curling and thickening into claws. Her ears drew back, growing to points. Lines of white fire scored her skin, radiating from below the songstress's navel piercing. She stopped singing when the microphone shattered in her fist.

"Aaawww..."

Clarice wasn't sure if the feedback whine came from Lonegan or the amplifiers.

Lonegan threw the remnants of the microphone on the floor and wailed. The fiery channels writhing across her skin widened and brightened and merged until she was completely engulfed in flame.

Melanie Lonegan flared and vanished. The air looked burned and soot-stained where she had stood.

Everyone in the room stood frozen: the caterers, the managers and PR people, the camera crew, the engineers. Heinman was pale, swaying on his feet. The only noise was the buzzing of Clarice's amp.

Clarice shrugged and bent to switch off the amp.

The door opened and Billy burst in, covered in sweat and carrying a large acoustic guitar case. He froze in the doorway and surveyed the room, wrinkling his nose. Clarice thought it stank of fear as much as sulfur.

"Am...uh...am I too late?"

"No," said Clarice, unslinging The Motherfucker and handing it to him. "You're just in time. Pack this shit up and load it into my car; we're done here for today."

7. Kiss of Death

"I guess there's not gonna be a Clarice and Melanie Christmas Album after all, then?"

They were in Heimnan's office at NimHyde's HQ, but the big man clearly didn't know what to say. He grunted and shook his head.

"So," said Johnny, smiling, "Melanie Lonegan was a demon from Hell. That's funny as shit."

"It's not just funny," said Clarice. "It's hilarious."

Heinman looked each one of them right in the eye and said, "I don't know what I saw yesterday afternoon, and I don't think I want to."

"You didn't look over the video footage? I'd love to watch it all again."

"I had the tapes destroyed," he said. "This kind of mess, NimHyde Records can do without."

Johnny nodded sympathetically. "Bad enough you lost Lonegan."

"Tell me," said Clarice, "Just how many other succubi are you employing as pop musicians? Right at this moment?"

Heinman shook his head and tried to look offended. "What happened to that girl was a terrible tragedy."

"C'mon, Steve, I know you're an agent of the Devil," said Clarice. "Just like me and Johnny."

Johnny smiled and gave the record exec a little wave.

"You have ten seconds to leave this building," said Heinman, reaching for the phone, "before I have you thrown out on your asses."

Clarice leaned over the desk, caught his hand, twisted it over, and yanked it toward her. Heinman lurched across the desk after it, yelping. "I'll break every bone in your arm if you even look at the phone again, Heinman." Clarice grabbed his elbow and forced him face-down onto the desk.

"What do you want from me?" Heinman managed.

"Answers," said Clarice. "I'll ask you again: how many demons you have on the payroll?"

"I—"

Clarice put more pressure on Heinman's captive arm, and he squawked.

"Six! Six!" Clarice eased off a little. "Six, counting Lonegan."

"Ah. Good old fashioned satanic magic," said Johnny. "Six, six, six. It's always a six."

"Aaahhh," puffed Heinman, shoulders bunching spasmodically.

"Okay," said Clarice, "so you clearly didn't know that Johnny is a witch..."

"Warlock," said Johnny.

"No, I didn't."

"Which makes all of this a bit of a coincidence."

"Other...powers...at work," wheezed Heinman.

"Yeah, no doubt," said Johnny.

"What I don't understand is your angle," said Clarice. "I mean, demonic pop stars? Mainstream music is awful enough already."

"...what...the public...wants..."

"No, I don't think so," said Clarice. "It's what you want to sell them."

"...same...thing..." Heinman looked up at her pleadingly. Clarice let go of his arm and he climbed back into his seat, trying to regain some of his dignity. "It's not the medium, it's the message."

"'Popsicle Heart' is your message?"

"I have specialist producers encoding subliminal commands into the mix."

"Heinman, I have to hand it to you," said Clarice. "That's the stupidest fucking master plan I've heard in a long time."

Heinman actually growled in response.

"What exactly did you intend to accomplish?"

"The Dark Lord favors those who spread evil in his name."

"Oh," said Johnny, disappointed. "So, nothing much, then."

"Do you really, truly believe that hearing the Devil's name backwards will make a person evil?" asked Clarice.

"It could induce you to evil acts."

"Bullshit," said Clarice. "Most people don't listen to the lyrics of the songs to begin with–how are they gonna hear voices masked backwards at the bottom of the mix?"

"Your subconscious hears. Your subconscious is—"

"Bullshit."

"It's magic."

"It's bullshit."

"Enough," said Heinman. "I tried to help you, I really did... but you ruined my artist and now...now you're standing in my chambers and insulting me?" He drew his hands from behind the desk. In his right fist he held an ornate dagger; in his left, a large black stone. "Who do you think I am?"

"Are you threatening us?" asked Clarice, incredulous. "With a knife and a rock?"

Heinman lurched to his feet. Green lightning arced between the dagger and the stone. "Of course not." He smiled. "This is just me voiding your contract, without going to the trouble of contacting your lawyer."

Clarice shook her head and rubbed her eyes. "You really are an idiot, Heinman."

Heinman kicked his chair away and raised the stone and the dagger above his head. Lightning crackled between his hands, arced into the walls and the carpet.

"Shall I?" asked Johnny.

"Yeah, go ahead."

Heinman started coming around the desk.

Johnny shut his eyes and murmured a few words. A black mark appeared on Heinman's cheek.

"Now you shall die," said Heinman, waddling toward them with as much poise as he could muster. The black mark had formed an imprint shaped like a pair of lips.

"Go to Hell, Steve," said Clarice.

As the black mark spread, the flesh beneath it started to glisten. Heinman's teeth became visible as his skin blistered away. The green lightning fizzled out, and the A&R man stopped where he stood.

"Uh, what's... uh..." He stopped talking as his jaw came loose.

Heinman's hair went crisp and started to drift from his scalp. His skin melted, and the fatty tissue beneath it liquefied. His eyeballs burst. His organs sizzled; his meat dried out and blackened. Stinking, greasy black smoke filled the air. The stone and the dagger fell from his hands as Heinman collapsed. His bones crumbled on impact, his corpse exploded into ash on the expensive Persian carpet.

"Well, that worked a little better than I expected," said Johnny.

"Shit," said Clarice, "I was hoping to keep his skull for an ashtray."

"We already had this discussion," said Johnny. "Cigarettes will kill you."

Clarice stirred the pile of cooling ashes with the toe of her boot. "So will obesity."

"Good one," said Johnny.

— BLOWING A GASKET —

1. Social Problems

Gabrielle Millner's mysterious case of syphilis dominated entertainment news for nearly a week. Then Melanie Lonegan's disappearance broke, and the diva's little "social problem" (handily treated with a course of antibiotics) was forgotten.

Lonegan had been scheduled for a jam session with Clarice Marnier from Bloody Waters, but she had failed to materialize at the studio. Lonegan's driver and security staff had, apparently, spent the entire morning waiting around for her. For all intents and purposes, Lonegan had vanished from within the walls of her own apartment. Police found puzzling gaps in her public records but, when no grasping relatives, lovers, or heirs materialized, the matter was quickly posted to the too-hard basket and forgotten.

Nobody cared enough about her to make up Elvis stories. Nobody suggested that she was a succubus who had been banished back to Hell.

Heinman's demise caused less of a stir. A receptionist at NimHyde thought he had left his office sometime after his meeting with Clarice and Johnny and never returned. Gossip circulated about Heinman and Lonegan, but most of the innuendo focused on a Texas billionaire who had publicly offered the missing pop star an undisclosed figure to spend a night alone with him and his webcam.

Clarice and Johnny were subjected to peremptory police interviews about each of the missing persons, but nobody really seemed to suspect them. Only hip-hop artists were considered to be capable of serious wrongdoing. Rock star crimes were usually confined to misuse of illicit substances or underage groupies.

Clarice was disappointed at the lack of conspiracy theories.

"Did you really want to see 'Satanic Rock Stars Banish Pop Succubus, Slay Evil Master' above your picture in the World Weekly News?" asked Johnny.

"Well, actually..."

Johnny laughed, but Clarice wasn't smiling. "This isn't the first time our involvement in weird shit has been conveniently overlooked."

"I guess big cuddly Satan is looking out for us."

"He's looking out for someone," said Clarice.

"Be fair. We bought a record deal from the Devil. Should we really have been surprised to discover that our A&R handler was a warlock?"

"No," said Clarice, "we should have been informed up front. The Devil is fucking with us."

"Another big surprise," said Johnny. "But I'm not too worried—we still owe him a favor, and that means we're worth keeping around."

"Yeah," said Clarice. "Thanks for reminding me."

"Besides," said Johnny, grinning, "he's probably grateful we removed Heinman from his organization. What an embarrassment."

"What you're saying is, we did his dirty work for him, free and gratis, when we could have been paying off our debt?"

Johnny's grin faded. "I hadn't thought of it like that."

Clarice stood up. "Well, I'm not letting this happen again."

"How do you propose to do that?"

"I don't know," said Clarice. "But I'll tell you one thing: we're not recording with NimHyde ever again."

2. New Dog

"I'm *sure* you will find a relationship with Blown Gasket Records to be far more...*harmonious*...than the one you had with NimHyde," said Dominic Wainer, shaking first Clarice's hand and then Johnny's.

Wainer was wearing a pair of designer khakis, rimless glasses, and a fitted T-shirt. His bleached-out hair had been artfully arranged into a mop. He was lean and gym-toned, and he flexed up every time Johnny looked in his direction. Wainer's office was decorated with framed posters of a number of SoCal punk bands and alt-rock acoustic balladeers, cherry-blossom prints, and nude sculptures.

"Convince me," said Clarice.

Wainer smiled a different record exec smile than Clarice was familiar with: one that promised different lies to those she had heard in the past. "I'm not privy to the exact nature of your quarrels with NimHyde, but, I *assure* you, at Gasket we put our artists first. Whatever your quarrel with them was, you won't have a repeat of it here."

"Terrific," said Johnny. He put his hand down heavily on Clarice's shoulder to prevent her from issuing the threat he knew was on her lips. "We're ready to start on the new album as soon as we have a new contract."

"I'd like to get you signed with *all* due haste," said Wainer. "Get your manager to call me and..."

"Oh, yeah," said Johnny.

"We need a new one of them, too," said Clarice.

3. Under New Management

Clarice wanted a manager with balls, so she hired a woman.

Helen Ingpen had started out as a dancer in Madonna's troupe in the mid-'80s. Using contacts she made there, she had broken out as a solo act and managed two minor soft-metal hits. After her second album bombed, Ingpen gave up performing and served the industry as a producer, publicist, and journalist. When she learned that Bloody Waters was looking for a new manager, she had contacted them. Clarice liked that.

They were sitting in the garden behind a café in Hollywood, drinking coffee and enjoying the not-quite-fresh Los Angeles air. It very quickly became apparent that they weren't interviewing Ingpen—she was interviewing them.

"So, when exactly did you sack my predecessor?" asked Ingpen, putting her latte carefully back on its saucer.

"When he allowed the record company to turn him into their mouthpiece," said Clarice. "When he told me I needed a fucking belly button ring." She took a swig of water from her glass.

"The ring was actually your idea," said Johnny.

"It's called 'sarcasm,'" said Clarice.

"You still haven't answered my question," said Ingpen. "How long have you been without a manager?"

"I dunno," said Clarice, looking across at Johnny. "Six, eight weeks?"

"Nine," said Johnny. "It was before the Lonegan session."

"Nine weeks?" said Ingpen incredulously. "And during that time, you agreed to go into the studio with Melanie Lonegan...*and* you negotiated a new record deal?"

"We still have lawyers," said Clarice, actually sounding a bit defensive.

"Did you sign yet?"

"No."

"You're lucky."

"No," said Clarice. "I'm smart, I'm talented, and I'm scary enough to get my own way. But it's a lot easier with a good manager behind me."

"That," said Ingpen, "is what I like about you." She smiled. "Your music ain't bad, either."

"You want the gig?" said Clarice.

"Yes."

"Why?"

"It'll make me the one person in the world who gets to tell Clarice Marnier what to do."

4. Heathens Burning

Once the new record deal was signed, the first thing Ingpen asked for was a publicity quote about the band Heathens Burning.

"Who are they again?" Clarice asked.

"They supported us on the *Razorblade Moon* tour," said Johnny, "between Tacoma and Chicago."

"Oh," said Clarice. "Did I choose them?"

"Yes," said Johnny. "We saw them playing in the Crocodile Lounge, and you asked for them especially."

"Don't remember."

"Well, they're the new 'it' band," said Ingpen, "and they credit you, personally, for their rise to greatness."

"That's lovely of them."

"Do you have a quote for me?"

"They're lovely?"

"Anything more?"

"They're lovely and talented?"

"I'll just make something up, then."

"Great. Is it okay if I forget them again?"

"No," said Ingpen, putting her hands flat on the table. "You're doing a press conference together next week."

Clarice recognized the Heathens' faces when she saw them again at the conference, but she could not remember any of their names. They were all uniformly tall and skinny, differentiable mainly by hairstyle and costume accessory. "These guys should have their own comic book," she muttered to Johnny.

"They do," he replied. "It sells better than ours did."

In the wings, the drummer told her that the Heathens really couldn't have managed this without her help. The lead guitarist told her how much he'd learned from watching her play. The bass player muttered that she was "real purdy."

The frontman said, "I'll never forget what you did for us. We'll repay you somehow, I promise."

"I may take you up on that," said Clarice. "My deal with the Devil is about to expire, and I need a fresh soul to renew it."

Ingpen ushered them into the conference hall, and the two bands seated themselves at a large, semicircular table facing the press gallery. Curtains emblazoned with guitars and skulls hung behind them. Clarice glowered at the popping camera bulbs.

The conference began with questions addressed to the Heathens. How did success feel? (Really Amazingly Awesome.) What inspired them? ('70s metal, '80s hardcore punk, Bloody Waters, and especially Clarice.) Did they think they'd ever make it this big? (Not in their wildest dreams.)

A reporter asked Clarice what it was that had drawn the Heathens to her attention in the first place. "Their music," she said.

Did she think they would ever make it this big? "If they didn't have potential, I wouldn't have asked them to support us."

Did she have any plans to collaborate with them? "Not at this time."

Was she proud of what the Heathens had accomplished? "They did this by themselves," said Clarice. "Full credit goes to them. All I did was let them share my stage a few times."

"That wasn't so bad, was it?" said Ingpen, when it was all over and done with.

"It was more fun than a root canal," said Clarice, "but that's about as far as I'll go."

"You'll go a lot further," said Ingpen. "And so will they. This was for your benefit as well as theirs."

"Whatever," said Clarice. "I'm pleased they have a career and everything, but it's time they got on with it so I can get on with mine."

5. Oh So Mafioso

"Remind me why I always agree to play these games with you?" said Johnny, pushing dominos around on the glass surface of the table. They were lounging by the pool in the early evening, drinking beer and killing time while the side of beef Johnny had prepared sat roasting in the oven.

"Because you're pussy-whipped," said Clarice, without looking up from the score pad. Instead of drawing houses to represent her score, she had drawn a large and highly detailed gantry.

"Am not," said Johnny. "I just know better than to say no to you."

"That's what I call 'pussy-whipped,'" said Clarice.

"It's more like a basic survival instinct."

"I hope I ain't interrupting anything," said a deep voice with a thick New Jersey accent.

The speaker was a heavyset, Mediterranean-looking man dressed in an expensive black suit. Black shirt, white leather tie. He stood with his hips forward and his hands in his pockets. Two more black-suited gentlemen flanked him. They stood with their hands clasped in front of them. Apparently, they'd let themselves in.

"Matter of fact, you are," said Clarice, sitting up and turning to face the men.

"Um, hi," said Johnny.

"I ain't gotta do nothing," the heavyset man told Clarice.

"Well," said Clarice, "in that case, I guess it's up to me." She stood up.

Johnny smiled mildly and stood up as well. "*Mi casa es su casa,*" he said.

The heavyset man laughed. "There's three of us, lady," he said. "You don't wanna make no trouble."

"You clearly don't know me very well."

"Hey," said Johnny, "it's a lovely day. Why's everybody so uptight?"

Clarice and the heavyset man both glared at him.

"Why don't we start again? I'm Johnny, this is Clarice."

The heavyset man considered that. Eventually, he took one hand out of his pocket and shook hands with Johnny. "Benny," he said.

Benny started to withdraw his hand, but Clarice stepped forwards and grabbed it. She caught him unready, grinned up at him as she crushed his fingers together.

"Lovely to meet you, Benny," she said. "Who are your friends?"

Benny scowled and put his hand back in his pocket when Clarice released it. "Vanni and Antonio," he said. Vanni was compact and broad-shouldered; Antonio was regular-sized and wore a tiny goatee. Neither of them came forward to shake hands.

"Well, now that we're all friends, why don't you fellas take a load off?" said Johnny, gesturing at the empty deck chairs. "I'll crack some beers, and we can all get to know one another."

"I think we'd rather stand," said Benny.

Clarice rolled her eyes. "Just tell us what it is that you want, already."

Benny grunted. "I want to offer you a gig."

"Me, or Bloody Waters?"

"Either/or."

"What kind of gig?"

"Private," he said. "Invitation only."

"What, like a wedding?"

"Birthday party."

"You think," said Clarice, "that we're a band you can hire to play at parties?"

"For this party? I think you can be hired."

"What if I say no?"

"Maybe I didn't make myself clear," said Benny. "For *this* party? I think you can be hired."

"We're not going to be able to play for you if we're dead or in traction," said Johnny in a helpful tone.

Clarice ignored him. "You think you got what it takes?"

"Oh, come on," said Benny, widening his stance and grinning. "You're a little rock bitch. What're you gonna do, slap me upside the head with a lawsuit?"

Clarice brought her shin up into his groin and followed it with an elbow to his chin. Benny went over like a sack of fresh Drakkar Noir-scented manure.

Antonio blinked, swallowed, and stepped back. Vanni grinned, looked down at Benny, and shook his head.

Johnny shrugged apologetically.

Clarice stood over Benny. "So, tell me about this party."

"It's a...surprise party for...Big Nicky's cousin," wheezed Benny.

"This cousin is a fan of ours?"

"Yeah."

"Well, you tell Big Nicky if he wants us to play at his bash, he should ask me himself."

6. Big Nicky

Big Nicky was waiting with Vanni and another goon in the booth in the back corner of Tony's Taverna, exactly as promised. Big Nicky was tall and obese and a good couple of decades older than his two companions. His suit was tailored. He had fingers like sausages and an ass like a pair of hams.

"Miss Marnier," he said, smiling and rising to his feet. "Mister Chernow. Welcome." He sounded more cultured than anybody Clarice had ever met in the music business.

He shook both of their hands. "This is Frankie C., and I believe you already know Vanni." Frankie C. had something of a Travis Bickle gleam in his eyes.

Clarice and Johnny shook their hands.

"Please," said Big Nicky. "Have a seat." He waved the barman over. "Tony, these are my friends, Clarice and Johnny. Make sure you look after them whenever they come here."

"Sure thing, Big Nicky." Tony inclined his head. "What can I get you guys?"

"Heineken," said Clarice.

"Guinness, please," said Johnny.

Tony did a little bow and backed away.

"Firstly, I must apologize for my associate Benito's rude behavior last week."

"Funny you should mention that," said Clarice, "I was about to apologize for kicking his ass."

"I am sorry that such an ordinary situation turned so unpleasant."

"Don't be," said Clarice. "I quite enjoyed it."

Big Nicky chuckled and nodded. Tony returned with their drinks.

"Well, you know, when I told Benny to see if he could get you guys to play at the party, I expected him to call your manager... the lovely Ms. Ingpen...but Benny always wants to do things the old-fashioned way."

"His mama used to be a nun," explained Vanni. Frankie C. nudged him in the ribs.

Big Nicky ignored him. "In any case, Vanni told me that you would still consider doing this thing for me, despite Benny being such an asshole to you," said Big Nicky, "if you'll pardon my French."

"The only French I have a problem with are the ones who sing in coffee shops," said Clarice. "And, yeah, we'll play this party for you."

"Excellent," said Big Nicky, grinning. "Mario Alonzo is my second cousin and I want him to have an amazing birthday this year. Shall we talk about the price?"

"Let's."

"I know you're big-time rock stars," said Big Nicky. "So hit me with a number and I'll see what I can do."

Clarice had given the matter some thought already. Would he write a check? Would the money come in an attaché case? A brown paper bag? Would her accountant know what to do with it?

"Know what?" she said. "None of us is short on cash right now. We'll play for free, if you agree to owe us a favor."

Johnny frowned at her. Big Nicky squinted. "How big a favor are we talking?"

"I dunno," said Clarice. "But, you know, we're only rock stars—how much trouble can we possibly get into?"

7. Birthday Bash

Mario Alonzo was turning twenty-one, and the party was being held at Big Nicky's estate in the Napa Valley. Mario was a skinny, olive-skinned guy, a bit on the geeky side. He seemed quite uncomfortable in the presence of the two hundred most influential members of Los Angeles's Italian American community. He was accompanied by a stocky, Anglo-Saxon girl in a black cocktail dress. She had dyed her hair dark red and wore it short with bangs, the same way that Clarice did.

Once Mario and his girlfriend had been hugged and kissed and provided with drinks, Big Nicky steered them toward the stage and threw his arms out dramatically.

As the curtains drew open, Clarice slammed on the opening chords of "Blood and Water," which had been the B-side for "Butcherama." Mario and his girlfriend were delighted.

After the show, Mario and his girlfriend came to speak to them. Wynokoff had already bundled Enrique and Beresford into the limousine, and Clarice and Johnny were in the downstairs library, packing away the last of their gear.

"Well," said Johnny, grinning, "if it ain't the birthday boy himself."

"Uh, hi," said Mario. "I'm Mario, and this is, uh, Gina."

"Pleased to meet you," said Johnny.

Clarice snapped The Motherfucker shut in its case and joined them. "Clarice," she said. They all shook hands.

"We're, uh, really big fans," said Gina.

"I figured," said Clarice.

"Thank you," said Johnny.

"Thank *you*, for playing here tonight," said Mario. "I know this isn't something you would normally do."

"Eh, I'm sure there's some extra notoriety to be had in it somewhere."

Gina laughed louder than she should have. Mario chuckled weakly.

"Well," he said, "we won't keep you. I just wanted to thank you guys and to, uh…ask you for your, um…"

"Autographs," said Gina.

"What do you want us to sign?"

Gina produced a huge, leather-bound guestbook with "Mario's 21st Birthday" embossed on the cover. Johnny found an empty page and drew a fairly decent cartoon of Mario and Gina playing air guitar. He wrote "Happy Birthday Mario!" above his signature. Clarice wrote "MA: HBD. MHR. CM" at the bottom of the page. Then, with her left hand, she wrote "alla besht love enrique n bereshford" below it.

"Here you go," she said. "Signed by the whole band."

Mario grinned.

"Oh, thank you," said Gina. "You got no idea how much this means to us."

"Sure I do," said Clarice. "It was the best evening of your lives." She paused. "It better have been, anyway."

"If Clarice finds out it wasn't," said Johnny, "she's gonna find you and make you pay."

Gina stifled a giggle, covered it with a guffaw.

Mario laughed. "I can die happy now," he said.

8. Accidents Happen

A week later, Clarice was having her mid-morning swim when Johnny came out through the screen doors and called her over. She swam to his side of the pool, and he held the newspaper down to her, folded open to a particular article.

Clarice pulled off her goggles, wiped her eyes, and read it.

Mario Alonzo and Gina Courtley had died in a fatal car accident. It seemed that three unknown individuals armed with MP5 assault rifles had opened fire on Mario's vehicle as he and Gina were driving home from a movie at 1 a.m., causing Mario to lose control of the vehicle and smash into a tree at fifty-five miles per hour.

Mario Alonzo, an Economics major at Berkeley, had been assassinated less than a week after his 21st birthday. Police would neither confirm nor deny that the killing was linked to organized crime.

Clarice raised her eyes from the newspaper when she finished the article.

"He seemed like a good kid," said Johnny.

"Seemed like it, yeah."

"It's a damn shame."

"Yeah."

"Well, at least we made him happy before he died."

"Yeah." Clarice pulled her goggles on.

"That's all you got to say?"

She shrugged. "I wonder who Big Nicky is gonna ask to play at his funeral?"

9. The Sound of Cyber

Clarice wanted Bloody Waters to start work on the new album as soon as the ink on the new contract was dry. Wainer was keen to get some new product out of them on Gasket's label, especially in light of their previous album's poor showing.

"It's not like *Razorblade Moon* bombed," said Clarice, pacing the length of Ingpen's office. Wainer and Ingpen faced her, sitting on the overstuffed couches across a coffee table. Enrique, Beresford, and Johnny were arranged in a semicircle on the couches facing them, their backs to Clarice. "Sales are slow all across the industry, particularly for rock bands."

"Yes," said Wainer, steepling his hands under his chin, "but it's the album that should have broken the charts for you, and it hasn't come anywhere close."

Ingpen said, "With a successful second album you've proved that you're not one-hit wonders, but on a sales chart, it looks like you've already peaked."

Beresford sat hunched over, staring sullenly at Ingpen. Enrique's eyes were half-lidded and his mouth was open.

"Can't help the market," said Johnny, putting his hands on his knees.

"So you're content to see your numbers slide?" said Ingpen.

"I didn't say I was content," said Clarice, "but I don't see *Razorblade Moon's* performance as a setback."

"It's a motherfucking *gold record!*" said Enrique, snapping out of his fugue with his eyes bugged out and his teeth bared. "That is not a setback." He settled back into the couch, blinked, and closed his eyes.

"All right, all right," said Wainer, diplomatically, "so, let's talk about the *new* album."

"You have some ideas yet, Clarice?" asked Ingpen.

"Of course I have some fucking ideas," said Clarice. "It's called *Sister to Dragons* and I've already written all the songs."

"Any particular producer you want for this?" asked Wainer.

"Can we get Neville Connors?"

"I can get you just about anyone," said Wainer. "I can get Butch Vig, I can get you Steve Albini, I can get you Rick Rubin—"

"I'm used to Connors."

"And Connors is used to Clarice," added Johnny.

Clarice shrugged. "He does what I say. We're doing some new stuff on this album, and I want someone who knows his place."

"What kind of 'new stuff' we talkin'?" said Beresford, suspicious.

"Digital stuff."

"I like it," said Wainer.

Enrique blinked a few times as the information tunneled through his skull to his brain. "No way, man."

"No fucking *way!*" shrieked Beresford, suddenly on her feet. "I will *not* be replaced with a drum machine!"

Clarice stared at the drummer until she unclenched her fists and sat back down in her seat, eyes downcast, but still visibly fuming.

"No one is going to be replaced," said Clarice. "I want to show what real musicians can do with all these new toys."

"I don't like it," said Beresford. "Drums and bass are the first to go when you bring in all that computer shit."

"Easy, easy," said Johnny. "Led Zeppelin did this thirty years ago."

"Yeah, and it was John Paul Jones who did all the keyboards and string arrangements," said Clarice.

"I don't play no *keyboards*," said Enrique. "I don't do no *string arrangements*."

"Nowadays it's just Page and Plant," said Beresford. "Jones is nowhere and Bonham is dead."

"Nobody is threatening either of you," said Ingpen.

"I promise," said Clarice, in a tone that brooked no argument.

"So, what cyberdork is going to handle the technology?" muttered Beresford. "You can rule out Enrique and me."

"I'm sure there will be DJs lining up down the *street* to be in on this," said Wainer, smiling broadly.

"No," said Clarice. "I'm the cyberdork. I'm doing it all myself."

"Oh," said Beresford, after a lengthy silence. "Why didn't you say so?"

— AXES TO ASHES, DJS TO DUST —

1. I'd Rather Burn

Although Clarice had expressly forbidden it, Blown Gasket Records went ahead and released a remix of "(Don't Piss On Me) I'd Rather Burn."

Clarice was furious, but it was hard to tell if she was more upset about the company's disobedience or the fact that the remix performed an order of magnitude better than any of the actual *Razorblade Moon* singles.

DJ Axolotl, the author of "Rather Burn [Death Spar Mix '01]," had added an insistent electronic dance beat to the stark blues-rock number. The chorus and the first verse were all that had been retained of Johnny's vocals, and a childish voice chanting "piss on me, piss on me" had been laid over the top of them. Most of Johnny's rhythm guitar was intact, but it had been pushed back in the mix to make way for drum and bass. Clarice's snarling, intricate leads had been excised altogether.

Wainer claimed that he'd authorized the remix in order to whet the public's appetite for the new album, which was taking longer to record than Clarice had expected.

"Well, you've now delayed the new album even more," Clarice told him. She took a week out from recording *Sister to Dragons* to air her outrage in any music journal that would give her column space. She ranted about the remix on the bloodywaters. net message boards; she fulminated about it in every interview or feature article that Ingpen could drum up for her.

When a pinheaded *Billboard* reporter commented that "she'd kept the money, hadn't she?" Clarice told him that she was going to donate most of it to organized crime and use the change to hire a squad of hitmen to exterminate the magazine's editorial staff.

2. DJ Bullshit

"Clarice, *honey*," said Wainer, "you can't be *serious*."

Wainer sat directly across the conference table from Clarice, flanked by Helen Ingpen and Neville Connors. Johnny sat on her right; Enrique on her left with Beresford beside him.

"I'm dead serious," said Clarice.

"I really *think* you're over-*reacting*." Wainer was not generally a nervous individual, but his dealings with Bloody Waters were becoming more and more unsettling. Since he had signed the band to Blown Gasket Records, he'd made some discrete inquiries about their issues with their old label, and what he had learned was... disturbing.

"I *understand* you're pissed about the remix, but that's no reason to *dump* the album you've spent so much time on."

"You know he's right," said Johnny. Clarice flashed him a spine-melting glare, but he just shrugged it off.

"Come *on*, Clarice, this is your *best* work yet," said Wainer. "You've said as much yourself."

Clarice clenched her delicate guitarist's hands into a pair of unexpectedly jagged-looking fists. "No," she said. "I want to start again. No studio tricks, no digital production, no filters, no loops, no keyboards...just four musicians in a fucking *room*."

"Sure," said Ingpen in her most soothing, managerial voice. "Next album. Why throw this one out when it's almost finished?"

"Because," Clarice grated, "I want the DJ bullshit *off* of there."

"Fucking drum machines," said Beresford. "I told you they were a bad idea." Enrique shushed her.

"I understand why you want to do this," said Johnny, "but you worked hard to sell us on the idea of this album, and you were right–it sounds great. Are you really going to let one stupid remix ruin a valid and ambitious project?"

"I want there to be no mistake—"

"You guys still sound like a guitar band," said Connors. Everyone stared at him. Hearing the engineer speak was even rarer than hearing somebody interrupt Clarice.

He stumbled on: "Maybe...maybe we could just mix the electronica back a bit. We could even add some...you know, strings. Brass. Sitars?"

"You want me to try *hide* the electronica? Like I'm ashamed of it?"

"If you're not ashamed of it, why are you making all this fuss?" asked Ingpen.

"The press will laugh at me, putting this out right after the remix."

"The press?" said Ingpen. "Didn't you just threaten to have them all assassinated?"

Clarice had no immediate reply.

"Clarice, you're not gonna get a lot of nice words written about you this time, no matter what you do."

Clarice stared at Ingpen until she looked away. She did the same to Wainer. When she turned to Johnny he only shrugged.

"You're right," she said, eventually. "I know it. We'll finish the album, and we'll take it on the road, and we'll put on one hell of a fucking show."

"Smart move," said Ingpen.

"Then why do I feel like an idiot?" asked Clarice.

3. Disk Monkey

It was still a hard slog to get the album finished. The recording was done, but post-production was proving a lot more difficult than expected. None of the technology was quite good enough for Clarice, so she wound up coding a lot of tools herself...which only added to the delays. Wainer and Ingpen spent another month convincing her to take on some extra help.

It did not take Wainer very long to find somebody to replace Connors. Connors took it well–in fact he seemed relieved that it was over. Clarice hadn't allowed him to do very much work, anyway.

Soon as the new engineer was signed, Wainer told Clarice that he wanted her to relinquish the rest of the mixing to him entirely. She didn't take it well.

"Come on, Clarice, *give* a little," said Wainer, once he'd persuaded Clarice to climb down off his desk and put down the fire axe. "Nathaniel is a talented artist. You have to allow him a little *room* if you want his best work."

"I don't care how talented this guy is," said Clarice, "it's *my* album."

"Nathaniel has his *own* artistic vision—"

"He's a disk monkey, for Christ's sake. What does he know about real music?"

"Clarice," said Wainer, "Nathaniel costs a *lot* of money and he's worth every penny. He's an *artist*, not a..."

"I don't care how much your precious 'Nathaniel' costs," said Clarice. "He'll mix the fucking album the way I fucking want it mixed, or not at all."

"I'll speak to him," said Wainer, "but he's *not* going to be pleased."

Clarice stared at him. Was it possible that Wainer was as scared of this DJ as he was of Clarice? "Who is this guy, anyway?"

"Nathaniel Ackerman," said Wainer, uncomfortably.

"Never heard of him," said Clarice.

"Well, you really *should* have," said Wainer, actually looking a bit incredulous.

"What's that supposed to mean?"

"Nothing," said Wainer. "Forget I said anything."

"Next time," replied Clarice, "don't say anything at all, and save me the effort of slapping you back into line."

4. Garters and Guitar Straps

"Nathaniel Ackerman," said Johnny, putting down his beer and cocking his head. "It's familiar. I should know it."

"I don't care if he's Elvis and Einstein reincarnated into the same body," said Clarice, knocking back her bourbon all at once. "If he crosses me, I'll have his guts for a guitar strap." She set the glass back down on the counter hard enough to make the barman jump.

"Easy," said Tony. "I'll get you another, all you gotta do is ask."

"Loud noises make you jumpy, huh, Tony?" said Johnny.

"I got no idea what you civilians are talkin' about," Tony replied.

They were spending a lot of time in Tony's Taverna these days. The clientele tended to be...furtive...so nobody ever hassled them for an autograph. And Clarice simply enjoyed hanging around in a bar full of made men.

"Just keep 'em coming, Tony."

"Aye aye." Tony went off to mix another.

"Anyway, it's nothing to stress about," said Johnny. "If you don't like him, you can always fire him."

"I am not stressed," she replied. "I'm teetering on the brink of a murderous rage."

"You haven't even met the guy yet."

"I just hate DJs."

"Oh, *come* on," said Johnny. "Wainer *assures* me he's a genius." His mimicry of the handler's voice was perfect.

"You notice how every DJ that releases an album gets called the g-word?"

"Yeah, well, the new music created by this horde of sudden geniuses is a whole lot less interesting than I might have hoped it would be."

Tony had returned with fresh drinks. "That's the whole attraction of it," he said. "You don't have to listen, you just gotta shake to the beat."

Clarice raised a skeptical eyebrow. "I have difficulty imagining you as a raver, Tony."

"I'm not," he replied. "I'm a professional. This place does a dance/trance night Tuesday of every week, and old Tony's gotta be here, tending bar."

"Disco night in the Goodfellas' bar? I admit, I'm having trouble seeing it."

"Well, Big Nicky only listens to Tony Bennett and the Three Tenors," said Tony, grinning, "but Little Nicky and some of the younger guys like to party down."

"Little Nicky?" said Johnny.

"No relation."

"I think we gotta find a new pub," said Clarice.

5. Sloppy Seconds

The new engineer had already been in the studio for a couple of hours by the time Clarice rolled in at 10 a.m.

"You must be Nathaniel Ackerman," said Clarice. She set down a cup of steaming coffee.

Ackerman looked up at her, smiling and removing the headphones. He rose to his feet and extended his hand. "Clarice Marnier! Lovely to meet you." Ackerman was just shy of six feet tall, toned, and handsome. He wore his blond hair clumped into spikes. He was fashionably dressed in linen pants, slip-on sneakers, and a short-sleeved shirt. A Celtic tribal design was tattooed around his left bicep.

"Yeah," she grunted and shook his hand.

Ackerman winced at her grip, smiled, and sat back down at the console. He passed Clarice a pair of headphones. "I listened through what you've done a couple of times, and I've just been putting down a few new ideas."

"What do you think of it so far?"

"It's good," he said. "Brilliant."

"Yeah, my mother thinks so, too. What do you like about it?"

"Well," he said, "you've got a lot of different stuff on there. Trad-rock numbers, an acoustic ballad, a couple of different varieties of metal, mutant blues…you do a bit of everything, but it doesn't ever sound like anybody else."

"Oh?"

"I also like that the songs are stories. Ballads, in the true sense of the word."

"No shit?"

"Well, super-ballads, really," said Ackerman. "It amazes me how you guys fit so much…*plot*…into a five-minute song."

"You actually listened to the lyrics? Are you sure you're a DJ?"

"I am," he said, grinning, "but I listen to all kinds of music. I know your back catalogue inside out."

Clarice grunted.

"Did I pass the test?" asked Ackerman.

"You didn't do too bad," she replied. She sat back in her seat and sipped her coffee. "For a disk monkey. Let's hear what you've done so far."

Ackerman offered her a headset. "'Executioner's New Clothes,'" he said, naming the song.

When the sound came on, Clarice closed her eyes, put her hands over the earpieces, and listened. When it was done, she removed the headphones and looked expressionlessly at Ackerman.

"Well?"

"Not bad," she said. "I like the layering, and you made some good decisions about where to bring up Enrique."

"Thanks."

"You mixed back some of the programming, I notice."

"Yeah," he said. "It sounds good, but the song needed more, you know...*meat*. You just can't get that with software."

"Agreed."

"I still think the song is a bit sparse. Needs more texture in the chorus."

"I've been thinking of adding another guitar overdub."

"Excellent," said Ackerman.

"What else you got?"

"Been messing around with 'Gantry Blues.'"

"Okay, line it up."

"I went a little nuts on this one," he said.

Clarice put on the headphones and made a rolling gesture. He hit play, and she closed her eyes again. She didn't open them for a full minute after the song was finished.

"You like it?"

Clarice just stared at him, expressionless.

He grinned. "I told you I went a bit nuts."

"There are Irish drums in it now."

"Yep."

"And...farm animals..."

"Yep."

"It's supposed to be a lo-fi blues number."

Ackerman shrugged. "I didn't think it fit with the rest of the album."

"It's there for contrast."

"I know that's what you intended," said Ackerman, "but it was fun to pump it full of crazy techno juju. Subvert the blues genre."

"You can't subvert the blues," said Clarice.

Ackerman leaned back in his seat and put his hands behind his head. "We're artists, we can do whatever we want."

"You want to mix this album or not?"

Ackerman grinned. "If I didn't want to mix the album for you, I wouldn't have asked for the privilege."

"Then you'd better fucking..." Clarice's eyes narrowed as her voice trailed off. "You *asked* to mix the album?"

"Sure," said Ackerman. "I had so much fun re-mixing your old single that I thought I'd come back for more."

6. Change of Service

Clarice threw down her racket and grabbed the bottle of blue Powerade off the courtside table. Johnny sauntered over from his side of the net with his racket under his arm and joined her under the shade of the umbrella.

"Four aces in a row," he said. "That's not tennis, that's a blitzkrieg."

She lowered the bottle and wiped her lips on the back of her hand. "I can't help it if you suck."

Johnny regarded her for a moment. "I know you're not mad at *me*," he said.

"Wainer should have told me the new producer was DJ Axolotl."

"He knew you would have refused."

"That motherfucker."

"He was only thinking of the bottom line," said Johnny. "They sold boatloads of the remix."

"I should have expected as much."

"Well, you got rid of him, and Connors even came back...it was a hiccup, and it's behind us now. Let's just get the damn CD out already."

"I want blood, Johnny."

"Can't you just let it go? Just this once?"

"No," said Clarice, picking up her racket and adjusting the strings. "It's not over."

"Sure it is."

"Ackerman knew I was going to get rid of him as soon as I found out who he was."

"So what?"

"So, he's fucking with us."

"For what possible reason?"

Clarice mulled it over. "He wanted to let me know who he is," she said. "He wanted to meet me, test me out."

Johnny looked skeptical. "What kind of agenda can he have? He's a DJ. His one reason for being is to make people dance by fucking up real music."

"I guess we're gonna have to wait and see."

"And then?"

"And then I'm going to bust open his rib cage and shit in his chest cavity."

"I don't feel like playing a second set anymore," said Johnny.

"Oh, yes, you do." Clarice slapped a pair of tennis balls into his hand. "Come on. It's your serve."

7. Salzing the Wound

Clarice and Connors had *Sister to Dragons* ready to ship within the month. While the album started making its way through the record company's distribution machinery, Bloody Waters began rehearsing for the new tour.

The music had changed since the band had been in the studio with it, and rehearsal required a bit of work—more work than the four-piece could manage. It quickly became apparent that they needed to add someone to the lineup if they were going to play the new material.

After a week of wall-to-wall auditions and interviews, Clarice selected a fifty-four-year-old concert pianist named Peter Salzman to play keyboards for them. Salzman was as accomplished with a bank of synthesizers as he was with a grand piano. He was used to playing music scored by other people, but he could improvise as well as any jazzman.

Clarice was not ready to take on a permanent fifth member for the band, and Salzman did not want a permanent gig as a touring rock musician–he just wanted to try something new and lucrative. He could play the music, he knew his place, and he wouldn't get grabby later on. He was perfect.

It didn't take long to rehearse him into shape. After the endless months of production delays, Clarice had set an aggressive promotion and touring schedule. The first pre-launch gig was already upon them.

Still, the band was ready, and the album was finally out the door. Clarice reckoned the worst of it was already behind them.

8. Axe Man Walking

It was the first time Salzman had been in the dressing room with them before a gig, and there was tension in the air. The new songs were more difficult than any of the old ones, and the new line-up was untested. Salzman himself seemed to be handling it rather better than the fidgeting, bickering rock stars. He stood quietly by himself, adjusted his tie, and waited.

When the familiar introductory music came on, Wynokoff knocked on the door and poked his shaggy head inside. "Time to fuck some shit up," he said.

"You ready?" asked Clarice. Everybody looked at Salzman.

"I'm ready."

"Okay, then." Clarice slung on The Motherfucker and took a last swig from her bottle of water.

The sound of a record being ripped from under a needle blared over the PA. The canned music stopped.

"That's not good," said Johnny.

"What?" demanded Clarice.

DJ Axolotl's Rather Burn Remix came on.

Clarice threw her bottle across the dressing room. "Oh, you have got to be shitting me."

Enrique and Beresford spun around to look at her, cowering. Salzman looked up, unsure what the alarm was about. Johnny brushed the hair from his eyes and sighed.

Clarice recovered herself. "Wynokoff, kill the music. Everyone else, follow me." The tour manager was already bulling his way toward the sound desk, bellowing.

The remix was still going when Bloody Waters stormed onto the stage. Frightened roadies scattered before them.

Beresford sat down behind her kit, drumsticks spinning in her hands like thresher blades. Clarice made a hand signal to Billy, and he scuttled onstage to trade The Motherfucker for a black-and-blue Flying V. He handed Johnny a Les Paul Special in the same tuning and Enrique a big Fender five-string bass. Roadies made some final adjustments to the setup, and then scurried away.

The remix cut out abruptly. Feedback whined.

Clarice stood at the front of the stage, The Flying V slung low behind her.

The audience booed.

"Shut your GODDAMN cake-holes!" Clarice roared into her microphone.

The crowd subsided to a soft muttering.

"Are you pissed off?" she asked.

The crowd continued to mutter amongst themselves.

"I said, *are you pissed off?*"

"YEAH!" the crowd yelled back.

"ARE YOU PISSED OFF?!"

"YEAH!"

"GOOD!" said Clarice. "Because so am I." She brought the guitar up, settled the strap across her shoulders. Raised her hands. "This first one goes out to the cock-sucking DJ *motherfucker* who engineered that remix."

Clarice stood back from her microphone and looked across at Johnny. He nodded and stepped up to his own. "This song is called 'Cross My Heart and Hope You Die,'" he said.

The crowd roared their approval when the song was done, but there was still a nasty vibe. There was no choice but to play it out, Clarice decided. She signaled for Billy to bring back The Motherfucker.

They followed "Cross My Heart" with "Hate You All" and "Davey Jones"–the heaviest songs in their repertoire. When the crowd finally started to settle, Clarice led them into "Shadow in the Valley" and then "Badman's Lament." By the time they had finished, the audience were waving their lit mobile phones.

Finally, she had them where she wanted them. "All right," Clarice told them, holding her guitar at parade rest. "You folks wanna be the first to hear something off the new album?"

The crowd surged toward the stage. Security goons repelled them. They surged again.

"Okay, fine," said Clarice. "We won't play it if you don't wanna hear it."

The crowd surged once more, stronger and more loudly. A half-dozen shirtless young men spilled over the crash barriers. Security hauled them away.

"Hell, we'll just keep playing the same old shit, if that's what you want," said Clarice. "I mean, you paid for the show."

"Maybe we should lip sync along with the remix?" suggested Johnny.

"Sure," Clarice replied. "I think that's what these lazy mother-fuckers want to hear."

Someone in the middle of the general admission area started chanting. "New stuff! New stuff! New stuff!" By his third repeti-tion most of the audience were yelling and clapping along.

"Oh, *now* you wanna hear the new album? Are you *sure*?"

"New STUFF! New STUFF! New STUFF!"

"Are you positive?"

"NEW STUFF! NEW STUFF! NEW STUFF!"

"Well, okay," said Clarice. "I guess we'll see what we can do." She turned toward Salzman, who had been standing patiently in a darkened corner of the stage. A spotlight shone on him. "Ladies and gentlemen, our special guest tonight–Mister Peter Salzman on keyboards."

There were a few seconds of silence as the audience took in the sight of the tuxedoed Salzman, standing in front of his array of keyboards and computers. He bowed formally, straightened up. Then, just as solemnly, he threw out a fist to the audience, pinkie and forefinger extended. The crowd went nuts.

Clarice and Johnny looked at each other. Perhaps they'd misjudged him.

Salzman sat down behind his keyboards.

"Hey! Hey! Calm down!" said Clarice. "We're trying to play some music here. *After* the song, you can go wild. Right now, I expect you to sit quietly and listen, like good little boys and girls. ARE YOU MOTHERFUCKERS GONNA BE GOOD LITTLE BOYS AND GIRLS?"

"YEAH!"

"Well, all right then," said Clarice, mildly. "This one is called 'The Executioner's New Clothes.'" She turned to Salzman. "Hit it, Pete."

Salzman put his hands on the keys. The sound of labored breathing—half sobbing, half laughing—spilled from the PA. Wood creaked. A sharp object whistled through the air, terminating abruptly with a heavy, wet *thunk*. Something *splatted* onto the ground and rolled away.

Beresford came in on drums, then Clarice. Johnny and Enrique roared in behind her.

"Executioner's New Clothes" was a rocking, up-beat, calculated piece: not quite heavy enough to exclude it from the playlists of mainstream radio, but odd enough to sit on the alternative charts. The song was about an executioner. A regular Joe who liked his job. Decent pay, good hours. He got to be out in the clean air and sunshine, and, when the volume of work was good, it was a pleasant way to keep in shape.

The rhythm guitar eased off every now and again to let Enrique's bass sound through. Clarice played fast, fluid leads over the top. Salzman added touches of piano and brass as well as the occasional special effect.

The crowd frothed up into a head-swaying, fist-shaking frenzy, trying to scream along to the words without knowing what they were.

The executioner's only problem was that he didn't like the way the uniform showed off his breasts. So he started to show up to work in Hawaiian shirts and cargo pants. Tails and Bermuda shorts. A tutu and tassels. The black hood went with everything.

They were about five bars from the main solo when Clarice noticed something amiss in the crowd.

A seven-foot tall-mountain of a man stood at the edge of the mosh pit. He was wearing a Hawaiian shirt, three-quarter-length cargo pants, flip-flop sandals...and an executioner's hood.

Johnny turned to her and mouthed "What the fuck?"

Clarice shrugged. She stomped on some FX pedals and started the solo.

The man in the hood was now crowd surfing the pit, buoyed up by a dozen pairs of hands. He was sitting upright, holding something high above his head.

An axe.

Johnny shut his own eyes and let his chords ring out.

Clarice kept her eyes fixed on the crowd-surfing axe-man as she finger-picked the solo.

He was deep into the pit when he was returned to his feet. The axe-man waded toward the stage, oblivious to the frenzied moshers bouncing off his arms and chest.

Clarice improvised some more leads to give Johnny more time to work his mojo. Enrique jumped and shook his way around the stage, filling in the space left by Johnny's stilled guitar. Salzman improvised a solo of his own when Clarice pointed to him. Beresford continued to hammer the skins like a madwoman.

Finally at the front of the stage, the axe-man stopped, looked around, and then jumped. It was like he was wired-up for a kung fu movie: his standing jump landed him right on top of the crash barriers. The axe-man stood there and posed for a moment, flexing up, putting his axe behind his neck to stretch his back. Then he swung around to face the stage and turned the weapon over in his hands.

Johnny opened his eyes. Looked at Clarice. Looked at the axe-man. Looked at Clarice.

The seven-foot axe-man hopped down onto the stage. The crowd frothed and boiled below him, laughing and cheering and butting into each other like enraged billy goats. The axe-man raised the weapon high over his head.

"I think," said Johnny, "it's time we ran away."

The axe-man spun the weapon between his hands and brought it around in a long, lateral cut. Johnny dropped his guitar and leapt backwards. His mic stand exploded in a shower of sparks as the axe struck it and swept it across the stage.

"Get the others off the stage," said Clarice. She slung her guitar behind her and stepped toward the axe-man. "I'll slow him down."

Salzman withdrew his hands from the keyboards and stepped backward, disappearing into the curtains.

Johnny grabbed Enrique by the shoulder, spun him around, and pushed him toward the wings. Beresford was still pounding the drums, oblivious to the action at the front of the stage.

The axe-man squared up to Clarice. His shoulders stood a good four inches above the top of her head. She took a step backward.

Johnny kicked over a snare drum and launched himself toward Beresford. She stumbled backward, upsetting her stool.

"Get off the fucking stage!" he yelled.

The crowd was screaming and roaring, clapping, stomping, and jumping. Many threw whatever was in their hands onto the stage.

The axe-man advanced slowly on Clarice.

"Come on, don't be shy," she said. "Big, bad axe-man like you can't possibly be afraid of a skinny little guitar bitch."

"HEH." The axe-man's voice sounded like a shotgun being fired into an echo chamber. He swung the axe.

Clarice zigged backwards, holding her guitar behind her. The blade sliced past her harmlessly, and she zagged back toward the axe-man, dropping her hips and slapping his forearms with her free hand. He stumbled around.

Still holding her guitar behind her, Clarice rushed through the curtains and bolted down the corridor, her sneakered feet sure on the damp linoleum floor. She caught up with the rest of the band just after the second turn. Johnny was herding Enrique and Beresford forward with his voice and his hands.

Clarice glanced over her shoulder. The axe-man was ten meters behind and gaining. His sandals made no sound as they slapped the floor. His breathing was inaudible, although Clarice could see his chest swelling with every inhalation. It was like being pursued by a cartoon.

A cartoon with an axe that could cut through anything.

The corridor forked.

"Left!" yelled Johnny.

Beresford went left. Enrique slowed and looked around, confused. Johnny grabbed the bassist by the arm as he skidded around the corner. The dressing room was up ahead.

"Get in the dressing room and do something!" yelled Clarice.

Johnny yanked open the door. "What are *you* gonna do?"

"I don't know," she said. She turned to face the axe-man again as Johnny herded the others into the little room.

The axe-man slowed his advance to a saunter, swapping the axe from hand to hand as he came on.

"Hello, sailor," said Clarice.

"HELLO, NURSE," said the axe-man.

"So that's how it's gonna be, is it?"

The axe-man raised the axe above his head and came on. The slash came from her left, as she had expected–there wasn't much space to maneuver a weapon that big in the narrow corridor. She jumped back, faked right. The axe cut a deep gash in the body of The Motherfucker as she spun out of the way.

The axe-man turned the weapon over and swung it upwards. Clarice sidestepped into the dressing room, and Johnny slammed the door behind her.

Silence.

Enrique and Beresford were huddled together at the back of the dressing room, near the dressing tables and the piles of street clothes they had shed before the gig.

"Hey, what is going on?" said Enrique.

"A seven-foot lumberjack just hacked up the stage," said Clarice. "What the fuck does it look like?"

Johnny was holding a large, black marker in his right hand. He had drawn a single line that crossed all four walls, continuous across the paint, the dressing mirrors, the doorframe, and the actual door. He had also put a hexagram on the door.

"Are we safe in here?" asked Clarice.

"For a minute or two, yeah," said Johnny.

"What is that thing out there?"

"Yeah, what the fuck is *going on*?!" demanded Beresford.

"It's magic," said Johnny.

"A demon?" said Clarice.

"No," said Johnny, "Just magic. It's not a monster, it's just a kind of puppet. A construct. A magical shell shaped like an axe-man."

"What the *fuck* does that mean?" said Enrique.

Clarice ignored him. "How long do we have?"

"Depends how long it takes the puppeteer to find a way to break in. The construct itself can't breach the warding circle, but something material would have no problem. The axe won't work, but if he tries to break down the door with a fire extinguisher or something..."

"Can you do something to the puppeteer?"

"Not without knowing who or where he is."

"Shit." She thought about it a bit more. "If the axe-man is just a spell, can't you just...I dunno, *dispel* it?"

"I'm a warlock, not a sorcerer. I can do demons and curses, but that's about it. That thing out there is being operated by a pro."

"What is *with* this Dungeons and Dragons bullshit?" demanded Beresford. "What in the name of *fuck* are you two talking about?"

"Shut the hell up, Beresford," said Clarice. "What *can* we do, Johnny?"

"I could summon something to fight it off, I guess," said Johnny, "but it would probably be just as dangerous to us as the axe-man."

"Crack cocaine," Enrique told Beresford. "The only possible explanation."

Clarice nodded. She slung off her guitar and turned it over to inspect the damage the axe had caused. "Sonovabitch," she said, glaring at the half-inch-wide furrow. Didn't look as though any of the hardware had been harmed, but it pissed her off just the same. She looked up. "Can you summon something and have *it* dispel the asshole with the axe?"

Johnny grinned. "Yes! Clear the floor."

"Where the fuck is security?" said Beresford, getting out of Johnny's way.

"Shouldn't we be calling the cops?" asked Enrique.

Johnny sketched a circle about the size of an extra-large pizza on the wooden floorboards. He drew a pentagram inside it and wrote the word "Mnemenarith" around its perimeter.

"You two better shut the fuck up, right the fuck now," said Clarice. "We'll explain later."

"Later," said Enrique.

"How much later?" said Beresford.

In the five triangular segments of the pentagram Johnny wrote "Will," "Magic," "Body," "Mind," "Spirit."

"*I said shut up!*" roared Clarice. Enrique and Beresford flinched back toward their corner.

Johnny stood away from the pentagram, looked down at it, and said: "*Mnemenarith*, Eater of Spells, manifest your *spirit* here. I bind you in *body*, I bind you in *mind*; let your *will* and your *magic* be subordinate to my own. Come."

The demon Mnemenarith manifested in the center of the pentagram as a foot-tall human hand. The hand stood upright on the end of a short section of wrist, clenched into a fist.

"Uh, maybe the pentagram was a bit small," apologized Johnny.

The middle digit of the giant fist slowly extended.

"Now, there's just no call for that."

A pair of eyes opened on the surface of the nail of the extended finger. A circular mouth filled with serrated teeth appeared on the tip of the digit. "Fuck you," said the mouth.

"*What the fuck is that?!*" shrieked Enrique, wedging himself right into the corner of the room. Clarice balled a fist and turned on him, bug-eyed. He quailed and shut up.

"Mnemenarith, I need you to dispel any magic that is operating within a hundred yards of your circle."

"Fuck you," said the demon, "and fuck the rest of you as well."

"Mnemenarith, I command you."

"I said, 'fuck you.'"

"Now, please."

"Fuck you," replied the demon, resignedly. Its fingers opened, and a small globe of pale blue light appeared in its palm. The globe collapsed into a disk, flared, and expanded until it had passed through the walls of the dressing room. The makeup mirrors shattered, but the silent explosion did not otherwise leave a mark.

Something heavy thumped onto the floor outside the door.

"Are you happy now, motherfucker?" said Mnemenarith.

"Much appreciated," said Johnny. "You are dismissed."

The demon clenched itself into a fist once more and re-extended its middle finger. "Fuck you all," it said one last time. Then it vanished.

Johnny stepped back and let out a long breath.

"What the fuck, what the fuck..." Enrique was muttering the same thing to himself, over and over.

Beresford shook her head, blinked, and turned to Clarice. "Now what?"

"What the hell do you think?" said Clarice, smoothing the gash in her guitar. "Now we get back on stage."

9. The Blame Game

"To make a really long story short," said Clarice, "our contract with the old record company came from a pact with the Devil."

They were sitting in the living room of Johnny's house in the Hollywood Hills. Enrique and Beresford–both of them stone cold sober–were seated on the leather-upholstered sofa. Johnny sat on the recliner, leaning forward. Clarice had the loveseat all to herself. The blinds had been drawn over the screen doors, occluding the view of the City of Angels and its light-stained night sky.

"*El Diablo,*" said Enrique. "That is some bad shit, man."

"But you ain't surprised to hear them say it, are you?" said Beresford.

"No," said Enrique.

"It was a last resort," said Clarice. "I got myself blacklisted with all the record labels and I had to do something."

"And the best way you could think of was to sell our souls?" said Beresford.

"Neither of you two are part of it, and Johnny and I both still have our souls."

"For now," said Enrique.

"It got us a contract, didn't it?" said Johnny.

"Yeah, an' look what else it got us," said Enrique. "A monster with an axe chasing us around our own fucking stage."

"I still don't understand how your deal with the Devil led to last night's fiasco," said Beresford.

"It's complicated," said Clarice.

"Of course it is," said Beresford. "So give me the short version."

"You remember Steve Heinman?"

"Yeah, of course," said Beresford. "The disappearing A&R asshole."

"Well…turns out, he was trafficking with demons."

"And then?"

"We had a disagreement. He disappeared in a puff of smoke."

"So Heinman sent the axe-man?"

"Uh, no, probably not," said Johnny.

"I think Nathaniel Ackerman is behind it," said Clarice.

"The producer?"

"Yeah."

"You think a DJ sent a giant magical axe-man to kill us because you fired him?"

"Pretty much."

Beresford had no reply.

"So, what we gonna do about it?" said Enrique.

"That," said Clarice, "is a damn good question."

"And I know who'll have an answer," said Johnny.

10. Black Magic Blues

It wasn't easy to get hold of Bad Jack Saunders and that was the way he liked it.

Bad Jack lived the rambling life of a bluesman, hitching from town to town with nothing but the clothes on his back and the guitar in his hands. Occasionally, he would play a stadium or a music festival. More often, he played anonymously in small clubs or on street corners. Sometimes he would check into his Chicago mansion, put together a backing band, and record an album. His name guaranteed a gold record at the least. But Bad Jack didn't care for gold so much as the road, where he was alone and accountable to no man. You couldn't find Bad Jack Saunders unless he wanted to be found.

Johnny Chernow had his cell-phone number.

When the bluesman agreed to see them, Clarice and Johnny chartered a helicopter to fly them out immediately, in case his feet got itchy before they arrived.

The bluesman was staying in room thirteen of a grubby motel on the outskirts of Nacogdoches, Texas. Before Johnny could knock on the door, Jack's rumbling voice told them to come right on in.

The room was dark and low-ceilinged and smelled of old cigarette smoke and new whiskey. The peeling walls were yellow, as if stained with nicotine. The bluesman sat on the narrow single bed, his guitar on one knee, a beaten-up laptop humming quietly in the corner. Spacemen floated jerkily across the void on its LCD screen.

"Johnny," he said. "And you must be Clarice. Find yourselves somewhere to sit."

Clarice hauled the chair out from under the writing desk and sat on it, adjusting her posture to offset the chair's list. Johnny leaned up against the doorframe.

"Appreciate your taking the time to see us, Jack," he said.

The bluesman ran his hand through his close-cropped, grey hair. No one knew exactly how old he was. Some days the bluesman told stories about paddling Robert Johnson's backside; other days he talked about whoring with Howlin' Wolf and Albert King. Some of the stories were almost certainly true.

"What can I do for you folks?" asked the bluesman, putting aside the guitar. The skin on the backs of his hands was thin and loose and threaded with thick veins. His fingers were long and strong and narrow.

"Got some trouble with a sorcerer. We figure you might be able to advise us," said Johnny

"You know the man's name?"

"Nathaniel Ackerman," said Clarice. "Calls himself DJ Axolotl."

"Oh, yeah. Young Natey Ax," said the bluesman. "You folks grabbed yourselves a double handful right there."

"He's good, huh?" said Johnny.

"Well," said the bluesman, "there's a bunch of musicians dabble in magic. You know the kind."

"Yeah," said Johnny. "Mostly they play guitar. Bluesmen or rockers like you and me."

"Right," said the bluesman. "Your problem is, young Natey ain't one of us."

Johnny frowned.

"Nathaniel Ackerman ain't no musician playing at magic," said the bluesman. "He a genuine first grade spell-slinger, playing at music."

"What he does isn't music," scoffed Clarice.

"You're right," said the bluesman. "I doubt he'd disagree with you, neither. All that boy cares about is power."

"So we're gonna need some heavy-duty protection?" said Johnny.

"I don't think you understand the situation exactly," said the bluesman. "Johnny, you a fine guitarist and a hell of a singer, but you ain't much of a witch."

"He's good enough to bargain with the Devil and come out ahead," said Clarice.

The bluesman grinned. "Oh, no," he said. "That Devil, he don't never come out second best. You might think otherwise, but he's a fellow knows how to get what he wants."

"I thought the Devil wanted souls?"

"If all the Devil wanted was souls," said the bluesman, "you wouldn't never hear from him. Way I hear it, he gets most of 'em just sitting at home in his underwear. He don't need to dicker for 'em one at a time."

"So what else do I have that the Devil might need?" asked Johnny.

"Clean underwear and a Tivo unit?" hazarded Clarice.

The bluesman's black, unblinking eyes shone in the dim light. "Whatever it is Old Scratch wants from you is gonna have to wait. You got Nathaniel Ackerman to worry about first."

"I'll—"

"There ain't diddly squat you can do against Nate Ackerman, son. Ain't no spell-ward you can raise he can't tear down. Ain't no beast you can summon he can't send away. Right now, he's just playing with you, but when he gets serious? Ain't no kind of magic gonna help you then."

"Just how powerful is this asshole?" asked Clarice.

"He's *powerful*," said the bluesman. "Ackerman could read your mind, dye your hair, fry your gizzards, cook your goose. He could fuck the sister you never had. He can *fly*. What *can't* he do? That's a much better question."

"What can't he do?" asked Johnny.

"He can't do too many things at the one time."

"So how do we stop him?" said Johnny.

"He's bulletproof, fireproof, waterproof, 100 proof. You can't sneak up on him, you can't spell-curse him. You can't find where he lives, you can't find what car he drives...you gonna have to do this the hard way."

Clarice leaned in. "He's got to have *some* sort of Achilles heel."

"You think this is some kind of fairy tale?" The bluesman chuckled. "Nate Ackerman don't have no Achilles heel–he got wings on his feet."

"He's really that good?" asked Johnny.

"One bad motherfucker, no two ways about it."

"That's all you got?" said Clarice. "That's bullshit."

The bluesman kept smiling. "That's all the shit I got. The rest is up to you."

Johnny came away from the doorway and moved in to shake the bluesman's hand. "Thanks, Jack, you've been helpful."

The bluesman shook his hand. "I been informative," he said. "I dunno as I been all that helpful."

Clarice tried not to glower when she shook the bluesman's hand. "Clarice," he said. "You may not be any kind of witch or mojo worker, but you still the baddest there is."

"I know," said Clarice.

"You know what to do," said the bluesman. "Maybe you haven't worked out the detail yet, but I can see it on your face."

Clarice nodded slowly. "Well, Jack, it's like they say in the classics: the best defense is a good offense."

II. South African Gigolo

Clarice had famously resisted all but the most basic security measures when it came to protecting the band. Venues and touring companies provided guards to keep the audience off the stage and out of the backstage area at concerts, but Clarice had never felt the need for bodyguards before.

"I can handle this shit myself," said Wynokoff, when Clarice asked him if he had any contacts in the security industry. "Running security ain't rocket science."

Clarice opened her mouth to reply, but Ingpen got in first. "Terry, you already handle everything. You don't have time to run security as well."

"Then get me an assistant."

"If you feel that you need an assistant, I'll arrange one," said Ingpen, "but I'm not hiring you an assistant because we need a security team."

"I don't need no assistant," said Wynokoff.

"Terry, you're an amazing tour manager," said Clarice. "Let some other schmuck run security for me so you can do your job the way it has to be done."

Wynokoff grunted his assent. "There's only one guy for the job."

—C●)—

Clarice met Thom De Villiers at the airport, right off the plane from O'Hare. He was about five-eight and probably weighed seventy kilograms. His head was shaved, and one of his ears was cauliflowered.

"Tell me your qualifications," said Clarice.

"Well," he said, calm and serious, "I was in the South African army for five years. Then I did five years with the Police Service. Since I moved to Chicago, I've been planning and controlling big events. Everything from crowd control to VIP protection." He smiled crookedly. "On the weekends I help underprivileged children learn to read and teach lonely women how to handle firearms."

"Oh, really?"

"Yes," he said. "I charge very low rates. Have you ever fired a gun?"

"Yeah. My Mom was a cop."

"You have a boyfriend?"

"Yes."

"Well," he said, "I won't tell if you won't tell."

"You'll find it difficult to talk with your jaw wired shut."

"Dirty talk–I like that," he said. "If I offered to take you out to dinner and a movie show, then maybe take you home and show you how to strip down a forty-five, would you accept?"

"No," said Clarice. "If I offered to take you to a gym and go a few rounds, would *you*?"

"I don't know," he said. "Would you kick my arse?"

"Probably."

"Then ja, I would," he said. "Oh, *ja*."

Clarice posed dozens of scenarios to De Villiers. He answered them all easily, managing to incorporate some kind of innuendo into everything he said. The scenarios got more and more elaborate as they went. After a while, De Villiers stopped her and asked: "Are you looking for a bodyguard or a mercenary force?"

"Maybe both."

"Are you serious?"

"As bowel cancer."

De Villiers smacked his lips. "You want to take me to the gym now?"

"No," she said. "I want you to start work tomorrow."

"Are you really expecting some kind of action, or are you just a tough cookie?"

"Both," said Clarice. "But, yeah, we've had some threats."

"Everybody gets threats, Ms Marnier."

"You can call me Clarice, or you can call me 'sir.'"

"Everybody gets threats, Clarice."

"Not this kind of threat, believe me."

De Villiers pulled off his gloves. "Why wouldn't I believe you?"

"Lately they've been...unusual."

"Unusual?"

Clarice looked at him long and hard. "Occult."

"You mean, like, hate mail written in blood?"

"I mean, like, monsters and evil wizards."

He grinned. "You need someone to fight monsters and evil wizards?"

She stared until his grin faded. "Maybe even go on a quest. Are you up for it?"

"Clarice, I'm from Africa," De Villiers said. "Of course I'm up for it."

12. Black Ops and Broomsticks

"Let me see if I have this right." Big Nicky straightened his white silk tie and leaned back in his swivel-throne, the leather upholstery creaking beneath his bulk. "You want a car, a driver, and three shooters, so you can pull a hit in a crowded nightclub."

Clarice put her right ankle on her left thigh and nodded. "Me and De Villiers will be in the car," she said. "Johnny will already be inside when we get there."

Big Nicky shook his head. "Have you ever done this kind of thing before?"

"No," said Clarice, "but none of your boys have ever pulled one quite like this, either."

"You really feel that you have to go in there with handguns? I know a sharpshooter, Zak Tyndall, who can thread a needle from a klick away, both eyes closed—"

"No," said Clarice. "That won't work. It's my plan and we're sticking with it."

"I don't know about this, Clarice," said Big Nicky.

Clarice let him sit for a few moments. "It's okay, Nicky," she said. "You can say no. You didn't expect this sort of thing when you promised me a favor—we both know it. Turn me down if you have to. I won't think any less of you."

Nicky sighed and slowly opened his eyes. "No. If I refuse, you kids will go to someone else. They'll make a mess of it, and I wouldn't be able to live with myself."

Clarice smiled and inclined her head.

"I'll give you Vanni and Frankie as well as Little Nicky. You'll have my own personal driver behind the wheel."

Clarice grinned. "Thanks, Big Nicky," she said, standing up. "You're the best."

"And you, Clarice, are the worst," he said. "Why else would I let you do this to me?"

13. Dying Like a Rock Star

Ackerman got in at 4 a.m. He spoke a short cantrip to prevent his girlfriend from awakening. It had been a good night at the club, and he didn't have time for small talk. He had to get down to his lab before his spell-traps started to degrade and the energy he'd harvested began to bleed away.

The basement looked as much like Mission Control as it did a sorcerer's laboratory: computer screens, mixing decks, and synth keyboards sat on the bench-tops alongside the skeletons of impossible animals and jars of luminous fluids. Fleshy plants, a disco ball, and odd pieces of cobbled-together stereo equipment hung from the ceiling.

Ackerman raised his hands and spoke a word. The coals in the brazier by the network server glowed; the scented oils in the burners took. Electrical cables writhed and sparked; the plants and skeletons twitched. The speakers hummed, and the disco ball began to revolve.

"Heh," said Ackerman. Magic felt good.

The club had been wild—the heat of summer, the start of the holidays. And the beat, of course. He'd been good behind the decks, and the crowd had responded.

Being a DJ was a nice, easy way to charge up his batteries. Tapping ley lines, bleeding faerie circles, siphoning demon gates, necromancy: all that tricky, traditional shit was difficult as well as dangerous. The yield from trancers and dancers wasn't as good, but it took much less effort to harvest because they gave it to him willingly. Eco friendly, too: they never dried up, and they kept coming back.

Ackerman's weekly gigs provided enough juice to work on all his pet projects, and there was always plenty left over for his savings battery. He estimated that if he hooked up all the power cells in his basement, he would have enough raw occult energy to level four city blocks. If he tapped his remote caches, he could do a lot worse than that. But why would he want to? He wasn't a bad guy. Okay, sure, he had killed people before, but never for fun–only for personal gain.

Besides, that was chump-change compared to what he had coming.

Ackerman smiled and thought of Clarice Marnier.

He'd been intrigued when he'd discovered what she'd done to his friend, Troutsmack'd, but it had taken him a while to work out his next step. Remixing that song had seemed like a good idea; he couldn't have known how badly she'd react to it. That had scotched the idea of him engineering a monster hit album for her, but that failure had inspired something grander.

Ackerman, of course, could take Bloody Waters out any time he wanted. He could cause an equipment malfunction, electrocute them live on stage. He could make them spontaneously combust. He could, if he wanted to, reach out and stop Clarice's heart without even leaving his lab. It wouldn't even be difficult. But there was no profit in that.

His new idea was to give her a rock star death like nobody had ever seen before. The axe-man was just a warmup. Ackerman wanted to raise the stakes. And then...*pow*. All that grief, all those broken hearts and shattered dreams: the wailing, the gnashing of teeth, the rending of clothes...

Destroying an icon was like splitting an atom. The energy he took from spinning records was *nothing* compared to that harvest.

Ackerman had developed a spell technology that he could imprint onto a CD. It was still a bit lossy, but those discs would capture some of the energy spent on the appreciation of one of those albums and transmit it directly into his batteries. There would be a lot of CDs sold when Bloody Waters went down in flames; a lot of new printings, remasters, remixes, tribute albums... and Ackerman was the record label's favorite new engineer.

He was going to make Bloody Waters the biggest act of all time, and then he was going to kill them.

14. Axing the Horse

Little Nicky was about half the age and half the size of Big Nicky, but he was still the largest man in the back of the limousine. "So we go in, we find this DJ guy," he said, "we cap him, we leave. Easy as pie."

"Ja, unless it gets weird," said De Villiers.

"I been meaning to ask about that," said Little Nicky. "What do you mean exactly, *weird*?"

"Black magic weird," said Clarice.

"You're kidding," said Frankie.

"Nope," said Clarice. "This guy is into demons and devils as well as shitty techno music."

Nicky scowled at her. He liked techno music.

"You're kidding," said Frankie, with even less conviction.

"Not really," said Clarice.

"So, so...hypothetically..." said Big Nicky, "*hypothetically*, what are we supposed to do if this guy starts shooting laser-beams out his asshole?"

"You're supposed to blow him away," said Clarice.

They sat in silence. Flashes of neon from outside the limo splashed over them periodically.

"Miss," said Frankie. "Miss?"

Clarice leaned back in her seat and smiled. "Yeah?"

"Miss, if this guy sends devils and spirits against us, will a crucifix be any use?"

"I was you, I'd be relying on my guns first," said Clarice, "but if you're a good Catholic, I'm sure a crucifix won't hurt."

Frankie smiled and nodded nervously. "Thanks."

Clarice grinned. "So, Frankie, when was the last time you made Confession?"

Johnny had drawn the summoning circle on the lid of the toilet. The accompanying control structures spread all over the bowl and the cistern, across the floor and up the cubicle walls.

He double-checked the spell, touching up the symbols here and there with a tiny brush, wet from a vial of pig blood. Then he checked it again. Johnny had never laid an enchantment on this scale before, and he wanted to be triply certain that the spell was correct.

He had drawn the Devil himself, of course, as well as some other minor beasts, but those spells were old and secure. This time, Johnny himself had authored the spell.

The plan was to summon a specific demon into a specific form, hardwired with specific instructions. Then he was going to turn it loose. Once the spell had been executed, he would have no further control over the beast whatsoever. That made him nervous.

It was ready.

He put away the brush and checked his watch.

The club had once been a very large multi-story theatre. The façade was covered with gothic turrets and gargoyles, but the newly added third level was all concrete and glass. The black limo did not draw a lot of attention when it pulled up out front.

Clarice put on a baseball cap and a pair of black leather gloves as the limousine pulled up outside the club. "Everyone ready?"

"Yeah, we're ready," said Little Nicky, cocking the slide of his massive .50 caliber Desert Eagle. The rest of his crew checked their weapons.

Frankie looked at Clarice. "You packin'?"

"I can handle myself," Clarice replied.

The driver opened the door. Little Nicky exited first, followed by Vanni and Frankie. De Villiers followed Clarice out of the limo. Nicky was already bobbing his head to the half-heard bass.

With De Villiers at her side and three mafia hitmen trailing behind her, Clarice walked straight up to the roped-off entrance to the club. A shaven-headed bouncer, six-five with shoulders as wide as his waist was narrow, moved to intercept her.

Clarice lowered her shades and looked up into his eyes. "Get the fuck out of my way."

The bouncer took a step backward, stunned.

"Nice," said De Villiers, as they swept on past him.

"Nice, my ass," said Clarice, her mimicry of De Villiers's accent making a rhyme of it.

The gunmen followed her into the club like a string of ducks.

Johnny raised his head and opened his eyes as he spoke the last line of the incantation.

The fluorescent tubes in the ceiling flared and dimmed. The urinals and then each toilet flushed, one after the other. The faucets went on, then off. The hand-dryer roared and fell silent.

When the lights came back on, an eight-foot-tall demon stood on the lid of the toilet bowl, balanced on one leg, hunched over. Its shoulders grazed the ceiling. It wore an executioner's hood over a black AC/DC tank top, olive-drab combat pants, and an enormous pair of boots. It carried a double-bladed axe.

The runes and line work Johnny had painted all over the stall streamed off the walls and spread, burning across the demon executioner's massive arms.

Johnny unlocked the cubicle door behind him and scuffed a breach in the remaining outer pentagram. "Cholschrak of Dis, come on down," he said.

The eight-foot demon leaned its axe on its shoulder and stepped down off the toilet.

The music grew louder as Clarice and her posse moved from the foyer into the club proper. Her phalanx penetrated the crowd easily, moving in past the bar toward the main dancefloor. The music for the ground level was canned: pop ditties, house-lite or disco classics. Proper DJs played hardcore techno and trance on the higher levels.

They elbowed their way up a spiral staircase and along a broad catwalk to the mezzanine. Two DJs, each with their own dancefloor, occupied the second level. Ackerman had the third level all to himself.

He stood with his back to the cavernous auditorium hall. A retractable glass screen kept out the music from the main dancefloor, two stories below.

There were no wallflowers on Ackerman's level. Everyone was dancing, but without the self-conscious cool or drugged-up abandon of the clubbers on the other levels. Ackerman's crowd was on another level altogether: shaking to the music, heads jerking, hands twitching; eyes staring, lips moist and open. The DJ was plugged directly into the pleasure centers of their brains and had completely disengaged their frontal lobes. The zombies, rather than the witch doctor, were dancing out this trance.

Ackerman turned to Clarice's crew and waved, scratching a record with his other hand. "Well, hello, nurse," he said.

Ackerman had been expecting them, of course. Soon as he'd arrived, he'd become aware of Johnny Chernow working some juju in the men's. He knew Clarice wouldn't be far away.

This was a ballsier move than he had expected of them. It was nothing he couldn't handle, but it did change the game a bit. He wasn't ready to play his hand, but he wasn't gonna let them have this round, either. Ackerman decided he would improvise, see what happened. It'd be more fun than spinning records, anyway.

Three of Clarice's goons were pushing their way toward the decks, brandishing automatic pistols. She and the runty one that he recognized as her new security chief hung back a little. The fat goon in charge of the mobsters was already grooving along; bobbing his head, lips pursed, shoulders swaying. Turning him was as easy as flipping a light switch.

Little Nicky stopped where he was and executed a *Saturday Night Fever* pirouette. He raised his arms and shook his ass, hips gyrating, grunting in time with the beat. His two companions stared at him.

"Welcome!" Ackerman's voice blared from the PA. "I'm going to try to put on a special show for you." Electricity arced from the decks into his fingers. His eyes crackled and sparked. "Get down and boogie, boys and girls. It's time to get this party started!"

The bass thickened, the tempo increased, and the dancers jerked with renewed energy. Little Nicky pointed his weapon at Frankie C. and squeezed the trigger twice.

Frankie went down with two in the chest. Vanni hesitated, then threw himself into the crowd and started clawing his way toward an exit, unprepared to fight with his boss.

De Villiers pushed Clarice behind him and pulled his own weapon. The security chief lined up his shot and put a round into Little Nicky's shoulder. The obese mobster dropped his gun and went down, clutching his injured arm. De Villiers swiveled and fired on the DJ.

It was only lead. Ackerman dismissed the bullets with a wave of his left hand. A bolt of electricity arced from his fingers, and De Villiers fell in a heap, jerking and twitching.

Ackerman juggled his two pairs of headphones. He dragged a finger over the record on his number two deck to sync with the number one record, then shifted the pitch across to it and let it go. Then he looked up at Clarice and smiled.

"Well, now," he said. "Are you ready for a turn around the dancefloor?"

The weird thing was, the dancers just kept on dancing. Gunfire and lightning weren't enough to snap them out of the DJ's trance. Worse, Johnny could feel the beat tugging at his own senses.

It had gone wrong already. The gunmen were supposed to pin Ackerman down so that the demon could do its work, but Ackerman had taken care of them before he'd even emerged. Clarice looked like she was about to wade into the crowd of dancers with her fists, but she knew it was hopeless and so did he. They still had the executioner demon, but Johnny wasn't sure how long it would last against Ackerman. Johnny got out of its way and let it go to work.

"What have we here?" said Ackerman. "A giant executioner. Where have I seen that idea before?"

"You stole the idea from a song *I* wrote," said Clarice.

Red eyes shone through the demon's mask as it advanced toward the DJ. Ackerman raised his hands from the decks and removed both pairs of headphones from his head.

"And now I'm supposed to fight it?"

"Why don't you just kneel down and let it slap off your head?" said Clarice. "I'm keen to get out of here before the music gives me a seizure."

"It might give you something worse, Clarice," said Ackerman. "It might even lead to *dancing*."

The DJ rose into the air inside a bulb of coruscating electricity. Lightning crawled from his eyes to his extended fingertips as he swung his hands in front of him. Static discharges earthed into the floor and the ceiling. His decks continued to operate themselves.

The executioner demon unlimbered its axe and lined up, like a batter stepping to the plate.

"*Zappo*," said the DJ. Lightning arced between his hands and forked out in the direction of the demon.

The demon caught the bolt on its axe. Tendrils of electricity writhed across the blades, down its arms and torso, and dissipated into floor through its feet.

Ackerman smiled. "*Zippo*," he said. He cupped his hands like he was making a snowball, turned them over, and extended them toward the demon, palms-first. The gasoline-and-mothballs stench of napalm filled the room and a ball of fire sailed through the air toward the demon in a beautiful parabolic arc.

The demon threw its arms wide and took it on the chest. The fireball did not even singe its T-shirt.

Ackerman turned his head toward Johnny and nodded approvingly. "Nice job on the conjury," he said. "You're getting good at this."

"Not bad for a dumb guitarist, huh?" said Johnny.

"Almost like a real magician." Ackerman's globe bobbed out from behind the decks and swung about to face the executioner. "*Avaunt*," he said, spell runes flaring in his eyes.

The demon raised the axe above its head and charged. Ackerman extended one hand, palm outward. Something invisible slammed into the demon with the force of a wrecking ball, blasted it off its feet, and sent it tumbling through the air. The demon unraveled into ribbons of red mist as it smashed through a picture window in the far wall. Ackerman grinned after it.

A shot rang out. The DJ went over backward with a fist-sized exit wound in the back of his head.

The knobs, dials, and levers on Ackerman's console stopped moving. The records on both of his decks spun uninhibited until Clarice kicked them over. There was a squawk, and then silence. The dancers kept on boogying, but slower and slower. Before long they started to drop, falling comatose on the floor like puppets with their strings cut.

"I've always wanted to do that," she said.

"What the fuck just happened?" asked Johnny, who was squatting beside De Villiers's unconscious form.

"I guess we'll have to ask Big Nicky," said Clarice.

15. Axe Me No Questions

Tony's Taverna was as dark and smoky as a villain could have wanted, but Zak Tyndall kept his sunglasses on just the same.

"I gotta say, that was one of the stranger hits I ever pulled," he said.

"Would you have taken the job if you'd known it would get weird?"

"Weird is my specialty." Tyndall exhaled a stream of smoke. "Besides, Big Nicky pays up front. I wouldn't have refused if he'd asked me to pop the Snuffleupagus when Big Bird's back was turned."

Tony sauntered up, smoothing his apron. "Hey, Clarice. Johnny. Zak," he said. "I don't even wanna know why you three are sitting together."

"Just having some drinks, Tony," said Clarice.

"What can I get you folks?"

Tyndall put out his cigarette and ordered for everyone. Tony served them up.

"Hey, Tony," said Johnny. "What are we listening to here? Burt Bacharach?"

"Yep."

"So Big Nicky's running the place again?"

Tony shook his head. "No, Little Nicky, still," he said, "But he had the jukebox removed and he shitcanned the disco night."

"Oh, yeah?" said Clarice.

"Yeah. Says techno music makes you a zombie, rock an' roll makes you a devil worshipper, and pop music rots your teeth. Now it's Three Tenors, Tony Bennett, Burt, or nothing."

"Sounds like somebody gave him a bit of an education," said Clarice.

"You say somethin'?" asked Tony. "I thought I heard somethin'. Must be my hearing aid needs batteries." The barman moved away.

Clarice threw back her bourbon. Johnny sipped his beer. Tyndall gulped down a few mouthfuls of Guinness.

"So, let me guess," said the marksman, lowering his glass and wiping the residue of white cream from his lip. "Big Nicky didn't tell you he was sending me."

Clarice stared at him for a moment. "He offered to, but I declined."

"Lucky for you he's a generous man, huh?"

"Lucky, yeah," said Clarice. "It didn't go down the way we planned it."

"Actually, it worked out pretty much the way the bluesman said it would," said Johnny.

Clarice put down her glass and licked her lips. "He gave us some answers, sure," she said, "but most of them had nothing to do with the questions we axed him."

— RETSPAN —

1. Bloodglass and Bonemarrow

Sister to Dragons was a monster.

"Executioner's New Clothes" debuted at number one on the alternative and modern rock charts and burned through into the mainstream Top 40. The album remained the highest selling record in any genre for weeks. It was platinum on the pre-orders alone, and they'd doubled that even before the tour started.

Even the critics liked it.

When Clarice told a fawning MTV journalist "It's just fucking rock music" live on the air, her fans adopted it as a catchphrase, which they repeated as if she had brought it down from a mountain, graven in stone.

Stories about the rogue axe-man at the preview show had become an urban legend. Ingpen wanted to hire a bodybuilder to smash up the stage with an axe all through the tour, but Clarice refused.

"We're a rock band, not a stunt circus."

Bloody Waters played to capacity crowds everywhere, and the album just kept on selling. Gasket Records released the second single, "Bloodglass and Bonemarrow," when the "Executioner" sales started to taper, and it, too, roared straight to the top of the charts.

"I think you're about to become the biggest rock band in the world," said Wainer, equal parts mystified and awestruck.

"We have been for years," said Clarice. "It's just taken the world a while to catch on."

2. Diagnosing Napster

Clarice was in a mid-tour press conference when the subject of Napster was first broached to her.

"What *about* Napster?" snapped Clarice from behind the lectern. She had been too busy with the album, with Nathaniel Ackerman and the new tour to air her opinions about the subject when it was hot, and she felt that anything she had to say had already been said.

"Well," said the journalist, blinking and waving his mic, "what do you, uh, think of it?"

"Um, uh, it's a decentralized technology for the unauthorized redistribution of recorded material."

"Um, yes...but how do you *feel* about it?"

"It's software, it's not my fucking pet dog."

"You have a pet dog?"

"No," said Clarice. "Irrelevant."

"How do you feel about people using Napster to steal your music?"

"It pisses me off a little," admitted Clarice, "But I'm not losing sleep over it. I earn most of my money from ticket sales and T-shirts, like every other rock band."

The truth was that Clarice didn't know or care how much money Napster was costing them. Her dislike of it had as much to do with the poor audio quality of the files exchanged as with the money. She didn't consider it a real threat and she was happy to let someone else deal with it.

Another journalist stepped up. "Any truth in the rumors that you're going to be contributing to some tracks on the new Heathens Burning album?"

"None whatsoever," said Clarice.

3. Caught Napping

They were sitting in front of the TV, watching an old Italian horror film, when the telephone rang.

Clarice thumbed the mute button as Johnny fumbled for the phone receiver. On the screen, a maniac with a butcher's knife chased two lesbians up the stairs of their home. His footfalls and their screams suddenly became inaudible.

"Johnny Chernow," said Johnny, into the receiver. He went quiet.

"Who is it?" Clarice mouthed.

Johnny covered the receiver with his left hand. "Satan."

"What does he want?"

"He wants to be on speakerphone."

Clarice put down her glass of soda and scowled. "Tell him to call back. We're watching a movie."

Johnny smiled wanly and pushed the speakerphone button.

"Hi, Clarice," said the Devil. "Can you hear me okay?"

"Yeah," said Clarice, "I hear you. What do you want?"

"Straight to the point," said the Devil. "That's my girl."

"We're trying to watch a movie here."

"Sorry to interrupt. You remember that favor you owe me?"

"No?"

"Don't be cute."

"Oh, yeah. *Now* I remember. I been meaning to speak to you about that."

"Uh huh?"

"Well, seems to me we did you a favor in putting a stop to Steve Heinman's hilarious antics. I say we're square."

The Devil chuckled. "Nice try," he said, "but I don't think so."

"It was you behind that, wasn't it?"

"Well, obviously."

"In that case, it counts."

"I didn't ask you to get involved."

"No, you *forced* me to."

"Be that as it may, you, yourself, excluded several kinds of 'favor' from the contract, and, as I recall, killing was one of them."

"Oh, come *on*."

"I think it was more like manslaughter," said Johnny.

"We banished Melanie Lonegan," said Clarice. "Does *that* qualify?"

"I didn't ask you to do that, either. And who do you think gave Johnny the power to accomplish that little feat, anyway?"

"The Easter Bunny?"

"Nope, he was busy hiding chocolate eggs. I did."

"That is true," said Johnny, glumly.

"Shut up," said Clarice.

"Now, if you're done trying to out-lawyer me, can we get on with this?"

"Yeah, okay," grated Clarice. "What do you want?"

"It's an easy one."

"Just spit it out."

"I want you to speak out in favor of Napster."

Clarice was silent for a good five seconds. "That is *so* fucking petty."

"I have my reasons."

"Pettiness is not a reason."

"You don't get a say. You just get to do what I tell you."

"Well, I already dissed Napster," said Clarice. "Sorry, too late."

"Yeah," said the Devil, "I saw you on *Entertainment Tonight*. I guess you're just gonna have to take it all back."

"I'd rather bear your children."

"Sorry, nope," said the Devil. "Come on, do this thing for me. It won't take long."

"Exactly why is Napster so fuckin' important to you?" said Clarice. "The courts are gonna shut them down any day now."

"It's not really about Napster, it's about digital distribution. No matter what the courts rule, this is going to be the biggest shake-thing in the record industry since...well, since the record."

"I thought you ran the entire business, anyway."

"Entirely beside the point," said the Devil. "I'm not just a businessman; you know me better than that."

"So now you're some kind of freedom of information revolutionary?" said Clarice, scorn dripping from her voice.

"Well, yes. Basically," said the Devil. "Always have been."

"That's not a good reason to screw with the livelihoods of every musician on the planet."

"Come on, Clarice," said the Devil. "You said that it's *not* going to hurt you very much. The only people who are really going to get hurt in this are going to be the middlemen. The suits who screw you out of sales revenue, interfere with your vision, and...well... turn on the radio and have a listen some time. The music business is clearly turning to shit."

"You made some good points," conceded Clarice, "but it's still *my* music being stolen."

"It's already being stolen–by the middlemen."

She shook her head but had no reply.

"What are you really afraid of, Clarice? That your fans will steal your music, or that a market that's friendlier to musicians will force some real competition on you?"

"All right," she said, "but after this we're square, okay?"

"Always and forever," replied the Devil.

4. Amendment

Ingpen wasn't impressed by Clarice's sudden interest in Napster. "Yesterday you were against it," she said. "Today, you're so thrilled by the idea that you *have* to go on record in its defense, right this instant, tomorrow is too late?"

"I changed my mind. You have a problem with that?"

"I don't have any problems with it," said Ingpen. "You have a right to free speech, and all that happy horseshit. I don't have any kind of problem, but it sounds to me like you do."

"The Devil made me do it."

"I don't care if it was the Easter Bunny," said Ingpen, "this is going against you, no matter what you say."

"I know." Clarice sighed. "Just set it up, please. I want to get this over with."

5. Under the Bridge

"Wow," said Johnny, looking away from the TV screen above the bar and across at Clarice. "That was…that was *good*, Clarice."

"They cut about ninety percent of what I said."

"So what? You made your point without backing down from your original position."

Clarice snorted. De Villiers laughed without looking around. He was leaning on the bar to Clarice's left, facing the door and the windows.

Tony wasn't on, and the duty barman kept as far away from them as he could. Johnny gestured for another round.

"You sounded like you really believed what you were saying."

"Well, yeah," said Clarice sourly, "I did, and I do."

"Whoa, whoa, whoa," said Johnny. "Did you just admit that? Out loud?"

Clarice grunted her assent. De Villiers put his hand over his lips and made a shocked face.

"But that's it," said Clarice, "no more and never again. We are more than square and our dealings with the King of Assholes are *over.*"

"Even though he was right and you were wrong?"

"It's not about who was right and who was wrong."

"Well, it's water under the bridge now," said Johnny. "The debt is closed, so what difference does it make anyway?"

"That's precisely the question that's bothering me."

— HOW SOLO CAN YOU GO? —

1. Groovetech 3000

After the *Sister to Dragons* tour was over, Johnny decided to celebrate Bloody Waters' biggest–and toughest–year yet by hosting a band-only barbeque at his place in the Hollywood Hills. The sun was out, the hamburgers were cooking, the Jacuzzi was hot, and the beer was cold.

Johnny was at the grill. Beresford had taken up position in a deck chair with a bottle of Jack Daniels. Clarice was standing on a short ladder, hanging a punching bag from a low beam in the gazebo. Enrique was nervous.

He drank some beer and stared out at the city rising up from the smog haze. Clarice stepped down off the stool and hefted the bag, supporting it on one cocked knee while she pulled the chain tight. It looked like the bag weighed more than she did. Enrique knew it was the best opportunity to speak to her privately that he was going to get.

He thought about what it would be like to die while he poured the remainder of the beer down his throat.

"Clarice, can I talk to you a minute?"

"Sure."

"Uh, is now okay? I got something I want to tell you."

Clarice glanced over her shoulder and saw the look on his face. She secured the chain with a carabiner and let it go slack. The gazebo creaked under the weight of the bag.

Clarice stepped down off the chair and looked at him. "Tell me."

Enrique told her. "I been invited to record with Groovetech 3000."

"What, exactly, is a Groovetech 3000?"

Enrique's skinny shoulders went up and down in a slouching shrug. "Is a kind of experimental music thing."

Clarice slapped the bag casually and stepped down off the chair. "Experimental? As in, you get to play along while the producer programs some beats, and then he goes and mixes you out in the studio?" Clarice's shades reflected the low sun with dazzling radiance.

Johnny looked up from the barbecue, hearing the tone of Clarice's voice from across the pool. He was wearing an apron with the legend "Kill the Cook" printed across it.

"Is just one track," said Enrique.

"I see."

Johnny turned the burgers, put down the tongs, and came over. "What's the story?"

"There's no story," said Clarice. "Enrique wants to do a track for an experimental techno album."

"Yeah," said Enrique. "It's okay?"

"You really want to do it?"

Enrique squinted at her. His reflection in her sunglasses squinted back at him. "Yeah," he said. "I do."

"So why are you asking my permission?"

2. Other Outlets

"You know," said Johnny, propping himself up against the headboard and putting a hand on Clarice's bare shoulder, "I think it's a good idea. Enrique going off to do this Groovetech thing."

Clarice was lying on her stomach with her head turned away. "Oh, yeah?"

"Yeah," he said. "Bloody Waters is pretty high stress; it'll be good for him to escape from it a bit."

Clarice snaked upright and turned to look at him. She *had* been running the band pretty hard. It had taken six grueling years to get them to where they were, and they were definitely starting to feel it.

"I guess it can't hurt."

"I think it will be good for him," Johnny repeated. He waited for a reply, but there was none forthcoming. "I'm thinking of starting up a side project, myself."

Clarice stared at him.

He looked her right in the eyes. "Bloody Waters is the best band in the world, but I'd like another outlet."

"Another outlet."

"Yep," said Johnny. "My own thing, where I get to call the shots."

"You call the shots."

"Yep." He had nothing else to say, so he just sat there and watched her. Her face remained expressionless, but he saw her shoulders bunch and relax three times before she spoke.

"Good," she said. "I'm looking forward to hearing what you come up with."

"It's probably gonna delay the next Bloody Waters album."

"Yeah, I know," said Clarice, "but that's okay. We could use the break, and I think I'm going to do some solo work of my own."

3. Red Jack Arisen

Enrique went off to record his track for Groovetech 3000. Johnny quickly recruited a bassist and a drummer for his new band, which he named Red Jack Arisen, and the three of them lit out for Florida to write and record some material. Beresford booked herself on a holiday tour of the hottest of hot spots in Eastern Europe and the Middle East: Gaza, Macedonia, Yugoslavia, Chechnya, the Czech Republic.

It didn't take long for rumors that Bloody Waters had broken up to begin circulating. Ingpen issued press releases that said otherwise, and Johnny was continually asked for comment about the matter, but nobody would believe it until they heard it from Clarice—but Clarice wasn't talking.

The music press went to Rex Munday in desperation. He claimed to have no idea what she was up to, either.

Groovetech 3000 was released before Red Jack Arisen had finished recording. It charted for a few weeks, then disappeared into the volume of lookalike, soundalike "experimental" techno that had flooded the record stores.

Red Jack Arisen's album *Lock and Load* rolled out to mixed reviews from the critics, but commercially it was an unabashed success, debuting on the modern rock album charts in the low twenties. The first single, "Dying Hard," got high-rotation radio play and sat in the top ten for more than a month. Some of the critics called Red Jack's sound "regressive," which, Johnny told Clarice, meant "retro" in a way that wasn't cool. Other critics were thrilled with Johnny's "previously unrecognized" guitar virtuosity; they tried very hard to compare him to Clarice without coming right out and saying that he was good...but not that good.

Guitar Magazine asked Johnny what his aims were with RJA.

"Well, modern rock is either really whiney or monstrously heavy," he said. "I have nothing against any of it, but...it's all folk ballads or nu metal. No one is playing straight-ahead, balls out rock'n'roll anymore."

"Including Bloody Waters?"

"You can hardly call Bloody Waters 'straight ahead.' Red Jack is not as...ambitious. We're not about pushing the envelope; we're not trying to *boldly go*. We're just here to rock out."

"So what's the plan for Johnny Chernow and Red Jack Arisen?"

"We're just gigging here and there, gearing up for the big tour. Having some fun. I'm enjoying the change of pace."

"And Bloody Waters is on indefinite hiatus?"

"Nothing indefinite about it. Bloody Waters is not something you can walk away from."

4. Demon Drink

The tattooed, steroid-jacked freak in the leather fetish outfit and the horror movie makeup grabbed a fistful of Johnny's jacket and shoved his metal-studded visage right into Johnny's grill.

"Tell me how to stop that Marnier bitch, or I'll eat the soul out of your ruptured heart."

The freak, Oliver Skaloniak, had been glowering at Johnny from his table in the back corner of the bar all night. Johnny knew who he was—the frontman of a mall metal band—but they'd never met, and Johnny didn't much care to. He'd done his best to ignore him, but it hadn't exactly been a surprise when Skaloniak had accosted him on his way to the bar. The real surprise was the discovery that this man who thought shaving off his eyebrows made him look scary, was, in fact, a demon.

"Stop her from doing what?"

Clarice was on the other side of the country, working on her mysterious solo venture. Whatever she had done to piss off Skaloniak, Johnny wasn't privy to it.

Johnny felt his feet leave the floor.

"Don't play games with me," snarled Skaloniak, in an appropriately gravelly voice. "You know what I am, and you know what she's done."

"I'd really prefer to discuss this from ground level," said Johnny, "if you wouldn't mind."

Skaloniak put him down. Johnny slowly, but firmly, pushed the demon's enormous hands off his lapels.

"Thank you," he said.

"You *know*," said Skaloniak.

Johnny held his ground. "I had no idea you had any connection to Clarice until right now."

Skaloniak's eyes flashed. "You lying *fuck*," he said. "I'll rupture your soul and eat your heart."

"That line was more effective the first time."

"I'll…"

"There a problem here?" The voice came from just below Johnny's shoulder. Jake Bradshaw, Red Jack's bassist, had his hand on Skaloniak's shoulder. Bradshaw was five-five, but there was a hundred kilograms of muscle on that diminutive frame as well as a short man's desire to prove his toughness.

A crowd had formed, and a couple of bouncers were wading through it toward them.

Skaloniak backed down. "This isn't over, Chernow," he said. "We still have business, you and me."

"You and me? Or you, and me, and Clarice?"

Bradshaw and Johnny returned to their table, where Caleb Haas was lounging back in his seat, swilling beer.

"What was that about?" Red Jack's drummer was lean, long-haired, and easygoing.

"Bring Out The Gimp over there wanted a piece of Johnny," said Bradshaw.

Haas raised an eyebrow. "I didn't think you swung that way."

"I prefer them a bit more demure."

"Riiight," said Bradshaw.

Haas took a swig from each of his beers and gestured toward Skaloniak with his chin. "Is he the dude from Spyteborne?"

"Yeah, Oliver Skaloniak."

"The one who sounds like he's vomiting?" Haas made some rhythmic vomiting sounds, then sang "Laaa, la laaa," in a warbly falsetto.

"No, that's the guy from Bescarred," said Bradshaw. "Spyteborne does more of a gurgle." He made some rhythmic gurgling noises, then sang "Laaa, la laaa," in a half-decent tenor.

"I'm still not sure which is which," said Haas.

"Who cares?" said Bradshaw. "End of the day, he's just another asshole who can't hold his liquor."

"It's a sad thing, what the demon drink can do to the weak-minded," said Johnny.

5. Up Uranus

"Well, that movie sucked donkey dick," said Haas. He popped a tiny quiche into his mouth and followed it with a slug of champagne.

They were hanging around at the reception after the premiere of the new Bruckheimer film, *Full Auto*, chugging the free booze and hobnobbing with Hollywood's Best and Brightest–or Youngest and Most Salable.

"Fuck you, I thought it was good," said Bradshaw. He put his empty glass down and looked around for a waiter with a tray. "Fights, hot women, exploding vehicles…that's what I paid my money for."

"You didn't pay a dime," said Johnny. One of Red Jack's songs had been used on the film's soundtrack, and they were attending the premiere as guests. Shitty film or not, it had been a pretty good payday for the band. Johnny had enjoyed hearing his own music in the cinema, too: Clarice had never allowed anybody to license any Bloody Waters' material for any purpose.

"Even the action scenes were lame," continued Haas. His tux looked clean and pressed, but he himself looked unshaven and bloodshot. "They tried to make it look like they got a fight choreographer from Hong Kong, but they always cut away before anybody could do anything cool. The stunts were fake, and the explosions were all CGI. 'No vehicles were harmed in the making of this picture.'"

"Stunts are, by definition, fake," said Bradshaw.

"You know what I mean. And the plot didn't make a lick of sense."

"Well, I ain't gonna argue that one. But you have to admit, Miriam Heathe was hot."

"I preferred the blonde. What's her name?"

"Johnny, what was the other chick's name?"

"Huh? What?" Johnny looked around, distracted.

"What was the other girl's name?"

"Look it up on IMDB," he said.

Someone was watching him. Johnny wasn't sure if his occult senses had picked up the vibe or if it was one of his regular five. Truth was, it was becoming difficult for him to tell the difference anymore. Whatever the case, someone or something was definitely scoping him out.

"Hey, you know where the men's room is?"

"On the left, past the bar," said Haas, gesturing with a handful of mini-quiches.

Johnny moved away.

"The acting was ass, too," Haas told Bradshaw. "Gerald Reilly is, like, the poor man's Paul Walker."

Johnny pushed through the crowd politely, moving around the bar and heading slowly for the men's. As he reached for the door, he glanced back over his shoulder.

A tousle-headed figure on the far side of the room froze, freaked out visibly, and tried to duck out of Johnny's line of sight.

Johnny folded his arms and watched his stalker flee through the thronging celebrities. Johnny followed him outside.

The stalker was standing out in front of the building, fidgeting while he waited for the valet to bring back his car. He was dressed in a vintage Ramones print T-shirt, checkered Extreme Sports pants, and flat-soled Converse skate shoes. He was also a demon. He did not notice Johnny moving up behind him.

"You're Matty Garton, right? From the Hoochstar Banditos?"

Garton jumped. "Jesus Christ!" He calmed himself with a few quick breaths. "You scared the shit out of me, dude."

"Sorry, pal. I'm Johnny Chernow."

Garton gave him a moist handshake. "From Bloody Waters," he said. "I seen you on Entertainment Tonight."

"Is that why you were following me around?"

"No way, dude," said Garton, the whites of his eyes showing. "That wasn't me."

"Who was it, then?" said Johnny. "C'mon, 'fess up. I know it was you, and I know what you are."

"Sure, man, whatever. I'm an ET from a flying fuckin' saucer."

"First Skaloniak, now you. I think you better tell me what's going on."

"They grow all the best weed up Uranus, did you know that?"

"Matty."

"That's why they do all that anal probing."

"Matty. Tell me what's going on."

"Nothing's going on."

"*Matthew.*"

"Are you going to tell Clarice?" Garton's voice cracked as he said her name.

"That depends on what *you* tell *me*."

"I...I gotta think about it."

"If you don't spill your guts, I'll go to Clarice myself."

"Oh!" said Garton. "Check it out. My car is here."

The valet driver pulled up in a beautiful, '60s-vintage Corvette.

"Matty."

Garton took the keys from the driver and slid behind the wheel. "Cool wheels, huh? Nice to meet you, Johnny."

"Matty."

Garton gunned it. The engine revved wildly as he shoved the stick into first and struggled with the clutch. He got it in gear and the 'vette lurched away.

Johnny sighed and went back into the reception.

"I don't care if she can act," Bradshaw was telling Haas. "She's got an ass you can crack walnuts on, a pair of double Ds, and she can sit on my face any time she—"

"Hey, look who's back."

"There's a queue for the men's room," said Johnny. "You wouldn't fucking believe it."

"Hollywood pussies, powdering their noses," said Bradshaw.

"You ain't wrong about that," said Johnny.

6. Rage Against the Answering Machine

"I don't care if it was based on a graphical fucking novel," said Bradshaw. "If it doesn't have dudes in tights fighting, it's not a comic book movie."

"You," said Haas, "are the kind of person that made a no-talent hack like Gerald Reilly into a multi-zillionaire."

They were sitting on the sofas in the hotel bar, drinking cocktails and eating buffalo wings while they waited for the air hockey table to free up.

"Are you two still having this argument?" asked Johnny.

Bradshaw ignored him. "We're gonna be zillionaires, too, if the album keeps selling."

"I spent long hours learning to play an instrument," said Haas. "I spent years humping my kit all over the fucking West Coast playing for peanuts and cat-piss. I *earned* my shit. All Reilly ever did was be born looking like a Greek god." He thought about that briefly. "Only more kind of…Aryan. Back me up, Johnny."

"You think you work harder than the guys who dig ditches by the side of the road?" said Johnny. "I know *I* don't."

"There's a matter of talent," huffed Haas.

"You don't earn talent, you're born with it," said Johnny. "Same as Gerald Reilly was born with looks."

"I got where I am on talent *and* hard work, man," said Haas.

"So did Gerald Reilly."

"Yeah, but that doesn't mean I have to like him."

A Souza march started to play, and they fell silent while Johnny checked his pockets until he located his cell phone. He flipped it open and raised it to his ear.

"Clarice," he said. "How are you?"

"Fine," said Clarice. "You?"

"Good, thanks," said Johnny, turning his back on Haas and Bradshaw and covering his open ear with his left hand. "What are you up to?"

"Business as usual."

Behind him, Haas made claws of his hands and shambled around stiff-legged, rolling his eyes and gnashing his teeth. Bradshaw made whipping motions, with sound effects to match.

"No," said Johnny, moving away from his bandmates. "It'd be business as usual if you were performing, interviewing, and recording while fighting off a bestiary of mythical creatures."

"Well, I guess it's a holiday, then."

"Glad things are going well."

"How about you? I'm reading good things about your shows."

"Thanks. We're getting pretty tight."

"You got that drummer under control, then?"

"Oh, yeah."

"No more surprise cowbell solos?"

"He has an odd sense of humor, that's all."

"That'd be great, if you were a comedy troupe."

"He's not gonna do it again unless we all agree to it beforehand."

"Democracy in action," said Clarice, making no attempt to conceal her contempt.

"Well," said Johnny, "Red Jack doesn't run like Bloody Waters. But everything's groovy now."

"No monster attacks on your end, then?"

"Let me get back to you on that one," he said. He settled into a quiet spot in the corner near the souvenir shop, behind the payphone. "It's still a bit early to tell."

Clarice sighed. "The shit we have to put up with... Hey, who the fuck is Oliver Skaloniak?"

"Skaloniak? He's the frontman from Spyteborne. I ran into him the other night."

"I thought I recognized his name."

"Why do you ask?"

"Well, he left an urgent message on your answering machine."

"You listened to my messages?"

"Hell, no. What do I care who calls you? I happened to be in your house when he called, and I heard the machine go on. Which wouldn't have happened, if you had voicemail like everyone else living in the 21st century."

"You were in my house?"

"I still am. I'm returning that old blues amp of yours."

"The one I found for sale in the window of that barbershop in Boro Park?"

"Yeah."

"It's a beauty, huh?" said Johnny. "I'd forgotten I even lent that to you."

"You didn't. I came in here on Saturday and took it."

"Well, I'm still on tour for five more weeks," said Johnny. "Not like I'm gonna miss it."

"Exactly," said Clarice. "Anyway, this brain surgeon wants you to call him back. He left a number."

"You write it down?"

Clarice read it to him. "He says to make sure that I don't find out he's talking to you."

"I'll be sure not to tell you."

"What's his beef with me?"

"He's afraid of you," said Johnny. "Like everyone else."

"Can't say I blame him."

"That's what I like about you."

"You ain't so bad yourself," said Clarice. "Anyway, I'm gonna let you go. I have work to do."

"Thanks for calling," said Johnny. "Try not to provoke any monsters or anything while I'm away, will you?"

"I'll try," said Clarice, "but I'm not making any promises."

Haas and Bradshaw had taken custody of the air hockey table while he was on the phone, and their boisterous competition had caused the remaining patrons to relocate to the far side of the bar.

Bradshaw scored a goal. Haas looked up at Johnny while he retrieved the puck.

"I see you survived ten minutes on the phone with the Bitch Queen of Rock."

"She's not as bad as you think," said Johnny.

"Yeah, right," said Haas.

7. Legacy

It was hot, cloudy, and oppressively muggy, but that wasn't keeping the tourists away from the Lincoln Memorial. Carts selling flags and militaria jostled for space beside those selling drinks and ice creams.

Skaloniak's companions were a diverse, if predictable array of singers: Matty Garton from the designer-punk Hoochstar Banditos; Mary-May Marjory, pop-country diva; Charles Summerland, frontman of the nuevo-emo band Self Inflicted; and boy-band survivor Jamison Achard. All of them were dressed in casual versions of their genre costumes. All of them were demons.

"Chernow," said Skaloniak.

"Hey, guys," said Johnny, thankful that none of them were quite famous enough to have attracted paparazzi stalkers. He, of course, had his own ways of eluding them. "Call me Johnny."

Garton shook his hand tentatively. "Hey again, Johnny."

"Uh, hi," said Summerland. His grip was weak.

"Bruh," said Achard with an easy, superficial smile. His grip was dry and faint.

Marjory looked at his hand as though it were some kind of reptile.

"So, we're all here in public," said Skaloniak. "Let's get on with it."

"Um, sure," said Johnny. "Get on with what?"

"Um, the parlaying, dude," said Garton.

"Why?" said Johnny. "Are we at war?"

"Your bitch killed our master," said Marjory, with the expected Southern lilt and an unexpectedly angry tone.

"The late Steven Heinman?"

"Yeah," said Skaloniak. "The Steven fuckin' Heinman. We're tired of waiting for Marnier to hunt the rest of us down, like Melanie Lonegan."

"You're afraid of Clarice, so you came after me?"

"It was a, uh, strategic decision," said Summerland, wiping his hands on the hem of his shirt.

"Shut the fuck up, Charles," said Achard.

"I see," said Johnny.

A flock of pigeons wheeled around the Washington Monument. Johnny shaded his eyes and watched them flap off in the direction of the White House. These five were weak; Johnny did not imagine that Heinman would have been capable of controlling anything important.

"So, what do you want from me, exactly?"

"We want you to call Marnier off," said Achard. "We want to be left alone."

They were minor celebrities on earth, but in Hell they were scum. Of course they wanted to stay.

"If she tries anythin'," said Marjory, "I will come for you, moment you leave her protection."

"We're in enough trouble already," said Summerland. He sniffed, took off his thick-framed glasses, and wiped the lenses on his cuff.

Out there in the daylight, each of the singers looked a little malformed. Skaloniak's skull was bumpier than it should have been. Something was wrong with Marjory's hands. Achard's tan did not look like it had come from a tanning bed any more than it had the sun. Summerland's shoulders seemed to have been assembled incorrectly. Garton's tattoos didn't look like they were rendered in ink.

Heinman's binding was unraveling. For the moment it had allowed the demons to slip their bindings, but sooner or later the spells would break down altogether and the five of them would be cast back into Hell. Being a rock star was a much better proposition than cleaning Satan's privy until the End of Days, Johnny guessed.

"I have a proposition."

"What?" said Achard.

"I'll rebind you."

"I'll return to Hell before I'll serve that Marnier bitch," said Marjory. "And I'll damn sure take you with me."

"Atta girl," said Johnny. "You're starting to sound just like a real demon."

Marjory lunged at him. Garton and Achard caught her arms and held her back—with some effort.

"No deal," said Skaloniak. "How can we trust her?"

"Clarice doesn't have to know about it."

They were taken aback. Marjory shook herself free and growled. "So we'll be serving...you?"

"Yep."

"Why should we?"

"You're between a rock and a hard place. If you walk away, you have the same problems as before. If you make a deal with me, they're solved, and you won't have to deal with *her*."

"What kind of service do you want from us?" said Garton.

"Good question." Johnny hadn't really thought about it. "For now, I want you to go on being musicians. I'll let you know if something comes up."

The five demons looked at one another uncertainly.

"That's the best deal any witch, priest, or sorcerer on the planet is gonna offer you."

The five of them nodded to one another.

"Okay, Chernow, you have a deal," said Skaloniak.

Since they had agreed to be bound, the spell-craft did not take Johnny very long. When it was done, Achard asked,

"What happens if Marnier finds out about this?"

"She'll kick my ass and send you five directly back to Hell."

They started to drift away, chewing that over.

"Oh, one last thing," Johnny said.

"Yeah?" said Skaloniak.

"If any of you need to get in touch with me, for any reason? Do *not* leave any message on my answering machine."

8. Wages of Sin

Jamison Achard tried to sing lower than his usual falsetto on his next record. His producer put his vocals to the usual unobtrusive, upbeat dance backing. It sounded like shit despite the wonders of Auto-Tune, and no one bought it.

Skaloniak's new album sounded like his previous efforts and sold about the same.

Charles Summerland disbanded Self Inflicted and took up whiskey, heroin, and sexual assault. Although he had been unable to record any new material due to lengthy periods in detox and lengthier courthouse appearances, his popularity grew wildly, and pundits predicted big sales for his new album—if he ever recorded one.

Seven new bands who sounded exactly like the Hoochstar Banditos broke, and their sales fell to one eighth of what they had been.

Mary-May Marjory wrote an album full of perverse and bizarre new songs, blasting her country-inflected vocals with a newfound operatic fury and adding distorted guitars and booming bass to the pedal steel and fiddles. Even Clarice was impressed. It bombed in the record stores.

Red Jack Arisen's *Lock and Load* was platinum by the time Clarice's new projects were ready, but that wasn't the big surprise. The big surprise was that Clarice's solo project was actually two projects.

9. Alone and Voidburned

Clarice's new record was called *Alone At Last*, and it was as solo as an album could be. There were no other musicians, no producers; every sound was 100% Clarice. Guitar, of course–eight of the sixteen tracks were single takes of Clarice playing unaccompanied. On the other tracks she also played keyboard or piano or drums or a variety of unusual stringed instruments. Some had overdubs and some had loops, but it was all her, from the ground up. There were vocals, too.

It was the first time she had recorded her voice on an album. It was more spoken word than singing, but there were a few songs in which it was hard to tell where the difference lay.

Clarice's second project was a 500-page hard science fiction novel called *Voidburn*, which was released simultaneously with *Alone At Last*. A hidden track on the album had Clarice reading a chapter from the novel with guitar accompaniment.

Album sales were hesitant, at first. The first single, "Burn for Me," got some radio play. It took about three weeks before people started to get it and sales picked up. The album went gold in the fourth week.

Voidburn was an instant bestseller. Clarice had a huge fan base, and they liked to read. She clipped the *New York Times's* review of it, though she'd never kept even the most glowing reviews written about anything she had recorded:

"Marnier's style is terse and evocative, her science is flawless, and her characterization is rock solid. A technological problem drives the story, but it's only on the last page that you realize that this is just as much a novel about people as it is about their ideas. Don't let the author's notoriety dissuade you from reading it: this is a damn fine book and it's well worth your time."

10. Burning Art

Clarice consented to an interview with *Rolling Stone* for the first time since *DIY Hemispherectomy*, on condition they printed it unedited.

RS: Clarice, you are famous for refusing to sing, but the first thing I noticed about *Alone At Last* is that you actually sing a bit on track thirteen, "Angel of Delight."

CM: I don't sing. I spoke the lyrics and then I vocoded them onto the melody.

RS: How did you record the melody?

CM: On guitar, of course.

RS: Wouldn't it have been easier to just sing it?

CM: I'm a guitarist.

RS: And an author, apparently. Tell me about *Voidburn*.

CM: It's a hard science fiction novel.

RS: Why did you decide to write a sci fi novel?

CM: Why does anyone ever write anything?

RS: So, um, what's the book about?

CM: Rockets and physics and astronauts and scientists. Did you actually read it?

RS: I did.

CM: You sound so proud of yourself.

RS: I liked it.

CM: I'm glad.

RS: Did you do a lot of research for the book? How did you find that?

CM: Yeah, I did some research. I do have a degree in Math.

RS: Oh, of course. Now, are these solo projects indicative of a rift between you and Bloody Waters?

CM: Absolutely not.

RS: Is this indicative of a rift between you and Johnny Chernow?

CM: I thought this interview was about my work, not my private life.

RS: It's about you.

CM: I'm going to walk out of here if you continue to be an asshole.

RS: Okay, okay.

CM: Okay.

RS: I believe that we can finally see you opening up to us in these new projects, especially *Alone At Last*.

CM: This project is a less intellectual enterprise than Bloody Waters.

RS: How do you mean?"

CM: Bloody Waters is about ideas. We want to make you think. *Alone At Last* is about pushing emotional buttons.

RS: So, this album is saying that Clarice Marnier has feelings, too?

CM: What's that supposed to mean?

RS: I just mean that, these songs are really affecting. "Dying for You," "He's My Baby," "Burn for Me." And they're told in your own voice. It seems really heartfelt.

CM: It's just good writing.

RS: You can't fake this depth of feeling.

CM: I can, and I did. It's called "art." Next topic.

RS: When are you expecting to go back into the studio with Bloody Waters again?

CM: Very soon.

RS: How about Heathens Burning?

CM: I have no plans to work with Heathens Burning and I never have.

The magazine ran the story as "Clarice Marnier: Alone and Voidburned." They put her on the cover, standing on a star field, her feet planted wide on the emptiness, a guitar slung low. A lengthy sidebar discussed Bloody Waters' "mentor-student relationship" with Heathens Burning, followed by her denial of the "Heathens Project."

11. Business as Usual

Clarice played solo gigs all over North America, in venues large and small. She fronted up to each gig completely alone. Johnny and Red Jack Arisen undertook a lightning tour of England, Western Europe, and Australasia. *Alone At Last* was platinum and still selling, and *Lock and Load* continued to pull in respectable figures.

On her way back from Eastern Europe, Beresford had gotten drunk with a jeans model named Jerome Kordely. They'd traded vodka shots all the way from London, passed out in each other's arms on the flight to LA, and had been shacked up ever since.

Enrique returned from the East Coast soon after with a plus-sized Irish-Italian mamacita named Maria O'Shaunessy, whom he installed in his San Francisco abode with all due haste.

Enrique and Beresford were rested and happy, and Clarice and Johnny were both enervated from their individual successes. It was time to get back to work.

— GODS AND MONSTERS —

1. Metal and Blues

When Bloody Waters' fifth album, *Metal and Blues*, went into production, the Devil rang Clarice to congratulate her.

It had taken just under a month to write and rehearse the material. It had taken five days in the studio to record it; just long enough to nail each song in a single, perfect take. Clarice and Connors took three weeks to mix and master it. And that was it.

Dominic Wainer was stunned. *Sister To Dragons* had taken more than a year to create, and despite its success, he had been dreading Bloody Waters' return to studio the way a smoker dreads lung cancer. Wainer was even more pleased once they let him listen to it.

"This is just *thrilling*," he said. "It's *revolutionary*."

"Tell it to the PR guys," Clarice replied.

Helen Ingpen was just as impressed. "This is good shit," she said. "It's raw, it's challenging, it's accessible, and it rewards every single repeat listen. You're going to do very well out of this."

"I'm delighted to have exceeded your expectations," Clarice replied.

"This album is going to make you the biggest rock band in the world," said the Devil. "I guarantee it."

It was four in the morning, and Clarice, wearing boxer shorts and a baggy old Lakers T-shirt, was watching TV, listening to the radio, and practicing the guitar.

"We already are."

"You're the biggest band there is now," said the Devil, "but that's not setting the bar very high. This album is going to put you up there with the Beatles, the Stones, Zeppelin, and Elvis."

"What do you care?"

"I thought we were friends," said the Devil.

"We were business partners," said Clarice. "Past tense."

"We still have a relationship."

"I paid you for services rendered; I don't owe you jack shit. Fuck off and leave me alone, I'm busy."

"You're up at four in the morning watching infomercials."

"You have five seconds to tell me what you want before I hang up."

"I want you to turn on Rex Munday."

It took Clarice a good few moments to reply. "Oh, *hell* no."

Munday was her only friend in the music industry, outside of the band. He was about the only other friend she had, period. He'd given her a start in the business when she was trying to break in. He'd come to her with the opportunity of a lifetime when she was at her lowest point.

"Are you trying to feed me straight lines?" said the Devil.

"I don't have to do anything for you anymore. We're square."

"You really think so?"

"I *know* so."

The Devil sighed. "You'd better wake Johnny up. He should hear this as well."

"What?"

"I'll call back in six minutes." The phone went dead.

"Fuck." Clarice threw the phone down on the sofa. She put down the guitar, turned off the TV and the radio, and stomped upstairs to the bedroom.

Clarice turned on the lights. "Johnny, wake the fuck up."

Johnny turned onto his back and sat up, blinking. He squinted at Clarice, nodded, and rolled out of bed. He followed her out into the living room in his shorts.

Clarice put the telephone on the coffee table and they stood over it until it rang. She put it on speaker. "Yeah?"

"Hey, Johnny, how you doing?" said the Devil.

"Good, thanks, and your own bad self?"

"Tell Johnny what it is you want from us," said Clarice, cutting off the small talk.

"I asked Clarice to turn on Rex Munday."

"I said no."

"Why are we even having this conversation?" said Johnny.

"Because, not to put too fine a point on it, you both owe me."

"We're square, dude." Johnny sounded a bit offended.

"The agreement was: a record deal for a soul, a spell for a favor."

"We gave you Hoben Rhys and Napster," said Clarice.

"You repaid the favor, but I'm afraid the first term has not been properly fulfilled."

Clarice looked at Johnny. He looked at her queasily.

"Explain," said Clarice.

"Rhys is a record executive," said the Devil. "Did I not mention that he might not have had a soul in the first place?"

"Of course he had a soul," said Clarice. "He was human, just like..." Johnny looked pale. "What?"

"Maybe Rhys had already sold it," said Johnny.

"You gotta be shitting me."

"Nope," said the Devil. "No shitting at all. Hoben Rhys had no soul for you to steal, because he had already sold it to me."

"You *thanked* us for when we handed it over to you."

"Good manners. You've never been given a dud gift before?"

"You lied to us."

"I've been known to do that."

"You could be lying now."

"I could be," said the Devil. "I'm not, but I could be, and there's nothing you can do about it."

Clarice stared at the phone. "Way I see it," she said, "we *might* still owe you a soul, but we don't owe you any courtesies. Why should I do your dirty work, if it's not going to ameliorate our debt?"

"I hate to threaten my friends, and everything," said the Devil, "but business is business. Scratch my back and I'll scratch yours. Do me the occasional service and I'll hold off on collecting what I'm owed while you sort out your options."

"You know what?" said Clarice. "Fuck you. You want your soul, come and get it."

"Aw, Clarice," said the Devil. "Can't you try to cooperate, just for once in your life?"

"No," said Clarice.

"Why not? Are you afraid that if you try it, you might like it?"

"I thought this was a business transaction," said Clarice. "If I wanted therapy I'd go to a professional."

"I'm cheaper than a shrink," said the Devil. "My advice to you is that, until you can pay up, you better do what I tell you."

"How you gonna make me?"

"I'm owed one soul and I have two debtors. Do I have to paint you a picture?"

Johnny stepped forward and took a breath.

She grabbed him by the shoulder before he could speak. "No, Johnny," she said. "No." She sighed and addressed the telephone: "I'll think about it, all right?"

"Atta girl."

"Oh, fuck you," replied Clarice.

2. Above the Vinculum

In the dead time between the completion of the album and the date it would hit the shelves, Ingpen came to Clarice with a new kind of proposition.

"I've been contacted by Vinculum Pictures," she said. "They want you to star in one of their movies."

"Acting," said Clarice.

"You up for it?"

"After we've toured the new album? Maybe."

"I wouldn't worry about the timing, if I were you," said Ingpen. "These Hollywood things take forever to put together."

"Fine."

"I'll set up a meeting for you."

Goldberg, the producer from Vinculum Pictures, was a portly, balding guy with the complexion of a well-scrubbed potato. He wore a Tom and Jerry tie and a suit tailored to minimize the protuberance of his belly. Clarice shook his hand across his big, cluttered desk and sat down in an overstuffed leather chair. His office walls were plastered with posters for some of the movies he had produced: romantic comedies, a rock'n'roll western, some old-school suspense flicks, and a couple of big-budget actioners.

"We've been waiting for you," said Goldberg, smiling broadly.

"I'm on time," said Clarice, without looking at her watch.

"No," said Goldberg, "we've been waiting for you to try break into the movies."

"We?"

"Hollywood."

"I'm not an actor."

"Nobody cares," said Goldberg. "How many A-list actresses can really act?"

"I'm not some brain-damaged starlet, either."

"We just want you to be yourself, in front of the cameras."

"Uh huh."

Goldberg pulled open a drawer and withdrew a sheaf of paper that was less than an inch thick and bound with a couple of brass brads. "I have a project that's just perfect for you."

"Hit me."

"It's about a tough young single mother—"

"Not interested."

"Uh, okay..." Goldberg licked his lips, opened the drawer again, and fished out another screenplay. "Maybe this one is better for you. It's about a rock band that—"

"Nope."

Goldberg frowned. Didn't she want to be on the big screen? Didn't she want to upgrade her status from Rock Star to Hollywood Heartthrob? He sighed and produced another screenplay. "Okay," he said. "Passionate young environmental activist takes on big business—"

"Not my kind of picture," said Clarice. "Tell you what: give me all the screenplays you got handy...other than the ones you just mentioned...and I'll pick one myself."

Clarice took them home in a box. A week later, she threw her selection down on his desk. "This one."

"Ah, yes," said Goldberg, flipping through it. "The caper picture." He flipped through it. "The assassin's young wife is a terrific choice. Start with a supporting role, build some chops—"

"I'm not anybody's wife," said Clarice. "I want to play the crime lord."

Goldberg's mouth snapped shut with an audible click. He put the screenplay down on his desk and straightened it so it was flush with the blotter. "Interesting," he said. "It'll need a bit of a rewrite..."

"I like it how it is."

"I think it could work," said Goldberg. "I'll speak to some people. It'll take some time."

"You got plenty of that," said Clarice. "Cuz right now, I'm pretty busy."

3. Apotheosis Now

The first *Metal and Blues* single, "Ice Shard Eyes," was launched a month ahead of the album. It received saturation play on the radio and TV and went to number one in its second week. The album debuted at number one.

A review in the *Washington Post* said:

Bloody Waters' follow up to the mega-selling *Sister to Dragons* is here sooner than expected, but more than welcome.

If its predecessor was a cluster bomb, this album is a nuclear strike. As suggested by its title, this album demonstrates an unquestionable mastery of everything from hill country blues to Scandinavian black metal, combining and then transcending these genres.

The first single, "Ice Shard Eyes," is a deceptively simple delta blues number that sets us up for the journey through the album's self-described continuum. The journey ends, literally, with "Evolve or Die." You really have to hear this one to believe it. It's not just a challenge issued to the music industry, but to humanity itself.

This album is the apotheosis of rock music, and I truly believe that it will remain so...until Bloody Waters cuts their next record.

"The album seems to be doing okay," said Ingpen, when Clarice looked up from the clipping.

"I guess so." Clarice dropped the review on Ingpen's desk and rose to inspect one of the other framed articles on the wall. It was a handbill from one of Ingpen's gigs as a solo artist. "I'm looking forward to taking it on tour."

"Which reminds me," said Ingpen. "We need to drop some of the dates."

Clarice spun around so fast that Ingpen had to lunge to prevent loose papers from fluttering off her desk. "Are you out of your fucking mind?"

"It clashes," said Ingpen. "You've been invited to headline the new Monsters of Rock tour."

"Monsters of Rock?"

"It's back. Bigger than ever."

Clarice's fists loosened. "Who's on it?"

"Everyone," said Ingpen. "The old guard, the new guard... everyone. And you're top of the bill."

"Are the DreadLords onboard?"

"Yes, indeed," said Ingpen. "You'll be able to party with your pal Munday from start to finish."

Clarice glared at her. Ingpen squared the stack of papers, seemingly oblivious.

"So, are you in?"

Clarice didn't answer.

"Well?"

"Yeah," said Clarice. "We're in."

4. Breaking Fast

There was a message on Clarice's voicemail when she got home: "Clarice, it's Rex. Hear you're gonna be headlining the Monsters this year. It's gonna be awesome. Call me back, it's been too long."

Clarice practiced the guitar for three hours. Then she cooked herself an elaborate dinner. Then she sat down to write some new songs. When the phone rang at 10:30, she knew who it was.

"Hey, Clarice. It's Rex."

"Hi, Rex."

"You get my message?"

"Yeah," said Clarice.

"You in LA?"

"Yep."

"I guess it's a little late for dinner, but I do want to catch up before the tour. Breakfast tomorrow?"

"Sure."

"Johnie's at eight okay?"

"See you there," said Clarice.

At eight in the a.m., Clarice and Rex were sitting in a red vinyl booth in the back corner of the diner. Sunlight streamed in the windows, bright enough to make both of them squint behind their sunglasses.

Clarice ordered pancakes. Munday ordered eggs and home fries.

"So," said Munday, "your first Monsters tour."

"Yeah," said Clarice. "First big festival in a long time. We've avoided them since *DIY*."

"Well, you're gonna have a blast," said Munday. "All the coolest bands in the world."

"I guess."

Munday looked at her over the tops of his shades, but a waitress in a white apron arrived with their meals before he could speak. "Here ya go!" she said. "Enjoy!"

Clarice shielded her eyes against all that brightness and nodded.

"Thanks," said Rex, smiling.

Clarice smeared butter on the top pancake on the stack. Poured syrup on it.

"Something's bugging you," observed Rex, loading up a forkful of egg. "C'mon, tell me."

"I have a bad feeling about this."

"That is so not the Clarice Marnier I know," said Rex. "Bad feeling, my ass."

"Thanks for the vote of confidence."

The waitress bounced back over to their table. "More coffee!" she told them as she topped up their cups.

Munday ate some of his breakfast thoughtfully. Clarice worked on her pancakes.

"It's the success, isn't it?" he said at last. "You're not the underdog anymore."

"You think I have performance anxiety?"

"No, never," he said. "I think you just need a new battle. You've won, and you don't know what to do with yourself anymore."

"Nah, I don't think so."

"You're afraid that's it, now. Nothing left but to get old and die."

"I dunno," said Clarice. She drained her coffee in five big gulps.

"Clarice, I've listened to *Metal and Blues,* and it says to me, 'there's always more.' Rock'n'roll can live forever and never grow old, but it has to evolve."

"Yeah," said Clarice. "Pretty much."

"You're the biggest star in the biggest band in the world. You're *the* rock star. You *are* Rock and Roll. Why should you be anything less than immortal, by your own definition?"

"No reason at all."

"You're a god, it's your rightful place…and you know it. So just relax and enjoy it!"

"I'm trying, Rex."

Rex grinned. "Atta girl."

Clarice smiled weakly. "Thanks, Rex."

The waitress loomed over the table again, almost luminous in the direct sunlight: a middle-aged angel in a starched cotton dress that was a size too small. She refilled their mugs and said, "Your meals okay?"

"Yes," said Clarice.

"Excellent, thanks," said Rex.

"Righty-oh!" The waitress receded back into the glare.

"Is it just me," said Rex, "Or is that waitress kind of... pathological?"

"If she doesn't fuck off she'll soon be pathologically dead."

"That's not very nice."

"Neither am I."

"I thought you were feeling better?"

"I am," said Clarice, "but filleting that woman would really make my day."

"After you've eaten her babies?"

"After I've fed them to her puppy dogs."

Rex laughed. "You're a true monster, Clarice," he said. "I'm proud to know you."

"Thanks, Rex," said Clarice, without a hint of a smile.

5. Bad Counsel

Bad Jack Saunders received Clarice and Johnny in the White Room of his Chicago mansion. A butler led them through the white doors, past a white-lacquered grand piano and a brace of white guitars, white cabinets and bookshelves, a white fireplace, and eventually to a sitting area where white leather couches were arranged around a white coffee table. Bad Jack shook their hands and directed them to sit.

He was wearing a white suit with a white shirt and white shoes. "Make yourselves at home," said the bluesman.

Johnny and Clarice sat down opposite him. The butler served them refreshments from a white tea service.

"What can I help you folks with?"

Johnny outlined the details of the deal they had struck with the Devil, although the bluesman already knew the basics. They told him about how one of the terms was unfilled, and how the Devil was now using it to extort additional service from them. The bluesman nodded and chuckled all the way through the story.

"Now he wants Clarice to turn against a good friend of hers," said Johnny, "which, obviously, she doesn't want to."

"It's a free world," said the bluesman. "Don't got to do anything you don't want to. But it's a rough world, too. Sometimes you just got to do what you got to do."

"I can't even work out *why* he wants me to end my association with Rex," said Clarice.

"Oh, he got a reason," said the bluesman. "Maybe just to see if he can get you to do it. But there's always a reason."

"So, what can we do about it?"

The bluesman looked up at her as though he was about to speak, but he just shrugged and smiled.

"You're gonna say something, spit it the fuck out," said Clarice. "I got no more time for your oracle bullshit."

The bluesman just kept smiling. "You think I'm the Magical Negro in your story," he said. "You think I'm here to give you the answers, and then die to save your skinny white ass?"

Johnny smiled good-naturedly. "Please," he said. "We're not asking you to put yourself in danger. We'd appreciate whatever help you can give us."

Bad Jack Saunders shook his head. "I'm a bluesman. I got some knowledge, I got some skill, but mainly what I am is a survivor."

"Pretty please," said Clarice.

"You can ask me as nice as you like," said the bluesman, "but there's nothing I can tell you. That Devil had his eye on you since the day you were born, and there ain't no one can help you with what you got coming."

6. Bloodymania

"Evolve or Die" followed "Ice Shard Eyes" to number one, and both songs occupied the top ten for months. They had high-rotation play across all the major American syndicates, and the video clips charted just as well.

The press started to call it "Bloodymania," at first with irony and then with alarm. De Villiers had to add four new guys to the security team. Johnny had to abandon his house in the Hollywood Hills. In LA, it became impossible for any of the band members to go anywhere without a swarm of paparazzi. They hid out in San Francisco as best they could until the tour began.

Peter Salzman agreed to rejoin them on the *Metal & Blues* tour, as well as for the Monsters of Rock, without a moment's hesitation. Every date was a sellout. Clarice would start each three-hour show with a song from her solo album before the rest of the band joined her on stage for the encore.

The *M&B* tour ended six days before Monsters of Rock was set to kick off. That was also the week that Clarice made the cover of *Time* magazine.

7. On My Side

Sonya Li, the journalist from *Time*, appeared backstage at the precise time that Ingpen had arranged. She was accompanied by a photographer, a lighting guy, and a makeup tech. Clarice waved away the makeup artist and told the photographer that he had five minutes. When his time was up, the photographer packed up his gear without complaint. They had been warned in advance about Clarice's lack of tolerance for dithering.

Clarice and Sonya sat alone in the green room, facing each other across a glass-topped coffee table.

"Bloody Waters is the biggest band in the world," said Li, without a hint of flattery in her voice. "And showing signs of becoming one of the biggest acts in history. Some journalists are crediting you with single-handedly saving the rock'n'roll genre."

"From what?"

"Irrelevance."

"Not true," said Clarice. "Rock was coming back sooner or later; the signs were all there."

"Signs?"

"Declining record sales, the fall of the divas..."

"Britney Spears covering Joan Jett."

"Exactly," said Clarice.

"Even Britney's people wanted rock back."

"They wanted to cash in on it, anyway. Nowadays you can become a pop star by winning a TV game show. That's all you need to know about how much value the public accords to what's now called 'pop music.'"

"So you don't think it was Bloody Waters that restored rock'n'roll's crown?"

"Maybe we hastened its return, but if it wasn't us, then someone else would've cycled it back into favor."

"Tell me about the cycle."

"It swings back and forth. Rock versus pop, art versus commerce."

"A pendulum."

"Yes. The last time the pendulum swung away from rock was when Kurt Cobain aced himself—"

"—due to those exact pressures—"

"—and that brought on a backlash against serious music. After that, less and less rock acts started making it big. Established bands started breaking up. The new breakout acts were girl groups, boy bands, pop princesses."

"Marketing forces split 'Pop' off from 'Rock.'"

"Right. Pop is now basically R&B, but with skinny white people singing lyrics written by other people, to music that's assembled by a producer," said Clarice. "It's 100% fake. The only remarkable thing about its decline is that it took such a long time for people to see through the forgery."

"Other 20th century musical forms have waned in popularity since their heyday, but rock always returns to reclaim its throne."

"I wouldn't say they 'waned,' I'd say they've been supplanted. Jazz, blues, and country all rolled up into rock."

"Why is that?"

"Rock music has power. Rock music is *about* power. That's why parents and church groups and governments and teachers are still afraid of it."

"Nobody was ever afraid of the Spice Girls."

"Exactly. Pop music is designed to sell hard and quick, then get out of the way for the next thing. It can't incite or empower or endure."

"And rock music can?"

"That's its nature. That's its mission: to inspire strong emotion. Rebellion. Subversion. Progress."

"All music is about emotion."

"Not technically true, but…okay, I'll run with it. Other kinds of music have been chiefly concerned with describing beauty. Maybe the beauty of sadness or whatever, but still…beauty."

"Go on."

"The blues was the first music to focus on the ugly. Rock took that ugliness and made it sexy and frightening."

"And pop music?"

"Pop music is a reversion back to the beauty; at its best, giving you a concentrated hit of joy. If there's an ugly side to it, it's concealed in the lyrics. It's meant to be slight. It's not meant to stay with you."

"Geddy Lee calls it 'empty calories.'"

"Right. Rock'n'roll will nourish your spirit. Pop will rot your teeth."

"Let's get back to the return of rock music."

"Okay, so, for a few years in the late nineties, rock was pretty hard up. Not a lot of new talent was breaking out–I sure as hell couldn't get a record deal."

"And then?"

"In, I guess, 1999, the band Korn had some mainstream success. That opened the gates for nu metal: big, tuned-down guitars; seven-strings, stacked and layered. Massive dynamic shifts. Growl vocals mixed with singing. Rapping, hip-hop beats; scratching and turntables. Korn wasn't the first band to go this way, but nu metal was the first time it became a coherent and commercial movement."

"So rock was already starting to come back."

"Right. Then we had neo grunge. Creed and Nickelback, playing kind of watered-down Seattle stuff. Staind."

"And the 'stoner rock' scene."

"Then the Beatlepunk set: the White Stripes, the Strokes, the Hives, the Vines. Suddenly there was a fairly diverse group of rock artists that were selling well, but it was difficult to call any of them 'pop' again."

"It's easier to sell something if it has its own category."

"Especially if it's a new category. 'Modern rock.'"

"Meaning, anything recent with guitars in it?"

"Right. It took less than a decade for Nirvana to become classic rock."

"I'm sure Kurt would have loved that."

"His own fault for skip-starting the next cycle."

"Bloody Waters started up during the bad years. You were never part of any scene or movement. The only other band we can really put you next to is Heathens Burning."

"I'd prefer it if you didn't."

"Why is that?"

"Nothing against the Heathens or anything, but we don't share a 'scene.' We've never recorded together, we've never jammed, we've never hung out...we played on the same stage a few times, but otherwise we have nothing to do with them."

"Really? That's not how it's presented in the press."

"Really. I gave them a support slot on the *Sister to Dragons* tour and now they're huge. That's the entire story."

"They look up to you. You are the Queen of Rock these days."

"Bitch Queen, is how I heard it."

"You're not renowned for being modest."

"I'm not being modest. I'm proud of what we've done, and I think there's a good reason we're the biggest dog in the yard."

"All right. Hyperbole aside, how would you assess your impact on the music world?"

"Hard to know. Hopefully we're pushing the genre to new places."

"Part of this resurgence is seeing a lot of old rock bands doing comeback tours, even recording new records."

"It's good to see," said Clarice. "Some of those bands are better than ever, and now they're being exposed to a new generation of fans. The kids who were listening to Limp Bizkit last year are wearing Led Zeppelin T-shirts today."

"You were a member of one of those veteran acts before you started Bloody Waters." From the way Sonya looked up at her, Clarice knew what was coming.

"The DreadLords."

"In fact, some say that your tenure there, however brief, was the apogee of that band's career."

"It was fun while it lasted."

"Why did they fire you?"

"My predecessor came back, and they didn't need two lead guitarists."

"Mondrian is a markedly smaller talent than you are."

"There were legal issues. It worked out for the best. I'm still good friends with Rex Munday."

"But it's been all downhill for the DreadLords ever since."

Clarice didn't have anything to say to that, so Li continued: "Were you a fan of theirs before you met them?"

"I knew some of their stuff."

"Would you have stayed if you hadn't been fired?"

"Probably not. It wasn't my band, you know?"

"Would it be fair to say that, unlike Bloody Waters, the DreadLords never, ever had anything new to say, or any new ways of saying it?"

"Fair to say?"

"They just copied what everybody else was doing as competently as they could. Yes or no?"

Clarice looked at Sonya long and hard. The reporter didn't flinch. All she had to do was lie.

Clarice wasn't afraid of the Devil. Let him come for her soul. Let him come for Johnny's. She wasn't afraid of him.

"Yes or no?" said Li.

Clarice wasn't afraid of the Devil, and she wanted to protect Rex. All she had to do was go on record saying something she didn't believe. Something that everybody would know was bullshit.

"Are you going to answer my question, Clarice?"

Clarice set her jaw. "The DreadLords were never greats," she said. "They never wanted to be. They just wanted to play some heavy shit, and they have accomplished that in spades. That's why they're still going strong."

"They haven't tried to change their sound since the eighties. Aside from the album you recorded with them, they've been repeating the same shtick for twenty years, with less conviction each time."

"They have their sound and people enjoy it."

"Do you regret your association with them?"

"Not a minute of it," said Clarice, quietly. "Rex Munday really is the nicest guy in the business. I learned a lot from being in his band."

"But being sacked from them was the best thing that ever happened to you."

"Yes."

And it was done.

8. All Apologies

Clarice rang up Rex as soon as the interview was over, but his answering machine said that he was on holiday "somewhere in or around the South Pacific." His management couldn't raise him, nor could his bandmates or his current girlfriend.

By the time he returned, the magazine was already on the shelves. *Time* hadn't needed to edit it very much to achieve the desired effect.

After that, Rex's answering machine went away, and his phone simply rang out. Soon after that the line was disconnected altogether.

The DreadLords' management announced that they had withdrawn from the Monsters of Rock tour.

9. Bumping Uglies

The Monsters of Rock tour was ugly from day one.

Although there was no open conflict between Bloody Waters and the DreadLords, the fractious rock community immediately polarized over the issue. Munday, being who he was, had friends in every band. Clarice, being who she was, did not. Bloody Waters were the bad guys, and everybody made sure they knew it.

None of the other acts confronted them directly, of course, but they avoided Bloody Waters like the bubonic plague. No one hung out with them before or after the shows. Nobody ate with them. The other bands insulted them on stage. Even their support staff—Salzman, the roadies, De Villiers's team—were ostracized. The entire crew was pissed off and demoralized and there wasn't anything Clarice could do about it. The Monsters organization was supposed to be managing everything, so Terry Wynokoff had remained at home. Clarice missed his influence badly.

None of this, however, did anything to diminish Bloody Waters' popularity with the crowds.

Ingpen called them up when she heard about their troubles. "You can drop out, you know. You wouldn't be the first."

"We're the headliners," said Clarice.

"Even so. The contracts allow for it with minimum penalties."

"No," said Clarice. "Fuck these assholes. I'm playing this tour to the end."

10. Unscripted Exit

Goldberg kept calling about the film he was putting together. When Clarice finally found time to speak to him, he gave her a lengthy status report. They were having difficulty finding a director and the script was in its fifth rewrite.

"I told you," said Clarice, "I liked the script the way it was."

"No film ever gets shot straight from the original screenplay," said Goldberg.

"Why leave the writing to some writer, huh?"

"We're trying to tweak it up so we can make best use of the available talent pool. It'd be a lot easier if you'd give us some feedback on the changes…"

"I *told* you, I liked it how it was."

"But—"

"I don't have time for this. Just do your job and let me do mine," said Clarice. "Right now, my job is touring with this band; yours is putting together a movie. Tell me when it's ready, and I'll show up on set and say my lines."

"Maybe you could take some time out from the tour—"

"I don't think you properly appreciate the situation," said Clarice. Her words were like marbles being dropped into a porcelain bowl. "I am a musician, not an actor. Music is my life; acting in your stupid film is a diversion."

"I don't understand," said Goldberg.

"I can't put it more plainly than that," said Clarice. "Wait. You know what? I can."

"Okay?"

"You ready?"

"Yes?"

"I'm out. Fuck you and your bullshit movie. Find a real actor. I have better things to do."

Clarice hung up.

11. Morning Glory Wine

The Ford Amphitheatre in Tampa, Florida was the last venue on the North American leg of the Monsters of Rock tour. The venue was packed and the audience was slavering by the time Bloody Waters hit the stage.

It had been a comparatively easy day for the band: the rest of the acts were too busy getting ready for the trip to Berlin to snarl and splutter at them. Bloody Waters were not leaving for a couple more days, however–they had a special gig to play before rejoining the tour in Germany.

The Tampa Theatre was a beautiful old building in the Florida Mediterranean style. Inside it was dark and quiet, encrusted with reliefs and gargoyles. It was a smaller venue than the band had played in a long time, barely 1400 seats.

The special show had been Salzman's idea: the theatre was home to a Mighty Wurlitzer with nearly a thousand pipes, and he was dying to lay his fingers on it. Scheduling was tight, but once Ingpen arranged a substantial donation to the theatre's refurbishment fund, the venue became free on the date they wanted for the show. It wasn't until they showed up for sound check that Clarice learned that the venue was rumored to be haunted.

Clarice accosted Johnny in the antechamber to the men's cloakroom. "Should I expect ghosts rattling the cymbals and goblins chewing on my cables?"

"Are you asking if this place is really haunted?"

"Given our history, I think it'd be prudent to find out."

"If you want to be prudent you should just cancel the show."

"I'm not feeling *that* prudent."

Clarice and Salzman rebuilt nearly two dozen Bloody Waters songs around the organ. Using some pedals and an EBow, Clarice rearranged some of the guitar leads to sound like strings or horns. Johnny abandoned his own guitar and belted out the vocals in an operatic baritone. Enrique tried to inflect the bass lines as a bassoon or tuba. Beresford was allowed to drum in her typical frenzy.

Suddenly free from the tensions of the touring festival, playing what they knew was to be a once-in-a-lifetime gig, the band was devastatingly, unrelentingly good. Omnipotent. They were gods on earth; beasts of the apocalypse; huge and terrifying creatures with hides of flame and bones of thunder. On that small stage, before that paltry audience, it felt like something new and massive had come into being. The ovation continued for a good five minutes after the band had left the building.

"So, Johnny," said Clarice, once they were settled into their limo and the vehicle was on its way, "you never answered my question."

Enrique and Beresford had emptied the ice in the champagne bucket out of a window and filled it with a fifth of bourbon and a quart of vodka. They were taking turns drinking from it while watching a baseball game on the in-car TV. De Villiers sat in the front with the driver. Salzman had remained behind at the theatre, deep in conversation with the conservators of the pipe organ. He would meet them at the hotel, he said.

"Was the theatre haunted?"

"Yeah," said Johnny, "I think so."

"Did you see anything?"

"It's not a sort of seeing, it's just...I don't know. It's a feeling." He shrugged. "Well, more than a feeling. It's a kind of knowledge. I *know* there were ghosts there, and I know they're pissed off."

"Why?" said Clarice. "They don't like rock music?"

"No," said Johnny. "They're pissed because the show's over and they know there's never going to be another like it."

12. Horse's Head

Clarice awoke to find her legs snarled in the bedding. Johnny was asleep beside her, lying on his chest with his face turned away. The pre-dawn light that filtered in around the drawn blinds was weak and diffuse. On her left, the glowing green digits on the TV clock showed 5:38 a.m. She had a headache.

She could smell blood.

Clarice kicked loose of the tangle of sheets and something heavy fell onto the floor. The distinctive *whiffle* of guitar strings slapping free snapped her fully awake. Naked, she slipped out of bed, blinking the sleep from her eyes. The carpet was wet beneath her feet.

The Motherfucker, which she had left secure in its case, lay at the foot of the bed. Someone had taken an axe to it.

The fretboard had been split into jagged chunks. Some of the tuning machines were still lodged in the head; others hung from what was left of the strings. Pickups dangled on coils of exposed wiring. Splinters of wood stuck out of the smashed-open body like the ribcage of some great jungle beast, slaughtered for the mystical properties of its liver or its heart.

"Clarice?" Johnny's voice was murky with sleep.

"Get up," said Clarice.

Johnny rolled his feet out of the bed and squinted at her. The carpet squelched beneath his toes.

"Clarice?" Johnny reached out and turned on the bedside lamp. He blinked and shaded his eyes for a moment. "Oh, Jesus."

Clarice's eyes were as clear as cut diamonds as they swept over the room. Latin had been scrawled all over the walls in what looked like brown ink. The drapes and every item of furniture in the room were just as sodden as the carpet.

Johnny squinted at the Latin. "An exorcism," he said. He raised one of his feet from the squelching carpet. "Holy water."

The police found nothing. No prints, no hairs, no fibers, nothing. The concierge did not remember anyone suspicious arriving the previous night. The hotel staff hadn't noticed anyone unusual wandering through the hotel late in the evening. The CCTV cameras were being serviced, so there was no video footage. All the police could establish was that someone had slipped sedatives into the drinks that the band had shared at the bar before going to bed.

The band moved to the Marriott while the investigation continued. De Villiers locked down their rooms. Nobody was allowed to eat from the restaurant or drink at the bar. The Monsters of Rock proceeded without them.

Clarice wasn't taking it very well.

Johnny stood in the kitchenette of Clarice's suite, pouring a bottle of pasta sauce into a saucepan. "Clarice," he said, "I know that guitar meant a lot to you, but... it was only a guitar."

She was sitting brooding in front of the TV set, practicing chromatic runs on her ancient Ibanez.

"Clarice?"

"Yeah, I know," said Clarice, without looking around. "It's only a fucking guitar."

The Motherfucker had been a low-end instrument. A cheap workhorse seven-string. The frets were soft, the sound from the bridge was muddy no matter what kind of pickup she put in it, and the instrument never held its tuning for long. It was a guitar, not a muse; not a sword from a stone, but it made her comfortable. Clarice just liked the feel of the instrument, the weight of it. It was familiar, like an old friend. Her oldest and most loyal friend.

Johnny dumped a packet of ravioli into a pot of boiling water and turned down the burner. "Who do you think is responsible?"

"If I knew, I'd have their head mounted on a stick."

"Well, in that case, I guess it's a good thing the cops are getting nowhere," said Johnny. He stirred the sauce with a tablespoon.

Clarice grunted a negative.

"It's either someone who knows about our first record deal or it's a religious group we've offended."

"Well, that narrows it down."

"Who else knows we're involved in black magic?"

"The DJ is dead," said Johnny, "and so is Steve Heinman."

"There were witnesses at the session with Melanie Lonegan," said Clarice. "Maybe one of Heinman's cronies?"

"Doubt it," said Johnny. He divided the pasta onto two plates.

"Heinman said he had five other demonic pop stars."

"I don't see demons sneaking in and splashing holy water on us."

"Fair point. Who else could it be?"

"Millner?"

Clarice snorted.

Johnny spooned some red sauce onto the steaming plates. "Maybe the DJ had an apprentice? A wife?"

"Maybe. Or maybe it's one of Big Nicky's boys?"

"They're good Catholics, I guess." Johnny offered her a plate. "Maybe the guitar was supposed to be a horse's head type deal."

"That was a movie," said Clarice. She set aside the guitar and accepted the plate.

"You don't think Big Nicky's boys go to the movies?"

"You seriously believe that the mafia arranged for a priest to break into our hotel room, destroy my favorite guitar, and write all over the walls with chicken blood?"

"Stranger things have happened," said Johnny.

"Well…"

"To us. Recently."

"I suppose."

"And *often*."

"All right, all right," said Clarice. "Let's go have a word with Big Nicky."

13. From Poland with Love

Clarice and Johnny joined Big Nicky in his business booth at the back of Tony's Taverna. The barman brought their drinks and retreated without saying a word.

"You heard what happened to us in Tampa?" Clarice asked, ignoring the bourbon Tony had left for her.

"Yes," said Big Nicky, "I heard."

"Well," said Clarice.

"Well."

"You know anything about it?"

"Officially? No."

"What does that mean?"

"It means I don't *know* anything. Florida's not my territory. But I have some ideas."

"Explain."

"Well, after your thing with the DJ, Little Nicky and his boys were unusually quiet. For several weeks. Then one day Little Nicky came to me and said, 'Big Nicky, I think Clarice Marnier is involved with black magic.'"

"What, did he see me with my head on backwards?"

"No, he didn't say anything like that."

"What did you say?"

"I said he was full of doo-doo, but I assured him that we were square with you and that he needn't worry about having to deal with you again."

"And that was the end of it?"

"Until a couple of weeks ago, yes."

"What happened?"

"We had some bigwigs come down from the Old Country. Little Nicky spent a lot of time with them. He's a full capo, you understand, but he insisted that he drive them everywhere himself. He made all of their arrangements; he was like their personal assistant. Nicky went everywhere with them."

"And?"

"Most of Nicky turned up in a dumpster last week, but there are still a few pieces missing."

"Jesus."

"The coroner says he was burned to death before he was butchered."

"Who are these bigwigs?"

"I can't name any names."

"Come on, Nicky. Give me something."

"Well," said Big Nicky, "I can't tell you who was here, but I did hear them saying they were going to report to someone they called the Polack."

14. Burning Heathens

Bloody Waters were delayed from rejoining the Monsters of Rock by more than a week and they missed all the dates in Germany and Belgium. As a direct result, attendance at the gigs was low and many patrons wanted their money refunded. Several of the other bands on the line-up tried to claim responsibility for driving Bloody Waters off the tour. When they rejoined the bill in Holland, attendance rose dramatically.

Hostility toward Bloody Waters continued to increase. De Villiers had them locked down whenever they weren't playing. Their audiences were rapturous, but the stress was starting to take a toll.

There were no incidents as the tour finished its European leg and went through to Brazil, South Africa, Japan, Korea, Hong Kong, and finally down to Australia for its final leg. The Brisbane and Sydney shows went without trouble, and there were only three dates left on the schedule after Melbourne.

The Melbourne show was staged on a tract of farmland an hour outside the city. It was April–autumn–and the skies were overcast, though it was mild and dry. Cars and buses had been trickling in from the metropolitan areas all day. Support staff searched every vehicle for concealed stashes of alcohol or weapons, but it was a huge site, and it was easy to sneak in from the adjoining properties.

Everything was running smoothly. Even the local security staff were cooperating with De Villiers' crew. The bands went on, played their sets, and went off, one after the other, without a hitch. Soon it was full dark, and only one more act remained before Bloody Waters was supposed to bring it home.

Shining his flashlight around, De Villiers led the band across the well-trodden and dusty area toward the backstage tents. He stopped and pointed it out when he saw movement in the big canvas maw of the Green Room.

The screen flapped open and five belligerent and very drunk musicians staggered out of the tent: Heathens Burning. A fit of giggling broke out amongst the Heathens when they spotted Bloody Waters standing in single file behind their security team.

"Hey, Marnier?" yelled the Heathens' frontman. Clarice couldn't remember his name.

"Yeah?"

"You suck!"

The rest of the Heathens laughed uproariously.

De Villiers's radio squawked. He moved off and gestured for one of the other guards—an enormous ex-Delta grunt who called himself Meataxe—to move up and take his position.

"You have a problem?" Clarice addressed the Heathens' frontman.

"Yeah," he said. "You."

"I'm real sorry to hear that."

"You *suck*, Marnier," said the frontman. "You fuckin' badmouth Rex Munday...you talk shit about *my* fuckin' band..."

"Rex had every right to be upset, and I'm sorry for that," said Clarice, "but *you* little pissants deserve a lot worse than what you got."

"You never helped no one," said the Heathens' guitarist.

"I put you on my stage," said Clarice. "How much more help do you want?"

De Villiers, done with his radio conversation, started to move around behind the Heathens. None of them appeared to have noticed him.

"Munday helped *you*," said the lead guitarist.

"Yeah," said Clarice, "and I gave the DreadLords their best-selling album ever in return, and *then* I helped out on his solo project. I don't owe shit to anyone. Not to Rex and certainly not to you."

"You owe your soul to the Devil," said the frontman.

Clarice stared at him.

Johnny put a hand on her shoulder. "Clarice. No."

Enrique and Beresford stood behind him, watching the action intently.

"Is there popcorn?" Beresford asked.

"No, just tequila."

Salzman stood off to one side, his hands in the pockets of his tuxedo, scrutinizing the darkening sky. It was still cloudy, but there was no sign of rain.

"Curse them, Johnny," said Clarice, without taking her eyes off the Heathens.

"Clarice, they're just a bunch of drunken idiots."

"I want to see them bleed."

"They don't know what they're saying. They're *really* not worth the trouble."

The Heathens stood there with their arms folded, sneering.

"What?" asked Clarice. "You want to rumble?"

Meataxe loomed at her side.

All four of them were suddenly fixated on the ground. Clarice waited a few moments.

"No? I didn't think so." She turned and walked in the direction of the warmup tent.

Meataxe blinked, shook his head, and rushed after her.

The Heathens muttered amongst themselves, glancing fearfully at Clarice's receding back. The lead guitarist turned abruptly–to find De Villiers standing right behind him. The guitarist screamed like a schoolgirl.

"You dumb fuck," said the frontman, turning on his bandmate.

"Douchebag," replied the guitarist.

The Heathens tromped away with their heads hanging low.

Grinning, De Villiers herded Bloody Waters after Clarice and Meataxe. "C'mon," he said. "We better catch up, she's already cross."

15. Meet 'n' Greet

A pair of enormous, black-suited security guards were standing outside the warmup tent when Clarice and Bloody Waters arrived. De Villiers demanded to see their IDs.

"VIP Protection Services," said one of them, raising the badge he had around his neck. He had his cinderblock-sized jaw so tightly clenched that Clarice expected it to squeak when he spoke. He had an American accent, so he wasn't a local rent-a-goon.

The badge was legit.

De Villiers asked, "Who're you minding?"

"The Hollywoods," said the second one. He wore his hair in a Marine-style crew cut that was almost a mohawk.

"The Hollywoods?"

Clarice scowled. "They're not supposed to be here."

"It's a surprise visit," said Cinderblock.

"They're about to get a big surprise, that's for goddamn sure," said Clarice, pushing through into the tent.

It was dim inside and smelled of dry earth and dusty tarpaulin. The mobile makeup mirrors at the back of the room were the only source of illumination under the wide expanse of canvas. Three people were waiting for them: Goldberg and a couple of other men whom she couldn't identify in the gloom.

"What the fuck are you doing here?" Clarice's voice was cold and flat.

"Thought I'd come by and give you the latest about the movie," said Goldberg.

"I told you I didn't want anything more to do with your goddamn movie."

"Got some surprise news." Goldberg came forward with a smile on his face. "In fact, I've got two surprises."

"You're gonna get a third and fourth surprise if you hold up my show," said Clarice. "My surprising foot lodged up your even-more-surprised ass."

Goldberg didn't falter. "A director and a leading man," he said. Goldberg's two companions moved forwards out of the shadows.

The director had graying, thinning hair and a beard. He wore squarish spectacles that had been fashionable in the '80s. The actor was bald and muscular, with a crooked nice-guy smile.

"I have to be on stage in thirty minutes."

"I just wanted to introduce you," said Goldberg. "To show you just how serious we are about this movie. These guys flew all the way out here just to meet you."

"Hey," said the actor, coming forward and extending his hand. "I'm—"

Clarice ignoring the proffered hand. "I know who you are," she said. "Nice to meet you. Now get the *fuck* out of my tent."

"I love it," said the director. "She's perfect."

"Get. The fuck. Out. Of. My. Tent."

"Perfect," the director repeated. "I'm dying to get her in front of the camera."

Goldberg grinned. "Well, soon as the new script comes in. I'm sure this will be the final draft…"

"OUT!" bellowed Clarice.

Goldberg looked at the director, who seemed taken aback. The actor made a "wow" shape with his mouth. They stared at Clarice, and she stared right back at them.

The actor led them out of the tent in silence, looking sheepish, but maintaining his sense of humor. The director looked stunned. Goldberg just looked scared.

When the flap closed behind them, Clarice turned to survey Bloody Waters.

"That was…" began Enrique.

"That was…" said Beresford.

"We've got twenty minutes to get ready. What the fuck are you standing around for?" said Clarice.

16. Onstage Presence

The crowd was mad to see Bloody Waters. Stark, raving, screaming, gibbering, climbing-the-walls, yanking-out-their-hair mad. Clarice strode onto the stage, the rest of the band following in lockstep.

Clarice and Johnny took their places at the front of the stage. Enrique found his spot between them. Beresford settled behind her drum kit.

Not bothering with any introductory remarks, Clarice swung her new, anonymous seven-string into position, raised her hands, and loosed a fast, thrashy riff that set the pit jumping. The crowd surged toward the stage.

Johnny and Enrique came in together, doubling and tripling Clarice's riff on different octaves. The riff split into a rising, two-guitar howl. Beresford came in, building a wall of noise and then smashing it down. Salzman beat the keys with both hands.

The audience pressed forward as its tide came all the way in: a solid, sweaty mass straining toward the band, never quite able to breach the security barriers and overrun the stage.

Johnny took the mic in both hands and sang about a very special girl in a voice that was high and delicate and loving. He sweetly threatened the audience on the girl's behalf, punctuating her heinous acts with rhythm slashes. Clarice splashed a jangling melody against the beat, as the special girl might've thrown a bucket of petrol onto a captive victim.

Beresford switched up to a brutalizing 5/4 beat, punching out a vicious combo on the snares. Her feet set the bass drum kicking and the hi-hat chattering. Johnny joined Clarice in a two-guitar call-and-response: he struck a sliding power-chord attack to which she responded with deadened strings, wahwah, and whammy. Salzman played a violent honky-tonk behind it all.

Johnny took up the second verse, his voice hoarsening with admiration and pain. He sang about the girl's deficit of ordinary emotions, about her wicked plans and hideous deeds. He screamed and barked how gorgeous were the atrocities she committed, how fine the horrors she wrought. His voice broke into an ululation that was at once a roar and a scream, exultant and agonized.

Clarice's solo was a teeth-aching melody constructed of pick scrapes and screeching harmonics. Her left hand clawed and scratched up and down the fretboard; her right hand gouged and hacked at the strings above the pickups. The solo rose like an electric saw, then collapsed into squelching feedback.

Johnny switched to a more labored version of the opening riff. He sang fuzzily of his undying devotion to the girl, his breath ragged and uneven. His guitar faltered and stopped, and his voice dropped to a repetitive murmur, chanting his pet name for the girl like a mantra or a prayer. Then a final choking sigh. He moved back from his mic and Clarice took her hands off her guitar.

"That was called 'Sick Bitch,'" she said. "I hope you fucking liked it."

The audience crushed itself against the stage, screaming and yelling, kicking and foaming.

"We've had a long fucking day and it's been a long fucking tour, so tonight we're gonna play the loudest, heaviest shit we got. I assume no one has a problem with that?"

Clarice listened to the crowd cheer. When they subsided, she raised her hands and glanced across at Johnny, but something on his face froze her. She frowned and turned around.

De Villiers was on the stage, coming toward her with his radio mic in his hand and tension on his face. He bent his head to her ear and said, "I've lost my perimeter."

Clarice nodded, her eyes on the crowd. They eyed her back. "And?"

"My whole team is offline."

"Are we under attack?"

"Ja, I think so."

"Can we play the gig?"

"I'd say yes…if I still had a perimeter. You have to get off the stage."

"Okay, prepare us a quick exit."

De Villiers went to it.

Clarice turned her back on the thrumming crowd and summoned the band to her. Johnny and Salzman came right over. Beresford stood up and walked around the drum kit, rolling her eyes, carrying her sticks. Enrique stubbed his foot on the side of an amplifier. He stumbled, caught himself, and limped up to the huddle.

A rumble came from the crowd. Small fistfights eddied in the loosening mosh-tide.

"Something's going down," said Clarice. "I want you off the stage, right now. All of you."

Beresford opened her mouth.

"No questions–go. De Villiers is waiting."

Salzman shrugged and made for the wings. Johnny shepherded the drummer and bassist after him.

Clarice went back to her microphone, slinging her seven-string behind her. "There's been a serious security breach," Clarice told the audience. "Show's over. Get yourselves out of here right now."

Some laughter, some boos.

"This is not a joke. Go."

Catcalls followed her as she stalked off the stage.

If this was a false alarm—if this was some kind of trick—then all of her bloody-mindedness had been for nothing. All of the pain and strife of this monstrous festival had been a waste. She felt like an idiot. Two dates to go and she'd just ensured that the tour was over for her. But the last time someone had disrupted one of their shows they had almost died.

The crowd stopped grinding against the stage. Angry muttering spread up the hillsides. People at the fringes of the crowd started to drift away, glancing back over their shoulders in case Bloody Waters returned to encore their single song.

Clarice caught up to the band backstage.

"I can't get the bus through," said De Villiers. "Too much foot traffic. We have to hole up 'til we know what's happened."

"Where?" asked Clarice.

"The rehearsal tent is empty," said Johnny.

"A tent isn't going to keep any bad guys out for very long."

"It's better than being out in the open," said De Villiers.

"All right," said Clarice.

De Villiers led them through the darkened backstage area, down the wobbly metal steps, and across the courtyard that lay between the stage and the rehearsal tent. There was no one around, not even lingering roadies. There were no signs that anybody had raised any kind of alarm.

Jarhead and Cinderblock were still guarding the rehearsal tent.

"Something's going on," De Villiers told them. "I've lost contact with my team. Cops are on their way. Keep your eyes open and do what you have to for your people."

"Right," said Jarhead.

"Sure," said Cinderblock.

They pushed through into the tent. Inside it was brighter this time. All of the interior lights were on and there were many more people present. Five men in black suits, armed with MAC 10s and automatic pistols, stood around the perimeter. The actor, the director, and the producer had been bound and gagged and were lying in the dirt.

De Villiers' sidearm appeared in his hand, but there were too many guns already out for him to be able do anything. Mohawk and Cinderblock followed them into the tent, blocking their escape.

"Put the pistol down," said a smooth, mature voice from the back of the room. The speaker was a whip-thin figure standing with his back to them. He was dressed all in black.

"Oh, Christ," said Clarice. "Are you supposed to be the villain?"

"The pistol, please." The speaker spoke precise English with an Eastern European accent.

The goons pointed their machine guns at De Villiers encouragingly. He slowly bent to put the weapon on the floor.

"Kick it away."

De Villiers kicked it away.

The figure in black turned and came toward them slowly, taking his time. His hair was white, neatly clipped, receding at the temples. His olive-skinned face was craggy and lined and tight. Clarice estimated that he was in his sixties, though he carried himself with the ease of a much younger man. He wore a priest's collar, and his shirtsleeves were rolled up to his elbows.

"I am Padre-Don Alfredo Nauk," said the priest. "I am here to purge you of your demonic infestation and send you on to Salvation."

"I knew it," said Clarice. "The villain."

"Padre-Don?" said Johnny. "As in, a priest...and...a mob boss?"

"Formally, I am an Archbishop," said Nauk, "but I prefer not to stand on ceremony."

"An Archbishop in the Cosa Nostra?"

"I run the Vatican mafia."

"What kind of gangster name is 'Nauk,' anyway?" said Clarice.

"Polish," said Johnny.

"I thought you had to be Italian to be in the Mafia," said Clarice.

"The last Pope was a Pole," said Nauk.

"Oooookaay," said Johnny. "I guess that makes some kind of sense."

"So, um, to what do we owe the pleasure of your company?" asked Clarice.

"I am here to purge you," said Nauk. "And to kill you."

"What did we ever do to you?"

"Little Nicholas Cabreze told some of my lieutenants about your adventures," said Nauk. He did not raise his voice, but there was fury in his eyes. "When I learned that you had involved my orga-nization...my *family*...in your deviltry, it was clear that something had to be done."

"And you had to wait until we got here?" said Clarice. "You had plenty of better opportunities to take us out in the States. Hell, you had someone in our hotel room while we were drugged asleep..."

"Politics," said Nauk. "Territory is very important to the Church and to the Family. Even I must be careful about where I choose to operate."

De Villiers stood ahead of the group, relaxed but alert. Salzman stood with his hands in his pockets, chewing his lower lip. Enrique and Beresford were looking around the tent, examining the gunmen, the fixtures, and the bound captives from Tinseltown.

"Is it worse than the axe man, do you think?" asked the bass player.

"Yes," said Beresford.

"That's fascinating, and everything," said Clarice, "but, if you don't mind, could you hurry up and start the exorcism? I'm getting bored."

"I am not going to exorcise you," said Nauk.

"Oh?" said Johnny. "Then who?"

"He probably has, I dunno...Torquemada, resurrected from the grave," said Clarice. "Ten foot tall and farting fire. It's bound to be something like that."

"I do not work with *Spaniards*," sneered Nauk. "I will call upon the Host itself to cast the rites."

"The Host? As in...angels?" asked Johnny.

"Angels," said Nauk. "They will come at my summons. They will do my bidding."

Clarice turned to Johnny. "Angels can be summoned?"

"Just the same as demons, I guess. I've seen the incantations." He looked across at Nauk. "What are you using, the *Clavis Salomonis*?"

"Indeed," said Nauk.

"I thought you had to be a Jew in order to use the Key of Solomon."

"My mother is Jewish," said Nauk. "According to Jewish doctrine, that makes me a Jew, too."

"Wait, wait, wait," said Clarice. "Slow down a second, I want to make sure I understand this right. You're a Polish Jewish Catholic Archbishop Mafia don?"

"No," said Nauk, unsmiling. "I am *the* Polish Jewish Catholic Archbishop Mafia don."

"You're a one of a kind, all right," said Clarice. She looked at Johnny. "What are the chances some IRA ninjas will show up and rescue us?"

"Not good," said Johnny.

"I do not concern myself with the activities of *Irishmen*," said Nauk.

"No," said Clarice, "I guess you wouldn't." She shook her head and sighed. "Johnny, why is it that we're beset by these goddamn morons everywhere we go?"

"I will kindly ask you not to blaspheme," said Nauk.

"Oh, excuse me," said Clarice. "I'll just stand quietly in the corner and masturbate with a crucifix."

Nauk put his hands together and bowed his head. He spoke briefly in Latin, and then in Hebrew. A booming basso voice doubled his words, and a soprano voice tripled them. Slowly the additional voices grew louder than the priest's own. The basso deepened until it throbbed in the cavities in Clarice's skull; the soprano trilled so high that the light bulbs shattered. The room did not stay dark for long.

Light flared so brightly that Clarice had to cover her eyes. When she blinked her eyes open, she found that seven angels stood behind Nauk.

The angels stood at attention: shoulders back, chins up, feet wide, hands clasped over the pommels of their burning swords. Seven identical statues cast from white light.

"Good Lord," said Salzman.

"Amen," said Nauk.

Clarice shaded her eyes with her hands. Each angel was about seven feet tall, with hair that blazed with blue fire. They were dressed in white jeans, white boots, and white T-shirts. Their furled wings were feathered with slivers of flawless crystal. Meeting an angel's gaze was like staring into the sun.

"Would it be rude of me to ask you to dim the lights?" asked Clarice. "I left my sunglasses on the bus."

Nauk came forward, flanked by two of the angels. The priest's black garments gave him some contrast, but it was still difficult to see him with the ambient light so intense.

"This will be unpleasant," he said. "But when it is done, you will be free of the demonic infestation that has corrupted your lives."

"I got to hand it to you–this is a new one," said Clarice. "Killer fucking angels. Who would have thought?"

"Still you blaspheme, beneath the gaze of the Lord's most holy?"

"I'm badass."

Nauk made a peremptory gesture. "Exorcise them."

Five angels flowed toward them, one for each musician. They moved with a frictionless grace that nothing human, nothing *material* could manage. Shimmering chords from an instrument that sounded like both a pipe organ and a harp rippled from their unfurling wings. The roar of their flaming swords filled out the unearthly music with a thick, staticky bass.

De Villiers threw himself in front of Clarice. An angel struck out casually with the flat of its blade and sent him crashing across the room. De Villiers slammed into one of the dressing tables and slumped beneath it, his shirt on fire, covered in shards of broken glass and splinters of wood.

Clarice raised her fists and faced the oncoming angels. Johnny bowed his head and started muttering under his breath. Beresford gnashed her teeth. Enrique backed away, raising his hands and pleading for mercy. Salzman shut his eyes and sighed.

"Now," said Nauk.

In perfect synchrony the angels struck out with their burning swords. An ethereal blade entered Clarice's head above her left ear and emerged below her right.

The five angels stepped away from the musicians and lowered their swords.

Clarice blinked.

Johnny looked up, frowning.

Enrique stood there with his mouth open.

Beresford was breathing hard, angrier and more terrified than before the attack.

Salzman looked up, across, down, like a bird that had just lit on the ground.

The angel that had struck Clarice turned to Nauk. "There was no infestation." It spoke with the voice of a children's choir backed by a host of gospel singers.

Nauk frowned. "I know they have trafficked with demons," he said. "How can this be?"

"Use your brain, asshole," said Clarice.

"You have bargained with the Prince of Lies," said Nauk. "His price is always the same."

"There's still some contention over what we owe him," said Clarice, "but your angel friends told you the truth."

"Well," said Nauk, "Possessed or not, you are still sinners."

"And proud of it."

"You have sinned against the Lord. You have sinned against his Host. You have sinned against your fellow man. And you have sinned against my Family.

"For your sins, the Soldiers of the Lord will strike you down with the Holiest of Fires."

"Well," said Clarice, "if the exorcism they just performed is anything to go by, I don't think I have very much to worry about."

Nauk smiled. "Last time, they struck at whatever demonic infestations you might have harbored. This time, they will smite your quivering mortal flesh."

"Quivering mortal flesh!" howled Beresford. "This dude fucking *rules*."

Nauk continued to smile. "You will burn forever," he said, "unless your master works an anti-miracle on your behalf."

"Funny you say that," said Clarice, turning to Johnny. "Can you frog this guy?"

"With two angels guarding him and five more breathing down my neck?"

"Can you summon something?"

"Something that can outgun seven angels?"

"How about some *one*?"

Johnny sighed. "Without wards and a circle?"

"He already proved to us that he can't be contained by them."

"I still need something to summon him *into*," said Johnny. "Some framework for the spell."

"Make something up," demanded Clarice. "Sing a Black Sabbath song backwards. Send a text message. Whistle Dixie. Whatever it takes."

Johnny took a deep breath, rubbed his nose, and looked down between his feet. "Dude?" he said. "Dude, a bit of help here?"

Nauk smiled slowly. "Your dark master will not attend to you now. But fear not–your festering souls will be dispatched to him directly."

"Man iron am I?" said Johnny, hopefully.

"Buddy," said Clarice, "if there's one thing you can rely on the Devil for, it's..."

The tent flap swung open and something dark blew inside.

"...a dramatic entrance."

The black mist coalesced into the shape of a man. He was wearing jeans and a leather jacket, running shoes, and a T-shirt that said "The Tea Party: Transmission Tour 1998." His head was a blurry mass that looked like a giant's fingerprint. The Devil sauntered into the room and spread his hands in a gesture that invited applause. "Hey there."

In the Devil's presence, the angels dimmed until they were little brighter than a battery of matching desk lamps. Sudden shadows flickered and shifted in the light of their burning swords. When Nauk took a step back, his pair of guardian angels moved with him.

"So you've come to aid your minions," said Nauk, cool as a refrigerated cucumber. "But what will they give you in return? If you let me kill them, their souls are yours."

"Has it occurred to you that these fine representatives of the popular music industry might be worth more to me alive than dead?"

"These creatures have no worth."

"Not in your eyes," said the Devil.

"Not in mine, nor in the eyes of the Lord."

The Devil sighed. "That's the problem with you religious types," he said. "Always presuming to impose your point of view on someone else. That's why so many of you end up coming to my barbecue." He turned to the angels. "And as for you boys and girls..."

The angels stood their ground stoically.

"You're pretty fucking stupid, getting involved in this."

"Your tongue is as filthy as your deeds, Lightbringer," said the first among the angels.

"You *know* I'm right," said the Devil. "Soldiers of the Righteous, taking orders from a criminal? This man is a murderer and a thief, and that's the least of it."

"He is a holy man, Lightbringer."

"A high rank in a human church does not make a man holy," said the Devil. "You're only taking his orders because you're afraid that your refusal will be construed as disobedience, and disobedience will see you Fall."

"Could it be, Lightbringer, that you yourself are beginning to believe the lies you were cast out of heaven for?"

"No, no, no, no, no," said the Devil. "That's not true, and it never was."

"What is true, Lord of Lies?"

"The truth is that *I* am the one who determines who has been good and who has been bad. I am the one who causes men to sin and angels to fall.

"I, Satan. I, Lucifer. I, the Devil. And no other."

"You have altogether too high an opinion of yourself, Lightbringer," said the first among the angels. "You are the strongest among the fallen, but that's all that you are."

"Uh-uh," said the Devil. "I am not, and never was, one of the Fallen. I was there before any of your brethren ever Fell. I was there before any of you were created. I am not one of you, and I never have been."

"What are you, then? Do you claim to be the Creator's equal?"

"I am the Devil, and I am nobody's equal. I am the one who brought the light, and I am the one who will take it away." He set his jaw. "Now, fall."

The angels liquefied. Their glowing skins splashed off like candles before a flamethrower. Their wings shattered; crystal feathers cracking apart with a harsh, unmusical tinkling. Their burning swords guttered and blew out. Their garments flaked to ash and blew away in the gusting breeze.

"That was bad ass," said Beresford.

The Devil raised one of his hands, palm upwards, and the seven gangsters raised their MAC 10s to shoulder height. He made a rotating gesture and the each of the gangsters turned to their left and took aim. As the Devil closed his fist, each one squeezed off a burst. The seven gangsters fell.

The Devil turned to Nauk and cocked his head. "Well, now."

The priest stared at him, white-faced.

"I'm afraid your demise isn't going to have quite so many pyro effects," said the Devil, "but I promise you it will be extremely painful."

Nauk stood his ground, only a twitch in his shoulders suggesting a firing flight reflex. He popped a switchblade and drew himself up into a knife-fighter's crouch, drawing his free hand to his chest and turning to present the Devil with his profile. He uttered a string of prayers and spells in Latin, Hebrew, and Greek.

The Devil caught Nauk's knife hand and twisted it until the bones splintered and the blade fell from his pulped fingers. A harsh sound escaped through his bared teeth. The Devil used the shattered hand to guide the priest forward and around, graceful as a ballroom dancer. He caught one of Nauk's knees, wrapped his free hand around his face, lifted him into the air, and broke the priest's back across his knee.

The Devil rolled Nauk's corpse off his leg and said, "Okay, then."

Enrique and Beresford stared, open-mouthed. Salzman clasped his hands in front of him and studied the far wall of the tent. Johnny folded his arms and tried to look nonchalant.

"I suppose you're expecting me to say thank you," said Clarice.

"I know better than that," replied the Devil, "but don't say I never did nothin' for ya."

"And now?"

"Now the police are here," he replied. Sirens warbled far in the distance. "I think it's time I headed out." The breeze stirred once more, and the Devil started to discorporate.

"See you later," said Clarice.

"I'll call you," said the Devil. His voice lingered long after his shape had blown away into shadow.

— SYMPATHY FOR THE DEVIL —

1. Cracking Up

The remaining dates of the Monsters of Rock tour were cancelled.

The Victoria Police found eight bodies, thirty-four firearms in various sizes and calibers, three of the biggest names in Hollywood, the most popular rock band in the world, and a Catholic Archbishop all together in the rehearsal tent. There was no way to keep the incident out of the press.

The official story went like this:

After Clarice had evicted them from her tent, the Hollywoods had gone to hang out in the green room. By the time Bloody Waters had taken the stage, the Hollywoods had given up trying to make conversation with the drunken and disrespectful musicians in the green Room and returned to the rehearsal tent. Nauk's men, who had infiltrated their security team, had then taken them captive.

When the band had returned to the tent, Nauk had declared his intention to murder them for crimes unknown, whereupon some kind of power surge had then caused the lights to go out. In the confusion, the mobsters had opened fire and killed each other. Miraculously, nobody else had been harmed.

"Sounds like a shithouse action movie," one Senior Detective observed.

The lawyers were not able to hush the story up completely, but there was enough money involved to convince the forensics team to overlook certain odd facts: the scorch-marks on the ground, the peculiar arrangement of the dead mobsters. The fact that, while most of the dead had been slain by gunshots, something had practically broken Nauk in half. De Villiers and Bloody Waters were remanded in custody, but no charges were laid against them. Their passports were confiscated, but they were cut loose within a day.

After a cursory questioning the other bands on the tour were allowed to go home – except for Heathens Burning. The police found copious quantities of marijuana amongst their gear and they, too, were taken into custody. In an interview with *The Age*, Clarice said she was surprised it wasn't crack.

Eventually, both bands were released. When they found themselves on the same flight back to the LA, the Heathens asked for their seats to be downgraded to business class. Business class, however, was full, so Heathens Burning flew back in coach.

When asked for comment about this in Los Angeles International Airport, Clarice said, "I didn't even know they were on the plane."

2. The Good, the Bad and the Ugly

Helen Ingpen wasn't very pleased about any of it. "Would someone like to explain to me *precisely* why this band is always in so much trouble?"

"Drugs and alcohol?" hazarded Beresford, wearing the best look of wide-eyed innocence she could muster.

"Most rock stars are content with that. Sex and drugs and booze. Sometimes, they challenge their rivals to fistfights they know will never take place. They go into rehab, they lose a sex tape, or they contract a venereal disease. But you guys? You guys have a body count."

"That's 'cause we the baddest?" said Enrique.

"Enrique, even 'bad' rock musicians do not have managers that disappear off the face of the earth. They do not evacuate their concerts and wander off into a mob war."

"We—"

"—have a lot more to answer for than just that. I'm still waiting to find out why a man with an axe hacked up your show in Boston a couple years back."

"That was kind of a practical joke," began Johnny.

"Oh, spare me."

"We've had some troubles," said Clarice. "Big deal."

"There's troubles, and then there are troubles," said Ingpen. "Did I mention the apparent gangland hit on that DJ you fired from mixing *Sister to Dragons*? Or, going back a bit further, the reported kidnapping Clarice filed for *you*, Enrique?"

Enrique shrugged and shuffled his feet.

"I've been studying up while you boys and girls were away, and it seems like there's an awful lot you haven't bothered to tell me."

"Did you know I was blacklisted in the biz before we signed with NimHyde records?" asked Clarice.

"I heard rumors, yeah. How did that happen?"

"I had a difference of opinion with an A&R asshole named Hoben Rhys," said Clarice. "He took it personally."

"You crossed *Hoben Rhys*?"

"What's your point? Are you tendering your resignation?"

"No," said Ingpen, "but I want you to know that I know you're involved in some real bad juju, and I don't like it."

"Do you want to know what's going on? For real and for true?"

"Absolutely not," said Ingpen. "Whatever it is, I doubt I can help you deal with it, and I don't want any part of it."

"Okay," said Clarice. "Consider us warned."

"No," said Ingpen. "I haven't warned you yet…but I'm warning you *now*. Stay out of trouble. If you assholes get me killed, I swear I will come back and haunt you."

None of them ventured a rejoinder.

3. Leather Pants

"Okay, you know a lot more about the band than most other people do," said Clarice. She and Johnny had taken Salzman to dinner at Spago's. They were sipping red wine while they waited for the main course.

"I expect so," replied Salzman.

"It's kind of awkward for us," said Clarice. "We didn't even let Enrique and Beresford in on it, until we had to."

"You may rely on my discretion."

"No," said Clarice. "This calls for more than discretion."

"Are you threatening me?"

"No," said Clarice, "because I like you and I respect you. So I'm offering you a full membership of Bloody Waters and a million dollars' worth of signing bonus."

Salzman nodded his head slowly. "Go on."

"But it's in for a penny, in for a pound," said Clarice. "If you agree, you're with us all the way. You get the same cut as everybody else. You get equal say in the writing of new material…"

"Which means, everyone is equally subordinate to Clarice," interjected Johnny. She did not dispute him.

"Understood," said Salzman.

"You get to share the money and the glory," said Clarice. "But whatever trouble happens, whatever shit goes down, you get a share in that, too. No whining, no tattling...or you're answerable to *me*."

"Okay."

"Johnny and De Villiers and I usually try to deal with whatever happens ourselves, but sometimes it spills over and affects the rest of the band," said Clarice. "That's going to continue to happen, whether we like it or not."

"I see."

"It's not a great offer, but it's the best I can do. What do you think?"

"Let me explain something to you, Clarice," said Salzman, considering his words carefully. "I've spent my life learning to play keyboard instruments. All my school years, all through college. I won my wife from her high school sweetheart at an orchestra rehearsal, and I lost her to a cellist twenty-five years my senior at a gala performance. I have spent my life playing other people's music in dusty rooms or improvising in smoky clubs. But now..."

They waited for him to collect his thoughts.

"But now, with Bloody Waters...for the first time in my life I feel like my work has really moved people."

"There's *nothing* like being a rock star," said Clarice.

"Of course, there are the...adventures...to consider," said Salzman. "I've been held prisoner by gangsters. I've seen angels die and demons run amok. I've been chased off the stage by a giant with an axe. How can I possibly go back to...to normalcy? Why would I even want to?"

"So, you're in?"

"Adventure, excitement, fabulous wealth, and a creative role in the most successful musical act in the world. How could I refuse?"

"Glad to have you aboard," said Clarice.

"Just so you know," said Salzman, smiling crookedly, "I've already bought myself a pair of leather pants."

4. The Strat in the Hat

Billy put the guitar case on the ground and knocked on the door of Clarice's apartment. After a while, he knocked again.

She wasn't in. Fine. Good, actually. He could go home without facing the Wrath of the Dragon. Wonderful.

Billy sighed and bent to pick up the case. When he straightened up, the door was open and Clarice was standing in front of it.

She was wearing a black tank top and blue jeans. Her feet were bare. A steel thumb-pick glinted on her right hand. "Billy."

"I...I have your, uh, your new axe," said Billy.

"Which one?"

"The '79 Strat you bought on eBay?"

"Oh, yeah," said Clarice. "How is it?"

"Well, the finish is scratched to shit, but I adjusted the neck and replaced the frets, and the sound is fucking beautiful."

Clarice took the case from him, opened it over her knee, and took out the old Stratocaster. It was covered in scratches, as he'd warned. The virgin white pickguard was plainly a recent replacement.

She handed him back the new-smelling case. Took the instrument in both hands. Looked down the neck, examined the machine heads, turned it over and inspected the back. Squinted at the pickups. Twirled the knobs, yanked on the whammy bar. Propped it up on one knee and ripped through a couple of scales.

"Well," she said, her attention returning to Billy.

"Uh, well?"

"Well, it looks like crap, but it plays like silk."

"It's a nice instrument," said Billy.

"It's almost as ugly as my old guitar," said Clarice. That was the way she now referred to The Motherfucker, although she had many old guitars. "If it sounds as good as you say, it's a keeper. Good job, Billy."

"Uh, thanks, Clarice."

She put it back in the case. When she looked up, she was surprised to see Billy still standing there. "Yeah?"

"Um, Clarice, you know my band?"

"Wretched Harvest?"

"Uh, yeah."

"Wretched Harvest. How are you guys doing?"

"Um, we're doing really good, actually. We just got signed, and we've got our first headline show at Le Mans in, uh, three weeks."

"That's terrific."

"And, um, then we're going on tour," said Billy. "In support of the Black Sixes."

Clarice raised an eyebrow. "Nice one."

"So, um, I think I have to quit working for you."

"Billy, that's terrific," she said.

"You're not, um, *mad*?"

"Well, I don't know where I'll find another guitar tech like you, but I'm really pleased for you."

He turned scarlet. "Um, thanks, Clarice."

"What day is the Le Mans show?"

"It's a, uh, Friday. If you're interested, I'll get you some tickets…"

"I can afford to pay for my own tickets."

"Oh," said Billy. "Um. Well. It'll be cool to, uh, have you along…"

"I expect an *amazingly* good show."

"You'll, uh, get one," said Billy, grinning stupidly. "Promise."

"Okay," said Clarice. "Thanks for taking care of the Strat for me."

"Oh, um, don't mention it," said Billy, backing away from the door. "See you. Um. Later…"

Clarice shut the door and took the Stratocaster back into the living room. She sat down on the sofa, crossed her legs, and put the guitar over one thigh. She strummed the open strings with the thumb-pick she was still wearing. It was perfectly in tune.

Johnny looked up from his copy of *Variety*. "It would have been polite to just accept the tickets," he said.

"What?"

"The tickets to Billy's concert."

"Oh," said Clarice.

Johnny returned his attention to the magazine.

Clarice played B-flat minor in all the different modes. Strummed some random chords in the same key. Made up a riff. Improvised a melody. The guitar felt good. The action was low, the new frets rang clear, the neck was smooth.

"Hey, check this out. Goldberg has just announced two new projects."

"Oh?" said Clarice, without looking up.

"One of them is pitched as *Goodfellas* meets *The Exorcist*. The other is about satanic rock stars."

Clarice grunted and tuned the guitar to open D. She slipped a glass over her left pinkie and played some slide blues, then some twangy hillbilly stuff. She stopped abruptly, dropped the slide, and started to fiddle with the machine heads. She hadn't decided what tuning she was going to, but she'd know it when she found it.

Johnny looked up again. "What's wrong, Clarice?"

"Hmm? Nothing."

"Bullshit."

"My sensitive artistic soul is giving me pangs," said Clarice. "What the fuck do you think? Nothing's wrong."

"Yeah? So what was all that with Billy?"

"Friendly chat."

"Oh, come on. You're Clarice Marnier, you don't do friendly chats. I mean, maybe this is you suddenly turning sociable–and hell, I couldn't be happier if that was the case–but we both know it's not."

"It's a tough life, being a rich and famous rock star."

"I'm sorry to see Billy go, as well." He frowned. "But that's not what's really bothering you, either."

Clarice sighed and looked away. "Well, I dunno."

"Yes, you do."

Clarice turned back to him.

"It's Our Friend Below."

"Yes." Clarice flipped the thumb-pick onto the coffee table. It landed in a ceramic fruit dish filled with plectrums.

"We went to him for a deal," said Johnny. "What did you expect it would be like?"

"I dunno. I never really thought it would work."

"Me neither. But we accepted it anyway."

"The deal was supposed to be really straightforward: a soul for a record deal. And then there was the favor for the spell thing, but that looked pretty cut and dried as well. And now..."

"Now we have endless, increasingly bizarre and life-threatening problems and an open-ended debt we have no way to settle."

"Now we have to do his dirty work whenever he asks...if he bothers to ask at all. But it's worse than that."

"How so?"

"I don't think he's doing this out of perversity. That asshole has a reason for everything, and I want to know what it is."

"How do you know that?"

"Bad Jack Saunders told us. And fuck-face himself said it, last time we saw him."

Johnny nodded slowly. "Right. We're more valuable to him alive than dead. Our services are more valuable to him than our souls. Something like that."

"Exactly."

"I want to interrogate the bluesman," said Clarice. "I bet he knows something."

"Bad Jack is not someone I want to mess with."

"You leave him to me."

"I'm serious, Clarice."

"He's just a geriatric bluesman."

"I think he's a lot more than that," said Johnny. "I like him, and I think he likes us, but he scares the shit out of me."

"Do you think he's the Devil in disguise?" said Clarice.

"I don't know."

"Does Satan really do that Kaiser Söze shit?"

"I don't know about that, either."

Clarice thumbed her chin. Her frown smoothed out, the tension in her mouth relaxed. She stared at Johnny, expressionless.

"What?"

"Are *you* the Devil?"

Johnny shook his head. "No," he said. "I'm just Johnny."

Clarice nodded slowly. "Good." She stood and picked up the Strat, then carried it over to the cluster of amplifiers by the TV. She chose a stack. Plugged it in. Switched on the amp, made a plectrum appear. Dialed up the volume. A low hiss rose as Clarice turned the knob.

"Get hold of Saunders," she said. "It's time we had the truth out of him."

5. And the Deep Blue Sea

"The fuck do you mean, you can't find him?"

Clarice's voice did not get shrill when she was angry, it got crisper and louder. Johnny had never heard it this crisp and loud before.

He held the phone away from his head, sighed, and rubbed his eyes. He sighed again, restored the phone to his ear, and said, "He's not replying to voicemail or SMS...email...I even tried fax."

"Can't you, I don't know, *telepathy* him or something?"

"No."

"There must be some magic you can use to track him down."

"Me. Track down Bad Jack Saunders."

Clarice was quiet for a moment.

"All right," she said. "I guess he's worked out what's going down and doesn't want to be involved."

"What *is* going down, Clarice?"

"We're taking on the Devil. What the fuck do you think?"

"We?"

She didn't dignify that with a reply.

He sighed. "How do you wanna proceed?"

"May as well go straight to the summoning."

"You have a plan?"

"Yes. You summon him, I kick his ass."

"Maybe we should take a few days to think this over..."

"No. I want to do it right now."

Johnny sighed. "All right," he said. "All right, we'll do it. Let me collect my books and I'll be right over."

"Well, hurry the fuck up," said Clarice. "I'd prefer it if you got here before he does."

6. Nativity in Black

Clarice was standing in the open doorway, tapping her foot, when Johnny stepped out of the elevator.

"Took you long enough."

"I ran three red lights."

Clarice grunted and moved inside. Johnny followed, pulling the door closed behind him.

Clarice sat down heavily on a couch, crossed her legs, and folded her arms. "Okay," she said. "Summon the fucker."

"And you're just gonna sit there?"

"Yes."

"Okay, okay." Johnny took off his jacket and put it down on an empty seat. He fished a book out of his satchel. Johnny walked into the middle of the room, opened the book, and flipped through it until he found the place he wanted. He raised his head and cleared his throat.

The front door creaked open a few inches.

Clarice turned her head.

Johnny closed the book and turned around slowly.

The doorway was empty.

Clarice stood up and walked to the door. Threw it all the way open. Stuck her head out in the corridor.

On her left, the five doors staggered across both sides of the corridor before the turn were all closed. On her right were four more doors, also closed. The elevators were both on the ground floor. The fire hose reel was still rolled into its snail-shell. The potted plant her neighbor kept beside his door sat quietly in its pot. There was no one around, neither man nor woman, child nor beast.

Clarice pulled the door closed and locked it. "You didn't shut the fucking door properly."

Johnny shrugged. "I guess not."

Clarice resumed her position on the couch. "Okay, let's get on with it."

Johnny leafed through the book...then snapped it shut. "Ah, fuck it. We don't need any books."

"Right."

He shut his eyes and intoned: "Great Lord Satan, O Dread and Dire Beast, so on, so forth...please, um...stop by?"

He looked up at Clarice and opened his eyes. "Uh, amen?"

"Sounded more like a prayer than a spell," said Clarice.

"It was." Johnny took a deep breath and looked around. Clarice just sat there on the sofa with her arms folded.

Unless the Devil was hiding behind the curtains, Johnny was pretty sure he wasn't in the room. "I don't think he's coming."

"That chickenshit fuckin'..." Clarice rubbed her eyes and sighed. "Try again," she said.

"Okay." Johnny lowered his head and clasped his hands over the book. "Um, please, Mister Satan? We really need to speak to you."

He raised his head and looked around, without much expectation. Nothing.

"I think he wants a formal summons."

"Well, shit," said Clarice. "A friendly holler isn't good enough anymore?"

"Huh," said Johnny. "I guess I'll go home and fetch the rest of my gear."

"No," said Clarice. "No. You were right, let's take some time and think about it. It's obvious we're not going to be able to solve this quickly."

"Okay," said Johnny, slipping on his jacket. "So what do you want me to do?"

"Dunno," she said. She rubbed her eyes. "I just don't know. Go home and get some sleep."

"I like that idea." He put the book back into his satchel and slung it over his shoulder.

"And close the door properly this time."

"Yeah, you got it."

Clarice heard the lock click into place when he pulled it closed. She sighed, yawned, massaged her forehead, stretched. She started to yawn again, but stopped herself and closed her mouth.

Clarice folded her arms and leaned back into the sofa. "Okay, you got me," she said. "Now, come out where I can see you."

Behind her, she heard the drapes move. Footsteps approached slowly. She did not look around.

"Chickenshit?" said the Devil with his oh-so-familiar voice. "I'm hurt." A massive shadow fell across her.

"Not yet, you're not," said Clarice, jaw set. "Quit the theatrics and look me in the eye, Munday."

The shadow shifted, and the footsteps came slowly around the couch.

Rex Munday was wearing jeans, sneakers, and a Black Sabbath T-shirt. His long red hair was tied back in a ponytail. His eyes were warm and dark, his smile was open and friendly. Clarice did not rise to greet him.

"Sit," said Clarice, gesturing at a lounge chair on her right.

The Devil sat down and propped a sneaker up on the edge of the coffee table. His smile was so familiar that she again had to remind herself that he wasn't, and never had been, her friend.

"You're supposed to give yourself a clever name," said Clarice. "'Louis Cipher' or some shit."

He looked hurt. "What's wrong with Rex Munday?"

"*Rex Mundi* means King of the Universe," said Clarice. "But you? You're literally the King of Shit."

"I'm the King of Mondays."

She stared at him.

"Everyone hates Mondays?" he added, hopefully.

"That's the kind of joke my Dad would say."

"I just liked how it sounded," said the Devil, crestfallen.

"You son of a bitch."

"I don't have a mother," said the Devil.

"Yeah, I know the story—you're a fallen angel. You might not be *the* son of a bitch, but you really are *a* sonofabitch."

"I was never an angel."

"I remembered you said that, so I went and read the Book of Job," said Clarice.

"And what did you find there?"

"Job says: 'The sons of God came to present themselves before the Lord, and Satan also came among them.'"

"'And Satan also,'" said the Devil.

"So, you're separate."

"Correct."

"Or it might just be weird grammar in a document that's been copied and translated repeatedly for more than 2000 years."

"Might be that too."

"Do I get a Girl Scout badge for Satanic Lore?"

"If you want one, sure."

"Look," said Clarice, "I don't really give a shit where you came from. I just want to know what you're up to."

"You're no fun at all," complained the Devil. Clarice gave him a look. "Okay, okay. Quibbling aside, my function is described pretty well in Job."

"You're God's prosecutor?"

"More or less."

"And the rest? Job doesn't say anything about demons or Hell or anything."

"Correct."

"But I've *seen* demons. Is Hell real?"

"Oh, there's a Hell, all right," said the Devil. "And there are demons in it, too. Some of them are even fallen angels."

"And you run the place."

"I do, these days, but it's not my real job."

"It's not?"

"It's just a bunch of extra administrative bullshit that got foisted on me by a bunch of dead masochists who feel that they need to be punished for their sins."

"If your workload is so heavy, how come you have so much time to fuck with the likes of me?"

"Well," said the Devil, "*that* is actually my real job."

"You're not making any sense."

"I am."

"Then why won't you give me a straight answer? What are you, and why are you fucking with me?"

"All right, all right," said the Devil. He sighed. "You really know how to take all the fun out of a conversation."

"Are you going to answer my question or not?"

He sighed again. "I'm the first creation. The first words spoken. I'm Lucifer, the Star of the Morning. I'm the embodiment of 'Let there be light.'"

"You're a lying fuck, is what you are."

"I'm not just the snake, I'm the apple and the tree. I'm the light in 'enlightenment'. The darkness of ignorance is my shadow."

"Do you practice in front of a mirror?"

"I'm energy, chaos, change, free will."

"You're the frontman of a third-rate heavy metal band."

"And that's why you love me."

"You wish. How does this 'light of reason' hooey fit in with the 'special prosecutor' bullshit?"

"I find the things that are fucked up and I draw attention to them. I stir the pot. Sometimes that fixes the problem, sometimes it inspires more bad shit. Either way, that's my function: to provoke change."

"And this makes it necessary for you to fuck with my life because...?"

"Well, you and Johnny did ask me to."

"Bullshit," said Clarice. "I've known you–Munday–longer than Johnny."

"That's true. I've had my eye on you for a while," said the Devil, "but I didn't do anything but help you along quietly until you came to me, asking for more."

"After you took away my other options."

"Perhaps."

"So, I'm what? A hobby?"

"Oh no," said the Devil. "You're work, big time."

"I just play the guitar. I don't go around...fomenting chaos, or... changing the world..."

"Clarice," said the Devil, "sometimes your cynicism upsets me."

"Oh, bullshit."

"It's not bullshit. Music is one of the most powerful media on the planet. Rock'n'roll has been an integral part of every major social change that happened in the last fifty years."

"Rock'n'roll was only the soundtrack," said Clarice. "Scientists and engineers and economists and doctors did all the real work."

"Now you're the one who's bullshitting," said the Devil. "You don't spend your whole life performing and writing and recording if you don't care who pays attention."

"I write about monsters and losers and shit blowing up," said Clarice. "It's just entertainment."

"Every story—every song—is a message, Clarice, otherwise no one would bother singing them. And Bloody Waters tell stories better than anyone."

"You make me sound like a fucking self-help guru," said Clarice. "I don't buy it."

"You don't have to," said the Devil. "I already did."

Clarice stared at him. "Whatever else I thought of you, I never thought you were an idiot. Now I see that I've been mistaken."

The Devil shrugged. "Maybe I just like your music," he said. "Now, do we have business to attend to, or were you just curious to see how many times you could insult me before I set you on fire?"

"I want an end to the debt," she said. "You tricked us when it came to Rhys's soul? Fair enough, you're the Devil. But I'm sure we've done enough of your fucking dirty work to pay that off by now. I want out."

"You have no idea how much a soul is worth to me."

"Yes, I do," said Clarice. "But you're the one who told me that you'd rather not be in charge of Hell, and I sure as shit don't see how stocking up on souls is relevant to what you claim is your true vocation."

"It's complicated."

"I heard you tell Nauk that my services were more valuable to you than my soul."

"Well, sure. I get your services as interest on the soul you owe. That's good business."

"Not if I refuse to serve."

"If I terminate your debt, you will have no reason to continue serving me, and then I'm out a soul. That's bad business. I'd then have to step in and take what I'm owed."

"You set this up so we would *have* to serve you."

"Is it really so bad? You made most of those choices yourself. I've never made you do anything against your principles. Even when I asked you to fuck over Rex Munday..." He grinned. "That was about your integrity, not about my demands."

"What about the Napster thing?"

"Even that. I made you go back on your words, but you came to see it my way in the end, didn't you?"

"Not the point," said Clarice.

"It's exactly the point," said the Devil. "And here's another: you've enjoyed the shit out of every one of your crazy escapades. Admit it."

"Yeah, I enjoyed them," said Clarice, "but it's interfering with my music, and I won't tolerate that."

"All right, fair enough. I'll try to keep any future issues clear of your concerts and studio time from now on."

"Not good enough," said Clarice.

"I don't see that you're in any position to bargain."

"I've gone along with you until now, but that's going to change. I will actively oppose your interests. If I can help you, it stands to reason that I can hurt you, too–especially now that I know what you are."

There was a silence.

"Okay, okay, I admit I've taken some liberties," said the Devil. "But I want you on my side." He sighed deeply. "And I'm willing to pay for it."

"Go on."

"If I annul the soul debt, will you give me your loyalty?"

"What does that mean?"

"You'd be an employee, rather than an indentured servant."

Clarice considered. "It's an improvement," she said. She thought about it some more.

The Devil crossed his feet at the ankles and clasped his hands behind his head.

"What's the salary?"

"Oh, the usual," said the Devil. "Protection. Luck. Simple immortality."

"Simple immortality?"

"You won't age, you won't get any kind of terminal disease, but you're otherwise the same as everyone else. You'll bleed if you're cut, you'll sprain an ankle if you trip, you're pizza if you jump off a building, you're spaghetti if you fly a spaceship into a black hole."

"A spaceship."

"Well, you know."

Clarice snorted.

"There's also an Unholy Intervention clause that means that I—or one of my agents—may actively manifest to help you, if you require it." He smiled. "And I'll continue to keep you out of trouble with the law."

"That sounds suspiciously like what's already been going on," said Clarice.

"If you accept, it will be formal," said the Devil. "That means that I will be *obliged* to look after you. You'll have the absolute best in benefits for your entire immortal existence, as long as you continue to serve me."

"I don't know if I want to hang around forever, getting irrelevant and obsolete."

"Clarice, you yourself said that rock music is about staying young. Reinventing itself. It never stops evolving–that's its job. If you accept this, you will be able to see to it...and *that* is what I really need you for."

"I still don't see why you need somebody to protect rock'n'roll from mobsters and demons."

"In an ideal world I wouldn't," said the Devil. "This is one of the other kind. I need someone to take care of that stuff for me, and you're the best."

"I don't know," said Clarice.

"What's it going to take to get you to sign on?"

Clarice rubbed her chin. "If I agree to this, I want to be briefed about what's happening in advance," she said. "No more of these seemingly random events mushrooming into some big drama. I want to know when I'm dealing with my own problems, and when I'm dealing with yours, and I want to be able to decide how to take care of these problems myself."

"Okay."

"And the same limits I set before. There's some stuff I just won't do."

"Okay."

"I want a guarantee that you won't use my band, my family, my friends or my business associates to force me if you *do* need me to step over the line."

"If I agree, is it a deal?"

"Do you agree?"

"Yes. And you?"

"There's one more thing," said Clarice.

"Yes?"

"Johnny."

"What about him?"

"The soul debt belongs to him, as well."

"You owe me one soul between the two of you," said the Devil. "If I annul your debt, I have to cancel Johnny's as well. I can't very well ask him for half a soul."

"I want some of that immortality for him, too."

"No," said the Devil. "This deal is between you and me, and no one else. It gets difficult when there are more than two parties involved as you might have noticed."

"I want Johnny."

"I told you, no."

Clarice was silent for a good minute. "Where is someone like me going to find another someone like him?"

"I could arrange it, if you want," said the Devil, "but I don't think that would please you very much."

"I don't want a new one; I want to keep the one I have."

"I'm not taking him away," said the Devil. "You'll still have him until he dies or you ditch him. This deal has no bearing on your relationship with him."

"You know that's not true."

The Devil shrugged. "And *you* know that's one of your own problems."

She looked away.

"Well?"

"I don't know."

"Look, I'm offering to clear your debt. You keep everything you have, and now you can have anything else you could ever want. You'll get to rock on until the end of the world, as young and as strong as you are today."

"I want Johnny with me."

The Devil stared at her. Eventually, he said, "Well, I'm not going to tell you that it can't happen. Perhaps he can strike a deal with me, separate to yours. Or perhaps somebody else will offer him something similar...but no promises. I've put everything I can offer on the table. Take it or leave it."

Clarice glowered at him. The Devil kept his poker face.

"All right," she said.

The Devil leaned forward and offered his hand. "Shall we shake on it?"

"We can shake on it," said Clarice, "but I want it in writing."

The Devil stood up and straightened his jeans. "I'll have the contract to you within six business days." He extended his hand again.

Clarice rose. "No more tricks. I want that in the contract as well."

"No more tricks."

She looked at the Devil's hand, then took it in her own and shook it stiffly, putting as much into the grip as she could—but he gripped her back just as hard. His eyes shone like black opals.

"Pleasure doing business with you," he said.

"It was all yours," she replied, withdrawing her hand and turning away.

"Yes," said the Devil. "It usually is."

— EPILOGUE —

1. Let There Be Rock

Hoben Rhys pulled up the collar of his jacket and adjusted his sunglasses. The Massachusetts wind was sharp, and the sinking sun glowered redly out of the clear autumn sky. Dry leaves crunched beneath his Italian leather shoes.

"So, you've settled everything between you and Marnier?" he asked.

"Yes." The Devil's footfalls were silent. His breath steamed from his mouth and nose. "For now."

"I still don't understand why she was a threat to you."

"No," said the Devil. "I don't suppose you would."

"C'mon, Rex, I did an awful lot of legwork for you on this one. At least, you can tell me what it was for."

They walked on in silence.

Rhys stopped to tear a branch from a young tree.

The Devil looked back at him. "What did that tree ever do to you?"

"Nothing," said Rhys.

"So what are you doing?"

"I want a walking stick." Rhys started down the path again, breaking the twigs off the limb as he went.

"Are you a cripple?"

"No, I just want a stick."

They walked on.

Rhys broke the sharp end off the branch and started to strip it, using a thumbnail to score the bark and then peeling it away in long, curling strips.

Eventually, the Devil said, "You know she can sing like an angel, right?"

"She can?"

"Yes."

"Then why won't she?"

The Devil sighed.

"What?!" said Rhys. "It was a fair question."

"If you have to ask, you'll never understand."

They walked on.

"Do you mean literally?" said Rhys.

"Do I mean what, literally?"

"Can Clarice Marnier literally sing like an angel?"

"No, of course not," said the Devil. "Angels don't sing."

"Oh." Rhys swung the stick about experimentally. "Well, how was I supposed to know that?"

"You weren't."

They walked on, Rhys twirling his cane, the Devil with his hands in his pockets.

"Are you going to tell me what all this was all about, or not?"

"Let's just say, it's better to have her walking the earth for the rest of forever than it would be to have her... elsewhere."

"Elsewhere, as in, dead?"

"Yes."

"I don't get it," said Rhys. "If she croaks, you get her soul and it's game over."

"No."

"You clearly have the best claim on it. But, for argument's sake, let's say she weasels out of it–then she goes to the angels. Or to purgatory. Or...anywhere. She's still dead."

"It's not that simple."

"Of course it is. At the end of the day, she's just one more loose soul to be claimed."

"No," said the Devil. "She isn't."

"Yes," said Rhys, jabbing his stick at an invisible opponent. "She is."

"No," said the Devil. "Souls are not currency. Every one of them is infinitely valuable."

"You already got bazillions of souls," said Rhys. "You're infinitely wealthy, a bazillion times over."

"True."

"Finally, we agree on something. Her soul is going to one of three places when she dies, and that's the end of the story. Right?"

"Not necessarily."

"You think she'll go to one of the other operations?"

"Oh, I wish," said the Devil. "I wish I could just palm her off on someone else."

"Hades would take her. Or Osiris. Those guys wouldn't say no. They haven't gotten jack shit for two thousand years."

"She won't go."

"She has to go somewhere."

"That's just it. She doesn't."

"What other options does she have? Reincarnation? Or, there's always the increasingly-popular Oblivion..."

"Not Clarice. She's not gonna start over and she's damn sure not going to go away quietly."

"So she'll be...what?"

"Independent."

"There's no such thing."

"There isn't...yet," said the Devil.

"How do you know?"

"I'm a primal force of the universe," said the Devil. "I have a certain amount of insight into these things."

"Okay, okay..." said Rhys, waving his cane around. "So what does it mean, if she were to become...independent?"

"I don't know."

"You don't know."

"Nope."

"I thought you were a Primal Force of the Universe," said Rhys, pointing his cane at the Devil. "I thought you had a certain amount of *insight* into these things."

"Give me that." The Devil grabbed the stick out of Rhys's hands. He snapped it in half, then he snapped the two halves again. Then he snapped the quarters into eighths.

"You're a vandal and a show-off," said Rhys.

"You didn't need it," said the Devil, discarding the pieces of stick.

"You're still a fucking vandal," said Rhys. "I made that with my own hands."

"No, you didn't. You just broke it off the tree and tore its skin off."

"You're still a vandal."

"I'm the goddamn Devil. You should expect that from me."

"Oh, yeah, I forgot. The goddamn Devil, primal badass, and all that shit. If you're so fucking primal, why are you afraid of some little guitar bitch?"

"I should have known better than to bring you into this."

"It's a record industry thing, isn't it?" said Rhys. "Indies versus the labels."

"You could look at it that way."

"There are more and more independent artists around, this last twenty or thirty years. Any of them started to do well, we would eat them…"

"Nowadays the opposite is happening. When an act gets big enough, they shake off their contracts and go it alone. Start their own label."

"Yeah, but none of those labels are as big as the corporate ones. None of them can survive without the distribution system we built."

"Less and less true every day, Rhys."

"That fucking internet."

They walked on.

"Anyway," said Rhys, "that's just the record business falling over. We were talking cosmic shit before."

"Everything falls, Rhys. Everything old has to end; everything new has to begin somewhere. The record business, the universe, everything."

"Are we talking about Armageddon, now?"

"Yes."

"I don't get it."

"Armageddon is…incremental. And perpetual. And inevitable."

"But you're in the driver's seat, right? Armageddon is *your* responsibility."

"Yes."

"So, you're still da Man."

"Rhys, the Jews made me their prosecutor. Then the Zoroastrians set me up as the Shadow, the Adversary. And then the Christians turned me into their jailer. I'm subject to change, just like everybody else."

"But…"

"I might govern change, but I'm not immune to it. I'm more susceptible to it than anyone."

Rhys cleared his throat. "What does all this existential claptrap have to do with anything?"

"If a soul declares itself apart...and has the integrity to remain so...well. That changes the balance of things."

"She's just a guitarist," said Rhys. "She's only human. Right?"

The Devil took a long breath and sighed it out as a double helix of steam. "Rhys, there is no such thing as 'only human.' They were given free will, they were given the capacity to choose and to change. That makes them capable of anything."

"I don't understand."

"Free will equals unlimited potential. I can't put it more plainly than that."

"She's not a witch, she's not a sorcerer, she's not a general or a priest or a politician. She's just a fucking rock star. There are plenty more dangerous people to be concerned about."

"Such as?"

"Such as that boyfriend of hers."

"Johnny? He has hidden depths, I'll grant you that. His power is more obvious than Clarice's, but it's not on the same order."

"So explain to me what kind of power Clarice has."

"True power is power over yourself," said the Devil. "And whatever else you might say about her, there is no power on this earth—or above it, or below—that will make Clarice compromise what she truly believes in."

"That's not true power, that's just rock'n'roll ego."

"Same thing. If your ego is big enough, changing the world is as easy—and as difficult—as changing your own mind."

"You made her give up her boyfriend, but she didn't want to."

"Yes, she did. She wanted what I can offer more than what he can, and she made her choice."

They walked on in silence.

"For argument's sake, let's say there's a new cosmic power," said Rhys. "Gods rise and fall, that's not news. Why is Clarice, specifically, a threat to you?"

"Because she will be ascending on her own self-belief. She doesn't seek power; she is innately powerful."

"Like you."

"Yes, but...I'm compromised, Rhys. Every time my function has been changed or extended, I've been weakened. Clarice won't change for anyone but herself."

Rhys stopped in his tracks. "You're afraid you'll be replaced."

"Yes."

"Well, fuck."

The Devil kept walking.

"No, no, wait." Rhys stepped quickly to catch up with him. "You *are* change, correct? How can change become something other than what it is?"

"How can it not?"

They walked on.

"You should have let me break her," said Rhys, wiping his fingers on his pants. They were still wet from tree sap.

"You. Break Clarice Marnier." The Devil spoke flatly. "Even I couldn't manage it."

"Well, you did manage to seduce her...I guess that's good enough."

"For now."

"No, I think it'll work out," said Rhys. "Making her immortal was a great move. Let time break her spirit for you."

"You think it'll work?"

"Sure. It's impossible to stay truly independent for an extended period of time. She'll go at it hard for a few years, but once the boyfriend dies and she doesn't have any more friends? Even Clarice is going to get lonely. May take her a few hundred years or so, but eventually she'll give in."

"That's what I'm counting on," said the Devil, "but I don't know if it's really going to work."

Rhys snorted. "I still think I can break her."

"You think you can do my job better than I can."

"No, not at all," said Rhys. "Come on, let me have her. Let me try it. Just for fun."

"You had your chance."

"One more try. Shall we make it a wager?"

"No."

"I thought we were friends," said Rhys.

"You don't have any friends, Rhys."

"You just confided all that stuff to me. We go back a long way; you know you can trust me."

"Oh, really?"

Rhys slowed up. "Well," he said, "maybe not. But that's why I'm so damn useful to you."

The Devil looked back over his shoulder at him. "You were useful to me for a long time, Hoben," he said. "But now?"

Rhys caught fire and blew away to ash.

"Nowadays you're surplus to requirements."

The Devil rubbed his eyes and sighed. "You would never have understood it, Rhys. I owned you because you believed that *you* could own Clarice. You sold your soul to me because you believe that everybody can be bought. But Clarice?

"She sold her soul to rock'n'roll."

BLACKENED SKIES

A novel by Jason Franks

(Excerpt)

— PROLOGUE —

Waiting for the Bus

The last time the bluesman ever went down to the crossroads, the Devil was already there waiting for him.

Someone had put a bus stop in there since the last time he'd been, and Old Scratch was sitting there under the sign with the bus number. But that wasn't the only thing that had changed. In all the many, many times the bluesman had come out to the crossroads, he'd never once gotten there second. The Devil liked to make an entrance, and the bluesman found it a mild cause for concern that he had given that up.

Dressed in denim and leather, red hair tied back and his face all a-shadow, his gleaming Dobro across his knee, the Devil himself hadn't changed. Old Scratch hadn't acknowledged him yet, so the bluesman stood and watched him play. The moonlight shone off the Devil's resonator guitar like cold fire, and the melody he drew from the strings vibrated under the bottleneck slide like the misery of the damned. Weren't nobody played the blues like that Devil.

When the music stilled, the Devil looked up, and though his face was still in shadow, the bluesman took it as his cue to approach. "What happened to your rock?" he asked.

The Devil spat in the roadway. "Damn thing was uncomfortable as hell," he said. His saliva sizzled on the blacktop.

"You could've used a cushion," said the bluesman. "I wouldn't have told no one."

The Devil shook his head. "Not how it works," he said. He considered for a moment. "But that doesn't make it a bad idea."

"I see."

The bluesman put down his own guitar case and sat on the bench on the Devil's right-hand side. The wooden slats were warmer than he was used to. "Things are changing, huh? Changing for real."

"The stone truth," said the Devil. He raked an arpeggio with his fingers, used the bottleneck to slide up to a high, fragile chord.

"Can you stop it?"

"No," said the Devil. "It's utterly inevitable and absolutely necessary."

It hurt the bluesman's neck to look at his companion, so he just looked straight ahead. "The girl," he said.

"She's a woman now," said the Devil.

"She grow up bad as you thought?"

"Worse," said the Devil. "By which I mean, she's even better than I expected."

The bluesman nodded his head. "That lady sure can play."

"You've met her," said the Devil. "What did you think?"

"She's still young, is what I thought," said the bluesman. "I wouldn't like to be her enemy, but I sure as hell wouldn't want to be her friend, neither."

"She doesn't need your friendship," said the Devil. "But her other half does."

"He can play, too…but he's still just a boy."

"No argument there," said the Devil. "That's why he needs it."

The bluesman nodded, made a sound in the back of his throat. "Just so happens I like the young man, but I ain't the right guy for it now."

"That's true," said the Devil.

"I know someone who can give him what he needs," said the bluesman.

"Thank you, Jack. I appreciate it," said the Devil.

The bluesman thought about it for a while more. "They both awfully white, you know."

"Their shadow's just as dark as yours."

"Well, ain't that some spooky-ass bullshit," said the bluesman.

The toe of the Devil's snakeskin boot rose upward, and he shifted the Dobro on his lap. "We gonna play together, Jack?" he said. "This one last time?"

"Sure we are," said the bluesman. He bent forward and withdrew his battered old steel-string from its case. It hurt his back to do it, but the way his knees were these days it was the less painful option. The bluesman was nearly 120 years old and it was finally catching up with him. He strummed a chord, made a minute adjustment to the tuning, strummed another. Right in tune.

"Just tell me one thing."

"All right," said the Devil. "What thing is that?"

"We play this one last song, and then what? What happens next?"

"Well, Jack, that's it," said the Devil. "This is the beginning of the end."

CHAPTER 1: A BRIDGE TOO FAR

Beverly Hills

Y ou bought a house and you never even thought to tell me about it?" Johnny didn't seem angry, but he didn't seem especially happy about it, either.

They were standing in the living room of Clarice's apartment in West Hollywood, and it was the first time they'd seen each other in three weeks. It would probably have been longer if Johnny hadn't shown up unannounced.

Clarice shrugged. "I must have forgotten." That wasn't exactly true. She knew she hadn't told him, but it wasn't because she had intended to keep it a secret. She just hadn't thought it was worth the bother. He would have wanted to come around and see the place, to help her move in, and...and frankly, she hadn't really bothered to do that, yet. She had been sleeping there for the last fortnight, but it wasn't like she'd bothered to furnish the place or anything. Aside from the recording studio she'd set up in the living room and the refrigerator in the kitchen there was still no furniture in the house.

Johnny would think that was weird. She supposed it was, a bit. But why should she have to explain herself?

"It's just a little—"

"It's a 12-bedroom palazzo on five acres in Beverly Hills."

Clarice shrugged. "I just wanted somewhere private where I could record in peace. I figured if nobody knew I had the place, nobody would bother me there."

"Including me?"

"Well, I didn't specifically exclude you," said Clarice. "How did you find out it, anyway?"

Johnny pulled a glossy brochure from his back pocket. He unfolded it and then unrolled it to reveal a map with the legend "Hollywood Constellation." "You didn't notice the tourist bus stopping at your front gate every afternoon at 3:45pm?"

Clarice snatched it from him and peered at it. There it was: her name and address and a little icon of a lightning-struck guitar. She scowled. "The realtor told me the sale was completely confidential."

"Well, I'm sure they paid off someone at City Hall," said Johnny. "These guys have been wanting you on their map for nearly a decade now."

"Guess it's time to invest in some attack dogs," said Clarice. "Maybe a small army of mercenaries." She turned and slouched into the living room. "How did you even know I was here, anyway?" she said. "I haven't been here in weeks."

Johnny followed her through. "Ways and means," he said. "And a lucky guess. But don't change the subject. I haven't seen you in weeks and—"

Johnny's pocket began to chime. He paused, frowned, reached back, and took out his phone.

Clarice picked up the Fender Jazzmaster that was lying on the couch and threw herself down in its place. The guitar fell across her thigh like an extra limb and her hands found their positions on its body and neck.

"Johnny Chernow," he said, in his usual equanimical baritone.

Clarice played a chord. Adjusted the tuning. Played another chord. Ripped a scale, then arpeggiated it. Johnny made concerned and affirmative noises into the phone.

Clarice slashed some power chords, squinted up at the head. She'd replaced the notoriously poor Jazzmaster bridge, but it still felt like the strings were slipping. Maybe she would try gluing in the saddle screws.

Johnny put away his phone, and she looked up at him. "What?" she said. She didn't like the look on his face.

"Bad Jack Saunders is dead," said Johnny.

Done Got Old

Bad Jack Saunders's wake was held in his massive Chicago mansion.

The bluesman had suffered a heart attack on his 120th birthday while riding the Greyhound bus to Jackson, Mississippi. He had $12.80 in his wallet and a driver's license that was nine years expired.

Bad Jack's immense white ballroom was filled mostly with musicians: famous and obscure, international stars and local talent. Blues, jazz, rock; folk; country, classical, funk, punk. About the only common thread Clarice could find was that they were confused. People were trying to trade stories about Bad Jack and finding that their accounts did not match up. Even now it was hard to know what was true and what was a myth. Clarice was sure Bad Jack would have found it hilarious.

"There's an awful lot of British accents in this room," said Johnny.

"I thought that was just an engine idling," replied Clarice.

Johnny gave her a reproving look, but the sound of somebody tapping on a microphone stopped him from saying anything. With the rest of the room, he turned to see a lanky man wearing a yarmulke, long, curling sideburns, and a business shirt standing at the lectern. White tennis shoes poked out from underneath his creased black slacks.

"My name is Ben-Ze'ev," said the man in the yarmulke. He sounded New York, by way of Montreal. "I'm sure you all have a lot of questions. Jack's lawyers have given me this letter to read to you, which, knowing Jack, may or may not provide you with the answers you're seeking."

The only one who did not smile at that was Ben-Ze'ev. He cleared his throat, looked down at the letter, and began to read. While his accent did not change, it seemed as though his voice fell by half an octave.

"I suppose y'all are wondering why you didn't get invited to my funeral. Answer to that is easy: I didn't have one." Ze'ev peered up from the letter and looked around the room. The murmuring had hushed down to silence.

"I been cremated and the ashes been thrown in the trash. I got no use for 'em, and I sure as hell don't want nobody trying to conjure with them.

"Didn't have no funeral service, neither. All I've seen and done, wouldn't feel right having some preacher speak over me in church. I wouldn't want to make a liar out of the man.

"By the time you hear this, I'm gonna be deep down in Hell. I only hope there's bad hooch and a good PA system down there, and maybe some roads to ramble.

"Eternity is a long damn time. I hope if you folks choose to remember anything about me, it will be the music. Never did give a damn about that other bullshit, if you'll pardon mon Francais.

"Enjoy the food and drink, and I'll see you in Hell. I'll make sure the party's good and hot by the time you get here.

"Your friend, Bad Jack Saunders."

Ze'ev looked up from the letter, then squinted at it one more time, then looked up again. "The date on the bottom is Friday last."

The bluesman had written the letter a week prior to his death.

"He knew he was going to die," said Johnny.

"We're all going to die," said Clarice. "What matters is how long it takes you to get old."

Secrets and Lies

Johnny wanted to talk things over with Clarice on the flight home, but as soon as they were in their seats she put her headphones on and went to sleep. Johnny knew better than to wake her.

He knew that something had happened. She was keeping something from him, and he knew her well enough to know it wasn't some little white lie. It probably wasn't urgent, but it surely was important if she was keeping it from him.

Not that Johnny lacked his own secrets, but he was willing to discuss them if Clarice was willing to ask. But he didn't think it had even occurred to her. Had she pressed him about how he knew when she'd be home, he would have told her that she'd tripped a protection ward he'd left in the apartment. Johnny's intention had never been to spy on her, but she'd been out of the apartment for so long that he couldn't help but notice when it activated and recognized a non-threat.

Secrets aside, Johnny had a genuine problem that he needed to discuss.

His power was fading. While Johnny's skill at composing spells and perceiving magical phenomena was better than ever, his ability to power his workings was starting to fail. His primary source of occult juice—provided to him by the Devil as part of their initial bargain—was drying up, and he didn't know why. He'd tried to raise the Devil a dozen different ways, but none of the summonses worked for him anymore.

The Devil had abandoned Johnny just when he was getting good at magic. He'd been intending to brace the bluesman for some clues, but now he was gone.

Johnny was sure they still had enemies out in the world. The music business alone was riddled with them. He just hoped that none of them would crawl out of their holes before he'd found a new way to squash it flat.

Or perhaps they were already flattened. Maybe it was time to give up the hoodoo and get back to being a rich and famous rock god. That wasn't so bad, was it?

In the limousine, Clarice smiled at him and said, "So, shall we go back to your place?"

Johnny thought about asking to see Clarice's new Beverly Hill mansion, but he was almost certain she hadn't bothered to furnish it yet, and he didn't want to argue about it. "Mine," he said, grinning.

His place was better warded.

Purple and Blue

They got to Johnny's place in the Hollywood Hills just in time to see the UPS truck coming down the driveway. There wasn't room for two vehicles abreast, so the truck had to reverse back up to the house with the limo following.

Johnny took the notice down off the door and the driver opened the back of the truck with a sigh. Johnny signed for the package—a guitar case, quaintly wrapped in brown paper and string—while

Clarice opened up the house and the limousine driver executed a thirty-point turn.

In the living room, Clarice gave Johnny a bemused smile. "Who's it from?" Usually she was the one who received donated guitars.

As soon as Johnny had stripped off the brown paper, they both knew who it was from.

Johnny opened the travel-stained case and took out the scarred old six-string with reverence, inhaling the rich, dark odor of the velveteen interior. There was a folded sheet of paper at the bottom of the case. Johnny set the guitar aside—he was surprised but gratified that Clarice didn't immediately take it and start playing—and picked up the note.

"What's he say?" said Clarice.

Johnny read the beautiful copperplate script through twice before he read it aloud.

"Johnny, I want you to have this here guitar."

"Obviously," said Clarice.

"You're getting pretty good now and I want to encourage you to keep on playing."

"You're better than good," said Clarice. "And everybody knows it." That was her way of saying that if she wasn't around, he'd probably get his due. She meant it as a compliment, though. "Why does he think you're quitting?"

"It's Bad Jack," said Johnny, looking up from the letter. "He's not talking about what you think he's talking about."

"Uh-huh?"

"Sometimes you just got to ask for help. Some voices are harder to silence than others."

"Well, that's definitely Bad Jack Saunders, talking riddles now," said Clarice.

"Till doomsday and beyond, your pal, Bad Jack Saunders."

"For a bluesman, Jack sure could be purple," said Clarice.

Johnny folded up the note. "The date on here is the day he died."

Clarice pursed her lips, looked at the guitar. He could see how much effort it was taking her not to touch it. "Is that magical?"

Johnny picked up the instrument, strummed a slow chord. Heavy gauge strings, slightly rusted from sweat and the Mississippi humidity. It was perfectly tuned. "Not in any occult sort of way," said Johnny.

She looked away so she wouldn't have to see him blink his eyes clear.

— ACKNOWLEDGMENTS —

The author would like to thank all the ladies and gentlemen of the guitar: Eric and Jimi and Carlos and Jimmy and Joe and Steve and Eddie and Stevie and Joni and Marnie and Kaki and Lita and Orianthe and Carrie and Suze... and, of course, Joan.

Thanks also to those who contributed feedback and encouragement from the earliest drafts through to the final version: Frank Curigliano, Karen Jacobson, Erin Marcon, David Richardson, Denice Luttrell, Steven Mangold, and John Tanner. Particular thanks to Jan Scherpenhuizen, who believed in the book enough to put his name and resources behind it, and Jason Fischer, who helped me resurrect it--twice.